THE
HUNGRY ONES

THE HUNGRY ONES

Elana Gomel

Guardbridge Books
St Andrews, Scotland

Published by Guardbridge Books,
St Andrews, Fife, United Kingdom.

http://guardbridgebooks.co.uk

Hungry Ones, The

This is a work of fiction. All characters and events portrayed in this book are fictitious, and any resemblance to real people or events is purely coincidental.

Edited by David Stokes
Proofreading by Laurie Hilburn

Cover art © Jackie Duckworth

ISBN: 978-1-911486-34-3

To my mother, Maya Kaganskaya.

"Where there is not enough to eat, people starve to death."
—Mao Zedong

PART I. THE CITY

Chapter 1. The Empty Hotel

I see a leaf. It is splayed-fingered, shot with a tracery of delicate veins. I reach for it, my hand shaking as if with old-age palsy as it slowly and reluctantly raises itself toward its goal. My hand, chicken-thin, baby-small.

Another hand intervenes between me and the leaf, and this enrages me so much I scream and beat at it. But, my blows are as weak as raindrops; my scream gurgles away.

The bigger hand returns, holding the leaf, which has undergone a miraculous transformation. It is luminous with warmth, shiny with dredging flour, dropping golden coins of cooking oil.

I reach for it. I am happy.

And somebody snatches it away.

And then she was dreaming of food again: trays of jewel-like sushi; puffy cakes with little cream castles on top; sizzling plates of roast meat. But, when she reached out, grabbed fistfuls of food, and crammed it into her mouth, it fell through her clumsy fingers in a shower of crispy burnt leaves. The dream was leached out of her memory as she awakened.

The bed was uncomfortable, the pillow so thin she could feel the bony hardness of the mattress dig into her neck. She lay back, staring at the white ceiling. Something was missing: there was no longer a light fixture at the center of it. Had there been? She turned her head, seeking a bedside lamp. It was there, on the table: a flat panel in the shape of a bird. Faint washes of pastel color ran across its surface.

Why did she need a lamp anyway? The room was bathed in the milky glow that seeped through the gauzy curtains. A rickety table, a fuzzy carpet, a closet. An anonymous hotel room. Not a place where one would luxuriate in bed, waiting for…Whatever she was waiting for eluded her. Breakfast, perhaps?

Getting up and doing some stretches to banish the kinks from her sore muscles, she dwelt on the idea of breakfast. She was ravenously hungry, emptiness pulsing under her breastbone, tugging at her like a fretful baby. She tried to distract herself by visualizing what she wanted to eat – and came up with nothing.

She walked into the bathroom. The snowflake-shaped fixture on the ceiling lit up.

"Hello!" she said. "I'd appreciate some privacy here!"

Who the hell am I talking to? The bathroom is empty.

The hunger was momentarily eclipsed by unfocused unease. Everything appeared vivid and disconnected. She wondered if she was still dreaming. No, the texture of her experience was real. Maybe too real.

She was startled by her own reflection in the mirror and it took a couple of rapid heartbeats to figure out why. She was so hungry that she half-expected to see an emaciated face and skeletal body. But, the black-haired, green-eyed woman staring back at her was strongly built, with wide shoulders, long muscular legs, and toned arms. Ridiculous! Just because she was starving now did not mean she had not eaten before…

And then she realized she did not remember when she had eaten last.

Probing her mind like a bleeding cavity left from a pulled tooth, she mapped out the blank – *blanked?* – areas.

She knew she was in a hotel. She knew what a hotel was. But, she had no idea how she had gotten here. And perhaps more importantly, she was not sure where *here* was.

The bathroom counter was filled with multicolored bottles of liquid soaps and lotions. She swiped them off and they cluttered down, breaking, surprisingly made of glass; a viscous wave lapping at her bare feet. The violence of this gesture eased the suffocating panic that was rising in her chest. She bit her lip and felt the skin parting under the pressure of her strong white teeth. A brief flare of pain like a match that instantly went out, a trickle of…

She could not taste her own blood.

She ran out of the bathroom, obliviously stepping on broken glass, and back into the room. She pulled aside the window curtain—

And stood there gasping, as if the view had suddenly sucked all oxygen out of the room.

The city reared into the white sky: slender stalk-like towers clustering in bright groves, studded with balconies, festooned with tubes that wound around them like giant sea-worms. Squat apartment blocks were piled upon each other in a dizzying profusion, with snaky alleys burrowing into the gloom between them. Buildings grew on buildings, like mushrooms and saprophytes in a tropical forest. Clovers of raised tracks bloomed above the high-rises; the stupendous mass of the city held together by a cat's cradle of walkways, escalators, bridges, stairs, and ramps. It rose up and up, a mountain of architecture veiled by the humid fog, glinting with shards of water, throbbing with hidden life.

She had never been here before.

But, she had been in…*a* city? She tried to remember which one, but the only image she could call up in her memory was of long rows of gleaming, curving, precision-manufactured huts. Metal and glitter and harsh light. A total opposite of this organic profusion. There was something indecent about the throbbing vitality of the cityscape and, at the same time, something menacing. Then she realized what it was.

The city was empty.

She saw no movement on the street below. The curving arc of the bridge to the right was devoid of pedestrians and vehicles alike. And somehow the cottony silence around told her that, apart from her, the hotel was unoccupied.

But, there was something moving in the sky, black silhouettes like papercuts against the yellowish vapors of the clouds. Birds? Big birds?

She squinted, trying to see across the body of water that lay close to the hotel. The visibility was terrible, the air thick and hazy.

Why was she wasting her time like this? She needed…yes, she needed to eat. Everything else paled in comparison to the relentless hunger that burrowed into her flesh like a tick. Perhaps her amnesia was simply the result of starvation. Yes, this must be it!

Hunger does strange things to you.

She would recover her memories once she was sated.

Checking in the closet, she found a black tunic crucified on the solitary hanger. Black tights, black underwear, and flat black shoes were laid out underneath. The clothes were clean but not crispy-new. They fit her perfectly.

The everyday familiarity of pulling up tights and wriggling her toes into a shoe calmed her down, so that the hot wave of dread bubbling in her chest receded somewhat. She forbade herself to overthink her predicament. Breakfast first. Then finding out where she was. One step at a time.

Haste makes waste.

The voice speaking in her head was her own, but she was still grateful for its companionship. *Everything will be fine*, she told herself. *Everything will be fine once I have eaten.*

Dressed, she ventured into the dim hallway lined with closed doors. She tried a couple of them, but they were all locked.

At the end of the corridor was an elevator alcove. She stared at it, frowning. Of course, a hotel would have an elevator, but there was something strange about it. It seemed familiar and unfamiliar at the same time. Finally, she realized it was because the sliding doors came together in a wavering line rather than the straight lock of honest metal, as if she were looking through a distorting layer of water. She blinked several times and shook her head, expecting that hunger was making her faint, but nothing changed. And the light…the light was coming from irregularly shaped and infrequent ceiling fixtures that seemed to be stuck at random throughout the hallway. She forced herself to think about her surroundings, because it deflected from the fear of the emptiness inside her.

She pushed the unpleasantly soft button and the curving lips in in the wall swooshed open. The cab dribbled flickering illumination onto the landing. The panel inside had numbers from zero to fifteen, but studying it, she saw that there was no fourth floor. She knew there was a reason for that but did not know what it was.

She was tempted, once again, to touch the gaping wound in her mind, to dig into what was left of her memory. To discover what was missing. But she forced herself to concentrate on externalities.

Surely, if there was a dining room or a restaurant here, it would be on the ground floor! She touched zero and felt her finger sink into warmth as the cab slid down with an asthmatic rattle.

The elevator shuddered to a stop and she rushed into the empty hotel lobby. There was a large reception desk, all sinuous curves and flowing surfaces. There were several shaggy armchairs. There was a flower arrangement, orange and purple. The flowers seemed to grow straight from the pedestal they were set upon. But, in contrast to the lushness of the décor, there was no sign of anything edible. And there were no people.

"Hello?"

She clapped her hand to her mouth. Her voice sounded obscene in the guarded silence. She looked around warily, but nothing stirred.

You want people, but you are afraid of people?
I want food.

At the end of the lobby was an archway and, beyond it, a large, brightly lit, familiar space. Abandoning her attempts to alert the hotel personnel, she ran into the mall. A mall was safe. A mall would have people. A mall would have food.

But, even as she exited the spooky hotel, sighing in relief, she realized that at least one of those assumptions was wrong. Despite its cheerful illumination, the mall was as empty of people as the hotel. All shops were locked. Not a single shopper, salesperson, or cleaner in sight.

But food was there, at least judging by the multiple ads, signs, and pictures that bloomed among the pillars and walkways like orchids in the jungle. Everywhere she looked, she encountered mouth-watering images: domed islands of rice in the sea of sautéed vegetables; piles of donuts colored like a child's balloons; porcupine dumplings winking at her from under the cocked bamboo lid. And meat: orange-tanned roast ducks; burgers preserved in buns like dried flowers in a book; stews bubbling in crocks.

Mouth-watering? Her mouth was as dry as a desert, though she felt no thirst.

She licked her lips. There was no residue of moisture left behind.

She found herself staring at a large poster of a crock of noodle soup, temptingly highlighted against the dark background scribbled with white letters. A new fear slammed into her. She could not read! The letters made no sense!

But then her gaze flickered to a shop sign and the fear abated, as she gasped for breath in relief. The sign was perfectly legible, though not very informative. The shop was called "Piggy-White". So, some of the signs were in a language she did not know – so what? It was to be expected because…She groped for an explanation, but it eluded her. Still, even the ghost of a memory was better than nothing. She walked by the Piggy-White, noting through the window a display of cute animal figurines in the front and large laundry drums in the back. The figurines seemed to move slyly in the corner of her eye but stood still when she looked back.

The emptiness inside nagged at her, pushing her forward, muting the questions that tried to rise to the surface of her mind. Hunger made everything simple. This was a mall. She had to eat. She had to find…She reached for the right word or image, but it wriggled away like a slick fish.

There was something wrong about the mall, even apart from the fact that all the shops were closed and there were no shoppers around. Was it a holiday? But the mall was brightly lit – except that the light was uneven, pooling in unpredictable corners, waxing and waning in spurts.

Hunger drove her on. She paused by a shuttered kiosk that sold snacks. There was a broken cracker left on the counter. She snatched it up, put it her mouth…and doubled up, coughing. The cracker flew out of her mouth, violently ejected. She clapped her hand to her mouth, as if trying to keep the food inside, but it was useless. Her mouth was empty. She looked at the cracker lying on the floor and felt no compulsion to put it back in her mouth.

This was ridiculous! She was starving. Starving people eat…anything.

And yet no appetizing picture made her salivate. She knew this was food, but it was an abstract, remote knowledge, much like her knowledge of what a hotel was. She desperately craved something to eat, but she did not know what this *something* was.

The panic was bubbling up again, threatening to drown her in its bright red flood. To keep it down, she walked faster and faster, as if trying to run away from herself.

Where is the bloody exit?

The mall was labyrinthine, like a dreaming brain, different levels dipping and tangling, linked by random walkways and unexpected little stairs. She saw a pair of swinging doors and went through. She found herself in a tunnel. Its walls were lumpy, deliquescing in long slicks of maroon and red. A couple of dim ceiling panels blinked desultorily.

She stopped to listen. Nothing.

The tunnel opened out into a larger space.

A train station.

An underground train station. This was another nugget of recognition which she hoarded eagerly because it proved, once again, that her amnesia was not total; that the occluded islands of her memory were surrounded by well-lit areas of common knowledge.

Hotel, mall, train station...

But with recognition came an unwelcome realization that trains cost money. And she had no money; nothing but the clothes on her back. There had been no purse or wallet in the hotel room. Or had there been? Should she go back and search the room again? No, no way! The idea of returning to the empty hotel gave her the creeps. Still, how had she expected to pay for food? She had not given it any thought. As opposed to train rides, food and money were not automatically connected in her mind.

The way into the station was blocked by hooded turnstiles, their gaping mouths eager for coins.

"Anybody here?" she called out, more to hear the sound of her own voice than to elicit an answer from the cavernous lobby. But an answer of sorts came: a ghostly echo of shuffling feet falling down like rain. She realized that there was another level of the city on top of the station.

She vaulted over a turnstile. Above her, multicolored displays shaped like sea-stars blinked and rolled rows of incomprehensible announcements on their gelatinous surfaces. The tongue of an unmoving escalator extended down, into the dark. But then she heard a whistle of an approaching train and more shuffling feet below. Passengers! People!

She started groping her way down – *why is there no light?* – when a rising wave of noise slapped her face. She could not understand what she was hearing: a mixture of slurping and sucking; wet sounds that were out of place in a train station, overlaid with a medley of screams and cries. There were people down there – and they were in trouble.

She hesitated. A hot draft touched her face. Why would she go down there? Something bad was happening. It had nothing to do with her, she was a stranger here, hungry and confused; she could not help even if she tried…But her body felt pulled by an invisible thread.

She took another step down and then another, trying not to stumble on the rounded ridges that pleated the surface of the escalator. And then a body smacked into her. Rushing up blindly, the stranger collided with her and almost sent the two of them tumbling down the escalator in a tangle of flailing limbs. She extricated herself from the person who had tripped her. It was a small woman, whose diminutive size did not prevent her from looking belligerent.

"What are you, daft?" the woman hissed. "Where are you going? Up!"

And the woman practically dragged her up the escalator. The slurping noise intensified, overlaid by a strange moaning, cooing sound as if produced by a flock of giant pigeons. She stopped, but the woman kept tugging on her hand until they were back in the main body of the station where the light was better, even though some displays had gone out and others pulsated with erratic waves of color.

She found herself edging back to the escalator. The moaning sounds reverberated deep in her belly where the hunger sat like a dead baby. But the woman barred her way. Finally, she was able to get a good look at her. The woman was tiny, almost child-sized, with delicate hands and a wrinkled face. She was dressed in a brightly colored padded jacket and trousers. There was something about her black hair and almond-shaped eyes that was familiar, but she could not put her finger on it, distracted by the moaning.

"We need to go!" the woman said briskly. Her voice was spiced with a sibilant accent that also sounded familiar. "There is a rogue train down there. Eating the passengers."

"What?"

"And the Hungry Ones are coming through. This entire district is evacuated. How come you don't know?"

"I lost my memory," she explained. "Amnesia."

The woman studied her, her head tilted. She looked like a tiny street bird.

"You are not a tenant," she said.

"What's that?"

"Later. We need to go."

Grasping her hand, the woman led her away from the escalator and back into the tunnel. She obeyed passively, exhausted by the roller coaster of her emotions and eager for the distraction of company.

And she finally realized why the woman looked familiar.

The Blades...

But the almost-memory instantly dissipated.

What are the Blades?

They got to the intersection of several passages. The woman placed her hand on the wall and a section folded in sagging pleats, letting in the misty daylight.

The smell hit her first: a mixture of tropical blooms and ripe garbage. And then the humidity. Her dress instantly stuck to her body. The hot wind blew purple petals and pieces of torn paper along the empty street. She picked up one piece, hoping it was a news bulletin, but it was stiff and blank. It crackled as the wind wound it around her fingers.

"The city is going to hell because of the tenants!" The woman sniffed. "Look at all the garbage! Derma wasted...Well, the

Hungry Ones can have them for lunch for all I care!"

She did not understand anything except the words "Hungry Ones" that sparked off a new spasm in her belly. She dropped the parchment that flew away like a huge butterfly.

"What is your name?" she asked the woman.

"Marika," the woman said. "And who are you?"

Horror flooded her again. How could she have forgotten her name? Or even the fact that she *had* a name?

Something stirred in the recesses of her memory, rising to the surface. She couldn't grab it – and then she could.

"K..." the sound caught in her throat, then it tumbled out.

"Kora," she said. "My name is Kora".

Chapter 2. On the Bridge

Marika darted across the road and Kora followed. Nobody in sight and yet she felt innumerable hostile eyes focused upon her, peeping from the windowless towers and the arching sweep of the overpass above their heads. The city brooded around them. The sky was draped with low clouds that reduced the slender high-rises to pencil sketches on the gray paper. They approached a wedge-shaped pink building, its bright color shocking against the smudged background.

She kept repeating her own name, filling her mouth with its reassuring nut-like roundness, her tongue caressing the hard ridges of the consonants, slipping into the grooves of the vowels. It was a sign that her memory was not lost. That she was not lost. She had a name. She was somebody.

The door of the building retreated and they rushed into another mall, this one smaller with a transparent ceiling. The door sealed itself behind them. Kora looked around and saw that this mall was not only deserted but trashed: display windows broken; merchandise scattered and trampled on the floor; garbage bins upended.

Marika scampered up the stairs to the mezzanine level that held a small eatery. It was in shambles: tables overturned, chairs scattered. Kora felt drops of warm rain falling upon her forehead. She wiped them away and stared at the red stains on her hand. She sniffed her fingers. The smell was pungent and salty like the reek of sea sludge.

Suddenly, the hollow of the mall boomed under the onslaught of many hands hammering on the door they had just passed through.

"Run!" Marika yelled. "Hungry Ones! The Pith won't hold them off. It's corrupted here."

Kora stood still.

"Come on!" Marika insisted. "You are human, not a tenant. I'll help you if I can, but I won't risk my life for you. Stay here and die or follow me and live. Your choice!"

She followed.

The viscous rain was falling off the edge of the mezzanine platform where dark puddles collected under the lone standing table. The table was piled with unwashed crockery, broken bowls, and splintered chopsticks. And mixed with the junk were hunks of raw meat, rivulets of blood drawing a river-delta map on the tabletop.

There was something under the table: a round ragged thing like a battered football. She stooped, looked into the torn holes of the missing eyes. Propped against the head was a menu with pictures of dumplings and steamed vegetables transformed into a carnivore's feast by splatters of blood. Kora wanted to throw up and realized she could not.

The door to the mall shuddered, and a wave of moans and grunts filled the empty space of the mall. Instead of being alarmed, she felt soothed by it. It was as monotonous as the sound of surf because there was no articulation to it. It just went on and on, at the same pitch, as if the lungs that were producing it were permanently locked.

Surf?

Kora shook off her fascination and ran after Marika. The mezzanine was connected to a slender gridiron walkway that crossed the mall. Marika was almost at the end of the walkway. Kora's longer legs ate up the distance, reassured by the boom of proper metal under her feet. All the materials she had touched this morning – from the soft elevator buttons to the sagging tunnel walls – had felt off somehow.

The entrance door crashed. Kora paused, peering back. Marika reached another door at the end of the walkway that swooshed open, letting in the foggy daylight. She pulled Kora through onto the thin strip of a catwalk suspended high above the pavement. The catwalk was connected to a bridge.

Or rather, bridges.

The bridge curved into infinity, dissolving into the muggy grayness of the tepid air. It soared and dipped, sometimes swooping above the tallest towers, sometimes snaking between their foundations, or burrowing into narrow alleys. Its many different styles were all joined together in chaotic and exuberant profusion. As a suspension bridge, it arced over the large reservoir that divided the city into two; and then it became an elephantine truss bridge, stomping upon the cancerous incrustations of makeshift huts; and then it wove around the flank of the peaked mountain that formed the backbone of the city…But anywhere she looked, it was there, in one form or another, stupendous, incomprehensible, overwhelming.

"What is this?" she breathed out.

"Skybridge."

The moaning came nearer. Marika rushed forward, her short legs pumping. Kora crouched, squeezed her eyes shut. The catwalk shuddered, swaying in the empty air. There was no railing.

"Come on!" Marika shouted.

I'm afraid of heights, she realized with dull surprise.

Marika paused ahead of her, her bright clothes as loud as a scream against the colorless sky.

"You're lunch!" she hissed.

The wedge of the mall hummed. There was a sharp clank of broken glass close, very close, behind her. She stood up, focused her eyes on her own feet and made a small step. Marika shrugged and walked on. Another step and another…

Something passed above her head, casting a moving shadow, but she was afraid to lift her eyes and risk another bout of vertigo. She bumped into Marika who cursed in a strange language as she fought to keep her balance.

"Slow down!" she hissed. "Khruts are here, they'll hold them back!"

Khruts? She was not sure that this was what Marika actually said; when agitated, her accent intensified to the point of incomprehensibility. But whatever it meant, it seemed to indicate that they were no longer in danger of pursuit.

She forced herself to unglue her eyes from the walkway and look down. Water like tarnished steel glinted below them. She made another mincing step and finally felt the reassuring hardness of the bridge deck under her feet.

"What are khruts?" Kora asked as they walked onto the broader surface.

"Guards. Tenants."

"Tenants?"

Marika rolled her eyes.

"You are not kidding about memory, are you? What happened? Somebody bumped you on the head? Raped you? Tried to sell you to the countryside?"

"I wasn't raped," Kora said indignantly. "And I wasn't sold. I was…given a task. But something happened. Maybe I got sick. Because I am really, really hungry. Like I haven't eaten in a long time."

Marika looked her up and down with cold appraisal.

"You look well-fed to me," she said. "But anyway, we'll straighten you out. Where I am taking you, we'll find out who you are. Because you are human. I have a nose for tenants. And just so you know: tenants are creatures who infest our city. And they have the gall to demand equal rights! Ha! Rights! They should be grateful that Grandfather did not exterminate them as he should have done when he led us across the Divide and into the city. It is ours now and will always be!"

Marika's words tumbled into her brain like an avalanche of pebbles, with sparkling gemstones of meaning lost in a jumble. She did not know what Marika was talking about, though she understood each word. And there was something about the woman that repelled and frightened her. But she promised to restore Kora's identity. What else could she do but follow her?

And perhaps when they reached whatever sanctuary she was taking Kora to, there would be something to eat.

Something I can eat.

The reservoir was long, sinuous, and dotted with small islands. The buildings on the other side were lower than on the side they had left, squat and pitted with blisters of shuttered balconies. There were other city levels above them, but Kora could not see them clearly in the haze; the visibility was even worse than before. The air smelled like the warm breath of cattle.

For a while, the walking was easy as the metal gave way to a smooth bone-like surface and the bridge broadened out into a flat ribbon. Despite the absence of a railing, Kora relaxed and gawked at the view. But then, they were suddenly confronted by a large hole fringed with jagged protrusions and dripping rags of some slimy material. It looked like the surface was eaten through by gangrene. On the other side of the hole, Skybridge rose up in a sturdy girder section, supported by a riotous jungle of beams. The question was how to get to it.

"Your mother's stinky underwear!" Marika cursed. "Bastard tenants! Suckling on the Pith until it rots! They won't rest until the city is dead, and then the Hungry Ones can pick our bones!"

Kora looked back at the mall. There was some commotion there, shadows rising and falling, but the thickening haze made it impossible to make out what was going on. Marika, meanwhile, sidled close to the hole. There was a narrow strip still spanning it on one side, but it looked impossibly fragile. Marika lay on her stomach and wiggled across the gap, propelling herself forward like a lizard. Kora grew giddy just looking at her. And then she was so much heavier than Marika; would not the treacherous substance of Skybridge give way?

"What are you waiting for?" Marika yelled.

Kora flopped down, clumsily imitating Marika, and screwed her eyes shut. She crawled on and her fingertips touched Marika's outstretched hand, indicating she was almost on the other side. And then something clutched her ankle.

She screamed and flailed, feeling the emptiness in her belly tilt sickeningly as her legs treaded air. Marika gasped and let go of her. The hold on her ankle ratcheted up into pain; something sharp pierced her flesh and she felt a drip of blood. Her nostrils were clogged by a cloacal stench. The strip of the bridge gave under her as if her body suddenly grew heavier. She clung to the edge with the dregs of her strength.

And then there was a shift inside her. A sudden spurt of energy blew away the cobwebs of confusion and fatigue that had wrapped her since the moment of her awakening. She threw herself forward, dragging her assailant with her as she reached the girder section. She rolled onto her back and saw, hanging above her like a desolate moon, a grey famished face with deep sockets into which dusty eyes were pushed as carelessly as dry raisins into a poorly made cake. Its teeth were broken and eaten by caries but sharp enough to draw more blood from the hand she instinctively raised to protect her face. It dipped its head again…and Kora grasped its pipe-thin neck and drew it to herself like a lover. She did not know what she was doing; some part of her cried out in disgust but another, stronger, part clicked into action. It was as if a fleshy flower unfolded inside her; she could almost see its blackish petals as they trembled and filled with meaty juices. An unclean warmth was spreading from the pit of her belly through her entire body.

The creature keened. Its tongue fell out of its maw, lolled upon its chin. Kora grasped it, vaulting to her feet. The creature twitched. She jerked the slimy rag of flesh, wound it around her wrist and easily lifted the squirming thing off the bridge, holding it aloft. It thrashed, and Kora realized that it was not trying to get at her. It was trying to get away.

She let the drained thing drop. It plummeted down, hit the water with a splash and sunk.

She met Marika's eyes and saw fear in them. Somehow the balance of power between them had shifted. She was feeling so much better: stronger, more alert, her body singing with…

What have I done?

The sucking emptiness in her stomach was gone.

"What have you done?" Marika whispered, unconsciously echoing Kora's thoughts. But even if she knew what to say, she would not have time to respond because the commotion at the mall suddenly grew louder and a knot of grey bodies erupted out of the haze.

"Run!" Marika yelled and sprinted forward, aiming for the short ladder up to the next section. Kora lingered, looking back, taking in the wolfish, emaciated bodies, some running on all fours; the grinning death-mask faces; the moaning, as monotonous as the humming of bees…

Unconsciously, she stepped forward, repelled and attracted in equal measure, eager to confront the creatures and horrified by her own eagerness, pulled and pushed by waves of conflicting impulses. Her shoe, still wet with blood from the wound inflicted by the creature, even though she felt no pain, slipped on the edge of the hole. Kora's arms windmilled as she fought to stay on the bridge.

A large shadow fell over her and she heard flapping of wings so close above that she had to look up. A fleeting glimpse of an enormous bird, or maybe a flying man, or both, and she lost her balance, pitched forward and crashed through the corroded deck. And then she was flying too, for endless seconds of heart-stopping terror, until she met the leaden surface of the water and plunged into the murky depth.

Chapter 3. The Buddha

Sputtering and coughing, Kora splashed around in blind panic. Finally, she realized she was not drowning. The water was warm, and though her swimming style would not win her any awards, it kept her afloat. She squinted at the tangle of girders high above her head. No way could she reach it.

She paddled away from the bridge that loomed over her, eerily silent. If Marika had seen what had happened to her, she had not stayed to help. Or perhaps she was still running away from the Hungry Ones. The thought of them cramped her guts, but she saw no sign of them or of the man-bird that had sent her into the water, though some indistinct shapes wheeled in the vapory sky.

She seemed to have fallen into the middle of the reservoir, equidistant from both banks. Kora trod water, trying to decide which way to go.

And then she saw it: a small island like a lush flower basket, an elongated oval of tropical greenery where stands of bamboo mingled with white-barked trees laden with large pink blossoms. A huge pylon supporting a section of Skybridge was planted in the middle of the island like a giant's leg.

A sweet smell wafted from the island, perfuming the haze. Rising above the trees was an orange-red tiled roof.

Kora swam toward the trees and hauled herself onto the shore that was covered in soft grass dotted with tiny star-shaped flowers. She shook herself like a dog, spraying drops of water in the warm air. Butterflies the size of her palm danced above her head. Their bright colors made the white sky look as dull as an empty bottle.

The building with the orange-red roof loomed through the bamboo.

It's a temple!

She stopped, gauging her reactions. Surely, she could not have lost her memory completely! She knew her name, after all. And the city, though strange, was *a* city; and she knew what a city was, what it was supposed to contain: hotels, malls, residential buildings, factories, jails, camps, weapon depositories, ironclad encampments. And temples. So, nothing surprising here. But temples were dangerous. She should not go inside.

And yet it did not quite match her almost-memories: familiar and unfamiliar at the same time, like almost everything else she had seen since her awakening. Before Kora could make a conscious decision, her feet carried her over to the building, swishing through the silky grass.

She searched for the scarlet pillars or rusty blades embedded in the threshold but there was nothing like that here. In fact, she started doubting her own determination of what this building was: it was too colorful, too pretty, like a confectioner's box. The pillars supporting the overhanging eaves were indeed red but of a cheerful doll-like hue and wreathed about with sinuous gilded dragons. The eaves themselves were elaborately carved.

She peered inside. Spice-smelling dimness, fresh flowers and fruit in porcelain bowls, a sand-filled vermillion cauldron with incense sticks…And a fat, golden-colored idol, its head drooping onto its ample chest, its round belly sticking out.

They are called eidolons, a memory whispered in her brain. *There is an engine inside. When they bring sacrifices...*

At this point, the memory abruptly shut down.

The eidolon lifted its head and looked at her.

Kora backpedaled in panic. Now, she saw what she had overlooked at first: the rhythmic rise and fall of its chest; the moist scarlet of its lips; the salty reek of its sweat underlying the sweetness of cinnamon incense.

Alive? How can it be alive?

"Hello," the eidolon said in a booming voice. "Who are you?"

Kora tried to swallow saliva and realized she could not. She coughed instead.

"And who are you?"

"A Buddha. Are you a tenant?"

She remembered what Marika had told her.

"No. I am human. I was…attacked on Skybridge. I lost my memory."

The eidolon nodded sagely.

"You may rest here," it said. "Perhaps you would like to light incense or make an offering?"

Kora had nothing on her except her sodden clothes but the idea of lighting an incense stick was, for some reason, appealing and even slightly titillating. She did so and looked back at the big creature. It appeared to be rooted in the fine sand of its lacquered box. And what she had taken for a conical headgear was in fact part of its skull.

"What are you doing here?" she asked.

"I answer questions of devotees. This is my job. If you make an offering, I'll answer yours."

Kora picked a china bowl from the floor and a small fruit knife lying on the altar. She made a cut on her left thumb. There was no pain, just a tiny burst of heat. Three drops of blood fell into the bowl. She put it in front of the Buddha. It looked startled, its irises rotating like spinning wheels, giving it a cartoonish expression.

The cut on her thumb closed neatly, the skin edges coming together with an almost audible gulp. In a moment, there was only a thin white line that faded even as she watched.

The Buddha cleared its massive throat.

"I'll answer three questions," it said.

"What are the Hungry Ones?"

"They are the doom of the city," it answered without hesitation.

"What am I?"

The Buddha hesitated.

"Come closer!" it commanded. When she did, he bowed its massive head and sniffed at her like a dog. And then it recoiled.

"What am I?" Kora insisted.

The Buddha was silent.

"I made an offering!" she cried. "You are bound to tell me!"

"We prayed to Grandfather to protect the city." The Buddha said slowly. "Or to destroy it, if it is polluted beyond redemption. I do not know his decision. But maybe you do. Or maybe you *are* his decision."

"Who is Grandfather? No, don't answer this. Just tell me: will I ever regain my memory?"

"Only you can know this."

"That's all you have to say? You are bloody useless! What a joke!"

She turned around, eager to be out. The incense aroma was suddenly suffocating, and she regretted disregarding her intuition that temples were dangerous.

The Buddha's booming voice stopped her.

"Consider," it said, "that there may be things you do not wish to remember."

Kora stood still, her back to the wheezing mountain of the alien body. Then she quietly left and closed the temple's door behind her.

The white sky had turned delicate gray-pink and the light was denser, making the tree blossoms crimson and the butterflies' wings black.

She walked aimlessly around the island and stooped to pick up some figs that had fallen off a sweet-smelling tree. They were purple and soft. She weighed them in her palm, brought one to her lips, bit into it experimentally. The muscles in her throat convulsed and ejected the choking mush with explosive finality. She tried to hold onto the residual taste but there was nothing in her mouth. She could not even taste her own saliva.

The dusk curdled into the indigo darkness, but it was still balmy. She watched the reflections of the city lights writhe in the dark water. Suddenly, she realized she was very tired. And with gratitude that this, at least, had not been taken from her, Kora curled up under jasmine bushes and fell asleep.

It is very quiet. The houses along the street, with their peeling paint and broken shutters, crouch in the dirty snow. They look abandoned, but I know there are people in them.

The only one outside is the crazy lady from down the street. She is sitting in the snow, her bare feet, purple from the cold, sticking out. The rags she wound around them have come off.

As I am watching her, she slowly keels over. She is now lying on her back, her toothless mouth gaping, her skeletal hands slowly opening like withered flowers. I edge closer, hoping to see what she has been clutching so tightly. I imagine a scatter of black seeds on the snow.

But there is nothing. Her hands are empty.

Kora woke up quickly and completely, a wrong sound reverberating in her ears. The sound had erased a welter of dream images that were an illegible signature of her lost identity. She tried to hold onto them, but they were gone, dissolved, and she focused on the present.

She listened. But everything was quiet now, the water splashing on the shore as the rising wind wrinkled the placid surface of the reservoir. The reflected city lights, a prodigious scatter of rubies, diamonds, and emeralds, were lifted in giant liquid handfuls by the waves and tossed around. The black sky blazed with golden towers.

She skirted around the shore to see the furthest end of Skybridge, leading to the part of the city opposite to the hotel. She could not suppress an exclamation of awe. If the slender skyscrapers had been impressive at daytime, at night, limned in shifting multicolored radiance, crowned with searchlights, alive with gargantuan scintillating images, they were resplendent. She was trying to figure out whether the images were ads, decorations, or messages when the sound came back.

It was the shuffling of many feet.

Kora listened intently. There was no doubt: the sound was coming from above her where the soaring arch of Skybridge cut through the blazing night like a scar. Hundreds of bare feet scraping against the pavement.

Then the sound stopped. The feet paused. A long silence.

It was broken by the smack of a body falling from a height. And then another and another. Dark shapes were falling off the bridge like ripe fruit from a shaken tree, slamming into the ground. In the riot of shadows, her eyes still blinded by the afterimages of the city lights, she could not at first discern what happened to them. But then she could no longer fool herself. Despite the considerable height of the bridge, they were not knocked out. Smudges of darkness rose up and shambled toward her.

She quickly ran the gamut of her options, which were not many. Scrambling up the pylon onto the bridge would bring her straight into the midst of the main body of them. Jumping into the water? There was no guarantee that they could not swim. Hiding? She saw how one of the dark silhouettes dropped on all fours, bringing its indistinct forequarters close to the ground. Were they tracking her by smell?

She turned around and raced toward the temple. Its interior was lit by incense sticks and candles; the Buddha's head rested on its fat chest, its eyes closed.

"Wake up!" she cried. "The Hungry Ones are coming!"

The Buddha jerked awake, just like a drowsing man. Its body quivering, it lifted his bucket-shaped head. The noises coming from the outside were now more than just shuffling; she could hear branches and twigs snapping under the weight of many bodies converging upon the temple.

"Can you do anything? Can you keep them away?"

With a rippling sound, the Buddha rose ponderously to its feet which had been hidden under his voluminous flesh. Its legs were short and stunted, giving him the appearance of a giant dwarf. As it stood up, its head, crowned with a lotus-shaped protuberance, hit the ceiling, which cracked, raining down pieces of plaster.

Kora cast about for a weapon. She picked up a decorative staff. It was hollow wood. Perhaps breaking a porcelain bowl…

A low gray figure appeared at the entrance, as feral as a street dog. In the flickering light, she saw the parchment skin, flaky lips, and dull eyes in the purplish sockets. Its limbs were spider-thin, but its belly was round and tight.

Kora tensed and felt the void inside her expand.

And then something huge and implacable closed over her midriff, scooped her up, and she was screaming and flailing until the kaleidoscope of images resolved itself into the debris-strewn ground below, filled with darting gray bodies. Her cheek was pressed into a soft golden wall smelling of cinnamon.

The Buddha had lifted her up, cradling her in its billowy arms like a mother carrying an infant. Its gait was rollicking but uncannily fast, its short legs devouring the distance. It was carrying her toward Skybridge and in the glow of the city lights she saw that the underside of the next section was crisscrossed by a tangle of beams and supports.

The gray bodies flowed after them, dividing into indistinct streams, closing in. In the semi-darkness, she could make little sense of what she was seeing. Quick shadowy forms were weaving through the trampled bushes, slithering through the bamboo stands. They ran like dogs – or did they? She saw some of them stand up and sprint after the Buddha, while others knuckle-walked like emaciated gorillas.

A couple of them fastened onto the Buddha's foot and the

giant grunted in pain, its blood rushing out with an obscenely loud slosh. But it had already reached the underside of Skybridge and heaved her up. She caught a beam and swayed like a pendulum until her leg hooked through another beam and she scrambled up into the webbing. Either her eyes got adjusted to the darkness or the lights blazed stronger, as if somebody turned up a switch on the entire city. She suddenly saw the melee quite clearly.

Spine-ridged backs and dusty gray pates milled below her as Hungry Ones leaped onto the Buddha's soft corpulent form and tore large pieces out of it. They made soughing noises like a breeze and the Buddha's cries of pain rang like wind chimes. Its golden skin hung in metallic tatters but the blood that splattered the ground was human-red. The Buddha flung off a skeletal body that hit the ground and instantly stood upright again, a huge mouth agape, and launched itself back at its prey. The Buddha tossed its head back, its eyes wide open as it met Kora's gaze. She wanted to yell at it that she did not need its self-sacrifice, did not want it, but it was too late. The golden body slumped down and was covered by the swarming pack like a piece of carrion covered by flies. Kora turned away, futilely trying to retch.

She climbed through the mesh of beams, her body strong and limber, acting on its own. She relaxed, letting it handle the challenge. And then jaws closed upon her ankle, the right one this time. She screamed, almost letting go of the plank. The creature thrust its death-head at her. Its teeth, even as they pierced Kora's flesh, seemed to be loose, rattling in its gums. Below, a knot of Hungry Ones were slavering and moaning, their skull faces strangely varied despite their uniform emaciation.

Clinging to the beam with one hand, she reached down and grabbed a fistful of its powdery skin. A flood of pure energy washed through her, washing away horror and disgust. The creature let go of her ankle and squirmed, trying to get away. She tossed it down where its mates tore it to shreds.

Kora kept climbing. She was afraid that the blood dripping down from the bite would whip them up into a feeding frenzy, but after a couple of seconds, the pain in her ankle disappeared and the flow of blood stopped. She did not stop to examine the wound and kept swinging through the dark beam-forest like a monkey, finding her next toehold by touch rather than sight.

A sack detached from the underside of the bridge and launched itself upon her. The odor of rotten grain made her gag and she saw a face like crumpled fabric and a hole of a mouth filled with needle-like teeth. She squeezed the face, crushing the elastic resistance of living flesh, and waited for a flow of energy. It came in indigestible dribs and drabs. She dropped the creature and it plummeted down into the gloom.

The web of beams thinned out and came to an end. The next section was a gossamer suspension bridge. She hauled herself up onto the deck and lay there, getting her wind back. The lights on the shore were so close she could distinguish individual lit windows in the megalithic blocks.

The shuffling was thunderous. She rolled over, her arms and legs throbbing. And there they were, a legion of them, so close that their stench – a mingled smell of dust, smoke, diarrhea, and rot – was like a blow. She scrambled up and fell again, balancing on all fours. *So many of them. Too many.* It was as if a reverse energy flow set in, the sheer number of them sucking strength out of her.

She had no time to think this through because the front ranks were reaching for her with clawed hands and, beyond them, the entire mass pressed forward like a wave.

She crawled forward, skinning her knees on the rough surface of the bridge. The weakness that engulfed her was insufficient to dull her despair. Her life had been so short, less than twenty-four hours, and yet she could not bear parting with it.

There was a commotion ahead, at the end of the bridge, where a mass of people congregated. Astonishingly, the rainbow-glittering sigils that she had taken for ads seemed to have detached themselves from the skyscrapers' walls and formed a line of free-standing branching pillars of light. But, she could not focus on them because the Hungry Ones were upon her.

With a superhuman effort, she shook them off and gained some ground, but they hung on to her, their nails digging into her flesh, energy flowing out of her as palpably as the blood from the opened-again wound on her ankle.

She tried to muster her recently-discovered power. Surely, it would come back, now that she was in mortal danger!

It was not a power, she realized. It was an appetite. And appetite cannot be forced.

She gripped a bony arm and yanked it, separating one creature from the squashed mass of its fellows. It tried to claw itself free, but she held on and felt strength pouring into her body. It struggled feebly and then was quiet. She flung it back and ran.

The crowd on the pavement milled restlessly, but nobody stepped forward. Until somebody did, pulled her off the bridge, and she glimpsed men in uniforms and luminescent sigils that, from close up, looked like some vast undersea creatures. But then a couple of people careened into her, pushed her to the ground. She struggled, afraid of being trampled. And then the same man tried to help her up; and she saw his face and mouthed his name; and a voice called "Daniel!" And the crowd surged forward, and everything went dark.

Chapter 4. Train-feeding

Mother is making soup. A tiny bunch of nettles and grass is lying on the draining-board, and she carefully pinches off one leaf at a time and drops it into the boiling pot. Metallic saliva floods my mouth, but I know what my body still does not: there is no nourishment in this pond-tasting water, and twenty minutes after gulping it down, I'll have to rush into the outhouse. And still I crave it.

The baby cries outside, a thin, mewling sound, and Mother's hand pauses in its monotonous stirring motion, and I see a familiar shadow cross her face. It is gone before I have time to be afraid.

Daniel Moylan woke up early, even though he had stumbled into his institutional bed long after midnight, shaking from the aftermath of an adrenaline rush. He had felt he would sleep forever. And here he was, the white morning sky staring through the un-curtained window like a cataract. The sun was a pewter disc in the east.

He tried to hold onto the disintegrating shards of his dream, but they slipped away. Good riddance. The dream was unpleasant, almost a nightmare.

He scrambled out of bed and did some push-ups. The barracks were mostly empty, the rows of iron bedsteads with scratchy gray blankets desolate in the flat light. Only two beds at the far end were occupied, the sleepers snoring in unison. They had been with Daniel at Skybridge yesterday. New recruits from low-levels. But good men, both of them.

As he walked by them, one of sleepers turned over and Daniel was startled to see a festering scratch on his cheek. Frowning, he hesitated but his bladder could not wait. Let the colonel deal with this!

The washroom was blessedly empty too. Having used the

urinal, he fiddled with the taps and was rewarded with a sigh of the pipes and a loud exhalation of hot air. He groaned. Another toads' strike?

But it was just an ordinary malfunction of the Pith; in a second, the shower-head coughed into action. Daniel smiled as the hot needles of water hit his upturned face. He would be ashamed to admit just how much these small city luxuries still thrilled him, even after all these years. Hot shower, the flowery smell of liquid soap, the white gleam of a clean toilet…The knowledge that a full breakfast was waiting for him in the canteen…

Somebody knocked on the steamed-up door of his shower cubicle. A vague face expanded and contracted like a balloon beyond the running streamlets. Daniel cursed quietly, motioned to the shower to cut off the water, and opened the door.

Max Rosen always reminded him of those pink crustaceans that hawkers in the Market sold from wicker baskets. It was easy to imagine him crawling into his uniform every morning like a hermit crab, shaping his shriveled body and sardonic face to fit the role of a militia colonel. There was nothing besides this role in his life. After the disappearance of his wife and daughter, he went on living in the married officers' quarters on the base, the higher-ups too busy with the chaos of internal squabbles and feuds with the Guards and City Corps to pay attention to this blatant violation of the housing code. He was never seen with a woman or a tenant, being as close to a Buddha in this respect as it was possible for a citizen to be. His men loved him and called him Shrimp behind his back.

"All ready to go I see," Rosen bleated.

"Yes, sir!"

"Train-feeding," Rosen declared after a longish pause. "Twenty minutes. Take Ivan Petrov and a civilian crew to the mid-level depot, hangar 25."

"Yes, sir!" Daniel responded crisply. That was better than he had expected. After last night's skirmish on Skybridge, it would be unfair to be sent to a cleaning-up operation in the Golden Flower, but since when was a militiaman's life fair? Still, Shrimp showed once again what a decent sort he was. He knew how Daniel felt about trains.

Max Rosen was at the door of the washroom when Daniel, a towel hastily wrapped around his midriff, called after him:

"Colonel, sir?"

Max turned around, his eyes glassy as if he had forgotten who Daniel was.

"What?"

"One of the men in yesterday's operation…"

"What about him?"

"He might have been bitten, sir!"

Max cocked his head.

"You do know, militiaman Moylan, that this is nothing but a vulgar superstition," he said in his scratchy voice. "All citizens are immune to the Hungry Ones' venom."

Yes, indeed. All citizens. But Daniel felt no desire to venture into the dangerous territory. His still-wet body was cooling off precipitously, his stomach was rumbling, and he had twenty minutes to get ready. Colonel Rosen was a stickler for time.

Lu Huan had probably just cut his face shaving.

"Twenty minutes!" Max Rosen reiterated and was gone. Daniel hurried back to the barrack. His stomach rumbled even louder. Twenty minutes or not, he was going to take full advantage of the breakfast spread in the canteen. Steamed vegetables, roast chicken, eggs, fresh bread…

The city provided.

The mid-level train depot was a huge, brightly lit space with a soaring derma ceiling over a white cavern where the off-duty trains rested, coiling like giant caterpillars. The platforms were immaculate. As Daniel, Ivan and their two civilian helpers marched in, the cleaning crew was straggling out: women in bright mismatched skirts and tops, their faces obscured by scarves. Bottom-feeders! One of the civilians made a rude noise; Daniel glared at him.

Only two trains were in, dozing in their cuttings, but even so, their presence filled the entire depot with an earthy warm smell and a wheezy breathing. Daniel smiled. He always felt safe around trains and snug inside their padded stomachs.

He walked over to the edge of the platform and patted the smooth gleaming pate of the smaller train. It was probably male, or juvenile, or both.

The train opened one round yellow eye, blinked sleepily and closed it again. Its breathing grill gleamed dully, vertical slats fanning. Many superstitious bottom-feeders who were afraid of MTT believed the breathing grill to be the mouth and the imposing slats the teeth, but Daniel knew better. The grill was merely an air filter, preventing particulates from fouling up the train's sensitive lungs.

He walked along the smaller train's length, checking the couplings of the cars, making sure the doors were shut and no juices leaked onto the rails. The train – now he was sure it was male as it lacked the terminal womb-car – was in great condition: his hide gleaming; the panels glossy and unscratched; the windows, covered by yellow derma membranes, without a single blemish. The black vertical lips of the doors made smacking sounds as the young train dreamed of his future journeys.

Daniel came to his last car. He had counted eight – too many for a youngster – but perhaps he had been given some by an older train. Indeed, the last two cars seemed slightly more worn. He examined the last coupling, a bony joint sticking out of the shaggy rear wall. The joint seemed all right, but Daniel was worried. Cars that had been passed too many times from one train to another eventually lost coupling capacity and could go rogue. Still, there was nothing he could do: an attempt to decouple a car would be met with a violent reaction from the young train. Trains were funny this way, so proud of their length that they would rather get sick or risk violent disintegration than give up extra cars.

Daniel forced himself to glance down at the tracks that snaked out of the depot. Officially speaking, it was not his purview: navvies, track-minders, and a whole army of other depot workers were supposed to take care of them. Daniel was glad: much as he liked the trains themselves, their tracks gave him the creeps. There was something off-putting about those blood-swollen, pulsating symbionts. They reminded him of fleshy-pink earthworms he had dug up…where? As usual, his memory shut down at this point.

At any rate, the tracks looked perfectly healthy: ruby-red, throbbing slightly, the snaking threat of the neuron cable at their center barely discernible. There was no leakage.

Daniel walked back and examined the bigger train. She was large and imposing, her golden face covered with the grayish fuzz that marked her age. Her womb-car was big and flaccid; she had clearly given birth many times. Her panels and trimmings were the same chocolate-brown as the smaller train, probably her son. Like him, she was soundly asleep.

Daniel made a decision. On his way, he had checked the supplies and cursed the City Corps; as usual, they had brought in less than was needed. Now, he and his team would be held responsible if the trains went hungry, refused to run, or in the unimaginably worst-case scenario, went rogue and ate their passengers. Being a natural optimist, Daniel did not want to think about this. But he had to consider how to divide the scant supplies they had. Normally, a female train would get more; and of course, she was also bigger. But he had made sure that there was no tell-tale pinkish swelling of her chassis. She was not pregnant and she was older, on her way to retirement. Her son, on the other hand, besides having the appetite of a growing body, also carried more than his normal share of cars. Possibly, he was being readied for a deep run into the countryside. And besides, Daniel was partial to the shiny-new youngster.

He explained his reasoning to Ivan Petrov, a young apple-cheeked recruit who trailed after him, hanging onto his every word. Daniel was flattered by his rookie admiration, if a little discomfited by having to play the role of a mentor. He did not like analyzing his own decisions: he just knew what had to be done.

He gestured to his civilian helpers, two nondescript middle-aged men, and they pushed open the depot's sliding doors and herded in the supplies.

Daniel covered his nose and mouth with a cologne-soaked handkerchief he had brought with him. His colleagues made fun of this sissy habit but they were just as revolted by the deadheads' diarrheal stench and only pretended to swagger through it.

The creatures milled along the platform, the civilians pushing them into lines with curses and sticks. The monsters had been neutralized: khruts had kept them in open-air pens for several days, starving them into listlessness. But a Hungry One was never safe to have around. Daniel and his team had to move quickly. He patted his 'arm. Wearing it gave him a sense of reassurance, even though he knew it was practically useless against so many of them. A single one, perhaps…but not a horde.

One of the smaller creatures brushed against him and Daniel cried out in disgust. It was the color of spoiled meat and its bulbous head on the reedy neck swayed idiotically as it clawed at Daniel's trouser leg. The protruding drum-like belly was cracked by a black fissure leaking foul ichor. He almost pitched the creature off the platform but restrained himself and shoved it into the line where a swollen female zombie, milky liquid leaking from her flattened dugs, caught it and held it close.

"Move, move!" Daniel yelled at the civilians who seemed to

be lost at what to do, desultorily poking at the zombies with their sticks and making the matters worse by aggregating them into big dangerous lumps instead of separating them into neat queues. Overcoming his revulsion, he started grabbing larger creatures and lining them up, while clubbing the smaller ones who could be mopped up later. He even used his 'arm a couple of times, just to show the civilians that he had one.

And then the mother train opened her big brassy eyes. Smelling food, she emitted a piercing whistle which silenced the shuffles, moaning, and curses of the melee. The Hungry Ones stopped resisting and let themselves be sorted out as necessary.

The juvenile train woke up too and added his breaking, adolescent whistle to his mother's triumphant call. The black-lipped doors slid open. Because this was a feeding-time, there had been no attempt to prepare for passengers or cargo: the exposed car interiors gleamed red and brown, the cartilage ribs flexing, the curving walls and ceilings dripping with sharp-smelling digestive juices that collected in slimy puddles on the floor. Some of the Hungry Ones moaned but most just dropped their ugly bald heads and let themselves be pushed into the maws of the cars. As he had decided, Daniel steered more of them toward the son-train. And he was glad to see that the mother-train was on board with what he was doing.

He brushed his hand gratefully along her warm, fuzzy flank. Trains were not only smart, they were good; better than most humans, to say nothing of toads and ducks.

In no time, the platform was cleared. The trains had been fed, and Daniel was free to go back home and rest, watch flambeau-casts, or play canasta with his mates.

Neither appealed to him. He decided to visit the Market instead.

Chapter 5. James Wingate

"Daniel!"

It was her own voice. Kora was mildly surprised when the response to it was something cold on her lips. A pinkish blob swam into focus.

It was a nurse dabbing her face with a wet cloth.

Kora tried to sit up and discovered she was still dizzy. She must have been asleep, but she could not remember any dreams.

"Drink?" The nurse offered her a glass of water. She was a young red-head with a thin mouth.

"No!" Kora pushed the glass away. "Who is Daniel?"

"How would I know?" the nurse asked reasonably.

Kora looked around. She was in bed in what appeared to be a hospital room. She swung her legs over the edge of the bed, her thin gown falling open.

"Hey, easy there!" the nurse tried to push her back. Her name-tag read "Sylvia".

"Where are my clothes?"

The nurse snorted.

"You wouldn't want to wear what's left of them!"

She felt a tide of rising panic at the threat of being trapped here. Hospitals were bad places.

"Give me something else to wear! I want out!"

"Come on," the nurse said soothingly. "Nobody's keeping you here against your will. We're just making sure you're OK!"

"I am OK! I want out!"

The door opened and another nurse, a plump middle-aged woman, looked in.

"A visitor!" she announced.

"A visitor for me?"

"Yes. Can he come in?"

He?

"Yes…no!" Kora looked at her state of semi-nudity, pulled the sides of the gown together. The idea of meeting a person who must have a clue to her identity in this institutional garb was, for some reason, unbearably humiliating. "I want my clothes!"

Sylvia sighed.

"I'll get you something to wear," she said.

It took fifteen minutes for Sylvia to fetch a pair of pants and a clean white shirt and for Kora to get dressed. During this time, her mind went through several cycles of anger at herself for postponing the all-important revelation of her identity because of vanity, and relief at the delay in confronting her past.

As she was tightening the belt in her pants, she debated with herself whether she actually wanted to know who she was.

There may be things you don't want to remember, the Buddha had said.

The Buddha was dead. It had sacrificed itself for her. Why? Did it know who she was? It had behaved like a living being but surely it could not have been!

Did she owe it to herself to find out who she was? Did she owe it to that strange eidolon?

She straightened up, took several deep breaths, and strode into the waiting room.

The man rose as she entered. She was simultaneously relieved and disappointed that there was no sudden jolt of recognition. He was a perfect stranger.

Buffeted by conflicting emotions, she missed his first words and had to ask him to repeat.

"How are you feeling?"

"I'm fine."

Not quite true. There was no residual ache from the bashing she had taken on Skybridge. But there was a tiny emptiness sucking at her innards like a leech. She tried to put it out of her mind by focusing on the man instead.

He was young, perfectly groomed, in a nice tailored suit. His sandy hair was expensively styled. His face was the least impressive part of him: it was narrow, with a jutting parrot-like nose and weak chin.

"I'm glad to hear it," he said with what she classified as a professional smile.

"Who am I?" she blurted out, suddenly tired of procrastination and uncertainty. If there was no avoiding the truth she would rather confront it head-on.

"Well…" the man blinked. "It's a rather long story and I'm not the one to tell it…"

"Do you know who I am?" she insisted. She did not like the man.

Daniel…

But she did not know who Daniel was.

"I am here to take you to one who does," the man replied smoothly. "But why don't we start from the beginning? I'm James Wingate."

He wants to know if I remember my name.

"I'm Kora," she said.

There was some bureaucratic procedure for checking out, but Wingate took care of it. She waited behind the barrier in the huge hospital lobby, smelling the pungent aroma of antiseptics and sick bodies, blindly staring at the large official portrait of a vulpine-faced man in some sort of ceremonial robe. She was still in shock.

He had asked her why she ran away from the hotel, sounding reproachful. She bristled.

"The hotel was deserted," she had said.

"We had to evacuate because of an unexpected incursion," he had explained. "It was not our choice. The militia and the Guards sealed the area and basically hustled all our personnel out, and by the time the chairman got in touch with Mayor Volk, it was too late."

Wingate finished his interaction with the clerk by signing some form and came over to her.

"Shall we go?"

She nodded.

She braced herself as they stepped outside, into the muggy, noisy ocean of people. Her first impression of the city had been very wrong. It was the opposite of empty. The street was a river of pedestrians, flowing between the cliffs of high-rises. She was buffeted, smothered, pushed and prodded.

Wingate grasped her hand and led on.

After the first disorienting moments, she realized the crowd was not the chaos it appeared to be. There was an etiquette here that allowed the smooth conveyance of this stupendous mass of people toward their various destinations. She quickly mastered the simple rules: don't stop suddenly, move at the same speed, never look anybody in the eye, do not apologize when you bump into another pedestrian. Wingate dropped her hand as she became more confident and walked a couple of steps ahead of her.

As she followed, eyes focused on the back of Wingate's head, anxious not to lose him in the press of bodies, she was trying to figure out whether she was remembering previous experience or adapting to a new situation. Had she been in the city before?

She could not decide. The size of the crowds was shocking and so was the height of the glittering towers that lined the street. But at the same time, being here felt right. She belonged in the city. She did not know how she knew it, but she did.

As the first confusion wore off, she became concerned about people touching her, or rather her touching them. It was impossible to avoid brushing against other pedestrians and nobody seemed to mind this casual bodily contact with strangers. Neither would she if it were about modesty. But it was not.

Her mind flashed back to the conversation with Wingate. She did not trust the man, but in the light of her experience on Skybridge, she could not deny that what he had told her made sense.

She had asked for a drink. It came out of her mouth automatically because she knew this was what people did in socially awkward situations. At the same time, even as she was saying it, the notion of drinking struck her as absurd.

It seemed to strike Wingate in the same way. He stared at her incredulously and before she could rescind her request, he walked out and came back with a steaming cup which he placed before her.

She had stared at the dark liquid, breathed in the bitter smell and coughed. She licked her lips. They did not need it; they were soft and pliant. Her tongue left no residue of wetness but neither did it feel dry.

She lifted the cup, sloshed the coffee around and poured a tiny amount into her mouth. And it instantly flew out like a stream of projectile vomit. She doubled up, coughing, the coffee splashing onto the floor, some of it ending on Wingate's immaculate suit. He dabbed at the stains with a handkerchief.

"You'll probably feel worse if you try to force yourself," he said.

"What's wrong with me?" she cried, trying to hold on to her anger because it staved off horror.

"Nothing. You're quite well. Better off than most people, in fact. No dieting, no bingeing, no bloat…"

"Are you saying I don't need to eat at all?"

"I'm saying you don't need to eat what others eat."

Not a power. A need. An appetite.

They have a name for those like me.

As they walked, she almost stepped on a legless man who had taken over a tiny portion of the pavement, displaying a collection of boiled sweets on a cardboard square. Other pedestrians expertly navigated around the cripple, respecting his tiny fiefdom. And he was not alone; there was a whole micro-economy by the side of the street: hand-sized carts hawking steaming noodles, a fat woman brandishing a clothes tree hung with bright scarves, a child offering boxes of pins. People were actually buying from hawkers, despite the endless row of shops in the ground floors of the high-rises. There was a brisk trade in seemingly worthless items. A young man was rooting through the basket of murky glass eggs, precariously balanced on a stoop. An older man got a sizzling pancake from a griddle and miraculously managed to finish it off without getting oil onto his white shirt. A girl dropped a coin into the legless man's cup and scooped up a handful of sticky bright candies, popping them into her mouth. Kora winced: wasn't street food unsanitary?

She almost laughed at the incongruity of this thought. For her to condemn the eating habits of other people when she herself was…She forbade herself to think the word, but it buzzed in her mind like a carrion fly.

Wingate stepped aside, waiting for her to catch up. She realized something was missing: the curb. The entire street was one pedestrian thoroughfare and the infrequent rickshaws managed the best they could.

As she considered the absence of transportation, something swooshed above her head and looking up, she saw the graceful arch of Skybridge against the grey sky and a sinuous caterpillar of cars crossing the gap between two towers and disappearing into the darkness of a tunnel. So there were city trains here.

"How far?" she asked.

"Not far. We'll take the mid-level escalator."

Somebody bumped into her, a woman with a child in a sling. Kora tensed but nothing happened.

Nothing will *happen! These are people. Not…Hungry Ones. Not zombies!*

Wingate had used this word and, when she asked what it

meant, laughed.

"Just a stupid label flambeaus invented."

"Zombies are the dead," she had whispered.

"Really? Well, the Hungry Ones are definitely not dead. We wish they were."

"So what are they?"

"Invaders from the countryside. Tenants of sorts, I suppose."

Tenants. Both Marika and the Buddha had spoken of them, but she still did not understand what they were. There was so much she did not know.

But one thing she knew by now and wished she did not. She knew what had happened on Skybridge.

A line of grey old people shuffled by, walking in a synchronized file like one body. As they were passing, Kora realized that they *were*, in fact, one body: the face of each grew into the back of the person ahead.

She was seized by sudden horror. Scanning the faces of the crowd, she saw what she had subliminally noticed already: many did not look entirely human.

She turned to Wingate, stabbed her finger at the shambling file.

"What are they?"

He shrugged:

"Toads."

"Toads?" It made no sense. But she had more pressing concerns than nomenclature.

"Can I…can I?"

He shook his head.

"I don't think so."

"You don't fucking *think* so?"

"Listen," Wingate said, his expression clearly saying that he would rather be scavenging in a garbage bin than acting as her chaperone, "why don't you just wait a little? Seriously, the chairman will answer all your questions. I'm just an employee!"

Kora took a deep breath, nodded and strode after him.

They came to a place where the street rose up sharply, snaking through the mass of smaller houses that clung to the slope like swallows' nests. An escalator under a bright canopy cut through the middle of the street: four lanes of accordion-pleated crawling stairs, carrying heavy loads of chatting, eating, staring passengers. Wingate jumped upon the lowest rung and Kora followed.

"How far?" she asked.

"Not far. This is the mid-level escalator. There will be a cable car to take us to up-levels. And then we go to the chairman."

She was squeezed by sweating bodies. She wanted to scream at them to step back from her but this, of course, was impossible. After a while, realizing that nothing was happening, she relaxed.

"Is he the ruler of the city?" she asked.

"What?" Wingate snorted. "Ruler? We have no 'ruler'. He is the founder and chairman of a private company."

"So who…you know…who is the head honcho here?"

"We have a democratically elected mayor," Wingate said primly. "You saw his picture in the hospital. Mayor Volk. But we'll have a new election soon."

The inside of the canopy was pale yellow, swirling with washed-out colors of the rainbow. Its ragged edges were pulling away from the hand rails, disclosing glimpses of the scene outside. The escalator crawled up slowly, occasionally accelerating with a jerk. The kaleidoscope of images and sensations beat against her: stench and perfume; tendrils of mist and waves of laughter; thousands of voices blending into the steady wheezing of the city.

The stalk-slender high-rises dominated the scene, but they were surrounded by the secondary accumulation of huts, sheds, walkways, and canopies. The towers glistened with snake-skin glamor; some had strange curlicue shapes clinging to their sides. Their edges were sharp against the roiling, cloudy sky.

Little else was. Skybridge flowed through the clouds like an estuary. The alleyways below meandered, collided and twisted around each other. Apartment blocks were covered with irregular growths of flimsy rooms, balconies, and canopies like fungi on a rotting stump.

Up and up and up. This much she had figured our already: the city was on a mountain or perhaps *was* a mountain. The humped shape on whose flank they were crawling like a pair of ants was a gargantuan heap of people, buildings, greenery, rocks, cable cars, markets, alleys, temples, all veiled and softened by the sulfurous haze.

One building stood out: a broad looming shape, bright with autumn colors - orange, yellow, sienna; bound with shiny ribs; crowned with a five-story-tall structure of toothy peaks and gables. Wingate told her it was the City Hall.

Below, reservoirs and lakes glistened like punctuation marks in the sprawling text that was the urban spillover onto the plain. And beyond it...everything melded into an insidious foggy background, but she thought she could see a brownish flat cut with black lines like giant crayon strokes. Fallow fields.

"How many people live in the city?" she asked Wingate.

"Five million humans. Ten million tenants, maybe."

She looked down into the dirty alleyway that stank of garbage and piss. There was a small stall piled with multicolored yarn. A mangy cat sat on the yarn, as if guarding it. As Kora and Wingate were carried above it, the cat lifted its head, looking straight at Kora. It had a flat human face with a fixed idiotic smile.

"A toad," Wingate said.

A hawker with a basket of rolls squeezed by, the rich smell of freshly baked bread wafting over the stinking fumes. Kora caught Wingate unconsciously licking his lips and envied him.

They finally got out onto a large platform suspended above a slope so steep that there were no buildings on it, only a tangle of luxuriant bushes with large purple flowers. Above them, the slope became shallow once again and terraces were carved into it with large houses clinging to the ledges, half-hidden by blossoming trees and shrubs.

"Up-levels," Wingate said.

The cable-car was waiting for them. As Kora walked toward it, she accidentally trod upon a crumbled candy wrapper, which unfolded itself into a flat sheet of tissue and flittered away.

"More of them now," Wingate said gloomily. "All the garbage in the Market…people are so careless, throwing stuff away. And the authorities are too busy, what with the invasion and all…"

Experimentally, she stepped upon another candy wrapper, but it remained supine.

Chapter 6. The Flambeau Hatcher

Daniel stopped on his way to the Market to buy dim sum from a street vendor and to watch a flambeau hatcher.

Munching on a turnip cake, he leaned against the wall as the bent old man lined up the fire-eggs on the dirty square of the pavement that he had fenced around with empty cardboard boxes. The flow of passers-by obediently detoured around the hatching island, respectful of the man's trade, which was supposedly established by Grandfather himself.

Each egg, a roughly shaped piece of murky glass, had a tiny flame inside. The hatcher placed some tattered good-luck pendants and a couple of incense sticks around the eggs and muttering incomprehensible incantations – or perhaps simply muttering – picked one and started chafing it energetically between his calloused, scarred hands. Nothing happened for a while and some onlookers moved on. Daniel bit into a shrimp bun and watched.

Putting the egg down, the hatcher dragged out from under a pile of rags a tiny briquette grill, splashed it with lighter fluid and lit it up. Then he picked the egg again and held it above the grill, slowly moving his cupped hands up and down, as if measuring the precise distance. Daniel winced: it looked like self-cooking and even though the man was clearly a pro, the shiny scar tissue that covered his palms was still painful to see.

The acid smoke got into his lungs and he coughed. The pollution today was worse than usual; you could hardly see ten paces ahead. Daniel contemplated walking away when the egg hatched.

The old man's involuntary hiss of pain was drowned in the flambeau chick's loud cackling as the creature shook off the hot slivers of its glass egg and danced on the grill. It was pale and ungainly, in the shape something like a convoluted letter "K" surrounded by curlicues. It was still as flat as a sheet of paper, but the heat from the grill was pumping it up with volume and color.

The hatcher tried to pick it up, but the sharp beak of the "K" pecked at him, drawing blood. Undeterred, the hatcher squeezed the creature's pinched waist and held it tight, its feverishly clacking arms facing away from him. The flambeau flushed angry red.

The hatcher clearly found it hard to control the writhing chick and passers-by started giving him a wide berth, afraid of his charge going rogue. But, fortunately, a buyer came just on time. A flambeau pole swayed and dipped down, its recessed head emerging from beneath its protective hood. It dropped some coins at the hatcher's feet and lassoed the hatchling with a loop of its vibrissae. It lifted the struggling youngster above the heads of the watching crowd and deftly tossed it to the overhanging roof of a secondary house where a small colony of lighters caught it and hustled it away.

The hatcher counted the coins and cursed under his breath.

"That's a hard work, father, isn't it?" Daniel asked sympathetically.

The hatcher mutely turned his burnt and calloused hands palms up. Gathering his equipment, he shuffled away into a narrow recess between the primary houses. Daniel went on. He had heard that there were big hatching factories in the country run by khruts. He did not quite believe it – just another silly rumor – but perhaps it would not be such a bad idea to give respite to the hatcher's seared hands.

Being in pain constantly…No, it did not bear thinking about.

The Market was booming.

Daniel wove in and out of side alleys. This was a near-impossible feat, considering that the crowd was packed into a solid mass. But since his arrival in the city, Daniel had spent so much time in the Market that he knew its ins and outs better than many jobbers born and bred in its stinking alleys. So now he popped into a lingerie shop, smiled at the girl named Candy with whom he had slept twice, ducked under the curtain of frilly undergarments and emerged, as he knew he would, into the Butchers' Plaza.

He breathed in the hot smell of dust and blood, and smiled. When he had first come to the city, he ate meat three times a day, intoxicated by the urban bounty. Now, he cut it down: a militiaman's pay only stretched so far. But he still loved seeing meat, raw or cooked. Sometimes he would just walk around, window-shopping, enchanted by the glistening wealth of scarlet cuts marbled with healthy golden fat, and by the garlands of roast ducks, chickens, and rabbits hanging from the hooks like exotic fruit.

The Butchers' Plaza today was relatively calm. The housewives, toting giant derma bags, bargained with no-nonsense purposefulness. The tiny eateries surrounding the plaza were only half-full since the lunch hour had passed. Daniel was not particularly hungry, but he looked at the price list in one of them – and stopped. What the hell?

A big fish flopped across the plaza, its mouth gulping asthmatically. The fishmonger whose tank it had escaped from ran after it, whacking it with a fly swatter, until it wriggled into a crevice slick with offal. The butchers in their spotted white aprons roared with laughter.

Still reeling from the prices that had gone up at least twenty percent since last week, Daniel searched for the fish's origin and was surprised to see that many stalls were now selling prawns, fresh-water fish, and even frogs and snakes. Normally, the butchers would not allow this inferior flesh to be sold in their precinct.

A hand touched his elbow, a purposeful touch different from the random jostling of the crowd. He turned back and saw nobody. Was somebody messing around with him? Just because he was not in uniform did not mean he was not a militiaman of the city! But then his eyes traveled downward and he frowned. A child? There were few reasons a child would be alone in the Market and none of them good.

She looked up at him. She was not a child at all.

Kora clung to the cage of the cable-car. The height sucked at her like a leech. So easy to let go, to plunge into the void, crush her bones, pulp up her flesh…She shuddered, remembering her funk on Skybridge. It would be easy to close her eyes, but she forced herself to look. She wanted to know the city and to know meant to see.

But she could see very little.

The higher they rose, the worse the smog became. The sky was fleecy-white, the sun a colorless ball, and the land shrouded in a dirty pall.

"Why is the pollution so bad?" she asked.

"The city exhales."

She coughed as she breathed in the humid, feathery air.

"Can't the government control emissions from factories?"

"They do. But they can't control the city."

The car bumped to a standstill. A uniformed attendant opened the door and helped her out. They were in a small terminal; beyond the open arch of the exit, lush tropical greenery waved in the fragrant wind.

"We'll have to walk," Wingate said.

"No more cars?"

"Nobody can see him who has not walked a thousand steps."

She thought it was a metaphorical flourish until she saw it was meant literally. In front of her rose a wide and imposing stairway shadowed by overhanging tamarind trees and flanked by rose bushes. And on each step sat a golden Buddha.

These were smaller than the creature who had saved her life

on the island, the size of a teenager. They followed her with their round eyes and adjusted their flowing robes. The sweet smell of cinnamon was overpowering.

Kora looked away. Feeling guilty about its self-sacrifice, she had tried to convince herself that the Buddha on the island had not been actually alive. Some eidolons were so cunningly made that they could fool a casual observer.

"What are they?"

Wingate, who had overtaken her by starting to ascend the staircase, shrugged.

"Well, they are just a welcoming committee. People think they can read minds and know if visitors come in peace, but this is just a Buddha-superstition. The chairman has his own Guards to protect him from assassination attempts."

"But what *are* they?" Kora's voice rose to a hysterical pitch.

"They are Buddhas!" Wingate tossed back, losing patience. "Listen, we have to go! It's not a good idea to keep the chairman waiting!"

Kora pivoted on her feet and rushed to one of the golden creatures. She grasped its flowing robe and jerked it roughly. The Buddha gave a piercing cry and she saw with horror that what she had taken for its robe was in fact a loose flowing skin that hung off its waist in soft billows. Her jerk had dislodged the creature from its pedestal but did not topple it because it was rooted in the gravelly soil by a thick copper-colored stalk that pulsated with blood. The webbed tendrils running like capillaries under the soil started bleeding as the creature bleated helplessly.

"What are you doing?" Wingate rushed back but stopped at some distance from her, apparently unwilling to tackle this large woman going berserk.

"I'm sorry," Kora whispered, horrified by the bleeding roots. She tried to straighten the Buddha up, re-plant it in the pedestal but it pushed away at her with its soft, ineffectual hands, all the time crying in pain. Its brethren stirred anxiously, twittering and clicking like a flock of birds.

"It's not supposed to be alive!" She whispered. "It's supposed to just an eidolon, an image!"

Wingate stared at her with incredulity, as if the full extent of her ignorance just dawned upon him.

"Everything in the city is alive," he said. "The city is alive."

He thought at first that she was a tenant, of an unknown variety to be sure, but there had been many such now, splitting off from the Pith. Some said it was because of the Hungry Ones.

But she behaved as if she was human and Daniel decided that she was. Her size – like a twelve-year-old – was exceptional but not impossible. Perhaps she was stunted by disease. Perhaps, like him, she had come from the countryside and had been starved as a child but, unlike him, carried the withering mark of hunger into adulthood.

She led him through the market crowd to an eatery under the red awning which, Daniel noted with some bemusement, was pleated paper, not derma. The owner sullenly served them with bowls of piping-hot rice soup. He was a dawn, as was the woman. Daniel was a dusk, but he never gave it a second thought. If people were good to him, he would be good to them – human or tenant, dawn, dusk, or noon.

"So, militiaman," she said with a sibilant lilting accent that many dawns had, "you have lots of work nowadays, don't you? The trains are calving, they're so stuffed."

"How do you know I'm a militiaman?" he demanded.

She shrugged and noisily slurped her soup, indicating it was a stupid question. He followed suit and burned the roof of his mouth.

"Lots of work," she continued, "and the pay is not good, is it? Not enough to feed a big fellow like you."

"Look," he said, "I don't know what you want from me but I'm telling you straight that you're wasting your time. I'm not going to do anything illegal. I value my citizenship and I respect my oath."

"Yes, the oath," she said musingly. "Lucky you. Not many countrymen get to swear it."

He flushed angrily.

"I'm a citizen, just like you!"

"Of course, of course!" she flapped her tiny hands. "No disrespect! Just saying. Many country people want to come here. Few do. Grandfather is watching over you."

Daniel rolled his eyes. The belief in Grandfather's survival was fine for bottom-feeders, but he was still amazed that so many regular people took it seriously. Grandfather had been a great leader, no question about it, but he had died many cycles ago. And dead was dead.

"Whatever." He finished his soup and was surprised when the owner plunked a tray with sliced roast duck served over rice on the table. This was more than just a token snack. But if they wanted to waste money on feeding him, why not? He picked up chopsticks and tucked in.

The tiny woman was watching him, sipping tea from a porcelain cup. Her hands and neck were smooth and plump, but her face was crisscrossed with deep furrows that did not follow the ordinary frown and smile lines. They looked as if they were randomly cut with a scalpel.

"Food is good in the city, huh?" she remarked.

"Just tell me what you want from me."

"So, you can say no?"

"So, I can say no and finish my duck in peace."

"Bad memories spoil appetite."

"What?" He dropped a chopstick.

"Nothing." The woman got up. "Eat your lunch. I'll talk to you later."

"Hey, come on!" he protested at her retreating back clad in

loud, flower-printed silk.

"Don't worry," she tossed over her shoulder, "it's on the house."

And she slipped out, leaving the bewildered Daniel contemplate the greasy remnant of his meal.

Chapter 7. The Chairman

She noticed that the higher she got, the more misshapen the Buddhas became. Some had giant flapping ears that spread out like batwings. Some had more than one nose. One creature who scowled at her had no mouth. Another's eyes had fused together into an hourglass shape, slowly rotating in its bucket-like face. Still another jabbed at her with an index finger as long as his arm.

"Why are they like this?" she asked.

"The chairman likes rare breeds."

It was one of those answers that Wingate seemed to specialize in: perfectly reasonable and devoid of any useful information. The man must be a consummate bureaucrat. She caught herself questioning the thought, worrying at it. How did she know what a bureaucrat was? How did she know what she knew? The wound of her memory was bleeding self-doubt.

Consider that there may be things you don't want to remember.

She glanced back at Wingate who was puffing and huffing below her. The man was badly out of shape. She did not even break a sweat.

The last couple of steps were broad and paved with white stone. Their Buddhas here were grotesque obese creatures with toothed maws in their bellies that clacked threateningly as she walked by.

The top of the mountain was leveled into a formal garden where decorative rocks, fretted and twisted like underwater reefs, were artfully scattered among rose beds and white-flowered bushes. The air was as sweet as candy.

There was a small pavilion with a red tiled roof, half-hidden in a stand of bamboo. But her attention was diverted as something flitted above her head. She looked up. Swooping and soaring over the garden were what she first took for big birds, no, giant birds. But then she saw that in addition to majestic wings, they also had stunted arms and legs, neatly folded and tucked into their feathered underbodies. One of them swooped low, thrusting an owl-like face with round yellow eyes and a curving beak at her. Nictitating membranes slid over the eyes as it banked away sharply.

"Khruts," Wingate said. "Guards."

They were like the creatures she had seen on Skybridge.

The pavilion had an open veranda. A man sat there, cooling himself with a gaudy fan. He got up when they approached.

He was trim and broad-shouldered, wearing a button-down white shirt and dress slacks. He was Asian like Marika, with a smooth, expressionless face and wary eyes shadowed by heavy lids.

She stared at him, disappointed and bewildered. Like Wingate, he was a total stranger.

He ushered them into the pavilion. The furniture was opulent: gilded chairs and overstuffed couches. But strangely, pictures on the walls were not in keeping with this ostentatious luxury. They had been seemingly cut out from magazines and newspapers and tacked on higgledy-piggledy, with no frames. They were all of human faces, mostly in close-up. All the faces were male.

He motioned at them to sit down. There was a box on the table with brightly colored cubes that she recognized as dice. There were also several dishes with assorted snacks, a bottle and glasses. The chairman poured a glass of some anise-smelling liquid for himself and after a moment pushed the bottle toward Wingate. He did not offer any to Kora.

Kora glared at him. He smiled. His face muscles barely moved and the smile looked painted on.

"How are you feeling?" he asked Kora. His voice came as a shock because it *was* familiar but then she realized, disappointed, that it was only because he spoke with the same accent as Marika.

"Angry," she spat at him.

"Not hungry?"

"If you think I'm hungry, why aren't you offering me food?"

"I tried to explain…" Wingate butted in, but the chairman waved him into silence.

"I will," he said. "You'll have more food than you can eat."

"Like the meal I had on Skybridge?"

"That was a mistake. We did not mean to abandon you. You ran away."

"Who are 'we'?"

"I," said the chairman. "I made you. I made you who you are."

She stared at him, torn by conflicting emotions. This was her creator, this smooth, impersonal businessman? No, this couldn't be. But why not?

He is not the one. He does not have…blades?

Nonsense. Delusion. I am here; I am now. I have to find out what has been done to me. And why.

"Why?" she asked.

"To fight the Hungry Ones. Consider – people fight because they want to. But you fight because you *have* to."

"I don't have to do anything!" she cried. "I am a human being, not a monster! I have choices!"

Something dark shifted in his eyes.

"We all have choices," he said, his voice dropping. "Or at least we want to. You are no different from me or him." He nodded at Wingate. "All who are living are in bondage to their hunger. You are made so that your hunger is your weapon."

She stared, blindly, at the dish of olives on the table, green and plump, swimming in oil, dusted with red paprika. Her mouth tasted of nothing.

She had known, of course, even then, on Skybridge. But she had not wanted to name it, waiting for others to do so. And yet, when Wingate had explained, she had still rejected his explanation because the man was so clearly a subordinate, a weakling. She had wanted to face the chairman and to defy him as if defiance could change what she was, what she had become.

"A predator," she said. "A zombie-eater."

A cannibal.

Wingate had not used that word. But he was clear enough about what had happened on Skybridge.

She had eaten the Hungry Ones.

She had not merely repelled their attack using some magical superpower. She had actually eaten them, consumed their energy, derived nourishment from their depleted bodies. And this was the only way in which she could sustain herself. All living beings have to eat and so did she. She ate zombies.

Wingate had been maddeningly vague on how this came to be. He did not deny that something had been done to her but insisted it was with her consent. He claimed not to know whether her amnesia was linked to whatever strange transformation had reshaped her bodily needs. Neither did he know her pre-transformation identity. Or so he had said.

He had fended off her inquiries with the assurance that the chairman would answer all her questions. And now here she was. This was the answer time.

The chairman shrugged.

"We are all predators," he said. "Life feeds on life. You're just better at that than others. More efficient."

Kora's fingers dug into her palms and she fought to control her breathing.

"What do you want me to do?"

"The entire city is shaking in fear of the Hungry Ones. Commerce is disrupted…refugees…the Pith is sickening. You alone can fight them easily. No, you have to fight them. Because if you don't, you'll starve."

"What if I don't?"

"You'll starve," he repeated.

"So I will!"

He laughed.

"People think that the Hungry Ones are the worst enemy of all," he said meditatively. "Not true. Hunger is. Hunger is the final enemy. You cannot fight it. Nobody can."

She wanted to shout that she could but remained silent because she knew he was right.

"On Skybridge, I was outnumbered," she said finally, realizing even as the words were leaving her mouth that she was giving in, accepting his rules. "This is ridiculous, like setting a lone wolf against a herd of stampeding bulls. What good is a single predator? If you made me, why not to make a whole army?"

He shook his head and poured some more liqueur for Wingate. The bottle hovered above his own glass; he glanced at her and put it down.

"No," he said, "not now. Not yet. We have the militia and the City Corps who can wear 'arms. Not that they do much good, to be honest. We have the khrut Guards too. Once this idiot Volk…once we have a new Mayor, the city can rally up, repel the incursions. But the Hungry Ones keep coming from the countryside. And nobody knows how or why. They swarm in the marshes, where the Divide is supposed to be, where Grandfather and his people came through. The countryside is in chaos. We send people and trains, but nobody comes back. You can do it. You can find out where they come from, who is sending them."

"And what do I get if I do?"

"Five hundred thousand wons."

She had no idea whether it was a miserly handout or a princely remuneration but Wingate's start indicated that perhaps the latter.

"I don't need your money. I want my humanity back. And my memory."

He stared at her and again she was stuck by how devoid of

expression his face was, like a mask.

"Do you, really?" he asked.

She looked at the wall of male faces silently regarding her: white, Asian, dark; smiling and frowning; handsome and average. There were no children or old men.

"I want to know who I am," she said.

"If you do what I'm asking of you, you'll know," he said. "So, deal or no deal?"

She was about to reply when the roof fell on them.

Chapter 8. Flying Roofs

When Daniel had come to the city and signed up for the militia, he had lived in the barracks. But no longer: now he had his own place, which he rented from an aging toad. His landlady was a squat whitish mass the size of a small room, which is what she had originally been. She lived in the center of a warren of tacky compartments, piled upon each other like a child's blocks, and linked by spidery ladders and creaky ramps. The place had originally been a courtyard, but one of the surrounding tenements died. Its flesh was stripped away by the city scavengers and its flaking skeleton was carried away illegally, to be sold for fertilizer in the country. Before the Mayor with his Planning Committee could decide what to do with the freed space, the landlady (whose self-chosen name was Felicia) had squatted on it. There ensued such a welter of suits, claims, and counterclaims that the neighborhood committee, tired of paying lawyers, decided to let her be on the condition that she take good care of her domain. She did. The warren was kept spotlessly clean and connected to the Pith, and any rowdy or unsavory lodger was summarily evicted. Daniel counted himself lucky to live under Felicia's wing and consulted her when the ways of the city puzzled him, which happened occasionally, even after fifteen years.

This time, he brought her a gift: a bottle of aquavit bought at an exorbitant price at the Market. Daniel was careful with money, putting aside a tidy sum every month in pursuance of his dream of becoming a landlord sometime in the future. But, this was an investment since the real estate he eventually planned to buy was in fact Felicia's warren. After all, she was getting on in years and, being what she was, had no natural heirs.

He navigated the cat's cradle of ramps and partially roofed

passages leading to Felicia's domicile, shaking his head at signs of disrepair: litter in the corner, peeling paint on the walls, a crookedly hung icon of Grandfather which he righted for the sake of symmetry if not out of respect.

It was evening, and the oppressive heat of the day had been transmuted into a golden haze that caressed Daniel like a lover's fingers. In the lavender sky, the slim towers of East Square One burned with the reflected fire of the setting sun. Some flambeaus were slowly crawling up their lower flanks, impatient to begin the night's work, even though their messages were all but invisible in the honeyed light. The curving hump of up-levels was outlined against the flaming sky beyond the jungle of mid-levels stalks.

Daniel stopped for a second, admiring the sight. The beauty of the city never failed to move him. And it never failed to bring home, once again, how lucky he was to be here.

He sighed contentedly and walked on, carefully holding the bottle and squinting against the glare. The ramp here was too steep; when he became the landlord, he would rip out this entire makeshift wooden structure and grow a proper bone stairway.

Felicia's domicile was a square yard in the middle of her warren, roofless and opened to the elements. Some toads (Temporary, Obsolete, Abandoned, or Derelict entities) affected sensitivity to the weather in imitation of more established tenants, but Felicia disdained such nonsense. Having been born of the Pith, albeit endowed with independent sentience and limited mobility, she was proud of her ancestral way of life, flaunting the fact that she was as invulnerable to sun and rain as the city itself.

Daniel shouted his greetings – sometimes the old toad would nod off and get angry when mobiles "sneaked up on her", as she put it. He noticed that the gravelly strip fringing her yard had become wider: Felicia was shrinking. Her original square shape could barely be distinguished underneath the sagging folds of her slug-pale skin. Clearly, it was the time for her to retire and for him to take over!

"Hello, auntie," Daniel called out cheerfully. "Fleeced many tenants today?"

"Killed many zombies today, hero?" Felicia replied in a hoarse, staccato voice. Her mouth was a puckered orifice low on her body. She pretended it had been a door; Daniel suspected it had been a cat flap.

Uncorking the bottle of aquavit, he placed it in front of Felicia. He poured a shot for himself and sat cross-legged in front of the toad, watching her rubbery, warty tongue slid out of the orifice and expertly wind itself around the bottle, pulling it inside.

"This is what I want to talk to you about, auntie," he responded. The address had initially been a joke as Felicia had teased him about his country-bumpkin ways, but by now, they both accepted it as a matter of course.

She made a noise like breaking glass – probably pulverizing the bottle in the depth of her mysterious inner works. It also managed to express derision and disgust in equal measure.

"You still believe that Mayor's crap?" she asked. "There are no zombies, I'm telling you! It's just a conspiracy to raise property taxes!"

"Huh?!" Daniel sipped the fiery liquor. "And who have I been fighting for the last two weeks? Tax agents?"

"Rogue tenants!" Felicia explained patiently, like a parent telling a stupid child for the umpteenth time that the chimney delivering gifts does not do it for free. "There are more and more of them each day. The city is falling apart, mind my word! And the Mayor and his clique are dancing on the rubble and lining their pockets!"

Daniel frowned. In the fiery fog of aquavit, Felicia's conspiracy theory sounded plausible for a moment. It was true that the number of rogue tenants had increased alarmingly and that every day brought new varieties. But, then he shook his head. The Hungry Ones were something else!

"No," he said slowly. "There is an army of them. And they are coming from outside the city."

Felicia chortled.

"There is nothing outside the city!"

"There is the countryside!"

"The countryside is simply the not-yet city. You're no less of a citizen, Daniel, just because you weren't born in some low-level slum!"

Daniel smiled and toasted her large whitish bulk.

"Thank you, auntie! I'm not concerned about my immigrant origin. Let Shrimp tease me about it, what do I care? But I'm concerned about two new recruits. They've been bitten by deadheads. And they're both countrymen like me, only much more recent."

"So?"

"They've been on sick leave for the last two days. And the colonel won't let me visit them. They're my men, auntie!"

"You don't have to nursemaid them. They're probably just faking to get extra-pay."

"They're good men, both of them. And there has been this rumor…"

"What?" The old toad was insatiable in her thirst for urban legends.

"Well, that country people are susceptible to the deadheads' infection. Not citizens born and bred but people like me. Immigrants. They say that if we're bitten by a Hungry One, we'll become one."

First, there was a rattling, gravelly noise. Both Wingate and the chairman turned to the window. But, Kora looked up at the ceiling because she realized that the sound was coming from above, despite how the pavilion was swimming in the empty air of the mountaintop. And this was when she saw a hairline fracture running through the plaster. It perceptibly grew even as she watched: a zigzag of darkness that rained dust.

"What the...?" Wingate shook his head, dust getting into his eyes. The chairman jumped to his feet and shouted something, but his words were lost in the roar, like the bellowing of a wounded leviathan that blew through the house.

The window exploded, slivers of glass flying through the room, a swarm of angry hornets. Kora threw herself down and rolled on her stomach to the floor, arms up to protect her head. Her exposed neck was stinging with bites of debris. Something fell upon her, smacking her painfully across the back. The crack of snapping beams and clang of breaking furniture were augmented by a hoarse shouting.

And then there was sudden silence. She lifted her head cautiously, peering at the devastation in the room.

The pavilion was in shambles, the furniture overturned, glass and china broken. The ceiling and walls were covered by a web of cracks. The chairman was nowhere to be seen.

Her pants stuck to her legs. She looked down, cheeks flaming in embarrassment at the thought that she had wet herself – but of course, it was impossible. The liquid soaking through her clothes was thick and red, but she felt no pain.

She jumped up and saw him.

Wingate lay on his back, his empty eyes staring at the crazed ceiling. A large piece of glass was sticking up from under his chin like a transparent fin of an exotic fish. Arterial blood spurted in feeble spurts.

The man had been talking and scheming just moments ago; he had been an adversary or a possible ally; he had been alive. And now he was dead. Kora tried to wrap her head around this brutal fact. As she stared, the piece of glass wriggled free from the wound. More blood gushed out. The glass sliver crawled away.

She snatched it up. It was simultaneously hard and yielding, slick and rough, brittle and elastic, as if it was fast-cycling through different states of matter. She flung it away and it shattered. Its fragments burrowed into the floor.

The noise started again and the entire pavilion shook dangerously, plaster dust rising in miniature cyclones, vases smashing, floorboards cracking. Kora rushed to the door but paused on the threshold, looking for the chairman. And she saw him.

He hung up on the wall. There was nothing to hold him up; he was just stuck there like a fly on flypaper. She thought that he was dead. But then his head rotated impossibly, a hundred and eighty degrees, and he looked at her. A curtain of blank flesh crept across his face. It was like a nictitating membrane of birds or frogs extending over the entire face. It clicked into place with a faint wet smack and something shifted under its damp skin. It withdrew. A new face was confronting Kora. It was pale and unhealthily swollen like a hydrocephalic child's, with staring eyes and slack mouth.

She rushed out of the pavilion into the humid heat of the afternoon. The garden was quiet and she thought that the earthquake, or whatever, was over. But then she realized that the shadows crawling on the ground were not of the trees. She looked up.

She had once seen an explosion frozen in time. (*Where? When?*) She remembered a spray of silver and black shapes hanging in the air, as delicate as a flower bouquet. This is what the sky looked like now, only the shapes were moving around.

It took her brain a couple of precious moments to process what she was seeing and by the time she did, they were diving toward her. She ran for cover, squeezing among the thick stems of bamboo that rustled above her head. But then a manta ray-like thing settled upon the bamboo tops that bent and groaned under the weight as it let gravity bring it down inexorably, threatening to crash Kora. The thing was heavy, as it should be. It was a roof.

The roof was flat and covered with tiles that slid over and under each other like oversized snake scales. Its underbelly was crisscrossed with bony slats. Kora could not discern any eyes, but she was sure the roof could see her.

As could the others, hanging in the air above her, swooping and diving, coasting lazily above the mountaintop garden or circling it intently. Roofs of all kinds: pitched, gabled, flat, tiled, shingled. Some floated in the air like flatfish; some flapped their eaves like ungainly birds; some seemed to propel themselves by streams of hot air ejected from their gutters. But she had no time for observation. The tiled roof above her was bearing down upon her bamboo shelter, stems cracking and breaking, the heavy underbelly coming closer and closer like a foot intent on squashing a bug.

Kora tried to wriggle free of the bamboo clump, but she was hemmed in. Tearing the skin of her arms, she managed to squeeze half of her body out, but her hips got stuck. Now, she was as helpless as a mouse in the trap and the roof was almost upon her.

And this was when the khruts swooped in.

Kora squinted into the dusty light. His nest was on the roof of an old low apartment block hemmed in by newer, taller buildings. People who lived in the apartments above clearly used the lower roof as a garbage dump: it was covered with heaps of junk. In this mess, his hideaway was well camouflaged. But, it was cleverly constructed in such a way that when she ducked under a skewed board-frame, she found herself inside a relatively large space, floored with scraps of carpeting and boasting a number of carefully arranged, if shabby, pillows. It looked clean but was filled with a hot stink. She realized that the stink was coming from its owner.

He was more human-like than other khruts. His body was covered in down, not feathers, and he had long thin arms with four-fingered hands and bent legs. Both fingers and toes boasted impressive curved talons. His wings were small, naked, and puckered like a plucked chicken's. His face was owlish, with big round eyes and a curving beak.

She was not sure he could talk but he did. At first, she could not understand much of what he said in his clipped voice.

"My name is Peter," he said.

"Kora," she mumbled, still dizzy from the roof attack.

The khruts had plummeted through the air like a flock of buzzards, landing upon the flying roofs and stabbing them with long spear-like knives. They used no projectile weapons, for which Kora was profoundly grateful as she scrambled away from the fray, having finally extricated herself from the bamboo. It was bad enough that she was bombarded with tiles and pieces of cladding that rained down upon her as she half-ran, half-crawled to the golden stairway. Even as she dodged this construction hail (some pieces were big enough to brain her), she marveled at how they seemed to be simultaneously inert objects and living creatures. Some tiles shattered on the ground, while others tried to crawl away. She saw a beam undulate toward her like a fat python. She stared, hypnotized, when a khrut landed on the beam-creature's back and broke it with a blow of his mace. The creature cracked open, its fibrous interior bleeding copper-colored liquid.

The khrut hissed at her; she shook off her paralysis and ran. From the corner of her eye, she caught a glimpse of another birdman carrying away the body of Wingate.

As she reached the stairway, one of the upper Buddhas reared itself on its fat stalk and tripped her with its long arm. She rolled down the stairs, her abused ribs screaming in pain, trying to grab the non-existent parapet only to encounter the shoving, grasping, clawing arms of the Buddhas. She was sure that what awaited her on the landing was a broken neck.

And then something caught her shirt, a purposeful grip different from the Buddhas' malicious mishandling. She clutched at her savior and felt sinewy arms like cables go under her armpits. She was lifted off the ground and spent the next fifteen minutes dangling in the void, her eyes screwed shut. She remembered the vertigo of Skybridge only too well.

And here she was.

"Koraa," he repeated. It sounded like a birdsong.

He offered her raw shredded fish.

"I can't eat," she said. "Something has been done to me to make me different."

Peter's eyes with their spindle-shaped pupils were hard to read. But she thought she saw a touch of fear in them.

"I know," he said.

"What do you know about me?" she asked eagerly.

"Chairman wants you to fight Hungry Ones."

"Is he alive?" she asked, surprised at her own question, remembering with a shudder of revulsion the pseudo-human body hanging on the wall like an enormous pupa. At the same time, she suddenly felt bereft at the thought that he might be dead.

Peter nodded, a strangely human gesture.

"He is alive."

"Is he looking for me?"

"Yes."

"Will you bring me back to him?"

"No."

And he explained.

His speech was so strange that she was not entirely sure she understood him correctly. A wave of fatigue suddenly rolled over her, a weakness not so much physical – her bruises and scratches faded as she listened to him – as mental. She fought a desire to close her eyes, curl up, sleep and forget…If her dreams allowed her to forget.

She gathered that there were two sides here. A war was brewing. And she was a pawn in some game whose rules she could not fathom because she did not know the board she was being moved upon.

A war? Between two cities?

No, he had said, between the Pith and the Divide. Between the city and the country.

It made no sense to her, but he kept talking in that strange clacking, abrupt way of his, insisting that the city was robbing his people, starving them, taking away their freedom.

Your people?

He fluttered his wings.

Khruts? But those who fought off the roofs…?

Guards. He clacked in disgust. Paid.

Mercenaries, then.

"And you?"

"Free," he said.

"What are the Hungry Ones?" she asked.

"Victims. An army. Of the countryside. Revenge."

Victims of what? Never mind, she did not believe him anyway. She was sure there was much more to the story than what he was telling her. But if he could help her, lies and evasions did not matter.

"Will you help me?" she asked. "Will you restore my memory? Will you make me able to eat ordinary food again?"

"Yes," he said.

She did not believe this either.

But, he promised to hide her away from the chairman and eventually smuggle her out of the city, out of his grasp. This she did believe because she wanted to.

The chairman wanted her. Not as a man wants a woman. But purely as a means to an end. To protect him against his enemies. To fight off the incursions of the Hungry Ones that interfered with his plans for the city. He had made her into…

…a cannibal

…a tool. A monster. Had taken away her humanity. Had sliced off her free will as if it were a tumor. Was there a greater crime than that? And if that golden-eyed birdman and his shadowy co-conspirators could help her and give back what had been taken away, she would go along. At least for a while.

"So," she asked, "where are you taking me?"

"Tomorrow. Market. Hide there until we are ready to take you to the country."

Fatigue suddenly crashed over her, drowning every thought and emotion in blank lassitude. She looked around. He pointed to a pile of rags on the floor. She lay down and was instantly asleep in the close stinky heat of this urban aerie, with the voices of the city whispering into her ears.

Silence. There is no sound except for the thin keening of the wind. And cold. It is so cold that my blood refuses to circulate, pooling peevishly in my limbs, swelling them into pasty pillows.

I am listening intently, trying to hear the wailing of the baby. But there is only silence.

I am trying to remember the barking of a dog, the meowing of a cat, the lowing of a cow. I can't. Have the sounds also been eaten?

I drag myself painfully off the earthen platform where I have been shivering under the cotton scraps tied together by dry grass. There should be a fire under the platform, heating it. But fire has been outlawed.

The mud floor rises to meet me and I am just lying there. It's so restful. But the churning in my gut forces me to my feet.

They say they found a dead mouse in the yard yesterday. Maybe there is another one out there.

"Koraa?"

A hot claw bit into her shoulder, silencing her scream. She sat up, her head swimming.

"I'm fine," she croaked.

What time was it? The light streaming through the openings in the canopy rippled with fluorescent colors. She dragged herself upright and looked out.

The splendor of the city wiped away the murky stains of the nightmare. Piercing the night sky, enormous spikes glittered with clusters of stars: golden, silver, red, green, and sapphire. Strung between them, winding through the high-rise jungle, were blazing vines of catwalks, studded with berries of luminescence the size of a man. Were they decorations, cars, gondolas? Below, the undergrowth of street lamps, stalls, huts, and kiosks covered the ground like a field of shiny moss. And a steady stream of tiny sparks flowed through the effulgent arteries: rickshaws plying their wares through the crowds.

As she stood there, basking in the sight, Kora noticed again the giant lambent sigils crawling slowly on the sides of high-rises, their many-colored curlicues overlaying the monochrome radiance of the walls.

"What are they?" she asked.

"Flambeaus," Peter replied. "Tenants, like us."

"What does it mean?" she asked. "My memory is…holed. I don't remember my past and I also don't remember some everyday things. Not all of them but some. Like I do know about high-rises, and bridges, and money. And rulers, like the chairman. But I didn't remember Skybridge. And I don't know about tenants."

"Tenants are everybody who lives in the city. Apart from humans. They are citizens."

"Where did humans come from?"

"From beyond the Divide. Brought by Grandfather."

Grandfather again. The name – if it was a name – should mean something to her, she felt, but it did not.

"So, humans have rights. Tenants don't?"

"Mayor is always human. The Pith is shaped by humans to serve them."

"The Pith is…?"

"The flesh of the city."

"So, the humans live in the city and the country is…tenants? People like you?"

Peter shook his head. Again, she was surprised how human his gestures were.

"No. There are khruts and khrut-fowls in the country, but humans too. The city bleeds all of us dry. Takes away our food. Starves us."

"And the Hungry Ones?"

"They are what's left."

When Daniel came to the gates of the base, he saw something was wrong. People were milling in the yard despite the pitiless sun beating down upon them. There was a knot of uniforms at the entrance to the HQ building. He recognized the diminutive figure of Colonel Rosen, but there were others whose insignia made his stomach lurch. He felt even worse when he saw the hunchback figure of a birdman among them.

The Guards!

Daniel was no bigot; having fallen in love with trains, he had high tolerance for other tenants. He had even acquired the reputation of a liberal among the human militiamen because he refused to participate in their drunken talk about exterminating the rogues and cleaning up the city. After all, the line between toads, such as Felicia, and rogues was rather fuzzy! But khruts gave him the creeps. They had a reputation for ruthlessness that was well-earned; their upper echelons were too cozy with Mayor Volk; and on top of all this, they were rumored to interbreed too freely with ordinary fowls, a rumor that was substantiated by the many strange hybrids flying and walking around. And yet, despite this shameful predilection, if any tenant group was de facto, if not de jure, equal to humans, it was the khruts!

Daniel hung back, considering whether he should just sneak back home and call in sick, but it was too late. The colonel saw him and beckoned him to approach.

As he squeezed through the groups of agitated men, he picked up snatches of conversation like a bad smell. And then a piercing scream rose from his own barrack, silencing the buzz.

A tall, thin man in the black uniform of the City Corps winced. He had a hatchet face the color of beets, as if it had once belonged to a much more corpulent person and kept its original flush.

"Shut them up, will you!" He turned to Colonel Rosen whose shrimp-like figure seemed to shrink even further under the staccato of the man's clipped words.

"Perhaps your people…" The Colonel addressed the khrut who stared at him disdainfully with his owlish golden eyes. At least, Daniel assumed it was a "he". Like many birds, the birdmen had no external gender characteristics, though unlike the Buddhas, they reproduced sexually.

"He goes," the khrut pointed at Daniel who gaped at him. He did not realize his approach was even noticed. Shrugging, he turned to walk into the barracks when the hatchet-faced man stopped him.

"Are you a country boy?" he inquired.

"And what if I am?" Daniel retorted pugnaciously. He could see from the man's insignia that he was not in his direct chain of command. The relationships among the human City Corps, the khrut Guards, and the citizen/tenant militia were complicated, to put it mildly.

The man snorted.

"Tell your hero," he said, demonstratively addressing the colonel, "that if he goes in, his friends will have him for breakfast!"

And as if to illustrate his comment, a low-running, emaciated figure burst out of the barracks and streaked through the yard, scattering militiamen like pins.

Daniel instinctively lurched forward but a hand clamped on his forearm.

"Stand back, you fool!" Colonel Rosen hissed.

A knot of bodies formed in the center of the yard, grunting and yelling. Somebody jumped back, clutching his chest that was painted with bright splashes of blood. Another man staggered away and flopped on the ground. With horror, Daniel saw that a chunk of flesh had been torn out of his cheek, leaving a bloody hole through which his teeth gleamed wetly.

Throughout the commotion, the khrut and the City Corps lieutenant watched impassively, making no move to help. Fortunately, it was over soon. The knot fell apart, the wounded were whisked away, and the sweaty, bloodied militiamen wrestled the creature down and literally stood on it to keep it on the ground.

Daniel shook off the Colonel's restraining hand and moved forward. The thing on the ground writhed and foamed but did not cry out; instead, it produced a monotonous uninterrupted moan, as mindless as wind. With growing nausea, Daniel took in the creature's dry, lifeless, cracked skin, sunken bruised eyes, and the giant fissure of the mouth. Its limbs were as wiry as a spider's but despite its gauntness, its belly was football-round, pressing against its tattered clothes. These clothes were the crowning horror because they matched Daniel's own. As its rabid eyes met Daniel's, he shuddered and turned away.

"Lu Huan," he said.

The City Corps lieutenant materialized by his side and studied the prone Hungry One.

"Your man?" he asked Daniel.

"Yes. There were two of them. Where is George?"

The lieutenant smirked.

"Inside. Whatever is left of him. They fought and our friend here is clearly the stronger one."

"He killed George?"

"He ate him."

Daniel managed to step aside, so the remnants of his breakfast did not splatter the lieutenant's shiny shoes. On second thought, he was rather sorry he did.

"Take him away," the lieutenant commanded.

The men who were keeping the Hungry One down reluctantly hauled it upright and put it in hand-cuffs with chains attached. It managed to snap at one of them, drawing blood. The victim paled.

"Not a countryman, are you?" the lieutenant asked.

"No, sir!" the man answered but Daniel caught a shifty expression in his eyes. There were many illegal immigrants in the city and their numbers were growing.

Daniel felt his face grow hot: how dare this bully harass his men? But before he could intervene, he heard the khrut's chipper voice:

"Oleg!"

The lieutenant turned around with a grimace: khruts refused to address humans by anything but their first names as they had no family or rank appellations among themselves, distinguishing hierarchies by subtle gradations of body shape or color. Most human who worked with them got used to this informality; some chafed under it. The lieutenant apparently belonged to the second category.

"What?"

"Look up!"

Oleg did and so did Daniel and everybody else in the yard.

Here, Skybridge was suspended high above the city, bearing MTT tracks. Its graceful arch stood out like a calligraphic stroke against the sparkling cluster of blue and green high-rises. As

Daniel's eyes adjusted to the blinding light, he gasped.

A knot of darkness appeared on the arch, insignificant at first. But as the stunned militiamen watched, the knot grew, expanded into a winged shadow, and took off; its distorted reflection in the mirror sides of the high-rises revealed its inconceivable size. The train on the bridge looked like a toy in comparison.

The bridge buckled and shook. A thunderclap rolled over the silent crowd.

And then it started raining stones, steel, and blood.

Chapter 9. The Market

Kora had never seen so many people.

No, she corrected herself: she did not *know* whether she had ever seen so many people. For all she knew, she might have spent her entire life in the Market.

The Market was a labyrinth spread over twenty city blocks in what Peter called low-levels. Kora still had only a vague idea of the geography of the city, but she had already figured out that it was built on the shallow slopes of a low mountain range whose tallest peak – called simply the Peak – towered over the rolling plains of the countryside. From Peter's curt explanations, she gathered that the city's social structure mirrored its vertical configuration: the rich lived on up-levels, the middle class on mid-levels, and the teeming low-levels were home to the variegated collection of inhabitants, human and not, collectively known as bottom-feeders.

The smell was the first thing that hit her; she breathed it in incredulously and started sneezing. Peter waited by her side, one clawed foot hooked nonchalantly through the railing of the tiny platform that jutted like a landing without a staircase from the side of a peeling hut. And the hut itself was perched on the roof of a narrow tenement that was squeezed into a crack between two gray high-rises that were joined at the top by a catwalk. Their lower stories were covered in a cat's cradle of walkways, pedestrian bridges, and passages that made it impossible to locate the street level. Or rather, Kora realized, there was no street level here. Life in the Market was three-dimensional.

The smell – a mixture of chemical sharpness and a warm, cow-like exhalation, with notes of fishy saltiness, meaty stink, orchid sweetness, and rotting flesh – made her eyes water. Blinking away tears, she tried to focus on the swirling crowds below, break up the sensory overload of sights and sounds into manageable chunks.

First, she noted that the crowds were not in random motion but rather followed certain patterns. They flowed through wider streets lined with shops that clung to each other like barnacles and spread through the delta of alleys, most of which she could not see into because they were roofed with pleated skin-like material. Even where the alleys were open to the sky, they were so clogged with marquees as to make whatever mysterious life was happening inside inaccessible to her. The delta was dotted with wider plazas where pedestrians swirled around in eddies and eventually ended washed up on the beaches of innumerable eateries. Some had sidewalk tables, each of which seemed to seat twice as many people as it was meant to. In others, customers just stood leaning against the wall or hanging onto pillars, devouring their takeaways from folding trays. The sight of so much food made her feel she should be revolted but she was not. Instead, she was trying to see what it was they were eating. But, from this height, all she could see were multicolored splotches. Noodles? Roast meat? Vegetables? Probably all this and more. And it was long after breakfast hour. Having spent the rest of the night in dreamless sleep, she was late to wake up. When she did, Peter was nowhere to be seen and she was beginning to suspect he had reneged on his promise and had flown away to bring back the chairman's Guards when he slithered through the entrance hole, licking his toothed beak with a long, sharp, maroon-colored tongue. He repeated his promise to take her to some hideaway. And so here they were.

"What is this?" she breathed.

"The Market."

She knew it because he had told her so but *what* was this? The city's stomach? Its heart? Its cancerous tumor? And what were the creatures infesting the maze of food, filling it to the bursting point? From where they stood, she could hardly distinguish humans from tenants; they all blended into a rainbow mass of dots flowing through the clogged arteries of the Market like sluggish blood.

"How many different kinds live in the city?" she asked.

He started counting on his supple, double-jointed fingers, folding them like a first-grader. She found this oddly endearing.

"Humans, trains, flambeaus, khruts, Buddhas, ducks. Five. Oh, and also toads. But I don't know if they are true tenants. Some say they are part of the Pith."

"What about the roofs?"

Peter's nictitating membranes slid over his golden eyes.

"Rogues." He spat and gestured to the fire escape precariously clinging to the side of the bigger building.

It was like wading into the ocean, she thought, waiting with bated breath till the next wave rolls over you, lifts you up, and throws you, blinded and out of breath, onto the beach.

The ocean?

Few passers-by even bothered to look up as Kora and Peter hung on the dangerously creaking ladder, waiting for a break in the flow of people to dive in. Nobody seemed to be curious about a tall woman and a small birdman descending from the fire escape of a tenement. Mostly pedestrians just seemed to be wary of objects falling onto their heads. This was not an idle fear. Something resembling a spiky football whistled past Kora. The crowd surged, people trying to get out of the way. The ball hit the ground with a wet organic smack and fell apart into slimy reddish segments. The segments tried to squirm away, but the implacable tide of the crowd rolled over them, grinding them into the dirty pavement.

Peter smirked.

"A little toad," he remarked. "A froggie."

"What's a toad?" she bellowed into his ear as the noise of the Market rose up to meet them: a cacophony of yells, music, touting, bells, clanks; a syncopation of thousands of conversations conducted at once.

"Temporary, Obsolete, Abandoned, or Derelict," he yelled back.

And then they dove in and the crowd closed smoothly around them.

Kora had been afraid of claustrophobia as she was swallowed up by the tide of densely packed bodies. But instead she relaxed.

A bulge pressed against her buttocks. A pervert? No, he slipped off her indifferently and another anonymous body took his place, washed against her like a random piece of driftwood by the surf of the crowd.

People...

She felt so good among them, she did not want to move. Just standing there, surrounded by their rhythmic surge...Warm energy flowed into her.

This was the Market. The place of food, the place of sharing and exchange.

But I have nothing to exchange for food.

It's all been bartered away...

"Koraa!"

She shook off her reverie and followed Peter, squeezing through the sweaty ranks of shoppers and hustlers.

They rounded a corner and found themselves in a covered arcade. It seemed older than the main thoroughfare. The skin (or derma as Peter called it) roof was desiccated; the ribs that supported it bent and sagging; and the gallery running above their heads was deserted, with boarded storefronts and broken railings. The stores on the ground floor, though, were all open, selling assorted junk. Kora thought about the gleaming mall to which she had escaped from the hotel and realized that the economy of the city was indeed pyramid-shaped.

Peter led her into one of the bigger shops. It sold yarn. Inside were shelves and shelves covered with balls and skeins of threads. The yarn was shelved by color and the interior was bright with a rainbow of reds, pinks, greens, and yellows. A faceless dummy stood at the counter, dressed in a hand-knitted shawl with pompons.

"Koraa?"

She turned around and literally felt her jaw drop.

Standing by Peter's side was something that looked like a hybrid of a snake and a rag-doll. A tall, willowy, thin creature, its body was composed of raw, complexly intertwined fibers of red, purple, and blue that glistened like the exposed muscle in an anatomy exhibit. Its boneless, uniformly thick arms hung loosely by its sides; its chest was covered by a ridged carapace. But its tiny triangular face was the most disconcerting thing about it, resembling a fly more than a snake. It had huge multifaceted eyes set in braid-fringed sockets and two small hooks sticking out of its mouthparts.

"This is Irene," Peter said. "Irene, this is Koraa."

The creature offered its hand, which looked like a bunch of cables with no palm to speak of. Kora shook it mutely. To her relief, it was warm and dry, not slimy as she had suspected.

"Irene does not speak," Peter continued matter-of-fact. "You stay with her. She takes care of you."

He made for the shop's exit. Kora, shaking off her surprise, rushed after him, caught him by one of his chicken-wings, feeling the frail bones under the thin covering of flesh. Peter flinched and she relaxed her grip.

"Who...what is she?" she whispered, casting a suspicious glance at the creature. Was it deaf? Would it take offence if it was not?

She did not care. She was fed up with being passed from one of the city's strange denizens to another.

"Irene is a duck," Peter said in his normal voice, apparently not concerned with the creature's feelings. "She takes care of you."

And he pushed the ancient door that chimed brokenly and

walked out, leaving Kora to speculate whether the amnesia had affected her linguistic knowledge as well, so that "duck" meant something entirely different from what she thought it meant. A water fowl? A darling? Irene certainly was not the former and Kora seriously doubted she was the latter.

Daniel rolled on the ground, throwing his arms up to protect his head. A piece of debris struck him on the forehead and he blacked out for a moment. When he came to, blinking blood and dust away, he looked up into the craggy landscape hanging over him.

For a dizzy moment, he thought that the giant rogue had flown over, picked him up and now he was like a fly stuck on Skybridge's enormous face…But wouldn't it be *below* him, in this case? And then the landscape dipped, he saw the crescent of dusty light framing it, and his befuddled brain shifted gears. He screamed and lashed out as the creature that was bending over him snapped its teeth and a thin dribble of saliva burned his cheek.

His kick pushed the zombie away and he managed to scramble to his feet. He caught a glimpse of the devastated courtyard, one of the barracks smashed like an egg, bodies strewn around. But he did not have time for observation because the Hungry One – his own team-man and good buddy Lu Huan – launched itself at him once again.

Daniel discovered he had lost his club in the shake. And because he was not supposed to be on patrol duty today, he was not wearing his 'arm. He tried to parry the zombie's assault, but its spider-thin body was as impervious to blows as dry wood. Even its round stomach was stone-hard. Fortunately, it was on its own and lacked the strength of a horde.

Backing off, Daniel stumbled over a broken beam. Lu Huan, its head hanging low, butted him in the chest, knocking the wind out of him. Its loose teeth snagged in Daniel's uniform. Groping on the ground, Daniel felt a sharp edge and his hand closed over a big sliver of glass. Disregarding the blood running down his arm from the cut, he brought it down sharply upon the creature's neck and stabbed and hacked the ropy muscle until the Hungry One gave a mewling sound and let go.

Daniel rose to his feet shakily. Lu Huan lay at his feet, its head almost severed from its body, a thin, greenish liquid seeping from the gash. A fecal stench hit his nostrils and Daniel gagged.

But he had no time for being sick. Now that the immediate danger to himself was averted, he was beginning to take in the magnitude of the catastrophe. The barracks were listing like beached boats, their walls cracked. In the debris-strewn courtyard, there were many bodies and only few of them were stirring. And as he lifted his eyes fearfully and looked up to Skybridge, he felt as if he were being choked.

But the suffocation of shock did not quite cushion the burning sensation in his lower chest. He looked down. His torn uniform was stained with the creature's ropy saliva; the stains were already drying out. But a fresh spot appeared even as he looked.

He tore apart the tatters and stared at the bleeding laceration where the Hungry One's teeth had grazed his skin.

Kora circled the yarn shop like a caged animal. After Peter had gone out and she had been left alone with Irene, she was too abashed by the creature's inhumanity to try to make a contact with her. In comparison to the "duck", as Peter had called her, the khrut himself appeared to be as homely as the boy next door. He had a face, after all; he could speak. But Irene had as little of a face as a fly. And when Irene just walked out the door, Kora was too late in reacting. Not until she heard the click did she realize she was locked in with nothing to do and nowhere to go.

She prowled the shop restlessly, pausing to look at the scuffed walls, tracing with her finger the convolutions of dirt. Had there been a human head resting against the discolored plaster? Had a human hand rubbed against the scratched counter? She realized she missed the crowds, the impersonal fraternity of strangers, and the press of anonymous bodies against her own.

The non-humans – the tenants – outnumbered the humans in the Market. If she got hungry – *when* she got hungry…

Could she…eat anything except Hungry Ones?

Anything? Anybody.

She did not know.

The chairman had told her he had made her to fight the Hungry Ones whom he described as monstrous invaders into the city. But if Peter was to be believed, they were pitiful victims of the city's war on the countryside. How could she, then, take away whatever leftover existence they still retained?

She would have to starve.

But even as she promised to herself that she would rather starve than be a cannibal, Kora knew it was an idle promise. Hunger was the one king whose rule could never be overthrown. Nothing withstood hunger: morality, idealism, love were like chaff in the wind confronted with the relentless pressure of famine. She did not know how she knew it, but she did.

The emptiness under her breastbone gave another tug, expanding, asserting its existence like a growing tumor. There was a twinge behind her eyes as she felt a headache coming on.

She wrenched her mind back to Peter's list of the kinds who lived in the city. Khruts, Buddhas…trains? And then there was the Pith, the living fabric of the city itself, the incomprehensibly enormous body stretched over the foothills of the Peak. Did it feed on sunlight like a plant or was it sustained by the effluvia of its residents like a mushroom? And hadn't Peter indicated that tenants, at least some of them, were splinters of the Pith who had achieved mobility and sentience?

She tried to bring back the sense of mission that had been so strong when she woke up in the empty hotel, but it was gone now that she knew she was a pet project of some rich businessman. Not a…weapon…

Blades. Rust. Blood.

The images dissolved into non-memory like the residue of a dream.

No, she would have to choose. Peter or the chairman. The country or the city.

Where was she from? The countryside was the source of the food that fed the Market. Kora examined her hands, strong and supple, with thick wrists and hard palms. Yes, she could have done manual labor. Worked on the farm. But tried as she might, she could not bring up any concrete images of when and where.

Tired of herself, she examined the merchandise on the shelves. She found a pair of knitting needles and tried to remember whether she had ever knitted and, if so, whether she had liked doing it. But the needles stirred no muscle memory; she had a general idea of how to use them but no unconscious aptitude.

Flinging them aside, Kora pulled at the old-fashioned cash register. It was locked, which she regretted. She had no money and would not be above filching some.

But what do I need money for?

Money was life because money could buy food. *Money equals food equals life. If you have no money, you don't eat. But what use is money to a creature who does not eat?*

Growing ever more depressed, she reminded herself money could buy more than food. Human beings were not animals.

But searching her mind, she found no wish for any of the amenities that lift humanity beyond the brute necessities of nature. She craved neither jewels nor art objects. She did not even want a home. Any shelter would suffice.

Am I an animal then? A predator that needs nothing but a lair?

She ground her teeth.

I am a beautiful woman, she reminded herself. *I need to keep myself beautiful.*

She was not sure why it was important, but this thought alone stirred some ambiguous desire. She needed to wash, to comb her hair, perhaps to use some cosmetics. Her body excreted no waste, but she still got covered in grime and dust. She needed to take care of herself.

There was a door at the back of the shop that opened onto a small lavatory. She stripped and cleaned herself with a washcloth, combed and plaited her long black hair. She took the hand-knitted shawl off the mannequin and threw it over her own shoulders. She felt chilled, even though the closed shop was stuffy and hot.

Is something wrong with me?

The emptiness inside answered her without words.

Kora shivered. And then the shop entrance door suddenly flew open.

Daniel lifted the wounded and the dead, and helped to clear away some of the rubble. Eventually, emergency crews arrived and took over. The lightly wounded and shell-shocked were directed to the impromptu medical stations set up in the undamaged barracks

Daniel tried to sneak away but was halted by the beet-faced City Corps lieutenant named Oleg who had escaped unscathed.

"Where do you think you are going, militiaman?" he hissed.

"Home," Daniel replied monosyllabically.

"No way. You need medical attention. Go to the pretty nurses over there; they'll take care of you!"

The "pretty nurses" were a pair of shapeless ducks, so Daniel supposed this was the lieutenant's little joke. He snorted and shook the man's hand off.

"Come on!" Oleg's face was so close that he could smell the man's garlicky breath and his fear.

"I saw how you dealt with our sunshine friend. Bravo! But

you're a country boy, aren't you?"

"So what?" Daniel snarled.

"You know what." Oleg pulled him even closer, speaking into his ear with odious intimacy. "But there is a way."

Daniel pushed him away.

"Go fuck yourself!" he enunciated as clearly and loudly as he could.

Oleg's red face turned purple as if he was about to have a stroke. But, at this moment, Colonel Max Rosen strode over. Daniel was glad to see him unharmed.

"What are you doing here, Moylan?" he bleated. "Interfering with the emergency crews? They don't need untrained oafs like you ruining the scene. Off you go and come back only when the general call is issued."

"Yes, sir!" Daniel saluted smartly and sauntered out of the ruined courtyard, casting a triumphant glance at the fuming lieutenant.

Irene walked in, carrying several bulging plastic bags. Kora noted how the fibers in her arms swelled with the effort.

Irene dumped the bags as if her guest was not there. Or was she looking at Kora all the time? It was impossible to follow the direction of her compound eyes.

Kora did not know what to say, so she just watched the tenant.

Irene started unpacking, lining up the contents of the bags on the counter. It was a selection of foodstuffs: bunches of small red grapes; some leafy vegetable Kora was unfamiliar with; a flatbread, somewhat damp from having lain on top of the grapes; and a carton of salted eggs. Irene turned her head toward Kora; now it was clear she was looking at her, even though her faceted eyes remained as blank and uninterested as dark mirrors. Kora saw her own distorted reflections stare through her.

Irene snagged a ball of green yarn from the shelf. Clearing

some space on the counter, she pulled the end of the yarn and lined it on the smooth surface. And then with a tip of her hooked finger she started pushing and pulling on the green line, transforming it into a wavy, complex tracing. The finger was flying so quickly, it blurred. And when Irene was done, the green thread spelled in a beautiful cursive handwriting: "Want to eat?"

Kora smiled, diverted from the touchy substance of the question by Irene's unusual method of communication.

"Is that how you talk?" she asked. And seeing that Irene's triangular head was still cocked inquisitively, she added: "No, I'm not hungry. But thank you."

Irene turned away and, with a quick economic gesture, speared the green vegetable on the tip of her finger. Her mandibles moved at an equally astonishing speed. When she paused, the vegetable had been chopped into a mound of tiny pieces on the counter, which the tenant proceeded to shovel into her small funnel-shaped mouth.

Watching it made the emptiness inside Kora stir.

"I'm going out," she declared. "I want to see the Market."

Irene deftly snagged another thread, this time yellow, and "wrote":

"Danger."

"I'll be careful," Kora promised. Freedom beckoned from the open door, through which poured the honey light of late afternoon, smelling of spice and sweat. The crowd-river still flowed in full flood.

She stepped into the alley. A distant sound like thunder rolled through the afternoon hum and the ground under her feet trembled.

Going home was easier said than done. Mid-levels were in turmoil, even though the destruction was not as bad as Daniel had feared. To avoid the milling crowds, he climbed the stairs to the Fragrant Lotus walkway, even though normally he tried to avoid its vulgar touts and aging whores. But now both touts and whores were standing in nervous knots, staring up at the ruined Skybridge whose sagging line was starkly outlined against the dark greenery of the up-levels.

Skybridge was in fact a collection of many different bridges, haphazardly joined together. But, by tradition, the entire thing was regarded as one entity.

The part that had been damaged by the Event (as it was already being referred to in the flambeau-broadcasts on the sides of skyscrapers) was in the modern suspension bridge whose tall pylons driven into the face of the Peak supported graceful spans of forty meters each. The spans bore the tracks of MTT whose trains – smaller and cuter than the countryside-bound variety Daniel tended – were now in their depots, no doubt being treated for PTSD. The dead train had already been removed from the damaged tracks, along with the bodies of other casualties, both human and tenant. Their names were given in a running sub-script of the broadcast Daniel was watching, but this happened to be a dawn-oriented one and he was not as fluent in their language as the city-born were.

Along with the clustered whores around him, some of whom were sobbing out loud, Daniel was staring at the giant figure that hung from the pylons of the bridge like a crucified bat. The rogue was inconceivably large; perhaps a hundred and fifty meters long with a two-hundred-meters wingspans. Its wings were a clumsy patchwork of broken beams held together by barbed wire and pseudo-steel cables. Its body was composed of dead train tracks wound around each other into a semblance of a rough trunk. One extended track jutted below, presumably as a leg. The second leg was nowhere to be seen. The rogue had no arms and its head was a cylindrical vat, sagging as if melting.

"…this toad," a woman was saying behind Daniel's back.

"It's not a toad, it's a duck!" a male voice objected.

"What duck? Are you crazy? Just look at this thing!"

The tempers were fraying, rattled by the catastrophe. The rogue – whether a duck or a toad, Daniel could not care less and in fact found the distinction largely irrelevant – had tried to crawl away from Skybridge and then to take flight. It had derailed an MTT train in doing so and warped the Pith, causing a slide that destroyed a small cluster of houses. It had in fact flown, at least as far as the barracks, which was a wonder in itself considering how heavy it was. Until today, Daniel would have sworn that the city had no capacity to lift that large an object. But then the rogue had lost altitude and somehow managed to return back to Skybridge where it now hung inert. Had it fallen onto the streets, Daniel would have been dead.

A clean death.

He shook himself roughly, chastising himself for dark thoughts. When this happened, the admonishing voice in his head often sounded like somebody else's – a woman's voice, both familiar and irritatingly elusive.

I am alive. The city is alive. Nothing happened.

The scratch on his chest throbbed faintly.

It doesn't mean anything. Lu Huan might have gotten it from anywhere.

Except the official line was that you could not get it at all.

The rogue twitched slightly; a mast sticking above it at an angle creaked alarmingly and listed even more. A chorus of yells rose from the crowd. But the rogue showed no further signs of animation, subsiding into an inert mass like a botched construction project.

Daniel swallowed. His mouth felt bone-dry. The scratch still throbbed. And he suddenly discovered he was extraordinarily hungry. Well, he had had nothing since morning and wrestling with a zombie was a tough job. He'd better get home, eat, lie down, and maybe chat with Felicia later in the evening…

A slight body was pressed against him by the rhythmical surge of the crowd. A hand was laid on his lower back. He turned around with a sharp retort that died on his lips as he looked down, into the quick bird-like eyes of the woman he had met at the Market.

"Who are you?" he yelled irritably. "Why are you following me?"

The woman dived into a passage off the walkway and sat, cross-legged, on the floor. Daniel stood, towering above her, feeling clumsy and conspicuous.

"You may call me Madam Wren," she said.

"It's not your name!"

She just shrugged.

"I have a proposition for you," she said. "A business proposition."

"Who are you working for?" Daniel bellowed. "Triads?"

She smirked.

"Think higher. Far higher."

"The Mayor?"

"Higher."

Daniel rolled his eyes and turned to walk away. Recently, weird cults had been proliferating like firestalkers in the dry season, whipped up by competing Buddhas and fueled by rumors spread by khruts. Some said the return of Grandfather was imminent; some argued that there was a new deity arising in the countryside and the Hungry Ones were messengers of his wrath. Daniel despised both groups with vengeance.

"Think about it, militiaman," the woman said in her sibilant voice. "This is the second time. The offer won't stand forever."

"There is not enough stolen money in Mayor Volk's coffers to make me break my oath to the city."

"Some betray by acting. Some – like you – by *not* acting."

"What the fuck does that mean?" Daniel felt an almost irresistible desire to shake the woman's doll-like body until her bones rattled. "I betrayed nothing and nobody! Ask my Colonel, ask anybody you want – my loyalty has never been in doubt!"

The woman smirked.

"They don't know you as well as Grandfather does!"

Daniel laughed. Somehow this superstitious nonsense calmed him down; his sense of superiority, momentarily undermined by the woman's snarky manner, was restored. She was just a credulous bottom-feeder, a small-time crook!

"If Grandfather knows me so well," he said mockingly, "he can talk to me himself. Surely, the one who led us across the Divide in time and space needs no messengers. Especially not messengers like you!"

He walked away, just catching the tail-end of the woman's retort:

"…need him more than you know!"

Chapter 10. The City Provides

Kora wandered around the Market that now seemed less crowded than it had been in the morning, the current of people flowing out of it, perhaps disturbed by the slight earthquake she had felt earlier.

The Market's layout was not completely haphazard, even though its general shape still eluded her. She decided it must be something like a many-armed starfish, with a central plaza and alleys, passages, and cul-de-sacs radiating from it. But, sometime during its evolution, the Market had spilled into the neighboring residential areas. Its tributaries now spread through high-rise-lined streets, so that families cooling off on their balconies could stare down into a display of underwear or inhale the aroma of dried shrimps. The central core was mostly about food, while the tributaries tended to specialize in clothes, jewelry, watches, and innumerable kinds of mysterious junk.

It was the food that drew Kora irresistibly. And she did not know why.

She felt no salivating frustration, like what must be experienced by a desperate dieter passing by a sumptuous restaurant. Her body remained inert; no remembered taste flooded her mouth as she passed the kaleidoscopic heaps of apples, plums, mango, and oranges; the jewel like displays of tiny puddings, each in its individual container; the stalls of smoked fish, gazing at her with their dim eyes; and the neat rows of roast fowls swaying on their hooks like exotic fruit. Her interest was more cerebral and, at the same time, more obsessive. She wanted to *see* that superabundance of food. And the more she saw, the more she craved the nourishment whose name she refused to utter in her thoughts.

She accidentally bumped into an elderly gentleman with a

bowl of fish soup, much of which ended in his lap. She muttered apologies but the gentleman, apparently used to such misadventures, waved her on and went back to the counter for a new portion. She smiled, her face muscles stiff as if unused to such an action.

She watched faces floating by from a corner of her eye. She was sure the chairman would send somebody after her. And she did not trust Peter. The more she thought about his explanation of the events, the less sense it made.

How did the khrut's mysterious employers in the countryside know about her? And why did they want her? If her only skill was killing Hungry Ones, wouldn't they try to keep her as far away from the country as possible? Or…wouldn't they try to get rid of her? Was Peter a would-be assassin, trying to lure her into a trap? He had not harmed her in his aerie but perhaps he had been afraid of her.

And what was the chairman's game? Now, beset by doubts and suspicions, Kora tried to squelch the strange attraction she felt for him and poke holes in his glib explanation of having been made into some kind of champion. Surely there were easier ways to kill Hungry Ones! Surely there would be assassins for hire in a place like this! Though she had seen a couple of people in uniforms, they hardly seemed enough to control this exuberant tide of trade, both legal and illegal. And assassins would have real weapons, wouldn't they? How could her…ability (*curse*) compare?

And then she realized she had not seen anybody with a gun, sword or any other weapon. Some stalls sold kitchen knives and hatchets, but that was all.

The humans in the Market seemed to be almost equally divided between whites, Asians, and blacks. Most spoke her language, though there were snatches of dialects she did not understand. But the others, the tenants, came in such a bewildering variety of shapes that any classification seemed inadequate. Only two kinds were familiar. Once, she felt rather than heard the flapping of heavy wings and looked up into the yellow eyes of a khrut flying low above the Market. She dove into a shop and squeezed between tracks of smelly garments, her heart hammering, but the khrut seemed uninterested in her. Later, she passed several tiny street temples glinting with the oily flesh of a Buddha. But the rest of tenants seemed to be composed of creatures who were *sui generis*.

She saw a pale, shapeless mass of flesh waddle by. Its means of propulsion was a broad corrugated muscle pad. But it had a face: a completely human face, big, drooping and melancholy, caught in a web of wrinkles.

She saw a whippet-thin woman, beautifully dressed in an elegant black suit. But her skin had a metal sheen and her high-cheekbone face lacked eyes: there was a blank expanse of flesh above the bridge of her nose.

She saw an elderly lady with a pet on a leash. The pet was merely a headless rib-cage on four legs. Another pet-owner walked by: a stooping, ungainly creature with a head like a bucket and very long arms attached straight to the trunk without the benefit of shoulders. Its pet was a miniature man in a jaunty fedora hat, perfectly proportioned but scaled down to one-sixth normal size.

The two pet-owners stopped and exchanged small talk. There was a constant buzz of social interactions in the Market. Complete strangers would toss casual remarks at each other; friends and acquaintances strode by in pairs and groups, talking and laughing. Their voices blended into a uniform background noise.

As the day curdled into dusk, she was beginning to see more and more creatures that looked like living neon signs. They floated through the crowds that parted around them: lacy arabesques and asymmetrical fretwork frames composed of the complex interweaving of tubes, flaps, valves, and conduits within a transparent membrane. All were as flat as a catfish. Some of them were as small as a child, others as big as a three-story building. They pulsated with the magical lights of rose, emerald, and gold, and she was suddenly convinced she had never seen anything like them. No amnesia could erase the enchantment of these living jewels.

Did it mean she had never been to the city? They were ubiquitous, these creatures that Peter had called flambeaus. They attached themselves to the sides of high-rises and scrolled pictures and headlines, too fast for her to follow. Some floated to the poles along the street and settled on their tops, folding their luminescent wings and shedding soft, even illumination on the crowd. Some took their posts on the marquees and displayed names of shops and ads for merchandise in lovely ripples of color and light. The city blazed with their effulgence. Apart from the glow of temple candles and incense sticks, she could see no other source of illumination and yet the night Market was almost as brightly lit as in daytime.

The spectacle diverted her from the emptiness that was nudging at her – not yet the monster that she knew it would become but just a snickering premonition, a mocking reminder of what lay ahead. Her rage at the chairman sustained her for a while and so did the wonder of the Market but those were petty distractions. At some point, everything else would fall away and only the hunger would remain.

The chairman said she had been made into a warrior. But it was a lie. She had been made into an animal.

A cannibal...

But there were still the Hungry Ones. She shuddered, thinking of their wolfish, low-slung bodies, their diarrheal stench. And yet they were her only lawful food.

Somebody bumped into her: a woman, her skin pearly-white in the shimmering light of the overhead flambeaus. She smiled, lingering for a moment, her silk skirt swooshing as her rounded hip pressed against Kora's. Seeing no response, she walked on. But the response was there, so overwhelming that Kora was paralyzed by its power. It was not, however, a doubtful flicker of desire. Instead, it was a glow of satiety, spreading through her like a warm unstoppable tide. Emotions can be denied and repressed; sensations are just there, brute facts of life. She had been hungry; she was now sated. She could pretend to be ashamed, but she could not deny the sensation of well-being that flowed through her starved body.

After a couple of heartbeats, she realized her hunger was not gone but only retreated. What she had taken from the woman was a tiny sip. It could not have harmed her; she probably did not even notice a sudden dip in her vitality. But it was enough to sustain Kora. For a while.

She scanned the crowd for the woman, trying to ascertain what kind she was, but it was impossible to locate any particular individual in the melee. The woman must have been a tenant, just look at her skin! Kora clung to that paltry self-defense – this was not cannibalism if she was not human! – knowing in her heart that ultimately it did not matter.

The city provided.

Something nudged her hand, a deliberate touch. She looked down. A creature like a big soft hedgehog nosed at her, a living tangle of strands. She pushed it away but a part of it wound itself around her wrist and tugged. The creature trotted ahead, pulling her in its wake and, as it went, it unraveled, becoming a thread that wove through the debris on the pavement, spelling out one word: "Home".

She followed.

Chapter II. The Dead

They are coming!

The white street is frozen; the air is so still I can even hear the baby's breathing, a small fluttering sound that seemed miraculous every time it is resumed.

The fresh snow squeaks. And again. And again.

I don't want to look out. I don't want to see them coming. If I screw up my eyes tight enough, they'll disappear.

Mother is dragging herself over to the cold stove, spreading the rags over the earthen floor to cover the uneven surface where it has been dug up and filled. She lies there and is quiet again.

They have bayonets. Mother is so thin. She cannot cover it up.

They have bayonets. Mother is so thin. But not too thin to bleed.

Daniel thrashed among his damp bedclothes, a scream forced back into his throat by the pillow that landed on his face. He blinked; his eyes sleep-crusted and dust-dry.

The sun shone straight into his face. At night, the flowery curtain affixed to his window had come loose and was now fluttering in the draft. The air was as heavy as smoke.

What a horrible dream!

If these were his childhood memories coming back, he wanted none of them.

But it could not have been. The terrible cold, the pitiless blinding light…How could he have gotten out of that frozen hell?

How, indeed?

He dismissed thoughts of the past. He had enough to deal with at the present.

He was unwell, for the first time in years. He shivered compulsively.

That was bad. Daniel hated being sick. And he was afraid of pain. He had never confided in anybody about this fear, knowing he would be made fun of by his swaggering mates. He often put himself in danger of an 'arm's sting precisely because his expectation of pain was so bad, he'd rather get it over with.

But the sickness did not put a dint in his appetite. He was ravenously hungry. He felt like there was a hole the size of the City Hall in his stomach.

He stumbled into the bathroom and stared at a minute crack in the wall while his body tried to squeeze out some liquid. He should tell Felicia; the old toad was getting careless about maintenance…Practical worries dissipated the sour aftertaste of the dream – until he came back to the present with a jolt and realized his bladder refused to cooperate.

He gulped some foul-tasting water from the tap and instantly retched it up. Food – that was what he needed.

He ran into the kitchenette, yanked open the small refrigerator and stared, spellbound, at the icicles that festooned the freezer.

On the window-sill, melting…

He touched the sharp point of an icicle. A perfect round pearl shone on the tip of his finger. A drop *pinged* on the floor. Then another.

The refrigerator was on the blink. The Pith had not been reminded to maintain the appliances in the apartment complex.

Felicia…But he could not wait to eat. There was a packet of sliced salami, a pot of cream cheese, some lettuce. He took them out, started to make a sandwich. The white curdles of the cream cheese glistened like a field of…what?

He stared dreamily at the empty pot. A lick of cheese was drying on his cheek. The salami was gone too. A couple of wilted lettuce leaves lay scattered on the counter.

He turned back to the defrosting fridge, rummaged in the freezer. His fingers encountered a slick bumpy surface. A roll of ground meat, bought long ago and forgotten.

He thought he should toss it out or perhaps feed it to the half-sentient toads that some charitable souls in the neighborhood were nurturing into a full tenant stature…

He was choking on shreds of the wrap. The taste and smell of blood throbbed in his sinuses. The meat was gone.

He rushed back to the bathroom, pushed two fingers deep into his throat. This time his body obeyed.

Staring blearily at the mess of raw meat and cheese in the bowl, Daniel pulled the chain. Nothing. There was no water.

Felicia. What the fuck was wrong with the old lumber-pile? She had never let her lodgers down before.

Daniel put on some stale clothes, wrinkling his nose at the smell but so incensed he did not care. He held onto his anger; it was important. It kept him focused. It kept him distracted.

Ice. Blood. Meat.

He walked out into the creaky labyrinth of walkways, calling to Felicia. The other units were silent: curtains drawn, doors locked.

He reached the open space at the center of the warren. His feet slid from under him but he managed to break the fall by grabbing the splintered doorframe. Cursing, he snatched away his hand and stared, uncomprehendingly, at the scarlet stain. He felt no pain.

He looked down. His shoes were splattered with red.

Felicia's domicile, always so neat, was cluttered with piles of rubbish, broken boards, chunks of…meat?

He touched the frame again. It twitched: a feeble dying reflex.

He looked down again, at the puddle that had almost sent him flying. He now saw what he had slipped on: a large burst eyeball smeared across the pavement.

Kora woke up in the nest of sumptuously knitted pieces piled upon each other with rainbow abandon: blue, green, and red;

smooth and cabled; patterned and monochrome. Last night she had been cold and burrowed deeply into the nest. But the morning was sticky and stifling. She kicked off a red-checked afghan. Then she picked it up again and pinched the shaggy surface. It remained inert.

When she had come back last night, the yarn guide having unraveled and reconstructed itself several times, two women were sitting at the kitchen table, snacking and gossiping: Irene and her friend Lola.

They were women as a matter of politeness, merely because they had feminine names. Lola looked a little more human than Irene, but this did not include such superfluities as gender. She was a slender cone-shaped being with the skin like a rough-pitted orange; her head, resting on her rounded shoulders without the benefit of a neck was another cone, hairless and smooth, slightly bulging at the tip. She had no legs and moved by contracting a powerful muscle pad like a snail. But she had a face with soft dark eyes and a Cupid's bow mouth. She had arms, disproportionately short and weak but boasting a pair of regular hands. And she could speak.

She seemed to be a little suspicious of Kora. But she was willing enough to chat, while shoveling candies into her pouting mouth (Irene was working on a head of lettuce). She did not ask too many questions. Perhaps Irene had already told her whatever she knew about her visitor.

Lola was a duck, just like Irene, and finally Kora found out what it meant. Ducks were those tenants whose form followed what had been their function before their acquisition of sentience. Irene had been a tangle of yarn. Lola had been a traffic cone. Like toads, they had split off from the urban fabric of the Pith. The difference – an insignificant one, in Kora's opinion – was that toads could become almost any shape, while ducks largely retained their original one.

It was very confusing: after all, Irene's shop was full of

properly inanimate yarn; there were traffic cones a-plenty clogging the streets where work-crews struggled with repairs; and the chairs on which they sat were just that, chairs. So why some objects became animate but not others?

She tried to pose this question to Lola, feeling vaguely embarrassed. Lola seemed to be taken aback, whether by Kora's rudeness or by her ignorance. She muttered something about the "will of Grandfather".

Grandfather?

Wasn't he dead? She had seen little altars with fruit and flower offerings scattered throughout the Market. Had Grandfather been deified? For some reason, she found the idea outrageous.

She tried to formulate another question, but Irene intervened. Pulling another ball of yarn from a shelf, she "wrote" on the table.

"Rest."

Kora smiled and hoped that gestures of friendliness would translate into a real feeling. She felt lonely. She *was* lonely.

"Yes," she said, getting up. "Good night, ladies."

As she turned off the light in the tiny bedroom where she had been directed by Irene, it occurred to her she was not being ironic. Human or tenant, female or sexless, these two were ladies.

Daniel walked very carefully, like an old man, bent and hugging his belly. There was something inside that he was afraid might burst and spill, tearing his flesh like sodden paper. He did not know what it was. Grief? Revulsion?

Satiety.

He was sated now and this was how it should be. This was how he should stay. Not waking up the beast that dozed uneasily, ready to stir and start clawing at his guts. Not waking up hunger.

Even though he had thrown up again when he saw what was

left of Felicia, emptied his stomach until nothing could come up but sour bile, this purging had miraculously reversed his gnawing need. Instead of hunger coming on the heels of emptiness, it was emptiness that made him feel full.

Somebody bumped into him, cursing in the noon language he barely understood. He lifted his bleary eyes to the stranger. The man was tall, slim and dark-skinned, wearing a colorful robe and a jaunty little hat. His lips peeled off his teeth like those of a dog.

Daniel took a step back, looked around. Somehow, he had wandered into low-levels. This was the part of the city he seldom went to because it reminded him of his own arrival in the city. Those first years of humiliation and poverty. And hunger.

He swallowed audibly.

He did not know where he was. How far could he have walked from home? The Pith was diseased here, the sidewalks covered with smelly blisters and suppurating potholes, the walls peeling in long scrolls of dry skin. There was a staggering amount of unoccupied space: deserted lots filled with debris; skeletal remnants of dead houses; poky dispirited courtyards. The houses were small and mean, standing apart as if disgusted by each other. The Peak and the high-rises of mid-levels were insubstantial ghosts against the yellow-gray pall of clouds. Shockingly, Daniel could see a great deal of the sky here, as if he was back in the country. The dirty void sucked at him.

"Whaddaya want here, frog?" the noon inquired in a growling voice.

As insults went, this one was ludicrous. If anything, the man looked more like a toad than Daniel. His grin was unnaturally wide, the lips curling over his cheeks and revealing worn-down gristle-like teeth.

"Nothing! Just let me pass!

"Frogs not allowed here! This is a human place!"

Daniel exploded.

Something broke inside him, as if a glass vessel just shattered, dousing his guts with liquid fire. Saliva ran down his chin. His body took over, doing the things it was trained to do and wanted to do now, while his mind was shoved aside, an ineffectual and shaky observer.

He felt hardly any impact as his 'arm connected, but the noon's face practically caved in. The jet of blood from his broken nose sprayed Daniel and he reflexively licked his lips.

With a bellow of rage, the noon charged again. Daniel sidestepped neatly and tripped him. The man collapsed on the scabby pavement. Daniel kicked him and ground his shoe into his hand, hearing the satisfying crunch of bones.

The noon keened.

A rabbit caught in a snare...

What snare?

He shook his head, trying to dislodge the hard nugget of an unwanted memory. The noon was scuttling away. Daniel licked his lips again and then licked his fingers.

What the fuck am I doing?

He ran down the unnaturally empty street, his head feeling as light as a balloon. He expected the noon's friends pour out of the moribund houses but all was quiet.

Dead. They are all dead.

All?

Felicia.

Yes, this is what he had to do. To report her death. Her murder. He was a militiaman, for Grandfather's sake! What was wrong with him?

He looked around, searching for an appropriate locus: something new and growing, a budding pylon or a fresh wall. A designated speak-to would be the best but he did not expect to find it here, in the gang-infested low-levels. They probably covered any exposed Pith with whatever dead junk they could find!

Nothing grew here. The houses were dwarfish, stunted and

pinched. Gaps yawned between them, filled with dirty tangles of coarse hair-wire.

He approached a blank wall the color of urine. Stucco boils hang on it like grapes. Litter blew against his legs. He grimaced, kicked it aside, and reflexively stepped back. There would be litter scavengers hiding in accumulation of garbage and they often bit.

The mess of flambeau molting and food wrappings passively absorbed his kick.

Daniel pushed his palms against the wall, searching for a spot where the ponderous, reassuring pulsation of the Pith would vibrate against his skin.

He felt nothing. The rough powdery surface was cold and mute.

Increasingly frantic, he rubbed his hands all over the wall. It was like caressing a corpse. The house was dead.

He ran to the next house whose balcony sagged like a limp dick. The first-story windows scowled with broken rails. He slapped the wall and got a cloud of dust in his eyes.

What was going on? Daniel looked around. Nobody else in the street. How was this possible? How could the Pith be so sick and nobody knew about it; no flambeau screamed about it in its broadcast; no emergency sessions were convened in the City Hall by Mayor Volk? If the Pith died, nobody could survive in the city, whether human or tenant.

Or they could all escape to the country: to the land of the dead patrolled by the Divide. Daniel had not thought of this name in years and its memory brought a chill that, for a moment, overrode both hunger and confusion.

He pushed the entrance door that hung, broken, from its hinges. He stepped into the muddy twilight. The interior walls had collapsed, leaving behind piles of rubble and bone. The floor gaped with toothless mouths.

But there was movement in the dim space. He squinted.

A leafless tree with curlicue branches stood in one corner. It was festooned with children.

They stared at him with big bright eyes, their faces shrunken and pasty, their bony fingers clutching bare branches. Their swollen bellies poked through their mismatched clothes.

Am I dreaming?

No. It was all too real, too obtrusive: the smell of dust and excrement, the heavy air, the creaking of the tree as it groaned under the weight of the clinging children.

Except…it was not a tree.

He had seen such a thing before as a rookie militiaman on one of his first assignments, investigating a fire in a flambeau compound. He had suffered from nightmares for months after walking into a field of ash studded with tortured tree-shapes.

It was a flambeau skeleton. These kids were clambering all over a corpse!

He stepped toward them, his mouth flooding with the taste of copper and bile. The children shifted and the skeleton groaned. They were light and small, nobody older than six.

Their faces. Marasmus. The mask of hunger.

The country. They are from the country.

He turned around, ran back to the door. It took ages.

Finally, he was out, one hand clapped over his mouth as if he was trying to keep a small vicious animal inside.

In the dusty daylight, he scuttled away from the dead house in the dead street.

Chapter 12. The Incoming

Kora developed a habit.

It was something she was proud of. A habit was the beginning of an identity. A habit was a building block of a self. A habit was something you could fall back upon.

Every morning, she would get up at the crack of dawn and help Irene stock the shop for opening. She quickly learned to sort out different kinds of yarn, to sweep the floor, and to toss out the skeins that started showing signs of animation. She found out that the main component to the overhead of the shop was the unpredictable fluctuation in the merchandise's degree of liveliness. The yarn that was delivered every week by Irene's supplier – a glum black man called Abidemi – was properly inanimate, comprised of skeins and balls of fibers in bright colors ready for the clacking needles of Irene's customers: a coterie of old ladies, human and otherwise, who faithfully bought their share of new patterns and corresponding materials every week. But occasionally, and with no regularity that Kora could discern, she would discover a ball twitching on the shelf or creeping away, caterpillar-like, under the counter. These incipient yarn-ducks had to be tossed out and to fend for themselves in the ecology of the Market. It occurred to Kora that it would perhaps be easier to kill them, but she did not dare suggesting it to Irene. For all she knew, the yarn woman had some fraternal feelings toward the creatures, even though she kicked them out irritably and entered losses into her ledger with a very human-like sigh. And could toads on the verge of sentience be easily killed? Kora did not know and did not want to find out.

After helping Irene, she would walk out into the morning rush at the Market. The giant place had its own rhythm, as predictable as the diurnal cycles of the human body. As the sun lit up the crown of the Peak, the flambeaus would slither away to their perches in their own districts. The bone shutters of shops and eateries would be raised with a screech, the derma marquees spread.

Of the eateries, the bakeries were the first to come awake with the bustle of workers inside and the warm aroma of fresh bread wafting into the morning chill. On her walk, Kora always stopped by one particular bakery, drawing in the sweet smells of vanilla and cinnamon, staring at the plump ruddy buns, the glazed crawlers, and the delicate pink-frosted tiny doughnuts. Something always stirred deep in the inaccessible recesses of her memory: a guilty pleasure, a sweet pain…She tried to translate it into actual appetite, but she could no more bite into a pastry than into a stone. Still, she told herself that trying to reawaken the human hunger helped to keep at bay the beast inside her.

The third time she stopped by the bakery, one of the workers offered her a coconut bun, so fresh it quivered like living flesh. She smiled at him, accepted the bun and accidentally brushed his hand. As her fingers lingered, he smiled back, coming closer. He was good-looking: a young copper-skinned man with dark liquid eyes.

He reached out for her. She pushed him away and ran, compulsively crumbling the bun, tearing it to shreds and tossing it to the semi-living garbage in the gutter.

But even her self-loathing could not repress the pleasure of a snack.

Next morning, she actually talked to somebody.

The Incoming Sun was one of the bigger coffee-shops: a vast cavernous space under the ribbed ceiling, decorated with curling posters. It was these posters that attracted Kora's attention as she sat at a corner table, nursing a cup of cold coffee for appearance's sake. They looked old; and though much in the Market was unkempt or dilapidated, she had not previously seen a sign of actual age.

All the posters were variations on a single image: a stocky man, wearing some sort of military uniform, his figure boldly outlined against the sulfurous sky, facing away from the viewer. There was a black jagged mountain towering over him and his arm was raised in what appeared to be a threatening and/or beckoning gesture. The style was rough and raw, the man's solid body and the mountain rendered in slashing strokes.

There were differences. In one poster, the sun was rising from beyond the mountain and its splayed rays lit the spiky lines of the summit and the foothills. In another, the man was surrounded by disproportionately small figures of followers who seemed to be genuflecting toward him. And in the one Kora studied most, the man had turned around. His face, under a funny little hat, was completely forgettable. But at his feet seethed a red-and-black mass like the convolutions of a brain or a looped pile of intestines. She could not make out what it was supposed to represent.

A waitress stopped by her.

"Anything else I can get you?"

Kora was not drinking the coffee, of course. But she felt bad about sitting in a coffee-shop without ordering anything and since Irene provided her with some money, she could indulge herself. Incidentally, looking at the prices on the menu convinced her that the chairman's promised reward of 500,000 wons was very generous indeed. Not that she was going to take him up on it!

She asked for a refill.

The waitress brought back a steaming cup and lingered by the table. She was young, a human female with a pasty face and makeup-encrusted round eyes. Her razor-cut hair was dyed an improbable magenta.

"You new here?" she asked. "We mostly get old-timers."

Kora had already noticed that the clientele of the Incoming Sun consisted mainly of old men who played checkers and Go, rustled derma-printed newspapers, and stretched out their mid-morning snacks well into the afternoon.

"Just moved to the Market," she said.

"How do you like it here?"

"I like it very much," Kora said honestly. "And you? Have you been here long?"

The girl smiled.

"Market born and bred."

Kora pushed the steaming coffee cup toward her.

"Take it. No, seriously, my stomach just went on a wildcat strike."

The girl laughed.

"I can take it back!"

"No, no! I'm fine. It's a pity to waste it."

The girl sat down.

"I've a break coming. Might just as well take it now."

She added two spoons of sugar to the coffee. Kora watched her enviously.

"I'm Alexandra," the girl said, pointing at the tag pinned to her orange shirt.

"Kora."

"Nice name."

Kora smiled gratefully. This was all she had.

"I was wondering," she said, pointing to the posters. "These look pretty old."

The girl nodded.

"They are. Folks from Art Museum came by a couple of times, but the owner won't sell. If I were him, I would charge a viewing fee but he…well, I guess he's too devout for this."

"Devout?"

"Yeah. Grandfather, you know?"

Kora did not know.

But she came back next morning and sat in the Incoming Sun, nursing her coffee, studying the lined faces of the customers, as if trying to decipher the writings of history in the hieroglyphs of wrinkles and folds. Irene had knitted a multicolored sheath for her that clung to her curves like a second skin. She liked it and so did the old men, apparently never too old for a wink and a smile.

Alexandra was ready to chat, but she imparted little useful information. She was not exactly a bubblehead, but her circle of interests was very narrow. She talked about flambeau parties, shopping in up-levels, relationships with her boyfriends, and the skyrocketing prices of food and rent. Her references to the city politics were casual and incomprehensible. She thought she was going to vote in the upcoming elections but did not know who for. Her favorite flambeau-caster was for Mayor Volk, so she would probably go with him. His challenger whose name was Malek something elicited little enthusiasm as being too pro-tenant.

Kora tried to ask Alexandra about the chairman but realized that she knew neither his name nor his position. The chairman of what? He was obviously rich and important, but the city was filled with rich and important people, living it up in their luxurious mansions high on the Peak. Mid-level people were squeezed into tiny apartments in the towers, but they had enough to eat, so there was little discontent. Apart from the low-level bottom-feeders, of course, but many of them were not city people at all. Not even tenants. Just…country.

She bought coffee and pastry for Alexandra on her next break. The waitress probably thought she was making a move on her and appeared not unwilling to carry on a flirtation. Kora found her doughy prettiness singularly unappealing. At least in the sexual sense.

Kora tried to bring the conversation round to the mysterious Grandfather but did not know how to phrase the question. Was the name of the café linked to the posters? Was the man in them Grandfather?

When she finally mentioned the Incoming, Alexandra giggled.

"Old Van!" she declared, pointing to one of the Go-playing pensioners. "He once had such a row with a duck over Grandfather that we had to call the militia! A real believer, he is!"

He was definitely old: a small, wiry, stooped man in nondescript clothes, his bald head as smooth as a billiard ball. His face was a mass of wrinkles that his poorly fitted dentures stretched like crepe paper. When he bent over the table, she saw a jagged scar snake out of the worn collar of his shirt, as if he had survived a near-decapitation.

He turned around abruptly and met her eyes. His own were narrow and dark, hiding in their creased lairs like suspicious rodents. Kora refused to look away; Old Van said something to his cronies, got up, walked over, and plunked himself down at her table. Despite his age and infirmity, he had the imperious manners of somebody who used to command.

"You're coming here every day," he said, his voice high, almost a falsetto. It was not a question and Kora said nothing. He continued to study her and then smiled unpleasantly, his false teeth flashing.

"Did he send you?"

"Nobody sent me," she said.

The chairman?

"You can tell him to fuck off," Old Van continued, as if she had said nothing. "The city is ours. He brought us here and now he wants to take it back?"

"Grandfather?"

He snickered.

"I'm a grandfather! He isn't! Never was!"

"They told me you were devout? Doesn't sound like it!"

"Who told you? Our pretty Alex? Have the hots for her, do

you?"

Kora flushed with anger. She hated his papery skin, the musty smell of him, and his shaky dentures.

"Careful, old man," she whispered. "I can eat tough meat too."

She was aghast at the words leaving her mouth. She wanted to apologize, to explain, to take it back...But Old Van did not seem shocked or even surprised. He cackled.

"We did," he said. "On the march...The things you do when you have no choice...Not that any of them would understand. Too cuddled, too soft, living it up in the city's warm belly like a babe in his mum's. What do they know of hardship, of struggle, of hunger? Those he left behind in that damned bog, though...that was different. We followed him like dogs. And he treated us like dogs. Fed us to that time-hole, the whirlpool..."

"The whirlpool?"

"The Divide," Old Van said and spat on the floor. "But I crawled out. Came here. Nothing he can do about it. I have proper metal walls in my place."

"Metal walls..." Kora repeated faintly. Something was brushing the edges of her mind, some elusive image, but it dissipated as she tried to get a hold of it.

"So, if he sent you," Old Van continued, "tell him to go to hell. Well, I guess he is already there, in a manner of speaking."

"Why do you think he sent me?" Kora asked.

"You have the look. The Marching Blades look."

"I don't know what you are talking about," Kora said. "I lost my memory."

An avid expression that was ghastly to behold came over Old Van's skull-like face. He leaned closer with odious intimacy.

"Have you crossed over?" he whispered. "Have they sent somebody – finally, after all these years...Years! I can only count them in wrinkles! This bloody Year Zero – that was his invention! He is afraid of time – as he should be! Time is his enemy's weapon! That's why it's making those meat-puppets! I bet he's shaking in his breeches! Funny how what goes around, comes around! He made us eat…that. And now they are coming to eat his get! Country against city; cannibals against cannibals' children!"

"Tell me!" Kora said.

"Tell you what?"

"The truth. Who is Grandfather? An eidolon? A god?"

"Eidolon? Nobody here knows this word. You did cross over, didn't you? You can tell me. I'm good at keeping secrets."

"I know nothing!" Kora cried, her frustration boiling over. The Go players paused, looked at them, and returned to the game. She lowered her voice.

"I really am an amnesiac. Please tell me…Who is Grandfather? Why do you hate him so much?"

"He brought us here. Incoming Sun…named after him! Ha! What a joke!"

"Do you worship him?"

He started laughing: spittle flying, dentures dancing, his bald head bobbling on his skinny neck as if about to fall off.

"Worship?" He pulled down his scruffy collar, revealing the scar. Kora gulped. She could not believe a man could survive such a wound. It went around his neck like a noose.

"This is what he did to me!"

"What's in the country?"

"Death."

"Isn't the food for the city coming from there?"

"Yes. The poor dolts of farmers…feeding the monster that sucks them dry! But now they have their own monster to fight for them. Or fight *with* them…depending on how you look at it!"

"I can kill Hungry Ones," Kora said.

Old Van's eyes opened wide.

"Weapons?" he whispered. "Real weapons?"

Kora shook her head.

"I'm a weapon," she said. "I eat zombies."

Old Van inhaled deeply and sat up. Something shifted in his face and for a moment a commanding presence looked out of his dull eyes.

"So, it happened…" he spoke to himself rather than to her. "The Blades have found us. I waited long. But not in vain."

"I don't understand!" Kora cried in frustration.

"No, of course you don't. I expect they took…precautions. Don't fret; I'll guide you. You're lucky that you found me!"

Kora was deeply skeptical about this "luck": the idea of being guided by this repulsive old man had very little appeal.

"First the khruts, then you…" she muttered. "I have more guides than I need. I would gladly exchange them for one guidebook!"

Old Van started.

"Khruts? Did they get to you?"

"Why are you asking?"

"Khruts are in cahoots with the thing in the bog…the Divide! Don't trust any of them!"

There was a commotion at the door. A couple of regulars tried to get out and were pushed back by a wedge of newcomers. An eddy of bodies formed, and the Go players, abandoning their stones, were sucked into it. Angry shouts attracted a couple of waiters who hovered uncertainly, not knowing what to do. Kora peered over Old Van's shoulder.

Above the shouting, she heard familiar clicking sounds like human speech chopped up and mixed with bird calls.

"Koraa!"

She jumped up; and so did Van.

The knot of people fell apart, and a khrut emerged, scuttling toward her. He had a raven head, its huge beak pulling it forward, unbalancing his shrunken feathered body. His arms were short with disproportionately large taloned hands.

She backed off. More khruts followed: a mix of scruffy feathers and pimply skin, of fluttering plucked-chicken wings and steel-tipped claws.

The raven-headed creature stopped. It was impossible to follow the direction of his sidewise gaze, but she was sure he was searching the faces of the patrons. It was early in the day; the café was not even half-full.

His beak clicked, a long crimson-colored tongue darting out.

Bony fingers clutched her wrists.

"Are they after you?"

"Koraa!"

"Don't go with them!" Old Van hissed into her ear. "He thinks he can control them, his precious Guards, but he is a fool! They have sold us out! To the Divide, the bog-thing!"

Kora's head swam. Who should she trust? The chairman who claimed to have made her; Peter who wanted to take her away from the city; this old man with his incomprehensible stories? She was supposed to be invincible, but she felt as helpless and out of control as a blind kitten.

"Run!" Old Van whispered. "I'll delay them! Tell the Blades that I'm sorry for what we have done!"

She scanned the advancing khruts, trying to find Peter. She thought she saw him at the entrance to the café, hanging back, his golden eyes lidded, but she was not sure.

She hesitated and Old Van stepped forward, positioning his frail body between her and the khrut.

"Run!" he yelled at her.

The raven-headed khrut lunged forward. His massive beak darted, barely missing Kora's temple. Wet warmth splattered her face.

Old Van collapsed on the floor, his bald skull leaking like a split watermelon. The raven-headed khrut pecked again and lifted his head, swallowed something, his feathered throat working.

Kora looked down, into the scarlet hole where Old Van's left eye used to be.

She backed off. Somebody was screaming in the background but it hardly registered. All her attention was focused on the khrut's rapidly rising and falling chest. She imagined the heart beating, the blood flowing, the surging vitality under the mangy feathers.

She bumped into a table; it wobbled, coffee spilling from the overturned cups. The raven-head jumped and floated above her, his wings vibrating.

She reached up, caught his bony limb. And she fed.

The hot rush ran through her body like water through the parched field, overriding everything else, silencing the horror and self-disgust. It was not like feeding on Hungry Ones: that was as simple and natural as drinking milk for a baby. Here, she had to force herself to adapt to unfamiliar and distasteful food. But it was nourishment. She felt her strength coming back.

She tossed the depleted thing aside and it lay there like a crumpled piece of paper.

The other khruts moved toward her, one of them lifting a long narrow knife. Another had a club.

She swiped at the one with the knife and drained him. She did it swiftly and unerringly as if the danger released something in her, sweeping aside the remnants of the inhibition that had held her back on Skybridge.

Just open up that void inside, just let it unfold inside you like a brainless, insistent, velvety-black flower, pushing through the stone with its wiry roots, reaching into the thin air with its grasping petals...Let it live, let it rule you, let it be you.

Survival.

She paused when a pair of round golden eyes looked at her. Self-disgust made her step back. She knew Peter betrayed her and was outraged, but it was a human emotion and it brought her back to her humanity.

He scuttled away.

She looked around. The khruts' bodies littered the floor –

four of them. One tried to crawl away and she stomped on it, snapping hollow bones.

She found herself at the door. The people had melted away. Frightened eyes, circled by heavy makeup, stared at her from under a table.

She pushed the door and stepped into the bustle of the Market. Nobody tried to stop her.

Chapter 13. Meeting on the Train

Kora walked through the Market as stiffly as a puppet, putting one foot in front of the other, mechanically moving through the gray world. The magic was gone. She saw the vendors and the shoppers, piles of fruits and vegetables, clothes and trinkets, but they were all disconnected from each other, broken fragments of the lost whole, meaningless monochrome smudges on the inside of her skull. The fragrance of fresh bread and flowers was as irrelevant as the stink of offal; the colorful crowds were merely an obstacle on her way. She was done with the Market, or the Market was done with her.

She briefly thought about going back to Irene's but shrugged and went on with the same measured indifferent stride. What was the point?

The duck ladies, Irene and Lola, she would keep away from them as much as she could. This was the only expression of affection she was capable of. Keeping away.

Peter has betrayed me...Was Irene in on his schemes?

She did not think so. But she could trust nobody, not even herself. Particularly not herself.

And she could be friends with nobody. She was a predator. Every living being in the city was potentially her prey.

But there was one lawful target, one acceptable source of nourishment that did not make her into...

Cannibal...

Hungry Ones were neither intelligent nor self-aware. Whatever they had been, by now they were simply dangerous animals. By feeding on them, she would do a service to the city, while simultaneously satisfying her own hunger.

She felt a glum admiration for the brilliance of the chairman's scheme. If he had truly remade her into what she was, he had acquired a tool whose very humanity depended on being used for the purpose she had been forged to fulfill. Obey and be a zombie-hunter. Rebel and become a man-eater.

The surge of anger that went through her felt good. She would show him…

Perhaps she should have gone with the khruts…

No!

Old Van's warnings aside, she did not trust birdmen. The couple of days she had spent in the Market did not restore her memory, but they helped her to find some kind of psychological balance, rooted in dreams and intuitions. She was now convinced she had encountered khruts before and this unremembered encounter was a source of fear and loathing. Killing them was the right thing to do. It was self-defense…

And dinner…

But she would be damned if she allowed herself to be manipulated further, battered by the events over which she had no control, targeted by schemes she did not understand.

There was one man who knew who she was, who could – or so he claimed – give her back her memory, her identity, her humanity. Very well, she would go and confront him.

The chairman.

Peter said he had survived the roofs' attack. She would find him. She was not afraid of him. She was not afraid of anybody.

Others should be afraid of her.

"Watch out!"

A vendor carrying live fish in a big glass jar strapped to his forehead and supported on his back by a harness pushed by her. Stinking water splashed onto her face. Round fish-eyes stared at her sorrowfully through the murky glass.

She wiped her face and went on.

Everybody has to eat. The Market exists so people can eat.

She reached the seam area where the maze of alleyways petered out, and high-rises with residential and retail floors began. The slender jade-colored towers were ridiculed by the Market vendors who called them "chopsticks". They soared into the pale sky, graceful and pliant, inclining toward each other as if they were gossiping. Perhaps they were.

She crossed a river of pedestrians going home from work. The sun was invisible behind the pall of vapors, but she judged it was late afternoon. A flat creature spreading across two floors was leisurely crawling up the side of one of the towers, the luminescent nodes embedded in its transparent flesh winking in soft blue and green: an adult flambeau, getting ready for his nighttime job.

She had no idea how to get back to the thousand-Buddha stairway. The city was bewilderingly complex. Where would she look for the chairman? She did not even know his name. The chairman of what?

A bright yellow sign caught her attention: black letters curling around a smiley. The letters said MTT, which Lola had told her stood for "Metropolitan Train Transit", the city's central transportation system. MTT tunnels ran under the entire city and into the countryside.

But Kora had never been inside a station. Well…apart from that first morning when she had met Marika…and she had not actually gone down.

Perhaps she could take a train to the chairman's residence. She tried to reconstruct her journey with Wingate. They had walked from the hospital whose name she did not know to the escalator snaking up the slope of the Peak.

The escalator! Wingate had called it the mid-level mover. And she was sure she had seen a yellow sign somewhere on the way!

She squinted at the sign. The smiley was not, she saw now, a stylized representation of a human face. It had round bulging eyes and its curving mouth had vertical strokes in it, like a grill.

The train is coming…

A worn-down remnant of memory stuck in her mind like a seed between teeth – tasteless but bothersome.

This station was called Bird's Nest. There must be a map of MTT inside. She would find the closest station to the mid-level mover and from there she would search the vicinity until she found the stairway.

She stepped through the glassy rippling doors.

Daniel shoved a handful of change into his back pocket and expertly maneuvered the tray through the crowd of late-lunch commuters. The tray was piled with four meat sandwiches, three taro buns, two cups of coffee, and a bottle of guava juice. He managed to squeeze through the crush of chattering secretaries and young city managers and find a free corner. Sweeping a pile of newspapers and dirty napkins into the nearest bin, he placed his meal on the counter and tucked in.

The tiny glass cubicle of the bakery clung to the yellow-tiled wall of the MTT passage, bathed in the buttery glow that did not rely on flambeaus but emanated directly from the Pith. People hurried to and fro; train displays flashed, turnstiles clicked briskly, swallowing coins; and half-sentient toad scavengers with bright carapaces and flexible arms scurried around, picking up rubbish. All was as it should be.

Chewing through the pickled beef tongue in his sandwich, Daniel relaxed. MTT always had this effect on him: partly because it was populated by his beloved trains, partly because it was such a clean and safe place, always brightly lit even in the depth of night, always humming with voices. Some immigrants found the stations and tunnels spooky because of their sense of being watched – which was perfectly justified since the Pith was at its most active throughout the complex and always growing labyrinth of the city's transportation system. It could not be otherwise: blood had to be pumped through the tangle of tracks; food had to be delivered to the trains; and petty criminals had to be dealt with. But though sentient, the Pith was not intelligent. It did not plot, hatch schemes, or single out individuals. It just took care of business. This was why Daniel always felt safest when embraced by the Pith, like a child in the womb. He tried to share this sense of security with recent arrivals, explaining to them that unless they felt more at home in MTT than in whatever low-level cubicle the municipality had allocated to them, they were not real citizens yet.

But he was; and sipping his sugary coffee, he felt the tension of this nightmare day drain away. Anything can be dealt with as long as one kept one's cool. How else did one survive?

How else did one survive in the hunger country?

But he was not in the country anymore; he was in the city, his adoptive parent whom he loved with all the passion of the second-best son. The city would provide.

He decided that it was probably for the best that he did not succeed in placing a call to the Shrimp in the dead street. Looking back, he suspected that much of what he had seen was a hallucination, brought about by shock and/or low blood sugar. All right, low-levels could be pretty dismal: he had stayed there after his arrival and had experienced the bite of poverty, but dead streets? Whole blocks of houses nothing but corpses? Children clinging to a skeleton?

Picking out the shreds of the flesh...

Was something wrong with him or with the city?

Bright eyes in the folded face, grey flaps of skin around fragile bones...

What was he thinking?

He bit into the soft taro bun and relished the calming taste of the grainy filling.

Now what? Felicia was dead. Tenanticides had increased dramatically in the last couple of months, fueled by the hysteria over the supposed "zombie invasion". There was no invasion, just sporadic incursions, but tell this to the news-flambeau guild who made money by flashing stupid rumors! Or to Mayor Volk and his cronies in the City Corps! Or to the birdmen who were so much in demand now as the rich folk on up-levels paid triple for the scrawniest Guard!

He swept the crumbs onto a napkin and funneled them into his mouth.

He had to report her death, of course. The boys in Serious Crime would investigate. And guess who would be their number one suspect?

He never made a secret of his plan to retire and take over Felicia's real estate mini-empire. She was his friend; he was willing to wait as long as it took until the old toad retired or died. But tell this to the snooty upper-level boys in SC! He knew they looked down on him: an immigrant, a country bumpkin! Not even twelve years of outstanding service could erase the stigma of his origin!

He reflectively bit into the remnant of a sandwich. The wrapping squeaked on his teeth.

But the Shrimp was on his side! Colonel Rosen may have been weird – and became even more so after his wife and daughter had left – but he was a fair man and a good officer who stood by his people. He appreciated loyalty and dedication. And Daniel had those in abundance – even if he was not smart enough to pass the stupid tests required for promotion to a Detective!

He chewed and spat out the scrunched-up wrapping when he could taste nothing but his own metallic saliva.

He would go and talk to the Colonel in private, explain the situation, and together they would come up with a way to report Felicia's death that would leave him out of it. As for the noon he had hit in the dead street…the bastard had it coming! Assaulting a militiaman (well, he was in civvies but still…)

His teeth jarred painfully on something hard. He discovered he was sucking on the empty bottle of juice like a babe on the tit.

Regretfully, he put it down and decided to go back for more.

Somebody was looking at him.

Nobody looked at you directly in the city. This was one of the worst gaffes you could commit: on the level with asking a khrut whether he fancied a chicken breast for dinner. The Pith watched everybody, of course, but people, whether human or tenant, gave each other privacy.

But this was no Pith surveillance.

Daniel looked back and caught the eyes of a girl in a trim suit who turned away blushing, her sleek black hair swinging around her face. But he had seen the expression on her face.

Horror.

He lifted his hand to his mouth and it came back speckled with blood. He had chewed up his lips.

There was nothing left of his meal, not even the wrappers, and the disposable cup and bottle. Everything had been reduced to pulpy mess. His tray was shining-wet as if somebody had licked it cleaned.

The rage at the busybody girl, at the lunch crowd, at everybody who had witnessed him, Daniel Moylan, as he was gobbling his food like an animal, was unbearable.

The skin on his right hand was smooth and tawny, darker than his natural color. He snapped his fingers and felt a springy kick.

His clothes were chafing against the graze that he had carefully disinfected yesterday. It was a superficial graze, hardly more than a scratch. But now he could feel a burning point of pain there like a predatory insect burrowing into his flesh.

He forced his muscles to relax, his 'arm to go quiescent. It was the hardest thing he had ever done.

Daniel carefully placed the empty tray on the stand and walked out of the bakery, ramrod-straight and dignified as befits a militiaman of the city.

Kora gaped at her surroundings.

She realized how limited her urban experience had been. She was too fascinated by the Market's abundance to pay real attention to the structure of the city itself. But if she were to find herself, she would have to search through its convolutions. And this was the real body of the city, its bloodstream, its veins and arteries.

The station was a curving, sweeping yellow space, lit by a golden glow emanating from the dome of the ceiling. The walls were tile-clad but when she peered at them, she saw that the tiles were slightly irregular and rough, like reptilian scales.

The tiles were separated by reddish seams. At intervals, a tile was missing and in these bare spots the reddish substance was more flesh-like, puffy and yielding.

A man stopped by one of these areas, touched it with his open palm.

The substance rose like dough and formed itself into a pair of pouting lips.

"Speak or see?" the lips asked in a liquid, genderless voice.

The man rattled off a string of numbers. The lips closed and reformed themselves into a stylized but unmistakable ear.

The man started talking into the ear, first saying something that sounded like a greeting in another language and then launching into a litany of complaints about some deal gone bad. Feeling Kora's stare, he turned his head and gave her a dirty look. She walked away.

The displays were bewildering: large flickering boards of red, yellow, and green with scrolling announcements and constantly changing timetables. She knew that the display boards were in fact flambeaus, specially bred for public service, just as others were bred to be ads, decorations, news-screens, or entertainers. Still, it amazed her that she had not realized they were sentient beings when she first saw them in the train station after her hotel awakening. Now, with her experience of the Market, she could see the ripple of muscle under the luminescent skin and tiny individual quirks that made each flambeau unique.

There were stalls and kiosks lining the station. The Market was only the most concentrated expression of the unrestrained appetite with which both the citizens and the tenants bought and sold, ate and traded. The abundance of the city suddenly felt suffocating.

She passed by a shop selling dry fish and paused by a newspaper kiosk. It screamed with giant headlines and pictures of an impressive wreck. Unfortunately, the text was in an unreadable spiky script.

She reached the place where the station was divided by a line of turnstiles that turned their flat eyeless heads toward her and opened their long slit mouths. She fed one of them a small coin. It withdrew its arm to let her pass. Beyond, the broad tongue of a flowing escalator was conveying passengers down to the tunnels.

She finally found a map of MTT and stood in helpless bewilderment, trying to disentangle the cat's cradle of multicolored skeins, representing different lines. None of the stations' names looked familiar.

Wait…here was something! Cat Temple! She remembered the small cat-faced toad she had seen while riding the escalator with Wingate. She had not seen one like it since. And Temple! Perhaps it referred to the thousand-Buddha stairway!

It was a very slender thread to follow but better than nothing. She stepped onto the platform.

Small toads dove in and out of the crowds, picking up litter. She saw one of them surreptitiously tug off a woman's scarf and scuttle away with it. Another toad clambered over her foot. She shook it off and the creature ran away.

The sunny glow of the ceiling petered out in the darkness of the tunnel. Even more people poured onto the platform, dangerously squeezing the crowd already there. Kora was pushed to the edge. She looked down into the pit of the tracks.

The pit was filled with blood.

The thick red liquid sloshed down below, reeking of the abattoir. The passengers on the platform stared at a couple of old flambeaus arthritically advertising a soft drink.

A rounded S-shape surfaced in the channel of blood, a thick purplish tube undulating like a giant worm. Then another. A venous segmented pipe plopped out of the liquid. Its sides were threaded by a stitching of black slits. The slits opened in unison like hungry mouths and sucked in the blood. The sounds of smacking, gulping, and draining filled the station.

Another pipe surfaced in parallel to the first one and proceeded to drink down the remains of the blood. The flatulent noise was deafening. Kora turned to the man whose briefcase was poking into her lower back.

"Excuse me, but…is this…normal?"

The man looked at her with disinterested eyes and gestured at one of the displays that informed her that the northbound train was 3 minutes late.

She looked into the pit again. The blood had been ingested, revealing the tough-looking floor, composed of tangled purplish fibers. There were two parallel indentations running along its length and the two verminous tubes, engorged with drinking, their slits closed, slid snugly into them.

And then she heard the soft rustle of the approaching train.

When the train entered the station, emerging from the tunnel with a soft purring sound, Kora gasped.

And yet, what else did she expect?

What else would the train be?

But there was something unnervingly human about its face, something altogether too quirky and animated. She had accepted the fact that the city was alive but only as a general notion. What she had seen of the exposed Pith did not seem too different from steel or stone: just another kind of building material. Toads and ducks were individuals, inhabiting the city. Flambeaus, she still had a difficulty in regarding as sentient beings rather than part of the urban infrastructure. But then flambeaus did not have faces. The train did.

The train had a large blunt head with a flat muzzle covered by dense, velvety fuzz like a mouse's. It was huge, snugly fitting into the tunnel. Its eyes blinked lazily, the wrinkled papery skin sliding over the recessed discs with cream sclera and dull black pupils, as inexpressible as fish-eyes. There were two prominent lumps above the eyes. Its skin was loose, hanging in folds and pouches but it did not appear old: like a puppy, it seemed not to have grown fully into its own hide.

Besides the eyes, the only other feature on its blunt muzzle was what Kora at first took for a toothy gaping mouth. But then she realized it was something else: a square opening, shored up by a cartilage frame and louvered by tough-looking white filaments. Stuck among the filaments were soft, blood-flushed protrusions, leaves of tissue growing in the forest of organic stems. An acrid smell wafted through the station.

Kora fought to back off, but the surging crowd carried her into the car.

The Skybridge line was still blocked because of the rogue and so Daniel had to take a roundabout route: by the Golden Flower line to the Pit where he changed to the Bird's Nest line that would take him to the base.

The train was surprisingly empty; there was not a single standing figure in the aisle. This made Daniel uneasy.

His eyes darted through the softly lit interior of the car. It was young and healthy: the inner skin moist and gleaming, the seats pleasantly plump, the loops hanging from the ceiling for the standing passengers to hold on to shining with the oily gleam of new derma.

He wished he had spoken to the train before boarding it. The

Transit Authority's rules prohibited trains from talking to the passengers, but this did not apply to him, surely. Chances were he knew this train's family.

The train lurched and Daniel's stomach lurched with it. Acid flooded his mouth.

Next stop – Bird's Nest. The closest station to the Market. Nobody knew why it was called that since there were no birds' nests in the vicinity. The carrion fowls that the khruts were so fond of nested in the countryside and on the barren slopes of the Peak above the urban habitation line. There was a silly rumor that some of them came from beyond the Divide. This was ridiculous since *nothing* came from beyond the Divide. Not after the Incoming led by Grandfather.

The doors whooshed open. Some people disembarked, more came in, shoppers burdened with bulging net satchels and derma-bags. One woman came in carrying nothing. He glanced at her: politely, from the corner of his eye as befits a citizen. But then he stared.

She was striking but this was not the reason for his shameless behavior. She was not his type: he liked his women small and petite, city-sophisticated, while she was big and strong, with wide hips and broad shoulders, saved from stockiness only by the deep curve of her slender waist. She was wearing a multicolored knitted dress that clung to her like a second skin, emphasizing her full breasts. But despite this alluring display, there was something off-putting about her; she was like a magnet whose poles kept switching, attracting and repelling at the same time. Her face was beautifully ugly, with slanted emerald eyes and a mouth so full it looked swollen. She looked like somebody you'd rather meet in a painting than in real life.

But Daniel was pretty sure he had in fact met her in real life. And he did not know when and how.

She was familiar and yet he drew blank trying to connect her to a name, place or circumstances. His city memory was excellent. He was not likely to forget somebody as distinctive as her. But clearly he had.

He suddenly felt claustrophobic, hemmed in, as if her presence drew oxygen out of the air. He got up as the train slowed down approaching the station and walked to the door, holding onto derma loops.

The woman's eyes fell upon him and her face lit up. Daniel could not decipher her expression. Joy? Surprise? Fear?

The train's headlights reflected off the fibrous walls of the tunnel. Suddenly, it shook, braking crazily, hurling the standing passengers forward. Somebody careened into Daniel, flattening him against the wall. And then the lights went out.

Inside, Kora began to relax, chiding herself for a fool. She *knew* that trains were sentient beings, for Grandfather's sake!

The popular Market expression popping into her head made her wince.

She remembered Lola singing praises of MTT. According to her, trains were much more honest and reliable than the khrut Guards or the City Corps who were universally condemned as corrupt and ineffectual.

Nevertheless, she was relieved that inside the train its (or was it *his?*) personhood was not too obvious. The long car was brightly lit by the narrow strip running along its curving ceiling, which was not a separate flambeau but part of the train's own anatomy. On both sides of the strip, leathery hand-straps hang down for standing passengers to grip. The car was not too full and she sat down on the warm red cushion.

Somebody was looking at her, practically burning holes in her with the intensity of his gaze. She looked back in irritation – men often stared but seldom so blatantly – and felt her breath stop.

She was struggling to her feet, a foolish grin spreading over her face.

"Daniel!"
And then the lights went out.

Chapter 14. The Rogue

Crawling in the thick darkness, Daniel was brought short by a blow to the head and instinctively lashed out.

His fist connected with something rotten-soft. Warm wetness splattered his fingers.

The car had been quiet at first but now a chorus of groans, cries and indignant exclamations was beginning to rise, a swelling music of fear.

He had been tossed onto the floor by a series of convulsions that shook the train after the lights went out. Somebody landed on top of him, a child by the weight of her, shaking and sobbing. He tried to comfort her, but she rolled off him and disappeared into the stifling darkness.

At least she could cry. Judging by the inert bodies he kept bumping into not every one of the passengers had been so lucky.

He tried to stand up, but his legs gave way. He gritted his teeth and crawled forward, a tiny insignificant parasite inside the body of a giant.

Something tickled the back of his head. It was a gentle tentative touch, almost caressing. He brushed it away, but it came back, more insistent that time.

He brushed it off again. His right hand was caught, pulled back and up, held at an unnatural angle to his body. He yelped and tugged at the restraint. The derma loop tightened around his wrist, cutting off circulation.

He hauled himself up, using the restraint as the leverage. His head hit the ribbed ceiling. He staggered but was held upright by the loop that was gradually pulling his arm away from him, threatening to wrench it out of its socket.

How could this be? The height of the car was enough to give ample clearance even to a man much taller than himself.

Who was he fooling? He knew exactly how this could be.

"Shut up, all of you!" Daniel yelled. "Shut up and listen!"

His voice rose above the hubbub of children's crying, adults' sobbing, confused unanswered questions flung into the void. Some woman's piercing voice was repeating a single syllable: a name? And underneath this babel of fear was the cause of it all: a whispering uninterrupted purl like a soft leakage of some viscous fluid from a giant open valve.

Daniel wanted to scream. The pain in his twisted arm was bad and growing worse as the contracting muscles of the loop inexorably pulled it up and back, forcing him to stretch until he was standing on his tiptoes, his head pressed against the ribbed ceiling. He groped in darkness with his free hand, trying to reach the base of the loop but his fingers fell short just a couple of centimeters.

He let the scream come out as a commanding shout.

The volume of noise dropped down a notch.

"Stop panicking!" he yelled. "You're making it worse! Help is on the way! Just stop moving around, hunker down where you are, and keep quiet! I repeat: don't move around, don't make a sound if you want to live!"

This got their attention.

"Who are you?" a cranky old man's voice snapped at him. And overlaying it, a woman's voice, as clear and familiar as an alarm bell: "What's happening?"

"The train is going rogue," he replied and instantly regretted his truthfulness as the voices erupted once again in a cacophony of horror.

"Shut up!" he bellowed again. "I'm a militiaman; I know how to deal with this! We'll be just fine as long as we don't whet his appetite! He feels live prey moving in his belly, he'll crank up stomach juice so much that we'll all be crap before you finish crapping your pants!"

A couple of gasps but the shuffle of movements went down.

Daniel bit his lip, tried to pivot around so as to relieve pressure on his shoulder. His left hand brushed the back of a seat and he winced: it was as soft as a rotting fruit and feverishly hot; the tiny vibrissae that should have been lying down to form the plush cover were all standing up agitatedly. A stinging wetness clung to his fingertips. He swore and waved the hand in the air, trying to shake off the acidic juice. He hit a weave of fabric that was so inert it must be a person's clothes. And then something clamped onto his free wrist, something that was not the guts of the train, and a voice whispered into his ear, so close that a warm breath ruffled his hair:

"Daniel!"

He jerked and cursed as the loop tightened again, cutting off the circulation even further. His hand felt like a blood-swollen balloon.

"Who's this?"

"Kora."

"Who the fuck are you?"

The person recoiled but now he could smell her: soap and shampoo and underneath it the heady, musky aroma of a woman.

"Never mind," he whispered through gritted teeth. "Help me get free. We have to get the hell out of here!"

"But help…"

"If they were to come, they would be here already!"

Amazingly, she did not flinch; she was so close to him that he could feel the swell of her breasts and the rapid beating of her heart.

"What can I do?"

"Feel up my right arm…careful…yes. Can you feel it?"

"The loop?"

"Squeeze it hard at the base…yes. Harder. They have a reflex. If you do it right, they'll relax."

Her body pressed against his, her arm sliding across his face.

"Yes, like this. Careful, don't let it loop you instead."

He heard a hiss somewhere close in this dense darkness filled with the smells and whimpering of frightened people and the stink of the rising gastric tide. The loop tightened so much he was afraid his wrist-bones would snap.

And then it relaxed and he was free.

He jerked forward, almost bringing her down, but she balanced herself somehow.

"Don't touch anything!" he hissed. "Especially the seats and the loops! And keep to the aisle!"

The darkness was so absolute he imagined his eyes had turned around, looking inside his skull. He blinked a couple of times, just to reassure himself it was not so. Was the entire system affected? Was the underground maze of MTT now a skein of lightless tunnels prowled by rogue trains?

Something splattered him, a spray of liquid from above, and there was a star map of stinging points on his face and bare neck. A child's voice wailed in the dark:

"Mummy, it burns!"

He put his hands onto the woman's shoulders, turned her around, so the swish of her long hair momentarily cooled the acid-burns on his face.

"There is a door about five seats from where we are," he whispered. "Go ahead. Then turn right."

He felt her nod and then she moved on and he followed, his right hand securely clamped on her shoulder, her fresh smell overpowered by the meaty stink of the train's gastric juices.

"Get up from the seats but don't move!" he yelled. "Don't move! I'll try to open the door!"

A scream, then another. A woman's frantic voice:

"My son…the seat won't let him up!"

Kora – if this was her name – bumped into somebody and he was brought up short, bumping into her. It would be funny – were it not for the fact that they were about to be digested by the train like a bunch of fucking zombies!

He still could not quite believe it was happening.

"Where do you think you're going?"

She just shoved the owner of the gruff voice out of the way. Daniel felt the swell of her muscles and the ease with which she cut through the press of bodies in the aisle.

A leathery tentacle whipped across his face. He pushed it aside and heard a gasp as it fastened around somebody else's throat, a death rattle of suffocation that was quickly drowned in the rhythmical puffing that now permeated the car. The walls, the floor, the ceiling throbbed in unison, releasing gouts of acid that flew through the shrinking cavity. The hand-straps thrashed around, catching people's arms, legs, and heads in their leathery embrace. Ducking and weaving in the dark, the panicky passengers congealed into a single hydra-like body, blindly flailing around, as the eager mouths opening in the swollen seats and dripping walls took bites out of them.

Daniel felt Kora push ahead of him like a battering ram, cutting through the chaos.

She stopped suddenly and he bumped into her again, hard. She molded herself to him.

"Turn right. Feel for the door!"

"What is this?"

He could hear it too: a liquid noise, like a loose-lipped mouth sucking drink through a giant straw, and then a grinding and a gnashing. He swore.

"What...?"

"He's growing intestinal surfaces! Find the fucking door!"

A tentacle brushed his shoulder. Kora's body shook.

"Don't let it touch your face!"

A confused scuffle; he was pushed aside, careening into somebody; a body slid from under him and sunk into a pulsating blister of a seat. A man was choking within centimeters of him.

A hand found his, clasped. Kora!

"Where is the door?"

She pulled him forward and then his fingers found the familiar rubbery seal, the vertical mouth with its tightly pursed lips. Only now the lips were hot and bloated, leaking saliva and the gap between them was filled with tiny gnashing teeth. He jerked away, his fingers bleeding where the serrated edges took off skin.

"Careful!"

He heard her heavy breathing as she explored the door. Her touch seemed to have driven the rogue into frenzy; the gnashing rose in pitch, becoming an intolerable drilling sound. The entire car shook.

"Let me…"

He needed to be out, to talk to the train! He was sure he could calm him down, but he knew trains did not have ears on the inside. It was unbelievably frustrating, to die here like a zombie when all it would take was the sound of his voice. He knew he could do it!

"Let me!"

But she was doing something; he did not know what – trying to pull the lips apart, perhaps. He wanted to stop her; she could not be strong enough…but then the car shook so badly that they were both thrown onto the floor, drowning in the effluvia. The acid on his skin was like liquid fire.

And then there was a gust of fresher air cutting through the stink.

The door was open! He clambered to his feet, grabbed the first handful of clothes his hands could find, and tumbled out, into the darkness of the tunnel, dragging a coughing, sputtering passenger with him.

Kora landed on her back, her wind knocked out of her, and as she was trying to orient herself in the pitch darkness, something else fell on her, strangling her, pinning her down to the hard floor. She pushed the burden away with all her strength; it cried out, smacking into…something and was silent.

She crawled forward and then scrambled to her feet, stepping in the yielding, twitching warmth. She was so disorientated that she did not even know whether she was still inside the train or outside, in the tunnel.

And then there was light!

She pivoted toward the bright spot that, just for a moment, made everything all right. It blinded her at first but as her eyes adjusted she realized it was quite dim and wavering. She stumbled toward it; stepped on a body; lost her footing and almost fell.

The light floated toward her. It was a flashlight held by a person. She squinted; the man was unfamiliar, thin-faced, in a long gray coat.

The beam swept away from her in a wide arc and she saw, with a shudder of revulsion, the blood-flushed worms of the rails writhing on the fibrous floor. Somehow, she had crawled clear of the back of the train that plugged up the tunnel with its asthmatically pulsating mass.

"Daniel!" She turned to go back but the man with a flashlight stopped her.

"It's eating them alive!" he said in a hoarse voice.

Several moving shapes detached themselves from the clot of darkness. She felt rather than saw that one of them was Daniel.

She rushed toward him. Dappled with shadows, his face was splotched and grimy. He was half-carrying, half-dragging a bundle of clothes.

He turned away from her and addressed the man with a flashlight.

"Can you light the way? We need to go forward, to his head."

"Why? This is the tail; we can just follow the tunnel back to the station."

"I can talk to trains, calm them down."

"If we get to the station, they can send a team…"

"Even if they do, there will be nothing left of the passengers by the time they get here."

And as if to lend support to his words, the massive black body shuddered, and a faint echo of screams and moans wafted toward them. She imagined people trapped in the steamy darkness, crying out, beating on the swollen walls, their flesh being dissolved by the acid glop.

She wished for the thousandth time that she could feel nauseated.

"But…"

"We have to do it!" Daniel's voice, so thrillingly familiar, calmed her down. The man with a flashlight hesitated, then shrugged and turned around, squeezing himself into the narrow gap between the train's flank and the wall of the tunnel. Daniel propped the body he was carrying against the wall – it was either a child or a small tenant – and followed him. Kora hurried after them, caught Daniel's arm.

"I'm coming with you!"

He looked at her blankly, his face masked by crawling shadows. It almost seemed as if he did not know who she was! But then he nodded and went on, Kora following.

They could barely clear the gap. The flank was heaving moistly, exuding steamy heat. But at least there were no writhing rails underfoot; they walked on inanimate gravel. The man with a flashlight had it easiest: he was very thin, almost skeletal. In the uncertain light, it was hard to see whether he was human or tenant.

He suddenly stopped and raised his hand. They could see the gleam of the flashlight's reflection on a train window, the transparent tissue puckering and twitching. It bulged forward as a fist slammed into it, again and again, from the inside. The window-skin stretched, limning the fist as if it were wearing a glass glove. And then the window snapped back with audible recoil, and its transparency was splattered by red.

"Should we try to open the door?" the man with a flashlight whispered nervously. Daniel shook his head.

"It'll only provoke him," he said grimly. "Trains can speed up their digestion…anyway, it's almost impossible to force the muscles from the outside…they just lock."

The train heaved again, its distended flank blocking their way.

"Give me the flashlight," Daniel whispered. The man hesitated.

"OK, just keep it down. They have eyes in their sides."

The man covered the flashlight with his hand, reducing the illumination to a weak admixture of gray in the black, and went on.

Eventually, they were in the open again. Daniel pulled on the man's sleeve.

"We're here," he whispered. "It's his head. Let me talk to him. What's your name, friend?"

So, he was human. Kora remembered Alexandra telling her that this was an old-fashioned way for humans to address each other. Tenants did not use it; nor was it used toward them.

"Sergei," the thin man mumbled.

"OK, Sergei. I'll talk to him. Cover my back. Don't make any sudden movements."

"What about me?" Kora whispered furiously.

Again, it was as he had forgotten about her existence and was reminded of it suddenly.

"You…you just stay there. Watch out for anything in the tunnel."

He rounded the flank of the train, stood in front of him. Kora, determined not to be brushed aside (*I helped him inside the train, didn't I?*) pushed by Sergei and peered over his shoulder.

She could see Daniel, vaguely outlined against the darkness, standing with his hands stretched toward the train, open palms up. She could not see the train's face and was glad of it. Those giant, flat, fishy eyes…

Daniel was speaking in a low, soothing murmur. She could not distinguish words because of the rumble that had started behind them, in the depth of the impenetrable darkness, and was steadily growing. The floor of the tunnel vibrated. There was a muffled scream coming from behind them, then another. Sergei's hand shook, the flashlight's beam dancing.

Daniel reached out slowly, his fingertips hovering in the air before the train's face.

Dogs! They gentle dogs like this.

And then they sic them on!

The rumble grew stronger, but the screams stopped.

Daniel put his hand onto the train's face.

And the train exploded.

The enormous creature buckled, humping up like a caterpillar, its back striking the ceiling. Its tail-end swished from side to side, hitting the walls of the tunnel with such brute force that sharp bone plates flew through the air. One whistled by Kora's head and embedded itself in Sergei's shoulder. He gave a high-pitched shriek and dropped the flashlight. In the crazy chiaroscuro of shadows, Daniel was lost: just another madly twitching black silhouette among many.

The train's flank hit her, driving her sideways and down, into the stinking, hot mud that was flowing through the tunnel.

Mud?

She crawled on all fours, aiming for the flashlight, shoving aside Sergei who was doubled up, crying in pain. Her hand tried to grasp a round object that slipped away but not before she knew what it was.

A skull. The train was disgorging the remnants of its meal.

Finally, her fingers closed on the dead metal cylinder of the flashlight and she stood up, her clothes soaked with the stinking, viscid substance. The train's convulsions were dying down, but the rumble grew. The tunnel shook.

"Daniel!"

She bumped into him.

"He wouldn't listen!" he repeated, sounding shocked. "He just wouldn't!"

"What is this? The sound?"

He caught her arm.

"It's another train! Also rogue, probably! We have to get away!"

She pulled ahead of him into the tunnel, but he doubled back, calling for Sergei. She had forgotten about the man.

Daniel re-emerged from the darkness, half-dragging, half-supporting Sergei. He pushed him toward her and turned around, to squeeze back into the gap between the train's flank and the fissured wall.

"What…?"

"The girl. I pulled her out. She's still there."

Kora opened her mouth to remonstrate – the girl must have been crushed by the train's convulsions, she was dead, and they were still alive and had to get away – when the tunnel was suddenly flooded with bright light.

Another train was approaching, his headlights in full luminescent mode. Coming from behind their train, he was invisible but its rush shook the tunnel.

"Fuck!" Daniel yelled.

It felt like the second train would slam with full force into the sluggish, well-fed body of their train that was beginning to undulate, its cars sliding on their bone couplings and smashing into each other. But in the last moment he paused, still hidden, his headlights playing uncertainly upon the ceiling that was beginning to bleed.

In the pitiless light, Kora finally saw the face of their train. His own headlights had slid out from their fleshy lids, poking from his sloping forehead like tumors but still unlit. His breathing grill was vibrating and leaking yellowish mucus, the pink protrusions swollen like leaches. His eyes were bloodshot.

Their lusterless pupils swiveled, focused upon her. And then the train buckled and charged.

"Run!" Daniel yelled and rushed forward, dragging Sergei. She stood still, the train's rancid breath hot and heavy upon her face.

They yell at us to go away. The train is leaving, leaving the station... Mama, why can't we go on the train?

"Run!"

The train's vibrissae touched her skin. Its innumerable busy legs scurried under the protective derma skirt, gripping the wormy tracks.

And then there was a crash from behind as the second train charged.

He butted the first train from behind and tried to clamber over it. But the tunnel was too low. Nevertheless, he succeeded in mounting the hindquarters of the first train. His huge, hammer-like head poked up in above the first train's tail, rising into the steamy air like an ugly sun, flooding the tunnel with the glare of his headlights. She stared at it, mesmerized.

Daniel caught her shoulder, spun her around.

"What the fuck is wrong with you? Run!"

The train's attention was no longer upon her as he tried to shake off the aggressor, twisting and thrashing from side to side, unable to turn around.

"What..." she whispered.

"They're both rogues!" Daniel did not even try to lower his voice anymore; it was lost in the thunderous grumble of the abused tunnel walls, though – even in her shock – she was surprised that the trains were silent, emitting only the wheezy breaths of combat.

"He is trying to steal cars! This will keep them busy for a while!"

Rearing up as far as the low ceiling would allow, the second train brought his entire weight to bear upon his adversary. There was a wet tearing sound of flesh and the crack of broken bone, and the first train finally screamed: a high-pitched muffled sound that originated somewhere below its low-slung chassis. It broke Kora's paralysis. She ran.

But they could not go fast because of Sergei. Daniel all but carried him but the man's thin body slumped, his feet dragging. They kept to the center of the track, avoiding the slimy rails – Kora because of her instinctive aversion, Daniel because he knew how dangerous they could be. But then Sergei slipped off Daniel's shoulder and hit the rail.

There was a long hiss and the wormy pinkish tube tore itself off the semi-living matrix in which it was embedded and reared up in a loop. The innumerable mouth-slits on its underbelly opened up, disgorging black hooks that tore into Sergei. Most of them got tangled in his clothes but some sunk into his face and hands. He screamed.

Daniel rushed to his side and tried to pull him free; Kora followed suit even though she knew it was useless.

They tasted blood. They won't let go.

They tugged at the man's limp body but all they accomplished was embedding the hooks deeper in his flesh. As she struggled with his blood-soaked clothes, something squirmed under her hands. She thought Sergei was fighting to get free but the movement was localized to one part of his body. She touched it and it bit her back.

She screamed; Daniel shone the flashlight. It was the bone plate that had wounded Sergei, still sticking out of the fleshy part of his shoulder. But it had grown long segmented legs and a blind snout that was burrowing deep into the man's muscles.

Daniel gave one mighty heave to the body and it popped free. It flopped over, staring at them with black holes where the eyes used to be.

The giant track caterpillar reared above them. Daniel lifted his right hand and something flashed in the air like a thin wiry whip, striking at the thing's underbelly. It hissed and fell flat into its groove.

The wave of grunting, smashing, and asthmatic breathing rolled through the tunnel as the two trains fought. More bone rained down.

Kora grasped his hand and pulled him forward. They ran.

Chapter 15. The Love Hotel

When they struggled out of the mouth of the Red Peony station, it was dusk. Stinking and bone-weary, they stood just outside the sliding door, watching the kaleidoscope of the flambeaus' multicolored lights blossom in the sky.

Daniel had unerringly led them through a maze of service tunnels. She would have been completely lost on her own. They had not met a single person, either human or tenant. The station, too, was deserted.

Once Daniel had stopped and put his palm on an exposed area of the Pith. He snatched it back as if burned.

She wanted to ask him what was wrong but did not dare. Her entire world had narrowed down to his hunched-up figure trudging ahead of her. The idea of losing him again was intolerable.

Again?

She did not know who he was.

He was Daniel.

Daniel who?

Daniel.

She realized she had not even tried to use her gift – *her curse* – on the train. She was pretty sure it would not have helped. The life-force of the rogue giant would have overwhelmed her, drowned her in a flood of its corrupt vitality. But she had not tried, even though people were dying around her.

But she had saved herself – and Daniel. This was all that mattered. She kept repeating this mantra until it dissolved in a welter of meaningless images, a buzz in her shell-shocked brain.

He was looking up at a flambeau display which she could not read. Then his head swiveled as if something else attracted his attention. He started down the street, Kora trailing behind.

He looked back sharply at her.

"Why are you following me?" he barked. "Go away!"

She stood still, watching his back disappear in the crush of the crowd. It was impossible, inconceivable, and yet it was happening. She looked around, at the meaningless fragments of the city, blank faces, and chaotic lights. It made no sense.

She willed her feet to carry her in the opposite direction, but they would not obey. She made a minuscule step and felt the weight of the city settle upon her.

Kora turn around and ran after Daniel, elbowing passers-by aside. The welter of stranger faces sucked her in; the fear of losing him, of having lost him already, caught in her throat.

And then she saw him. He was standing by a food cart tucked into a corner of an arcade, slurping noodles from a carton.

He lifted his eyes and saw her. An ambiguous expression flickered over his face.

"Why don't you go home?" he said gruffly, tossing the empty carton aside.

"I've no home," she said.

He shrugged and turned away, but she knew she had won.

"Do you have money?" he asked.

She rooted in the pocket of her filthy sheath, found a pocketful of change, gave it to him. Daniel sniffed.

"Not much. I have some…I don't want to use credit."

"Why?" she asked.

"The Pith will know where I am. I need to talk to my Colonel first."

He was scanning the street and finally located what he wanted. In a narrow alley between two sparkling malls, there were a couple of stalls selling cheap clothes and trinkets, their owners curling up like aged lizards under the red lanterns. He went there, beckoning Kora to follow.

When she caught up with him, he was rooting through a heap of frilly dresses and men's gaudy shirts.

"Come on," he said impatiently. "You stink. So do I. Get something!"

He was right. Her clothes were stiff with the train's reeking juices. She realized that even the impassive stall-owner wrinkled her seamy face when she approached. The city was vain. Clothes were cheap and plentiful, and even the poorest tenants loved to dress up.

Daniel pulled out a black-and-pink shirt and denim pants for himself, started bargaining with the old woman in a rapid-fire dialect she had heard used in the Market. Desultorily, she grabbed a flowery, flouncy dress. Would he like this?

He ended his negotiations and dropped a handful of coins into the woman's leathery hand. He eyed the flowery dress dubiously.

"Won't it be too small for you?"

Blushing, she dropped it back, grabbed another: loose, red, high-waisted, with a big silly bow on the side. He pulled her deeper into the alley where the light from the malls' stationary flambeaus filtered through the torn marquees, throwing a net of lacy shadows on the garbage-strewn pavement. A fat scavenger looking like a hairless rat was slowly eating its way through a pile of fruit rinds and noodle cartons.

Daniel pulled off his shirt and pants, tossed them at the garbage-eater who emitted an indignant squeak and started munching on the pant-leg. Kora turned away from his wide shoulders and smooth pale chest, a heat-wave blossoming in the pit of her belly and rising to her face.

"What are you waiting for?" he barked. "I've enough of this stink!"

The heat-wave turned into a fiery flood, but she said nothing. Pulling off the stained knitted shift, she balled it up and threw it onto the pile of garbage. She put on the red dress. It was too big, sloping awkwardly off her shoulders; the uneven seams chafed, and the bow sat in her armpit. She discarded her underwear as well but did not dare asking Daniel for more money to buy a pair of panties. All the while she kept her back to him, hoping that he was watching.

When she was done, he was already out of the alley, striding toward a tall needle-thin building that loomed over the malls. Its lower floors were covered by a garish medley of flambeaus but even she could see that they were old and decrepit, their lights flashing and dimming erratically, some crawling aimlessly over their brethren.

Only when he was at the entrance did she ask:

"Where are we going?"

"We need a place to stay. I don't know about you, but I'm pooped. I can't think straight."

"Your home…is it too far?"

He shrugged without looking at her.

"Yes, too far to walk…I'm not up to taking MTT again; are you?"

"What…what is this place?"

"A love hotel."

"A *love* hotel?"

"Never been to one?" he smirked. "It's cheap."

Inside, there was a brightly lit lobby with a thin woman sitting under a garland of fake flowers.

Daniel talked to the woman in low tones; her disinterested gaze slid off Kora as she pushed a key toward him.

"Twenty-fifth floor," he muttered. "Fine; I'd rather be as far above the ground as I can."

He strode toward the bank of elevators, Kora tagging along, feeling acutely aware of her large body (*like a fat red trapeze!*). Daniel suddenly stopped and turned back to the concierge.

"Is there a news flambeau in the room?"

"Five wons," the woman muttered and Daniel dropped another handful of small change onto the scratched counter.

"I'll send him in," the concierge declared, her eyes shifting to the transparent door through which she was watching the nightly flambeau display, in which the biggest of the tribe, sparkling giants thirty meters tall, stood on top of high-rises and let coordinated waves of emerald, crimson, and gold wash over their flat bodies. Only when they were inside the opaque cage of the elevator did it occur to Kora that it was strange the city was allowing such an entertainment despite the disaster in MTT. But she could not spare too much thought for this; not even for the realization that she had, once again, escaped death. The proximity of Daniel was just too overwhelming, blotting out everything else. She could not force herself to look straight at him and yet she was aware of every minute shift in his posture as he fidgeted during the interminable crawl up.

The door swooshed open and they walked into a dimly lit corridor. The blank doors stared them down.

Daniel unlocked door number 2515 with a big clunky key. Kora gasped.

The room was tiny, but it did boast an impressive view of the city. It was the highest she had ever been. Below her, the city blazed like a frozen firestorm, its scintillating tentacles crawling up the flanks of the Peak and magnified by the broken mirrors of its reservoirs and waterways. But she paid little attention to the stunning view.

The room only had one bed, which was round.

"OK," Daniel said, business-like. "Who is the first to shower?"

She was too flustered to answer. He shrugged and walked to the bathroom's door, throwing over his shoulder:

"We'll have to share but that's just the way it is. No money for a twin – even if they had it here, which I doubt. Oh, and when the flambeau comes, let him in but tell him to wait for me. I want to see the entire newscast."

He disappeared into the bathroom. She heard the flush of the toilet and then the rush of water. She sat on the edge of the silly round bed, feeling tired and dislocated. And bereft. There was a pink rug near the bed, decorated with the inscription: "My fair rabbit."

Somebody knocked on the door and she cautiously opened it. A small flambeau minced in, his skin thin and pale, strained by over-exposure, his squashed head turned sideways, showing his perpetual profile, the one round eye blinking tiredly, as if he was half-asleep or on drugs. He hopped onto the stand in front of the bed and prepared to display, bands of colors flickering on the work-surface that comprised most of his flat body. His edge was no thicker than a man's wrist.

"Sorry," Kora said, shy in addressing somebody who could not answer back. "Can you wait till my…my husband is done?"

She instantly felt stupid because of the lie but the flambeau showed no reaction besides folding into himself like the shadow of a sleeping bird. The bathroom's door opened and Daniel walked out, naked but for the towel around his waist.

"Your turn," he said cheerfully. "Don't go stingy on soap; it's already pretty ripe in here!"

She walked into the tiny steamed-up bathroom and firmly closed the door. Standing under the hot jets of water, she discovered that some drops on her cheeks were tears.

When she came out, swathed in all the towels she could find – at least the love hotel did not economize on those – she saw that the display had already begun. The flambeau was standing erect, his small legs locked into position, the beak aloft and aligned with the stand, the bleary eye closed. The quality of the picture was quite good for such an old workhorse and the sound was clear.

In the lit-up oval of one of the local stations, a pretty newscaster was reading from a page in front of her. Behind her, in an embedded oval, which the flambeau thoughtfully colored up for contrast, were stills of an MTT station cordoned off by orange tape and surrounded by uniformed men. Kora recognized the station where she had entered MTT, though she did not remember its name.

"…technical difficulties," the newscaster was saying. "MTT consortium released a statement denying an unexpected upsurge in rogue infestations and promised the normal schedule restored by tomorrow. When asked to comment, Mayor Volk expressed full confidence in his Transportation Officer, Madame Lu. And now for business news…"

Daniel swore and threw a pillow at the flambeau who clacked in distress, fading the picture.

"Bastards!" he raged. "No rogue trains, no passengers turned to turds! Who are they fooling?"

Kora touched his arm diffidently. To her surprise, he stopped raging and just sat on the edge of the bed, breathing heavily. She motioned for the flambeau to leave. He loitered at the door, perhaps expecting a tip, but seeing that none was forthcoming exited with a loud farting noise.

"I have to talk to the Colonel," Daniel repeated. "I…"

He tried to get up, but Kora restrained him.

"You need to sleep," she said firmly. "So do I. I just…I can't take it anymore."

It was true; the entire weight of this horrible day suddenly fell upon her. Daniel sighed but lay on the bed, his feet sticking out from its edge, and dimmed the light. The effulgence of the city blazed in through the un-curtained window but neither made a move to get up and pull down the blinds.

Now, lying so close to his naked body, Kora discovered she could not fall asleep. Fatigue and excitement combined into an intoxicating brew in her veins; she felt as if she were flying. When Daniel turned his back on her, she finally spoke:

"Why are you treating me like this?"

"What?" his voice was sharp with irritation but not drowsy; apparently, he did not find it easy to fall asleep either. "What are you talking about?"

"As if you didn't know me…"

"I don't know you! Listen, lady, we've been through a lot together today! You helped me. I'm grateful and all that. But I don't know you from Grandfather! I don't even know your name!"

The rainbow-dappled room seemed to revolve around Kora. She drew in her breath.

"But I do, I do know you! Your name is Daniel! I called you on the train, didn't I?"

He sat up, kicking the blanket aside, and she could not bear to look at him.

"It's true. And…?"

"And what?"

"What else do you know about me? What's my family name? What do I do?"

She mutely shook her head, afraid that if she started to cry she would not be able to stop.

He sighed.

"OK, let's start from the beginning. What's your name?"

"Kora."

"Kora what?"

"I don't know. I lost my memory."

"You *lost* your memory? So how do you say you know me?"

"Because I do. You're the only face I know in the city. When I saw you…in MTT…I knew you! You saw…I went to you…when the lights…"

She was beginning to babble and shut up. He was silent.

"You knew me too!" she cried in desperation. "I saw you looking at me!"

"My memory is just fine," he said dryly. "I don't know you. Except…"

"Except what?"

"Your face does look a bit familiar," he said reluctantly. "But listen…Kora, the way you talk…it's as if we were lovers, or relatives, or…something. And it's just not true. I may have met you at a party, maybe. Or a restaurant...whatever. You are a striking woman. I *was* looking at you, there, on the train. But you're not my long-lost soul-mate, or wife, or sister. Forget about it."

She bit her lip, deeply, to keep the sobs in. He patted her shoulder awkwardly.

"I'm not very nice to you, I know," he said. "I'm sorry. But listen, it was a hell of a day. For you too, it seems. We need to sleep. We'll talk tomorrow."

She nodded and watched his back and listened to his even breathing for what seemed like a very long time. And then she slept.

The ground is as hard and cold as iron; it seems that if you stepped harder on it, it would ring with a hollow boom. But our dragging feet touch lightly on the frozen dirt: there is no weight to put into them.

Mother walks in front of me, her rags-swathed back hunched into a shapeless hulk that seems to float in the clear air. I feel angry. My own rags are sliding off me, knots perversely undoing themselves even as I walk, layers of casts-off refusing to stay together. The glass fingers of the cold cut through the worn fabric and touch the bumpy skin that offers no resistance to their probing.

"Mama!" I wail. "Cold! I'm cold!"

She does not stop, does not look back. Cradled somewhere deep within the musty layers is the baby. It is sleeping there, cozy and warm.

"Mama!" I cry again.

She stops, looks back at me. Her lips are like the land broken by drought: fissure upon fissure. A drop of blood is slowly oozing down her cleft chin.

"Not far," she says.

The ground rises ahead of us: a shallow slope covered by burnt rocks the color of rust. She tries to climb the rise, but her rags-wrapped feet keep sliding, creating miniature avalanches. The baby wakes up, starts crying: a thin, almost inaudible sound that pierces me with pure hatred.

She gives up trying to climb and just walks along, following the curve of the embankment. But I surprise myself by clambering on top. She looks at me with reproach for wasting my energy but would not waste her own by voicing it. She rocks the baby.

I turn away, look down into the indentation on top of the embankment where two parallel streams run away into the dazzling distance, reflecting the pale winter sun. I touch the tracks: they are warm and humming.

It is a road to freedom. But I can't take it.

She woke up screaming.

The blaze of city lights streamed into the room, undimmed, but now it was reinforced by the full moon that had risen above the black hump of the Peak, its skull face grinning at her.

Daniel reached out, touched her, and she threw herself into his embrace, sobbing. She molded herself to him, his body big and warm and reassuring, every muscle, every fold of skin and jutting of bone deliciously familiar and utterly strange. His arms closed around her, his hands slipping down her back, fondling her buttocks. They were sleeping naked and with a sweet sense of inevitability, she felt him growing hard against her…

And then his erection dwindled and he rolled away, leaving her breathless with disappointment and doubt. For the first time, she began to question her recognition of him. What if her mind was playing tricks on her?

If the chairman could wipe away my memory, what else did he do to me?

Was she throwing herself upon a stranger who might have a wife and family?

Or maybe he just finds me repulsive.

"Bad dream?" he asked.

"Yeah."

"I also had a bad dream. No surprise, after…that."

She was silent, her body throbbing with the heat of frustrated desire. The frightening thing was she was not sure what this desire was *for*.

"I'm sorry," he mumbled awkwardly. "I'm really tired…out of sorts. And sick. I think I am getting sick."

It was a ridiculous apology in a ridiculous situation.

But somehow it calmed her down. The molten wave receded and she patted his naked shoulder.

"I understand. I'm also…I mean…we've been through a lot…"

"What time is it? This fucking place doesn't even have a clock…or no, here it is!"

The red numerals showed 1.15; the clock, a low, primitive flambeau, only lit up when somebody asked.

"Too early," Daniel said, sounding disappointed. "There may be a round-the-clock food court somewhere, but I don't want to wander around. Not a good neighborhood!"

"Are you hungry?" she asked.

"Starving! Aren't you?"

"No, not really."

"I guess I can wait a couple of hours," Daniel said unconvincingly.

"And then…after you eat, I mean…what are we going to do?"

She was instantly afraid of her own boldness – what if he would suggest, again, they just go their separate ways? But he did not. Instead, he shifted uncomfortably in the round bed, pulling up his feet.

"I need to talk to my commander," he said finally. "Weird things are happening…and they're keeping it all under the covers. I need to talk to somebody I trust. He's a funny guy but he is smart. He can figure out why not one but *two* MTT trains just went rogue and ate their passengers. And more importantly – why there is no hue and cry about it!"

"Are you a City Corps?"

"No, a militiaman. I was on furlough…the last days had been just plain crazy, even before the train thing. Ever since that skirmish on Skybridge…Wait a second!"

He sat up in bed, the blanket falling off, and she dropped her eyes, afraid to awaken the dormant desire.

"I saw you on Skybridge!" he said triumphantly. "Yes. This is why you look familiar. It was you, wasn't it? The woman we pulled away from zombies!"

"I was on Skybridge," Kora said. "You may have been among the militia who helped me. But I didn't see you there. I didn't see anybody. That's not why I know you!"

But he paid no attention, caught up in the excitement of his discovery.

"Yes! That was one crazy fight, this one! So many of them, so deep into the city! This had never happened before! This was when Lu Huan…" he suddenly stopped and lay back, staring at the ceiling.

"I don't remember you!" she insisted. "I was…I lost consciousness. Somebody pulled me off the bridge, but I don't know who."

"What were you doing there anyway? How come an entire horde of deadheads was chasing one woman? Where did you come from?"

"From a hotel…on the other side. The closed sector. But it's no use asking me what I was doing in the hotel. I don't know."

He looked at her dubiously.

"You've really lost your memory, haven't you? It's not just a trick?"

For the first time, Kora felt like slapping him.

"No, no bloody trick! Do you think I'd fake it just to get in bed with you?"

"OK, OK! Go easy! But do you know…do you have any idea who you are?"

She told him about the chairman.

Why not? Maybe he knows something I don't.

Something? Anything would do.

She told him about James Wingate, about the roofs' attack, and about staying in the Market. She said nothing about her conversation with Old Van in the Incoming Sun café. Nor about what happened after that.

She did not mention Peter or his promise to smuggle her out of the city because she did not want to leave anymore. Especially not with khruts. She simply said she had been hiding in the Market for the last couple of days and then decided to find the chairman and confront him.

Daniel seemed to be totally absorbed in her tale. Gradually she nestled close to him and he did not pull away.

"That's a weird story," he said. "The chairman…This house you describe…it's like nothing I've ever seen or heard about."

She sat up:

"Are you saying I'm lying?"

"Hey, calm down! Not at all! But you said it yourself that you were confused. Those Buddhas, for example…I'd say it was impossible."

"Why?"

"Because Buddhas are solitary. They grow out of the Pith in some districts and then believers build temples around them. But if there are two Buddha stalks growing close together, one of them will die."

"So how do they reproduce?" Kora asked.

"They are like plants. They have no sex. Still…I heard rumors about new varieties being bred by rich folks on up-levels. This chairman…you don't know his name?"

"No."

"He might be Malech. Adam Malech."

"Who is he?"

"Chairman of the Malech Corporation. They do growth-construction mostly but also food and drugs trade. He is rich. And famous. Meddles in politics too."

"Have you met him?"

"No. Only saw him on 'casts. But he is the kind of operator who would pull something like that."

"He said I had asked for it."

"Did he show you a signed release form?"

"No."

"So he is lying. You should complain."

"Complain to who?"

"Us. The militia."

She laughed; she could not help herself.

"So are you going to take my deposition now?"

Daniel grinned.

"I'm just a lowly sergeant. No, we have a Serious Crimes division. You come with me and talk to Colonel Rosen. He'll take you over to the plainclothes boys. It sounds to me like you can claim abduction and grievous bodily harm, at the very least. This will take Mister Malech-the-Golden-Leech down a couple of notches."

It was as good a plan as any.

Lulled by his warm body, she tumbled into sleep again. And neither of them dreamed.

The morning found them down in the street, navigating through the piles of semi-animate garbage chased by scavenger tenants. Kora saw that they came in all shapes and forms. Alongside the multicolored turtles were creatures like skinned cats and hairless rats, pouncing upon skittish wrappers and cartons.

It was so early that the street vendors were not out yet. Kora was sorry; she wanted to buy something else to wear. As they had been going down in the elevator, a couple joined them: a fat gentleman in a business suit and a slender woman whose name he clearly did not remember. The woman had looked Kora up and down with undisguised amazement, making her vow to get rid of the scarlet dress even if she had to go naked.

Daniel was also looking around. He seemed antsy, barely

talking to her. Suddenly he dove into a narrow alley. Inside, a tenant was loading a food cart with stacks of tiny pancakes and jars of condiments. Daniel tossed several coins into his three-fingered palm and got a plate loaded with pancakes and preserved vegetables. He turned to Kora:

"What do you want?"

She shook her head and watched in amazement as he devoured the entire plate in seconds, scooping vegetables with pancakes and stuffing them into his mouth, barely taking time to chew.

Was he a glutton? No, impossible. There was not an ounce of fat on his muscled body. But he was a big, strong man; he needed nourishment. Perhaps, in some distant past when she had worked in the fields she had also eaten like this.

He turned to her, his eyes still bleary, as if the food failed to give him energy.

"You really don't eat, do you?" he said with a mixture of disbelief and something strangely like envy.

"No, I told you."

"You hunt…"

"I hunt Hungry Ones," she said bluntly and turned away, not before seeing him shudder.

They resumed walking. The streets were gradually filling with pedestrian crowds, extinguished flambeaus slithering down the skyscrapers' walls and heading for their perches, their flat silhouettes like giant origami against the faded sky.

They started climbing up a flight of stairs.

"This chairman," Daniel asked. "Is he a dawn?"

"A what?"

"A dawn. Adam Malech is a dawn."

"I don't know what it means," Kora said.

Daniel pointed at an Asian noodle-vendor.

"Like him!"

"The chairman is an Asian, yes," Kora said.

Now it was Daniel's turn to stare.

"I've never heard this word!"

Another divide suddenly gaped between them.

"Well, people like him…you know, black hair, eyes like this…they're Asian!"

"What does it mean?"

Kora considered.

"I don't know," she said. "It's just a word."

Daniel shook his head.

"We call them dawns," he said. "I learned it when I came to the city. And people like him," he nodded at a tall dark-skinned businessman, "are noons. And people like you and I are dusks."

"Dark-skinned people are Africans," Kora said. "And people like you and I are Caucasians."

Daniel burst out laughing.

"It's the funniest word I've ever heard! 'Caucasians'! Where did you get this from?"

"I don't know. Where I got all my other words from, I suppose."

"You said you *lost* your memory. Now it seems you also have something *added* to it!"

Kora shrugged.

"Whatever," she said. "But why do you call us dusks when we're just as light-skinned as As…I mean, dawns?"

Daniel frowned.

"It's a good question!" he admitted. "I honestly don't know. Just another city thing. But it makes no difference, really. Dawns have their own dialect, and noons too. I speak a little of both but not that well."

They ran into a slow-down, a crowd of passengers exiting the MTT station, and the conversation ceased. But Kora kept thinking about what he had said.

I learned it when I came to the city…

Chapter 16. The Colonel's Cellar

When they came to the barbed-wire fence of the militia base, Daniel perked up.

The base consisted of a rectangle of dead, human-built huts and a couple of larger city-grown buildings, arranged around an empty plaza and overshadowed by a clutch of high-rises. The gate in the fence was manned by a bored youngster in a khaki uniform. Daniel barely paused when they approached.

"Hey, Rooster!" he called. "Double duty again? Caught smuggling Golden Flower girls in? Is Shrimp in the HQ?"

The boy stared at them.

"Daniel?" he said incredulously.

"Sergeant for you!"

The boy fidgeted.

"We thought you were…Colonel told us…"

"What are you talking about?"

Rooster's right hand sneaked up onto the flat panel in front of him and closed around a shiny knob. The gate slid aside.

"Come in," he muttered, staring at his feet.

Daniel marched in, Kora following close. The place gave her a shivery feeling of something almost-familiar.

They were halfway across the plaza when a shrill bell tore through the hum of the city. People spilled into the yard, khaki uniforms topped by blank faces. Daniel stopped.

"Guys…" he said uncertainly.

A man stepped forward and lifted his right hand, palm forward. From the center of the palm protruded a tube like a giant wasp stinger.

Kora grasped Daniel's shoulder.

"Don't move!" the man said. "Hands up, slowly. Drop your 'arm!"

He has no 'arm! He has nothing on him, except second-hand clothes!
Daniel's face purpled with rage.

"What the…"

"Sergeant Moylan!" the big man went on, as the others stood uneasily behind him, refusing to look at the couple. "Raise your hands and drop your 'arm. You know the drill. Don't make it harder. And tell your companion to do the same."

She could feel Daniel's body shake with suppressed rage as he lifted his hands and made a strange gesture, as if pulling off an invisible glove. The skin of his right hand split, bloodlessly and neatly, peeled off and fell onto the ground where it contracted into a five-legged spider that skittered away toward the line of militiamen. One of them picked it up and shoved it into his pocket.

She stared at Daniel's hand: it was unmarked, the same as before.

She scanned the militiamen's faces: some white, some dark; some young, some older; some human, some tenant. All nervous and embarrassed.

"Tell her to step aside!" the man said.

"Stick close to me!" Daniel whispered. And then, loudly: "She is a civilian. She has nothing! She is my girlfriend!"

Girlfriend!

Somebody caught her shoulder from behind and pulled her away. She gritted her teeth, willing herself not to retaliate.

"Step aside, lady!" the boy who was holding her said.

"Leave her alone!" Daniel lurched toward her. "Where is the Colonel?"

"He'll talk to you," one of his captors, an older heavyset man said. "Don't make it harder!"

His shoulders sagging, he let himself be marched away.

She was locked in a featureless cell with a bunk-bed and a toilet. She was given a bottle of water, which she used to wash her face, and a plate of mashed potatoes. She amused herself by shaping them into peaks and valleys with a fork.

And then she found herself staring at the miniature landscape she had created. She had piled up most of the soft mash into a massive peak and flattened the rest of it into a flat plain. And beyond it, touching the edge of the plate…

Nothing. She had scraped the mash away, leaving a featureless clean surface, as shiny as a bone.

She stared at it, feeling goose-bumps rise on her skin.

This must be the Peak, the central mountain whose slopes the city covered like the growth of lichen. The flat plain? The countryside. But what was the bare edge?

The country of the dead.

She threw the plate against the wall. The mash trickled upon the floor.

A man opened the door, shaking his head.

"Didn't your mother teach you not to play with food?" He grumbled. "Look at the mess!"

"So clean after me!" she said rebelliously. "I didn't ask to be locked up!"

The man clicked his tongue disapprovingly and withdrew, locking the door. The mess on the floor now seemed to form a distorted face that stared at her in rebuke.

Didn't you mother…?

She cleaned up the best she could. Afterwards, she tried to sleep to pass the time but failed. She was pumped up with nervous energy. And she was hungry.

Finally, the door screeched open. She was instantly on her feet, hoping to see Daniel.

But it was an unfamiliar man, small and wizened, his head thrust forward on the wrinkled neck. He wore the same khaki uniform as the militiamen in the courtyard but with different insignia.

"The guard says you refused food," he said in a low scratchy voice. "Why? Do you have special requirements?"

She almost laughed. Almost.

"Where is my boyfriend?" she challenged him. "You have no right to keep us here!"

The man walked into the cell, sat on the edge of the bed. His eyes were bloodshot, as if he was not sleeping well.

"Ah yes, your boyfriend!" he said. "How long have you known him?"

"What's that has to do with anything?"

"Sergeant Moylan is very sick. We need to inform his family. Would you be willing to do it?"

Sick? Daniel's sick?

"Yes, of course. What's wrong with him?"

The man's eyes narrowed.

"Sergeant Moylan has no family," he said.

She kept standing, towering over him. The temptation to provoke him was almost overwhelming. If he charged her, she would defend herself.

She would feed…

She remembered the strange 'arm Daniel had worn and sat down.

"Are you his commanding officer?" she asked. "Daniel talked about you."

"I'm Colonel Rosen, yes."

"He was coming to see you, to tell you what happened. We were caught in the train accident at MTT. A train tried to eat us."

Colonel exhaled sharply.

"The Bird's Nest incident? You were there?"

"Didn't Daniel tell you?"

He did not answer, still looking at her with his tired, bloodshot eyes.

"What's your name?" he asked.

She hesitated; on the other hand, what did she have to lose?

"Will you take me to see him?"

"Maybe. What's your name?"

"Kora."

"And…?"

"Just Kora."

He looked away and then nodded.

"Come with me." He got up and she followed him out of the cell.

They walked through the barracks. She was too tense to pay attention to the environment besides the general impression of minimalist sterility that, for some reason, frightened her deeply.

Colonel Rosen led her to a metal door with a lock on the outside. A militiaman slumped on the stool by the door but quickly snapped up to attention when he saw the Colonel.

The Colonel peered through the fish-eye lens on the door and then beckoned Kora to do the same.

She looked and saw a narrow white bed, distorted by the lens into a long catafalque. A man was strapped to the bed.

She was rattling the door before she knew it; when the militiaman tried to stop her, she shoved him into the wall.

The Colonel put a hand on her forearm.

"He is dangerous," he said. "Do you still want to go in?"

"Dangerous? Daniel? What a joke!"

"He is changing into a Hungry Ones. He was bitten by one."

"I eat Hungry Ones!" Kora cried, no longer aware of anything except her overwhelming need to be on the other side of the door.

Rosen started but unlocked the door.

She walked in. Daniel's head was rolling on the pillow, swinging right and left with the precise rhythm of a metronome. His face was flushed and swollen; his fists clenched; his eyes shiny with a wet glaze.

She reached out and touched him.

Behind her, Rosen moved closer.

She squeezed Daniel's shoulder, pulpy like a rotten fruit. He lurched toward her, one of the straps snapping. And then he fell back, his face beaded with sweat, the sick flush receding, leaving an ashen pallor behind. He moaned and lay still.

She drank deeply, feeling the delicious rush of energy through every starved cell and every cramped muscle.

You never know when you're hungry just how *hungry you are...*

And then she pulled herself away, her body screaming in protest, muscles seizing, ready to drag her back to finish the meal. She fought it, and the hunger subsided reluctantly.

Daniel's eyes closed, his breathing slowed down. She wanted to run away from this room, from the stink of sickness, from herself. She wanted to vomit herself up.

Daniel's eyes snapped open.

"Kara," he whispered. "Not right, not right...Don't do...Kara!"

"What?" she cried. "What did I do wrong?"

Rosen's hand closed on her forearm and she followed him, exhausted by her emotions.

He did not take her back to the cell but led her to his house. It was inside the fence but separated from the plaza by a patch of sickly grass. She stared at it with dull surprise: single-family dwellings were uncommon in the city.

It was cozy inside, with pale pink-washed walls and overstuffed sofas. There were two house flambeaus snoozing on their perches who woke up when Rosen unlocked the door. One rolled a newscast on its flat stomach and the second one winked at them with the temperature inside and outside the house.

Rosen showed Kora into a guest room, which must have belonged to a woman, judging by the perfume bottles and scarves draped around the mirror. He left her alone and did not lock the door.

She realized she had given herself away. Now, he knew she would not try to escape. Daniel was here. She was as safely confined to this place as if she were handcuffed and chained. But what would he do with her?

She lay on the bed, watching the sunset sky flame with the giant brush-strokes of crimson and purple like the script she could not read. And then the flambeaus crawled up the skyscrapers and the nightly show begun. She felt empty.

And then she slept.

The creature totters toward me, its face tapering into a giant beak, its swollen belly borne on its matchstick legs. When it comes closer, I realize it is a child. Its face is so gaunt it looks like a bird's.

It is making tiny mewling sounds. It is disgusting.

It comes close and starts pawing at me with its claw-like hands. I push it away. It keels over and is still.

The sun is coming up over the empty fields, a misty rosy ball in the matte-glass sky. It is very quiet. The fields are bare earth, quietly golden in the sunrise.

There was a patch where some heart's-ease was growing. Mother said it was poisonous.

Why should I listen to mother?

I stumble toward the hedgerow of spiky bushes long ago denuded of their leaves, pull them aside. My hand is scratched and I stare at the bright beads of blood.

I should not stare. Hunger makes you stupid, she says. I won't be stupid.

The patch is empty, the dry earth dug up and scattered around in clots. Not even a single wormy root remains.

The tears won't come. Something else comes; I don't want it inside me, this thing. I don't know what it is. I know fear, hunger, pain. I even know anger. But this is neither of them.

I hear shuffling behind me. I turn around, my fists clenched so tight that the bones rasp against each other. If this is the beak-headed child, I'll kill it.

I WILL kill it.

Kora clawed up from the dream, her body bathed in sweat. Her nightmares were getting worse.

Today, I buried my mother.
Yesterday, I buried my father.
I buried my grandparents...oh, who the hell remembers?
I have boiled my mother's slippers. They fell apart in stringy pink goo. Can't eat that.
My father's shoes are gone. Leather.
The girl is here again. Knocking on the door, bothering me.
What does she want?

Daniel's eyes snapped open. They were so dry that the movement of the lids over the sclera scratched it.

He moaned. His tongue lay in his mouth like a big furry animal.

He tried to sit up but the straps jerked him back with the brute indifference of inanimate matter. They were dead. Everything was dead here.

He turned away his head, trying to shield his eyes from the pitiless glare of the flambeau on the ceiling that was sucking the last dregs of moisture out of his desiccated body.

"Please," he croaked. "Please..."

The flambeau did not as much as twitch to show that it heard his appeal. Was it under orders not to talk to the prisoner?

He squinted into the pale unwavering light.

The flambeau was dead. They had a corpse pinned to the ceiling.

This profanation would have shocked him into screaming and tearing at his bonds if there was anything in him left to shock. He felt gutted, hollow, and as weightless as air.

And he was hungry – desperately, humiliatingly so.

The door slammed open and a man came into the room.

Daniel stared at him, hoping for a friendly face.

Since he was roughly thrust into the sickbay after his arrest, divested of his clothes and badge, probed with medical instruments and tied to the cot, he had been surrounded by strangers. They must have brought in a new unit, perhaps from low-levels. Did they go into so much trouble just for him? The thought chilled him to the bone.

The man was definitely low-levels: a grubby creature, with hair as thin as cobwebs. He was carrying a tray with a couple of covered dishes and a jug of water. Daniel felt saliva flood his mouth and flushed in shame as if he had wet himself.

"Hey, friend," he croaked, "what gives?"

The man gave no sign that he even heard. Placing the tray on the side table, he whisked the covers away with a flourish of a waiter. A strand of saliva wormed its way over Daniel's unshaven chin.

One of the dishes held a generous portion of glass noodles with steamed cloud-ear fungus, bok choy and ginger. The second was piled high with chunks of raw meat swimming in clotted blood.

Daniel choked.

"What the fuck?" he cried indignantly.

"Which one?" the man asked economically, his accent reeking of dead housing.

"Water."

Without batting an eye, the man lifted the jug to Daniel's mouth. He wanted to remonstrate against being treated like a baby but the touch of moisture on his chapped lips silenced him.

"Food?" the man inquired.

Daniel nodded and tugged ineffectually at his restraints.

"Which one?"

"What do you think I am, a fucking butchers-row scavenger? Noodles! And fucking untie me first!"

Impassively, the man produced a pair of chopsticks, snagged

up a clump of oil-oozing noodles with a black sliver of fungus on top, and brought it to Daniel's mouth. He briefly thought of spitting it back at the low-scum's skeletal face, but it was impossible. The food slid down his gullet and his body welcomed it, shutting out the indignant screaming of his offended brain. He gulped down another portion and another, barely bothering to chew, the crispy softness of the noodles and the rubbery tartness of the fungus exploding on his palate. He came back to himself only when he realized the bowl was empty.

The man stared at him with his pale spidery eyes. He experimentally nudged the dish of raw meat toward him. Daniel spat.

The recruit got up and walked away despite Daniel's protesting cry. Left alone, he kept tugging at his restraints, swearing and yelling at the flambeau corpse, until his food-fueled rage was spent.

What happened to him? Was he still on the base? Had he been transferred somewhere else? Probing his memory as gingerly as a loose tooth, he discovered it contained gaping holes. He remembered coming to the base with…with the woman.

Kora.

He had been arrested. His 'arm had been taken away.

It wasn't much use in the tunnels anyway.

He remembered being questioned by…was it the Shrimp himself? No, couldn't have been. He dimly remembered unfamiliar faces swimming in a blinding light. Human faces, no tenants.

What did they ask?

He slumped back onto his cot with a sigh. Who was he kidding? He knew exactly what they had been asking.

They had talked about Lu Huan. They had questioned him about any unusual symptoms he had been displaying in the last twenty-four hours. They inquired about his appetite.

They all but asked him if he was changing into a Hungry One.

And he was. He knew it now. Strangely, this realization brought no horror or revulsion but only acceptance, almost a relief. He had known what was happening. The strain of denying the obvious had been too great. Easier to acquiesce, to give in, to go with the flow.

He thought of the zombies he had fed to the trains. The idea that he would become like these creatures was too enormous to encompass and he simply rejected it. He was sick. He was probably dying.

But even as he was sinking back into sleep of repletion, his body temporarily satisfied and his brain shutting down in denial, he remembered the woman.

Kara.

5.30 am. She had not slept since her nightmare. The sky was pearling outside, the night splendor fading. The advertising flambeaus had retired, and only the flat winged creatures that perched on the underside of curved pylons like giant silvery moths dutifully shed their pale glow onto the pavement. Some were cheating, dimming their light to conserve energy for mating during the day.

Kora thought, not for the first time, how her inability to eat was leaving her with huge chunks of empty time. Ordinary people's schedule was neatly subdivided into manageable portions by three meals. She had no routine to anchor her in the everyday.

"At least I still sleep," she muttered.

But what if her insomnia was a sign that she was changing, that even this human capacity was being taken away from her?

Sighing, she went into the bathroom to take a shower, glad that her body still needed the daily ritual of cleansing.

The water was icy cold.

Irene had explained to her that the Pith took care of the utilities. She waited, confident that the city would provide. But the water dribbling out of the snakehead showerhead was barely warmer than ice melt and not getting any better.

Kora snatched a robe off the hook and stormed out of the bathroom, feeling ragged. There were three doors on the landing: the guest room, the bathroom, and another one. She knocked and when there was no answer, irritably pushed it open. The room was empty and looked like it had not been used for a long time.

She went down to the ground floor, peered into the empty kitchen, and spotted stairs leading down into the basement. Since she could not think of anything else to do, she went down.

The basement door was unlocked. The windowless room, lit by a decrepit flambeau, was long and low-ceilinged, its walls sagging in oozing folds of the raw Pith. Kora had never seen it uncovered before in such quantities and was shocked by its meaty vitality. There were some articles of furniture scattered about: a couple of packing boxes, a stool, a military cot. But Kora's attention was riveted by what was right in front of her.

At first, she thought it was some sickness of the Pith, a bulbous tumor hanging from the wall. But then the tumor stirred and looked at her.

The girl's upper body protruded from the Pith, surrounded by a crusty welt like an inflammation around an untreated scratch. Even though the body existed only down to the waist, it was not naked – a clean t-shirt had been forced upon its swollen contours and the flesh squeezed out in pasty rolls. The arms were rudimentary sticks, in shocking contrast to the bloated appearance of the rest of the body. The head rolling on short fat neck was sparsely covered by thin strands of blond hair and the face was hardly more than a blob of unformed fat.

Colonel Rosen appeared out of the gloom.

"What are you doing here?"

She shook her head, unable to take her eyes off the half-girl who stared back at her as unblinkingly as a cornered rat.

"Meet my daughter, Lucia," Rosen said.

The head lolled; the half-girl squeaked.

Rosen lifted a framed picture from the table and showed it to Kora: a pretty blue-eyed teenager with a shy smile nestling between her beaming parents.

Gently, Rosen patted the half-girl's balding head. She snapped at him, her teeth small and discolored.

"How…" Kora whispered.

He shrugged.

"We had this basement, see? One of the perks of military housing. Few people have storage space in the city. Anyway…we just piled it up with junk. One day, Lucia went down to fetch her old school uniform because she had spilled coffee on her new one. When Mar…when her mother and I sat down to dinner, she still had not come back. We called her; no answer. We went down. And…this is how she was."

"But why?" Kora cried. The meaninglessness of this disaster struck her as a personal insult.

"Nobody knows. It happened before. Not very often. The Pith just…just goes crazy, I guess. More often now."

The half-girl's head went up, her bloated face screwed up in a babyish grimace. Her small mouth opened and she let out a shrill, keening sound, as mechanical as the whine of a drill. Rosen patted her again and when it made no impression, he fetched a baby bottle filled with yellowish liquid. He stuck the nipple into the half-girl's mouth. She stopped keening and started sucking with the greedy bliss of a newborn.

"Sugar water," Rosen said. "It calms her down."

"What…I mean, does she talk?"

"No. Not anymore."

"How does she ask for food?"

"She does not need food. The Pith is keeping her alive."

The last word struck Kora as grotesquely inappropriate.

"Where is her mother?"

Rosen shrugged.

"Gone."

She wanted to apologize for intruding upon his personal tragedy, but she did not feel apologetic. She felt suffocated. Suddenly, she realized she did not want to spend a second longer here, in this claustrophobic chamber of horrors, fenced in by the walls that quivered and reeked of raw meat. She was about to dash up the stairs when she heard footsteps.

Coming down into the basement was the chairman.

Chapter 17. Madam Wren's Offer

Daniel woke up when a hand was pressed against his mouth.

"Shhh!" the attacker hissed angrily.

He tried to lash out but the restrains jerked him back. The dead light burnt his dry eyes. Finally, the blurry silhouette of the intruder came into focus.

"Ivan!"

The boy shook, his hands so unruly that it took him several tries to cut the restraining straps. When he finally did, Daniel groaned as, with a rush of pain, his circulation was restored.

"Come on!" Ivan Petrov whispered, his face pale and glistening with perspiration.

Daniel stared at him, his sluggish brain unable to process the new recruit's presence here. The last time he had seen him was on the day of the train-feeding in the mid-level depot. He swung his legs over the edge of the cot and stood up unsteadily. The door was open.

"Where is everybody?"

"They're all gone," the boy whispered jerkily. "An emergency in up-levels, the Virgin's Veil precinct…a rogue…"

"What rogue?" Daniel asked automatically, though he had more immediate things to worry about.

"A firestalker."

"So what are you doing here?"

"You must go to the Market! You must go to Madam Wren!" Ivan whispered.

Daniel finally woke up.

"She sent you? Paid you?"

The recruit looked aside. Daniel felt like tearing off the uniform he was disgracing. Bribes! Corruption!

The city is rotten.

And so am I.

He peered out. The plaza was empty, the main gate ajar.

Was Rooster bought too?

"They're all gone," Ivan muttered. "It must be bad."

Daniel stood still.

The militia had been his home for twelve years. If he did not belong here, he belonged nowhere. If he was not Sergeant Moylan, he was nobody.

You are *nobody.*

"Go!" Ivan urged.

Daniel looked at his country-fresh, round face, his small eyes blinking.

Stupid chicken-shit!

Stupid...chicken...

The boy's apple cheeks quivered, bursting with lively juices.

Daniel shuddered and turned away.

"Go! I'll tell them I was asleep...didn't hear anything."

Daniel snatched the flambeau's corpse from the ceiling. Stuffing it into his pocket, he sprinted across the gray void of the plaza and into the city.

For a moment, they just stared at each other.

The chairman's face was smooth and immobile. Wearing a bespoke suit, his black hair slicked back, he looked like one of the richer merchants of the Market. But surely, he was somebody...something else! The memory of what she had seen – or thought she had seen - after the roofs' attack felt as elusive as a dream. But strangely, she was glad to see him.

"I'm glad to see you, Kora," he said, echoing her feelings and instantly making her angry.

"It's good because you have some explaining to do."

"I know. I would have told you before but for the attack."

"Take her away, Mr. Malech," Colonel Rosen interrupted. "And hope she's worth it!"

Kora glared at him:

"So, you told him I was here? Taking bribes, are we? Aren't you an officer of the law?"

Rosen straightened up, put his hand on Lucia's lolling head.

"I'm sworn to protect the city," he said. "It is sick. Mr. Malech is the only one who can cure it. He promises that what happened to my daughter won't happen again. This is all the bribe I need."

"This is very noble," Kora retorted "but I'm not going anywhere. Not while Daniel is here!"

Daniel stumbled through the dark streets.

Skulking in the dark...

Hungry Ones, in fact, often attacked in daylight but it did not matter. He did not want anybody to see him; did not want to watch the dawning horror on the passers'-by faces as they shrunk from what he had become.

Am becoming.

He did not know whether his appearance had changed. He passed by a mirror display in a shop window and deliberately averted his gaze. The night-duty flambeau did not react to him, but he hastened his steps.

The flambeau corpse in his back pocket felt like an admission of guilt. He had not killed the tenant but here he was, hauling the corpse around like a ghoul. Why? He did not know.

He looked at his hands; they appeared unchanged, strong square fingers lightly dusted with freckles. He stared at them, almost expecting the nails to grow into crooked claws, the skin to roughen into a blue-gray hide. Nothing happened.

No, he was lying to himself. Something was happening all right. Hunger tore at his gut like a ferret, lacerating him from the inside.

With whatever was left of his willpower, he put the beast down. It felt like an actual physical effort, like wrestling down an animal. The attack was repulsed but the enemy did not retreat.

Instead, it settled down into a dull ache at the pit of his stomach, more intolerable in the long run than the active pangs of starvation.

The big flambeaus were crawling down the skyscrapers' sides as their night shift was ending. He looked around. He had wandered into the Grandfather's Street Bazaar. It was empty, the stalls wrapped up in wrinkled derma. But some enterprising peddlers were already waking up their stalls and unpacking their wares.

A noodle stand would open up soon. He still had some money.

He negotiated with his hunger. He pictured a steaming bowl of glass noodles swimming in golden broth, slices of fish-cake piled on top. He tried to force himself into salivating.

Useless.

The image that filled his mind was of the dish he had rejected in the sickbay: chunks of raw meat, the blood sweet and cloying, congealing around the rim of the bowl. It was so vivid he could smell its rich stink. He wanted to vomit in self-disgust but could not summon enough bile.

He needed a place to hide. A tiny blind alley debouched from the main thoroughfare. The pavement was bare Pith but covered in the damp fuzz of new growth. A small colony of fire-stems clung to the gutter, their cone-shaped heads turning when he squeezed through the opening.

Daniel glanced at them blearily. A dumb relative of flambeaus, fire-stems were considered pests and rooted out by the municipal exterminators out of fear that some would achieve mobility, becoming rogue firestalkers. Citizens were called upon to stomp them out wherever possible or at least to apprise the authorities of new clusters.

No matter. He was done with the duties and privileges of a citizen. Going back, divesting himself of the title he had so proudly borne for over fifteen years. Thinking that the city would truly accept him and love him back.

Sham, all a sham. He was country trash. He belonged here, with all the other trash. Wait until the garbage collectors start sniping on his carcass, dragging bits and pieces of him away into the belly of the city, to be tasted, digested, and excreted. Dust to dust? No, shit to shit.

He leaned against the blood-warm wall that gave slightly, accommodating him. It gave him a measure of comfort.

Something poked into his buttocks. He reached down and pulled out the pathetic dead flambeau he had snatched from the base. It was a young one, hardly more than a baby. Its rubbery flesh was beginning to acquire a sickly fungoid sheen of decay; its delicate gills were shriveling into blackish powder that stained his fingers.

It was the most delicious thing he had ever seen.

Daniel raised his arm and pitched the dead flambeau as far as he could within the narrow confines of the alley.

"Who is Daniel?" the chairman asked. Kora opened her mouth and closed it because she did not know what to say. But what happened next blew the question out of her mind.

The half-girl was waving her claws in the air, making a sound like water in a blocked pipe. Her father stepped up to her, calling her name

The wall surged, a wave of muscle ballooning forth. Lucia screamed. With a wet smacking, she tumbled out from the wall. The lower part of her body was a tapering root like a bleeding carrot.

The half-girl crawled toward them like a snake, her belly scraping the floor, her root smacking down. Her face was changing: the dull features running together into a ball of wrinkled skin that was split by the gaping fissure of a mouth. Thin needle-like teeth sprouted from the upper jaw. Before stunned Kora could move, the chairman clutched her arm and pulled her toward the stairs.

"It's the Pith!" he cried. "You can't fight it!"

The Colonel stepped between them and the half-girl, reaching out to his daughter, trying to lift her like a baby. She jumped into the air, a huge ungainly tadpole, her root winding itself around his legs, tripping him. Her teeth fastened on Rosen's throat and bit into the jugular. A spray of blood peppered Kora and the chairman. He pulled her up the stairs, hoarsely yelling to his Guards.

The half-girl shook her father's body and dragged it toward the wall. The Pith retreated, forming a gullet-like tube. She wriggled inside, pushing her prey before her. With lightning speed, they both disappeared into the matrix of the city, only the wriggling end of her tail sticking out as the aperture closed.

Daniel squeezed deeper into the folds of derma. The fire-stems flinched away from him.

All of them but one.

Daniel stared at the fat golden growth, taking in its bulbous shape, its rounded head, its two beady eye-spots staring back at him…

This was not a fire-stem. This was a baby Buddha.

Daniel leaned closer, examining the creature. Buddha-sprouting was rare enough to warrant a spot on the news and to spur pilgrimages of the devout who would immediately start raising money for a new temple. He knew that there was an association of Buddha-worshippers but for the life of him could not remember its name. Mysticism of any kind held no appeal for him.

Still, he had never seen such a tiny Buddha before. And here, in this dump, of all places…He wondered idly if the resulting temple would be named after him. He chuckled.

"Not funny," the Buddha chirped. Its voice was very high, in the upper range of human hearing.

"I agree. It's rather sad that my last conversation should be with a talking mushroom."

The Buddha snorted.

"Have any better candidates?" it inquired.

This gave Daniel a pause. Killing oneself was easy, available to any citizen at no cost: just whoosh up to a viewing platform or open-air café and take a dive. But since a suicide was likely to have an involuntary company by landing on somebody's head, self-killing was discouraged by levying heavy fines on the surviving relatives and close friends of the jumper. What made Daniel's dry eyes prickle with insipient tears was the sudden realization that nobody would be found to pay a fine for him.

He had no blood family. His militia mates were his family and his friends. Or so he had thought until his buddies looked the other way as he was being arrested, humiliated, stripped of his 'arm – for no fault of his own.

Then who? The girls he had slept with? Pearl, Zoe, Candy…He might just as well be ticking off the names of his favorite dim sum.

Felicia, who had taken him under her wing, had given him a place he called home?

Felicia who was dead, torn apart, perhaps by himself, in the delirium of his transformation?

His Colonel who had ordered him strapped down like a rogue?

The sudden emptiness at the center of his carefully constructed life hurt so much that he was almost glad of the coming release. A stray image floated through his mind, a tall woman, broad shoulders and curving hips, sleek black hair swishing across his face…but he shied away from it with a shudder of dread.

The baby Buddha's tiny piercing eyes never left his face.

"Daniel Moylan," the Buddha said.

"How do you know my name?"

"Daniel Moylan," the creature repeated. "Born in the village of Edenberry. Came to the city at the age of 16. Has been in the city for 15 years, has served in the militia for 12. Has two days left."

Two days? Shockingly, it came as a relief. It was longer than he had expected.

"Will I die after two days?"

"No," the Buddha said. "But others will."

Daniel looked away.

Emerald Needle, he thought. *They have an open-air deck. I've always wanted to go there. Too expensive. And now I won't even have to pay the tab.*

Hysterical laughter bubbled in his throat. The Buddha fastidiously rearranged the hanging folds of its loose golden skin.

"How do you know all of this? Do the Buddhas know everybody in the city?"

"Grandfather knows everybody in the city."

"I don't believe in Grandfather!"

"But Grandfather believes in you. This is why he urges you to accept Marika Fu's offer."

"Marika Fu? Who the hell is she? I've never heard of her!"

"You have had two conversations with her. She made you an offer which you rejected twice. But Grandfather is willing to grant you the third opportunity. This will be your last."

"She called herself Madam Wren..." Daniel said slowly. "She wanted me to work...for somebody. The Triads? But she never actually said what she wanted me to do."

"You'll find out," the Buddha said imperturbably, "Marika Fu who occasionally calls herself Madam Wren for luck, offered you money. Now, she has something much better. She has an antidote."

"An antidote? To what?"

"To what ails you."

"The zombie plague?"

"It is not a disease. But yes, she can preserve you – your mind, your soul, whatever makes you Daniel Moylan."

Daniel jumped to his feet.

"Are you serious?" he demanded. "It's not some stupid dawn medicine made of rats' asses? It's real?"

The Buddha nodded.

"It's real," it said.

He still did not quite believe it. But, so what? He had nothing to lose. Nothing. His oath was null and void. He had no home, no friends, and no identity.

"I'll do it," he said. "Whatever it is. Where is she? In the Market?"

But then he hesitated. "Whatever it is?" He knew there were things he could not, would not, do. He was not sure he could name them, but the image of a flambeau corpse suddenly rose before his eyes.

I would not...eat...

"If it means becoming an assassin…" he said slowly.

The Buddha tittered.

"Just the opposite," it said. "You have to track down a criminal."

"Me? I'm not a detective."

"You're a militiaman. You've been trained. You'll become a Hunter and hunt down the person we need you to find."

"And she'll give me the antidote? She really has it?"

"She does. And she'll give it to you. But there is very little time. If you wait any longer, it won't work."

"It's either a dive or her," Daniel said. "I'll try her first. Where is she?"

"You'll have a guide," the Buddha said.

One of the walls of the alley bulged toward him.

"This criminal?" Daniel asked. "What has he done?"

"The unforgivable."

Chapter 18 Lost Names

"She was after us. After me. It has happened so many times. You saw. The roofs. The Pith…something in the Pith is rotten. Sick. Breeding rogues."

They were standing outside Rosen's house. Kora heard a beating of wings above her head and shrunk back into the doorway. The chairman – Adam Malech – put his hand on her arm.

"These are my Guards."

The two khruts landed noiselessly. Kora looked away.

"We must go," he said.

"I'm not going with you!"

"You need me! You won't survive in the city alone!"

She shrugged, started walking.

"I need you!"

She looked back at him.

"Is it why you made me?"

"I didn't make you. I found you."

The grey derma of the alley-wall bulged, forming a blister in the shape of a person like a child's sketch: whip-thin arms and legs, the oval of a head, two round eyes that opened with a smacking sound, revealing weeping black irises. No mouth. The blister detached itself from the wall and beckoned to Daniel to follow. Before leaving the alley, he looked back at the Buddha. It was whispering something to the fire-stems who bent toward it attentively.

The guide creature deftly maneuvered through the early-morning crowds, eliciting only few glances. Daniel, following, thought that there were many more rogue tenants now – unique toads and ducks, random slivers of the Pith, suddenly acquiring sentience and blundering through the streets, falling into the hands of the Triads or washing up in the Market. When he first came to the city, things had been much more orderly. There had been the traditional five kinds of tenants: trains, flambeaus, khruts, Buddhas, and toads. The toads came in few versions: mostly sentient houses like Felicia or walking struts and crawling beams calving off Skybridge. Ducks were few and far between.

And of course, there were no Hungry Ones.

Daniel bit his lip and savored the saltiness of blood. Something the Buddha had said nagged at him.

Born in the village of Edenberry.

The name was familiar and as he let his mind wander, images floated up. Not quite memories but more than dreams.

The pungent odor of manure wafting up from the pile on the barn's floor...Flies buzzing around his head, attracted by the stink of sweat – not animated bits of the Pith but actual insects...The dull ache in his muscles, the sharp pain in his gut...A woman, her face grey and crumpled like a piece of paper, holding a covered dish, as she is calling out to him...

His mother.

He could not – or would not – remember her name because it would come as a reproach. But he remembered the fragility of her worn body as she hugged him, the bones poking through the papery skin.

He knew she was dead. As was his entire family. He did not want to remember how they died but knew the memories would come eventually. If he stayed sentient.

But there was still a black hole of oblivion in his mind. The hole was shaped like the woman named Kora.

They ended up in the Market. The smells of food assailed him. He covered his nose with the hem of his shirt and followed the guide through the labyrinth of side alleys. He thought he knew the Market, but this area was unfamiliar. His guide led him through a sagging doorway that dribbled ropy liquid onto their heads. There were four closed doors on the landing, which was dark because the flambeau station on the ceiling was abandoned. When Daniel's eyes adjusted, his guide was already reduced to flatfish outline on the wall.

One of the doors suddenly swung open, letting him into a dark room smelling of garlic and feces. There was an empty futon in the corner.

Or was it empty? He came closer. The bumps on the futon resolved themselves into a flattened outline of a human body. The face was a gaping fabric mask, the shallow indentation of the eyes striving to open, the mouth issuing a bleating sound. Daniel tugged at the futon, but it was hopeless. There was no telling anymore where the fabric ended and the skin began.

"Lucky day to you, officer," the voice startled him into letting go of the futon who moaned pitifully.

The tiny silhouette stirred and Daniel recognized the bird-like tilt of the head.

"Madam Wren," he said. "They told me it was not your real name."

"Old names don't matter anymore," she said. "Grandfather will give us new ones."

They were still standing at the door of Rosen's house, flanked by the two impassive khrut Guards. A stalemate.

"Found me where?

"At the Divide."

"The Divide," she repeated numbly. She remembered the dish of mashed potatoes she had been given in jail. And the shiny clean edge of the plate, where she had scraped off all food. "Where is it?"

"Deep in the countryside. Far away. It's not a place; it's a guardian. Nobody can cross it. Not anymore. Most people can't even see it."

"Why not?"

"They say that after the Incoming, they closed the gate behind them."

"Who did?"

"Grandfather and his people."

Kora squeezed her forehead, her thoughts scattering.

It does not matter. Only Daniel matters.

"I don't remember any of this."

She was, according to Malech, found wandering in the deadly swamps by his hired khrut scours, bedraggled and emaciated.

"They tried to feed you, of course, because you seemed malnourished, but you rejected everything. This is how they knew you had some power. Everybody feeds, human or tenant."

"But did I talk?"

"Yeah. But not much sense. Except you claimed not to remember who you were."

Double amnesia. Is there such a thing?

"They kept you in a small outpost until they could transport you to the city. They sent a khrut to tell me about you. I wanted to see you. There were some deadheads there, captured. For my experiments."

"So this is how…"

"Yes. You fed. They were happy, the Guards. They were afraid you'd die."

You fed.

"How many..?"

He shrugged. Indeed, what difference did it make?

"And then…"

"You slept. And when you woke up, you looked much better but remembered nothing again. So, they brought you to the Golden Flower precinct, left you in the hotel. Wingate was supposed to pick you up, but he screwed up. It's lucky for him that he is dead."

She was shocked by his callousness. And yet he claimed to be risking his life for the sake of the city?

"We thought you woke up with no memory every morning, but after Wingate talked to you in the hospital, he called me and told me you remembered the hotel. So, I decided to play it this way."

"You lied to me!"

He sighed.

"I know, Kora. I made a mistake. Please come with me."

She shook his head. He was looking at her intently and then something strange happened, his features momentarily obscured by a wet-looking membrane like an all-face blink, and when it retreated, another man was there. No, it was the same man, the same broad-shouldered body, the tailored suit, even the same black hair, but the face was totally different: younger, fair-skinned, with chiseled features and pale grey eyes. Not an Asian – a dusk, not a dawn, as they said in the city.

She was not shocked by the transformation but by what it implied. Vulnerability. Trust.

"Yes," he said, "they don't know. Nobody knows. You do. Please come!"

She hesitated for a moment, then shook her head, and ran across the empty plaza toward the sickbay. And stopped short when she saw the door wide open, the room inside empty, Daniel gone with no thought, no sign or message for her.

PART 2. THE COUNTRY

Chapter I. The Abandoned Village

She could never get used to the empty sky.

Everything else was acceptable. The flat terrain passing unchangeable outside the train's window. The familiarity of the faces she did not want to become familiar with. The rocking, sliding, monotonous motion that had at first made her light-headed and now acted as a soporific, allowing her to sleep as the train sped through the countryside.

She even got used to eating regular meals. When Malech and his lieutenant, a piebald khrut who called herself Fiona, sat down to their sumptuous lunch or dinner, she would slip away, walk across the bony couplings of the train cars, and open the door to the holding pen. There were always a couple of new Hungry Ones there, picked by the Guards on their daily stop as they flew above the devastated fields and burned-down villages. She had requested they do not bring in children. Now, after five days of being snapped at by smelly maws, of staring into the flat eyes that grew flatter as she drank their owners' energy, she was not sure it mattered.

But the sky made her shudder. An expanse of gray or blue, lightly dusted with herringbone clouds or pale with the relentless sunshine, it made her feel tiny and insignificant. When she stared into its void, something brushed the edges of her mind: a non-memory, as delicate and deadly as a disease-bearing mosquito. At least, she had no more nightmares. She attributed it to not sleeping alone.

But she missed the city, missed it with the intensity that surprised her. Why would she miss the living garbage in the smelly alleys; the swollen, inflamed tissue of the Pith; the endless crowds, the pollution and the noise? And yet she did.

She was standing at the window, watching the countryside roll by. Adam walked in and stood behind her, so close that she could feel his breath on her neck. The train was slowing down.

"Another dead village?" she asked without turning around.

"Perhaps."

She finally looked at him. He was wearing his favorite face – bland and fair, eyes of icy blue, smooth and faintly contemptuous. She preferred the dawn (*Asian*) face she had seen him with the first time they met. Even though she knew it was not true, she thought of it as the *real* Adam Malech.

"I thought you'd want to get to the Divide as soon as possible."

"I have to find it first."

She started. That was new. Until now, every time she had asked about their destination, he became so elusive that she had come to believe he was prolonging the journey in order to spend more time with her. She wanted to believe he had feelings for her – but then, how would she know? What did she know about men, human or otherwise? Whatever sexual and emotional experience she had had – and she must have had some, judging by the impeccable working of her body when left to its own devices – was lost to her.

Fiona came in. She was less human-looking than the khruts Kora had met in the city. Certainly, less human-looking than Peter. Her hunched body was thickly feathered, gray and brown. She had actual wings, not the plucked-chicken travesty of Peter's. Hers were long, with ragged pinions, which trailed on the floor unless she discreetly folded them on her back as she normally did.

But not now. The saw-toothed feathers were fluttering like torn banners. Fiona's yellow beak clacked. She could talk pretty well but not when she was under pressure. Then she would switch to the khrut language, consisting of whistles and clicks, which was as incomprehensible to Kora as birdsong. Adam, on the other hand, claimed to understand it.

Fiona was clacking away until Adam lifted his hand. The khrut made a strangled sound and dipped her narrow head. When she spoke again, it was in words:

"Village. Empty. But two survivors."

The train rolled down a ramp-tongue and they descended onto the dry crumbly earth, thinly covered with wilting grass. The wormy tracks stretched ahead, looping around a ragged copse and disappearing from sight. Tracks were semi-sentient, though Kora could not figure out whether they were extensions of their trains or independent organisms. Trains needed tracks for several reasons: to protect their sensitive multiple legs from rough terrain; to provide nutrients when there were no humans or tenants to feed them live prey; and to guide them toward a destination. On their own, trains were rather dumb.

Daniel loved trains...

Don't think of Daniel.

A gust of wind cut through her shirt and she shivered. The city's balmy warmth had spoiled her; now, even the tiniest bite of chill made her uncomfortable.

The day was raw and unfinished. The air smelled of dusty hay and dry earth.

Or maybe something more. She sniffed: a corrupt sweetness brushed her face.

By her side, Adam fidgeted. He was a city creature, made uncomfortable and defensive by the countryside. The urbanity of him was one of his most attractive features in her eyes. She was not sure about the rest.

The village sprawled beyond the naked fields: a cluster of mean huts, seemingly leaning into each other for warmth. But Kora knew it was an illusion. These were dead buildings: man-made contraptions of wood, straw, and tile. There was no Pith here.

The first house they entered was a flat-roofed white-washed

box surrounded by barns and outbuildings. The yard was surprisingly clean and totally empty.

Adam and Fiona disappeared into the house, but Kora lingered outside, staring at a bony tree planted in the corner of the yard. The tree was dead. Its bark was stripped off the trunk to the height of a man.

Adam and Fiona reappeared, and he said: "Nothing here!" But she peeked into the house anyway.

The bodies of two adults lay on the sleeping platform in front of the stove, dressed in their best. A couple of disappointed flies circled above their caved-in faces. The bodies were little more than skin-covered bones.

Searching the rest of the village, they found a couple more corpses, one of them of a child, and that was that. Very few possessions, mostly broken and scattered. No sign of any farm animals or fowls. Nor was there any evidence of the hulking agricultural tenants that the city sent to the country in exchange for food requisitions. Adam had told her they were nicknamed Aunt Harrow's by the country people because they were used for plowing. In one yard, there was a small pond that, once upon a time, might have held a couple of ornamental fish. It had been dredged, even the scum gone.

As the search progressed, Adam became more and more impatient and distracted. It was as if he were looking for something he had become convinced was not to be found here.

Eventually, they went back to the train. The two survivors were huddling together, shying away from the knot of khruts who stood nearby.

Another khrut came out from the train carrying a jug of wine and a dish of roast meat.

"Don't!" Kora ran forward. The survivors looked up blearily. They were two women, perhaps in their mid-forties, but it was impossible to tell their age from their skeletal faces.

"Hungry!" The khrut impatiently pushed by Kora. One of the

women reached a tremulous hand to the plate and snatched a chunk of meat.

"No!" Kora pulled the dish away. The khruts stirred. They did not care for humans, famine victims or not, but they hated Kora. The feeling was mutual.

The woman turned away and vomited lumps of undigested meat. The khruts stopped.

"Give them a little soup. No meat, no wine, no bread. After prolonged starvation, they can't take solid food."

Kora walked into the train, tossing this piece of advice over her shoulder as the women slumped on the ground and the Guards looked uncertainly at the chairman.

Adam came to her two hours later as the sky outside deepened to the color of bruised plum. With his back to the meager light, she could not tell what face he had on.

"Nothing?" she asked.

"Nothing."

"What are you going to do with them?"

"They are sisters. An uncle in the village of Lotus Pond. About twenty kilometers away. Left them some food. They'll go."

"Will Lotus Pond be any different?"

He shrugged.

She thought he was going to touch her, but he did not. As the pause lengthened, she suddenly longed to be outside, walk into the thickening twilight. But just then the train shuddered, the tracks contracting as they woke up and unspooled forward, worming their way through the countryside.

"You knew not to overfeed them…" he said. It was not a question.

"Common sense," she said drily.

Chapter 2. The Hunter

Darkness. Light. Then darkness again.

This is how time was now: sliced into chunks of different colors. He dimly remembered something from his childhood, a home-made dessert, striped layers of chocolate and angel-food cake. He did not remember its name, or whose hands had placed it on the table, or whose other hands battled his own as they fought silently over the thin slices. But it had been delicious.

Time was like this dessert now, with layers of different smells and tastes piled up on his plate. And like the dessert, it was running out.

He had been hiding in an outbuilding for most of the day, surrounded by rusty spades and hoes. They looked as if they had not been used for some time. He tsk'ed disapprovingly, running his fingers along the dull edges, and then forgot about them. He found some hay, stale but clean, and made a nest for himself. He only moved twice: when the dusty sun rays fell through the chinks in the roof; and when he heard the rustling of a mouse. Sunlight hurt his eyes, so he retreated into the shadows. He caught the mouse and ate it.

At dusk, he came out. The sun was low in the pinkish sky, hiding behind tattered clouds. He looked at it for a long time. This was a sickly and forgettable sunset; he suddenly longed for the bright colors of…what? The word eluded him, and he decided to hunt it down.

But not right now. Another hunt was more urgent.

The outbuilding belonged to a largish farm that stood apart from the village. He had determined that there were people on it. But he had not heard much noise during the day, at least not animal noise. A farm this size had to have animals; he was certain of it, though less certain of what kind. But perhaps this was irrelevant.

He slunk toward the farmhouse, easily gliding through the thickening evening air, finding shadows everywhere. Shadows smelled differently; he had recently discovered this. As his eyesight was failing, the other senses stepped in.

The house was a white shadow among the gray ones. It smelled of jasmine and blood. His nose twitched.

He was about to bound up the wooden steps leading to the porch when something cricked. He hunkered down in the low bushes.

A clot of darkness appeared on the porch. It smelled young.

Light was spilling from the open door, a soulless orange light with an unpleasant odor.

The girl (*yes, a girl, it is a girl!*) tottered down the steps. Her legs were fat, swollen with liquid, supporting a shrunken body. Thin strands of hair obscured her face.

She stood for a moment as if she had forgotten what she was supposed to be doing and then dragged herself toward the outhouse. He rose up from the shadows, blocked her way.

She stared at him dully. But then something sparked in her extinguished eyes, a hint of excitement.

"Grandfather?" she exhaled.

He stood still, taken aback. It took him longer and longer to understand language. He had lost none of the words and their connections; it just felt as if they were put away in an old chest whose rusted lock was harder to open every time he had to. Now, he had to rummage in the chest to figure out what she meant and, while he was doing it, she acted.

"Mam!" she yelled.

Another, bigger, clot of darkness separated from the gaping doorway. A woman walked toward them, her wrinkled face held together by the tightly knotted head-scarf. The woman looked at him and screamed.

Several more people crawled out of the house, one holding a

flaming torch. He flinched away from the fire.

There were all women and children, he noted; no men. Not that it mattered. He was not afraid of country men or their paltry 'arms.

He turned to the girl who was staring at him with rapt fascination.

"Where are your animals?" he asked, trying to enunciate clearly.

"Taken away."

"Agatha!" he mother screamed. One of the children started crying.

"Shut up! I won't hurt you!"

It was easier to talk now, even though his mouth still felt wrong and he licked his lips to make the sounds coming out of him clearer, more urbane, as befits a militiaman of the city. It occurred to him that he felt no bristles as his tongue probed his upper lip and he was glad: the regulations on facial hair were quite strict, even though he could not, for the moment, remember the last time he had shaved.

"Where are your men?"

"In the village hall. Are you from Grandfather?"

He disregarded the question which, now as he had his words back, was revealed as completely meaningless.

"I need to see your hetman," he commanded. "Lead me to the hall!"

"Agatha!" the mother cried again, but this time her voice was softer, as if the long habit of helplessness just reasserted itself. He glowered at her and she slunk back.

Agatha nodded. There was a feverish light in her sunken eyes and he decided she was only at the first stage of starvation when the body is drunk on its own self-consumed tissues. She took the torch from her brother, and the Hunter wrinkled his nose at the smell of smoke. The folds of skin moved heavily on his cheeks.

"The hetman has 'arms!" the mother warned.

"I know."

He followed Agatha but turned around (his neck contracting sluggishly) and looked back at the farmhouse. The smell of blood had faded somewhat and now, as the immediacy of it receded beyond the barrier of regained words, he realized it was quite old.

"No animals?" he repeated, looking at the clutch of thin children. "Poultry, geese, cats, dogs? Harrows?"

One of them shook his head; the others just stared dully through him.

In the dark. The soft whisper of the train's multiple legs skittering on the wormy flesh of the tracks.

Kora lay with her eyes open, watching the subtle patterns of shadows shifting on the car's ceiling. Adam lay beside her. The bed had broadened and stretched to accommodate the two of them in comfort. He could command the train with a simple vocabulary of taps and strokes. He had tried to teach her, but she refused to learn.

It would not work anyway if the train went rogue.

He had retained his dawn face and she appreciated it. Normally in his sleep, the face-membrane would blink into place, shutting off the current human features with moist blankness. But once she had walked out of the bedroom when it happened and after that, he tried to accommodate her. She never told him that the walking out had nothing to do with him.

Daniel.

She repeated his name under her breath until it lost its sweetly wounding edge and dissolved into a meaningless sound.

Adam explained that the fact that he had left out of his own free will meant that the zombie poison did not take hold. For a reason nobody understood, citizens and tenants were immune to it; only country people were susceptible to various degrees. This had nothing to do with heredity since a prolonged residence in the city conferred immunity even upon immigrants. The length of the requisite stay varied in obscure ways; but since Daniel had been in the city for a fairly long time, he must have been on the cusp of it. So, he must have overcome his infection, somehow got out of the restraints and just walked out, as the base was convulsed by the attack of a firestalker nearby.

She knew better but she did not correct his explanation. It made for a satisfyingly simple story and she wished she could force herself into believing it. But she knew. He had left because he did not want to go back for her. It was that simple. He did not want her, never had.

She stirred restlessly. The car was stifling; there was a faint milky smell in the warm air coming from the walls.

She sat up, and Adam woke, blinking off his face, bringing up another: an olive-skinned face with a generous mouth and smoldering back eyes. She winced; it meant he was amorously inclined and she was not at the moment. She would not touch him unless she felt desire – *the other desire* – in her flesh.

He saw her reaction and brought back the blue-eyed face. She did not know how many he had; there were four or five he used most often but there may have been more.

"Dreams?" he asked economically.

"No. Not anymore."

The train was slowing down. Perhaps they were coming up against an obstacle: a hill or a brook. Then the tracks would scout ahead, find a new route.

"What are we looking for?" she asked bluntly, tired of the games they played, of the subterfuge, of her own fear.

He sat up in bed, naked, drew up his knees, looked at her. The ceiling flambeau, alerted by the movement, turned up its light and Adam waved it down impatiently.

"There is a war going on," he said.

"Who with?"

"I don't know."

She stared at him. He sighed.

"Look," he said, "I love the city. I'll be Mayor when this imbecile Volk is done. This is *my* city. And it's under attack."

"The Hungry Ones…"

"They're mindless. Dangerous, of course, but mindless. Somebody is sending them. Somebody is *making* them. And the city is…sick. The Pith is splitting off rogue tenants faster and faster. And now it has also started eating humans, taking them in, melting them down…You saw, in Rosen's house. It has never happened before. Not since Grandfather's time."

"When was it?"

He blinked on another face: a perpetually smiling, almost a clownish, countenance. Where humans would change facial expression, he changed face.

"It's a good question. Nobody knows."

"How is this possible?"

"There was no time before he came. No mind."

He explained, leaving her even more bewildered than before.

"You mean, there were no tenants in the city before the humans came?

"No. Just the city. Alive but not aware. Like a body. Khruts and Buddhas and trains – its cells, its tentacles, its epidermis. Growing on the Peak, spilling into the valleys."

"What did it eat?"

"Khruts hunted, Buddhas sucked nutrients from the soil, trains brought plants and animals in."

"And when humans came…"

"We woke up."

"How?"

"I don't know. Some say consciousness is a disease. The city was infected."

"Is that what you think?"

The smiling lips pursed thoughtfully, the face contorting into an awkward approximation of contemplation. She saw a human

Adam Malech – the man he wanted to be.

"No. I think it was a gift. Many tenants hate humans but they're stupid. Without humans…what would I be? A piece of meat pulsing to the heartbeat of the Pith? Without memory, goals or desire? This is why I'm trying to save them. To save the city."

Suddenly, she believed him, believed in his sincerity. It was an overwhelming and not altogether welcome sensation.

"So what year is it now?" she asked quickly, averting her eyes so he would not see the trust in them.

"Year Zero. It is always Year Zero. We count back to the past, forward to the future. The problem is, the tally in the city and the country never coincide."

Chapter 3. Agatha

The village hall was a sturdy building set in the middle of the green, with a little pond in front of it. The water sloshed lazily, ruffled by the night breeze. The broken reflections of the torches swam like the ghosts of dead fishes.

He was still surprised as to how primitive the country life was. No flambeaus, no…At this point, his word-chest clanked shut.

The girl led him to the double door and stood aside. He pushed the door; it was unlocked. But as he stepped into the smoky fug of the interior, something long and sinuous shot at him, winding itself around the place where his neck sloped into the shoulders.

It did not hurt him; he barely felt it. He pulled it off, his nails piercing the tough muscle. Somebody grunted.

The hall was big, running the length of the entire building. There were benches at the sides where a clutch of sleeping men were stirring, woken up by the commotion. But he instantly zoomed in on his assailant.

The man backed off against the podium where a large table piled up with papers stood. He was as flabby as an empty sack, his once-stocky body sagging listlessly. But his 'arms were uncommonly long. They undulated on the floor, two sagging pythons tipped with clawed digits. One of them was retreating, hissing and coiling itself around the hetman's waist. The other one reared threateningly.

"Stop it!" he yelled and seeing that the hetman did not understand, articulated painfully, "STOP IT!"

The second 'arm fell down but did not withdraw.

"Friend," he repeated. "No danger. Help. I will. For information."

The men on the benches were all awake now and he smelled their fear. And hunger.

They were better fed than the family in the farmhouse but not much better.

He strode forward and the hetman's 'arms spooled back, drooping off his bony shoulders. 'Arms drew nourishment from the body of their bearer. He remembered that.

He had no 'arms now and did not need any.

"Who are you?" the hetman cried fearfully. "What are you?"

"I'm a Hunter," he said.

They found something.

The train stopped in the middle of a denuded field, while the tracks snooped ahead. Whatever had been growing here had been harvested, leaving only brown stubble behind. The village loomed beyond a straggly copse, apparently deserted.

But in the middle of the field lay a body.

Adam, Fiona, and a couple of other khruts gathered around it. Kora pushed by them.

The body was that of a flambeau. He was flat and squashed, his lumens extinguished. Like most of its brethren, there was nothing human-like about him; he resembled a large piece of soiled lace. But she knew he had been an intelligent, self-aware creature. A tenant, a city dweller.

And here he was, in the middle of the countryside.

Adam straightened up, frowning, wearing a long scholarly face with wrinkled forehead and squinting eyes. He said something to the khruts and they lifted the body and walked back to the train, Kora trailing behind.

She caught up with Adam and Fiona as the latter was saying something in the click language.

"What?" she demanded. "What does it mean?"

"Flambeaus never go so far from the city. They can't. They suckle on the Pith and their eggs are hatched by humans. They hate the country."

"So?"

"I heard of the hidden farms. Illegal hatcheries. Somewhere around here."

"You think he was escaping?"

"I think it is a she."

Kora refused to watch the autopsy performed by Fiona: not so much because she was fastidious but because she was afraid to find out that she was not. Anyway, the intricacies of tenant anatomy were beyond her. But Adam told her that the dead flambeau was undoubtedly a female, and a gravid one to boot. Her egg-sack was full.

"She was trying to escape," Adam said. "From somewhere around. Flambeaus can't move very fast."

"And that means?"

"There is a bootleg hatchery around. Somebody was keeping her prisoner."

It was, of course, illegal to restrain flambeaus' freedom of movement. They were full tenants, with all the rights and privileges of their second-class status. Only humans were first-class citizens by the decree of Grandfather.

"Why would they do it?"

"Only one reason. Somebody is preparing an army, out here, away from the city, hidden from the militia and the City Corps. Flambeaus are slow but they can be deadly. They can spit fire in self-defense. And if they are turned into firestalkers…"

"But who would be doing it?"

"There is a legend," Adam said. "Among the tenants, mostly. People of the Market tell it to their children. They say that before Grandfather, before history started, the city was not alone. There was something else here, in the countryside. The guardian. The wild khruts and khrut-fowls are still keeping in touch with it. This is why they resent the human villagers and attack them. The city used to provide protection, to send City

Corps and hire Guards to protect the food supply. But this imbecile Volk…"

Kora raised her hand to stop him. He could go on about the shortcomings of the current human Mayor for a long time, as if practicing his future election speeches. But she was not interested. Some dark stain in her memory was spreading fast but she could not focus its outlines: it remained a blob of anxiety and fear.

"This other…thing. Does it guard the Divide?"

"Perhaps."

"But where *is* the Divide?" she cried in frustration and Adam did not respond. He had already explained it to her and it still made little sense.

The Divide was not in any specific location. It moved across the countryside, popping up in various places. Humans could not even see it, though khruts and their bird cousins apparently could. When she had been found by Adam's Guards, they had sensed the Divide nearby.

So, had she crossed over? From whatever lay beyond…

Grandfather had come from beyond the Divide. That was all anybody knew about it.

She remembered Old Van and cursed under her breath. He had known…something. Something important. He was about to tell her and then the khruts came. She tried to remember what he had said but it was lost in the horror of that attack and of her own response. What was it? The Marching Blades? The knowledge hovered at the edge of her mind, as annoying as a key dropped down the drain, and just as hopelessly out of reach. And the more she tried to grasp it, the deeper it fell into the well of her occluded memory.

Fiona ran out of the train, and a low moaning sound rose from a nearby copse.

The hetman was stupid.

He had not bothered to dig grain pits because he had not believed in Hungry Ones. Whatever gossip khrut-fowls were disseminating, he did not listen. The village had always been prosperous, the requisitions paid on time, the winter seed stashed in granaries. They did not bother with the city and the city did not bother with them, except sending Guards every fall to collect the taxes and bring in Harrows and other goods.

Well, last fall, the Guards did arrive on time. But the Hungry Ones had gotten there first.

The Hunter was not interested in the details of the village's affliction. It took him longer and longer to pry open his word-chest. And he found the villagers weak and contemptible.

But the girl Agatha attached herself to him, despite her family's horrified protests. He was not surprised. Once he walked in on the family when they were eating their supper – traditionally the largest meal of the day, currently the only one. Agatha's parents and their five children, three boys and two girls, were seated around the scrubbed table laid with chipped plates, a couple of pitchers of sour beer and water, a misshapen loaf of bread puffed up with chaff, and some leaf pancakes, which he recognized for what they were: bits of indigestible greenery rolled in oaten flour and fried. The mother, her lined face sagging so much he vaguely expected it to slip off like a mask, served the food. She cut up the loaf into uneven chunks and proceeded to give her husband the biggest one, followed with smaller portions for her sons. The men also got all the beer. The girls were given leaf pancakes and water. She left the crumbs to herself. Nobody protested but the Hunter caught the expression on Agatha's face as she carefully chewed the tough leaf. After that, he let her tag after him when he went around scouring the countryside in search of his prey. He also hunted for food, which was obtainable, though not plentiful. This increased his contempt for the villagers who were passively starving instead of switching to alternative sources of nourishment.

Agatha had more gumption. She gratefully accepted his leftovers, even though the first time she saw him hunt, she was shocked. She wanted to cook the game, silly girl! He told her that khrut-fowl was very good raw, as long as one plucked out the tough indigestible feathers.

"But they speak!" she protested.

He did not see the relevance but allowed her to roast the garrulous bird next time. He had to agree it tasted better.

He had commandeered her family's empty barn for his own headquarters while he scouted around. He could sleep in the open but some part of him still craved a roof over his head.

Agatha crept into the barn at dusk, carrying a handful of dried berries.

"My brother found those last year," she whispered. "I dried it for him and he gave me some, so I would keep my mouth shut."

The Hunter made a questioning sound. He did not realize that the famine had been going on for so long.

"No," Agatha explained, having become quite adept in understanding his limited communication repertoire. "He went where he was not supposed to. Was away for a week. Dad spank him. But he would kill him if he knew where he had been."

The Hunter grunted again, rolling a dry berry around in his mouth. It tasted of dust. He was beginning to be repulsed by plant food.

"The village is empty. And cursed. Nobody goes there. But my brother is a fool. A pretty name and he thinks it's safe."

"Name?"

"It was called Edenberry."

Chapter 4. Dinner

Adam pushed her into the car and went outside, summoning the khruts. She watched through the contracting window as the train reacted to the threat by lowering its lids and pulling in its legs. She gagged on the acrid smell of its fear.

Or was it her own?

The Guards landed, forming a loose ring around Adam. Fiona, who had taken off to scout the enemy's movements, landed as well in a flurry of clicks. She was the nav of this khrut flight, whether appointed or elected Kora did not know.

There was no longer any need for scouting. The moaning rose to such a pitch that Kora stopped her ears. And then they emerged from a scraggly wood, a line of bony silhouettes against the pale blue sky. The details of their appearance that she tried to overlook while feasting on them now forced themselves upon her with intolerable clarity: the peaky faces, mouths transformed into ululating holes; the rounded bellies; the stick-like limbs. But the worst thing was the appalling contrast between their emaciation and their unnatural energy. They looked as if they should be barely crawling around. But, instead, they were running through the denuded field like a pack of feral animals.

Fiona and the other Guards swooped upon the Hungry Ones, their clubs and spears rising and falling. Kora knew that khruts could not use the living 'arms that humans wore. Normally, they also distrusted dead weapons and preferred their own talons and teeth. But these were of little use against deadheads.

Several Hungry Ones bunched together, forming a tight little knot. One of the khruts plunged toward them, his club aloft. But he miscalculated, coming too close. Clawed fingers reached for him, pulled him down. Feathers and blood sprayed out as the creatures tore him apart, stuffing chunks of raw flesh into their mouths. Fiona strafed them with a hail of stones, but they had little effect.

Kora forced herself to walk out.

Adam was standing by the train's head, watching the carnage. His face was the one she had seen only once, when the rogue roofs attacked: swollen, expressionless, and barely human.

"I'm going to try," she said, hoping he would say no. He nodded.

By now, the Hungry Ones had pushed the khruts back by sheer numbers. Several gray corpses lay scattered in the field like bunches of sticks, but more active ones were emerging from the wood.

She scanned their groupings and located a lonely deadhead that had strayed away from the rest, edging closer and closer to the train. It looked bloated, its belly sloshing.

If she could vomit, she would. But instead she felt a faint stirring of appetite.

She grabbed the creature and its tepid energy poured into her like warm sour milk. She tossed the husk aside. But then a bunching group of them ran her way and the sheer number of them reversed the current, drawing upon her energy, draining her.

Think! Think like a predator!

She ran away, her meal singing in her veins, allowing her to move faster than any zombie. And then she doubled back, caught the smallest one of the group, whisked it away, drained and dropped it. They turned upon her, but she was too swift for them, as eager now as a wolf circling a deer herd.

Another zombie. And another.

She was full, could not eat any more, but she could still kill. And she did. The energy she drunk spilled out of her in sparks of static electricity, dancing around her like luminescent wasps.

And then something sharp tore into her arm, the pain breaking her focus, pinning her down. She screamed.

The creature biting into her was like no other Hungry One. Its head seemed to have sunk into its globular body giving it the shape of an upright spider. Its bony arms flailed from the top of its rounded body but there was an auxiliary pair of stunted arms emerging from its sides. Its giant maw gaped in the middle of its belly. Kora struggled, trying to taste it, to find that invisible spigot from which its life could be drained, but found nothing. The creature shook her, worrying her like a cat with a mouse.

She cried out to the khruts whose flapping wings she could dimly hear but they did not come. Something else did.

Giant maroon arches rose above the brown field, fell down, and rose again, falling apart into a multitude of shorter, mobile segments. Bunching up like inchworms, the tracks crawled into battle.

A verminous underside scuttling with multiple legs slapped her attacker and it let her go. Kora rolled aside, sobbing, terrified at the unstoppable rush of arterial blood that soaked her clothes. But then the rush dwindled to a trickle and stopped. Her healing capacity reasserted itself.

The tracks fell upon Hungry Ones, crushing them to the ground or seizing them with their innumerable scampering limbs and tearing them apart. Tracks had no head or tail and could move in any direction; their mouths were in the middle of each segment, and now these mouths opened up and bit into zombie flesh. Chunks of this flesh were carried over by waves of vibrissae toward the train who stirred, emerging out of his funk. His stomach-car parted its vertical lips.

Remembering the rogue train in MTT, Kora turned away.

But she could not afford introspection. Even though the Hungry Ones had been scattered by the tracks, there were still too many of them. The creature that had been biting into her was only stunned by the tracks and managed to scamper away. She could see its low-slung spiderish figure heading for the trees.

Fiona and another khrut swooped down on it, their clubs

rising and falling.

Kora saw another knot of Hungry Ones nearby and headed for it. This particular group was strangely immobile: just a clutch of slate-gray bodies pressed together, their backs turned. When she caught one of them and pulled it out, the entire clutch fell apart and she saw that they were pressing around a crouching zombie, its bony arms wrapped around its knees. It lifted its bald head when Kora cut through their throng. Though most of Hungry Ones lacked any discernible genitalia, this one looked female.

She backed off. The crouching zombie made grunting noises that sounded like chewed-up reminders of words. Kora wanted to turn around and run but another creature careened into her and she automatically drained and tossed it aside. And then it was pure instinct to take another, and another... She let the khruts deal with the female.

She limped back to the train, feeling bloated and depressed. The train had been feeding too: she saw a steaming pile of excreta on the ground and turned away. The tracks had lain down, satisfied: the twin lines of pinkish flesh stretching into the gathering dusk.

Adam was waiting for her, but she pushed past him, went to the bathroom, stripped off her clothes and stood for a very long time under the boiling-hot jets of water. Her skin grew red and puckered, and still she could not feel clean. This water was a by-product of the train's metabolism.

She lived inside a living being, just as there were innumerable living beings inside her, engaged in their endless and futile cycles of eating, breeding, and dying. Life was all about eating and being eaten: a mindless and meaningless chain of horror. She shuddered in disgust.

Adam knocked on the door.

"Are you well?"

She was about to snarl at him but something in this quaint

turn of phrase stopped her.

"I'm fine," she said.

He was waiting for her in the dining car, the table set with candles and a bottle of wine. She could no more drink wine than she could drink water, but she asked him to have a glass in the evening while they sat together. It was another almost-memory, a ghost of some civilized ritual she had engaged in…somewhere. He obliged, even though his own preference was for anise liqueur.

The train started moving when she walked in: a swaying, gliding motion. He had dimmed the lights but not enough to disguise his new face: an older man's, round and broad-cheeked, with scraggly moustache and deep crow's feet radiating from his small eyes. A dawn's face but unfamiliar.

"Change it," she breathed.

He slid his nictitating membrane over his new features. It used to spook her; now she thought no more of it than of blinking. When the membrane withdrew, the blue-eyed face looked at her, handsome and reassuring.

"Why didn't you like that one?" he asked. The one thing that never changed was his voice: a little hoarse and spiced with a sibilant accent.

She shrugged.

"No accounting for taste."

He smiled.

"Then I'm happy I can please you."

They sat together, and he drank his wine. She fidgeted.

"How are we going to find the Divide?" she asked.

"A guide. I know where to get one."

"When?"

"Soon. Unless…"

"What?"

"Unless you tell me you don't want to go there."

Her breath caught in her throat.

She had been dreading the idea of the Divide: not just because of its dangers, not just because she had no image of it except a blank space she had created in her unused plate of prison mash – a white expanse of nothingness. She was afraid that crossing the Divide – if she could do it – meant regaining her memory.

There may be things you don't want to remember...

But what was the alternative? The invasion of the Hungry Ones would be repulsed sooner or later. More Guards would be hired; the City Corps would eventually get their act together; even trains and tracks would contribute to the war effort. And what would she become then? A predator without prey?

She would starve. And like the starving villagers, she would eventually turn to the forbidden fare.

Nobody can withstand hunger. Nobody.

She looked at Adam.

"I want to go to the Divide," she said.

He offered her his arm and led her to their bedroom car. At the threshold, he paused.

"This face you did not like," he said.

"What about it?"

"There is only one extant portrait of Grandfather. It's his face."

She frowned, struck by an unwelcome recollection.

"I met a man," she said uncertainly. "A very old man. He said that he...remembered Grandfather. It is possible?"

Malech shrugged.

"I don't think so. He was lying. Or demented."

Kora was relieved. That was what she had been telling herself. Old Van had been senile. It was horrible that he had died protecting her but perhaps it had been time for him to go.

"So, is there a book about Grandfather? An official account or something?"

"Many. But they all omit the most important thing about him."

"Which is what?"
"His grave is nowhere to be found."

Chapter 5. Dividing-the-Divide

The Hunter was frustrated.

He had lingered in the village far too long. But he did not know where to go. He had lost his prey's spoor.

He decided he would scout the plain in widening circles until he hit the foothills of the mountains where khrut-fowls dwelled. He did not think his prey would venture there. On the other side of the plain were the marshlands. He did not want to go there but knew that eventually he might have to. And just a couple day hikes to the east was *that place*, marked on his mental map with an illegible warning. The village of Edenberry.

He could not read the warning and was glad he could not.

Another problem was Agatha. She clung to him with passion that made him itchy and uncomfortable. She had filled out with the meat he had brought her. Her edema had receded and her body assumed her normal proportions. Even her straw-blond hair regained its gleam. She now looked her age which was fifteen.

And she was determined to follow him.

He tried to explain that there was no way he could take her with him but she would not listen. She burst into tears, pleaded and kissed his hands. She even tried to seduce him, which was totally useless. His transformation made him indifferent to such trifles as sex. Her childish attempts to awaken his discarded desire made him remember something else, something he definitely did not want to remember, and he pushed her away roughly.

But it would not stop her. She just pleaded some more.

He could not understand her desperation. The weather was good, the hetman had released some seed stocks, and people started planting late-summer vegetables and collecting edible herbs. Others dug up their emergency caches.

Agatha finally told him what she was afraid of. She showed him a couple of anonymous graves in a disused hayfield and told him that the remnants of children and old people were buried here. The remnants were all that was left after the cannibal meals last winter. Two families even exchanged their ailing children, so that parents and siblings did not have to consume their kin's flesh.

"The hetman put them in stocks and three of them died," Agatha said. "One woman survived."

The Hunter had seen her around the village, a muttering gray-haired shade, shunned by all.

Agatha's story made him uncomfortable and only increased his desire to leave the village. But he still could not take her with him, and yet the idea of simply leaving her behind also seemed wrong.

Fortunately, the dilemma was resolved for him.

He had gone scouting. Most of the countryside was featureless and flat, dotted by small trees and cut by shallow creeks, dried by the drought into wrinkled gulches. But, to the west, the land rose, broken by rolling hills and narrow gullies, and the vegetation became denser, coalescing into thickets of thorny bushes and banks of creeper-choked shrubs. He came to a swift river whose yellowish water was diverted to the neighboring villages through a system of canals that had been left untended and started silting up. He had watched the burbling stream for a while, searching for a word to express what he was feeling. Not finding any, he caught some crayfish and ate it on the spot.

He almost decided not to return to the village but, at the last moment, his feet declined to obey, and he found himself slinking through the denuded trees on the outskirts of the village green. Even before he saw the commotion, he smelled it: the unmistakable zombie stench.

They were all over the village, scrambling through the clouds of dust raised by their feet, weaving in and out of yards, pushing into houses. By itself, each creature could be killed, albeit with difficulty. In such numbers, they were invincible.

He saw two of them tear a woman apart. Fortunately, they bit through her throat first, so her screams were drowned in gurgling of blood. He saw another one devour a rabbit and dimly wondered how the family managed to keep it hidden. He saw several pull out the sweet potato shoots and stuff them into their gaping mouths.

The Hunter felt nausea rise in his throat and his word-chest shut tight, cutting off the flow of concepts that would befuddle him. He needed his strength and cunning to run away from the overwhelming danger. He did not need extraneous things like "horror", "disgust" and "guilt".

Crawling on his belly through the dust, he started moving away from the carnage.

A small stinking body careened into him. He grasped the child-zombie and hurled it against a barn wall. It lay still in a spreading pool of tarry liquid.

The door of the barn opened, and Agatha rushed to him, sobbing, her face smeared with blood.

"I come with you!" she cried. "Mam and dad are gone!"

He lifted her to his shoulders and ran swiftly through the barren fields, occasionally dropping on all fours.

It was the fowls who told them where the flambeau hatchery was.

The "guide" Adam had talked about turned out to be a khrut "cousin", as Fiona put it. A cousin? Kora remembered the scandalous rumors in the city that khruts bred with ordinary birds to produce hybrids. But, when he asked Adam about it, he got offended on behalf of his mercenaries. Unions between tenants and humans were widespread in the city but no tenant, he protested, would dream of mating with a dumb beast – or bird. It was said that the original khruts had occasionally procreated with birds, but it was before the Incoming and so did not count. Contemporary khruts and khrut-fowls were sentient creatures with high moral standards. Any other suggestion was anti-tenant prejudice. The explanation did not make Kora like khruts any better but endeared Adam to her a little more.

She kept thinking about Peter. Adam told her that a Guard by this name had been in his employ but had been dismissed when his flight requested it because of some internal squabble. He had no idea why he would try to hide Kora in the Market or what his final plans for her might have been. Before they left for the country, Adam had tried to find Irene's yarn shop. The only one that corresponded to Kora's description was dark and abandoned. The neighbors knew of a duck named Irene Nitka, but nobody knew where she had disappeared. Some blamed human vigilantes.

Peter had told her there was somebody in the country who wanted her. Some central intelligence that opposed the chairman and his plans for the city. Somebody who knew who she was?

Thinking about it, she realized that the last part was perhaps something she had inferred rather than heard.

Adam was skeptical. He believed that the main problem was in the city; that the starvation in the countryside was merely the result of the bad policies of Mayor Volk who refused to mount a military expedition to stop the depredations of the country khruts. But the Hungry Ones were a wild card thrown into his calculations. He wanted to find out their source and stop them, so he could deal with the city's problems as he saw fit. But now, Kora thought, he was changing his views. The catastrophe in the countryside was far worse than what he had imagined.

She went with Adam and Fiona to the khrut-fowl colony out of curiosity and was stumped by what she saw. She had expected something like the high-density tenements in the city. But this was very different.

They climbed the steep hill covered by bristly yellowing scrub and desiccated grass. The day was unseasonably hot, with swollen rainless clouds pressing down upon them, and Kora felt out of sorts. When she heard a dim rhythmic hubbub, she thought it was blood ringing in her ears. But the noise increased until there was no doubting its reality. An acrid reek floated in the air.

They crested the top of the hill.

Below lay an irregularly shaped lake. Its raw, undisguised naturalness was shocking: ugly brownish water fringed by the smelly mud-flats and clumps of canes and horsetails. But the most striking thing about it was the rocky island stuck in the middle.

For a crazy moment, she thought the island was covered with snow.

Snow?

But the white splotches on the gray rock were too thick and too dirty, speckled with black, brown, and green. And they were in constant motion as flapping shapes rose into the air and settled back, redrawing the fluid geometry of the colony. The stench was unbearable.

Adam wrinkled the aquiline nose of his new patrician face.

"They stink," he declared to Fiona. "Are you sure they're civilized?"

The khrut nav nervously shifted her pinions. She was saved from answering when a flock of birds separated from the cloud above the island and headed their way.

Civilized? Hardly!

The fowls wheeled above their heads, obscuring the daylight and peppering them with loose feathers and perhaps something worse. Finally, they settled down. Kora stared at them in wonderment. They were just ordinary birds as far as she could tell, ranging in size from as big as a goose to as small as a robin. Their plumage ran the gamut from drab to dull. They clacked and shuffled.

Fiona plunged into a furious series of clicks when one of the birds interrupted her:

"Is it true that the city is at war?"

Kora gulped and even Adam appeared to be taken aback. The bird that spoke was in the middle-size range and just as underwhelming as its brethren. Nevertheless, it spoke not just clearly but with a clipped accent that Kora knew characterized the up-level elites.

It was Adam who answered:

"Yes."

"Who with?" the bird persisted, scrabbling in the dirt with its scrawny feet.

"We are not sure. The enemy is cunning. It is weakening the city's defenses, so the Hungry Ones can come in. We need to find out more. This is why we are requesting your help."

"If the enemy is unknown, how do you propose to fight it?" the bird asked. The rest of them stared at the visitors – or at least, Kora thought they did. It was impossible to follow their sidewise gazes.

Adam seemed to be surprised by the question. He hesitated. Fiona chipped in with another series of clicks.

A smaller bird, as plump as a dove, suddenly took off. It flew straight at Kora who ducked instinctively. Remembering that the creature was intelligent, she forced herself to stand still. The plump bird chirped something and alighted on her shoulder, its scrabbling feet messing up her shirt.

"You have one with you who has the power to unlock," the speaking bird commented.

Adam and Kora spoke simultaneously.

"Unlock what?" he asked.

"Do you know who I am?" she asked.

"We will take you where you need to go," the speaking bird said after a pause. "But one of us will come with you. She will follow the person who has the power to unlock."

And then, as if obeying an inaudible signal, the entire flock rose into the air, mingling with the stream of birds perpetually rising from the colony like a column of smoke. But the bird that had alighted on Kora's shoulder stayed there.

The Hunter and Agatha spent the night holed up in a cave.

Actually, it did not even qualify as a cave; it was just a measly overhang in the jumble of limestone rocks. The land rose beyond Agatha's village, becoming a wilderness of gullies presided over by the rocky pinnacles that flamed up in rose and peach at sunset. The view was magnificent after the flatness of the plain but Agatha, sniveling throughout their trek, was not impressed. The Hunter was but even though his word-chest was somewhat loosened by the need to talk to Agatha, it no longer contained names for aesthetic responses.

Having carried her on his shoulders, he finally set her down and ordered her to find shelter.

"Don't leave me!" she cried in paroxysm of fear.

He grunted. Of course he was not going to leave her, stupid girl! But they needed to eat, so he went hunting.

It was not good. The countryside was swept clean by the depredations of the Hungry Ones and the desperation of the villagers. Still, he managed to snatch up a couple of field mice and a lethargic lizard. A feathery, bright green fond caught his attention and he remembered that this wild relative of carrot was edible, though not to him.

He ate the two mice immediately. Still hungry, he gathered the lizard and the tubers and went back to Agatha.

She had been surprisingly resourceful. She had found an overhang, cleaned out the mess left by birds and bats, and arranged sleeping pallets of branches and grass. When he showed up, she was building up a cone of dry twigs at the entrance to the shallow cave.

Her face lit up when she saw him. In the rosy evening light, her skin shone like pearl and the color of her straw-like hair deepened to bright yellow.

He snorted to hide his discomfort and gave her the lizard and the tubers. She reached into the pocket of her smock and withdrew a square box. Taking a tiny stick out of it, she flicked it on the side of the box. A bright orange flame blossomed in the dusk.

He instantly trampled upon the fire, scattering embers.

"Firestalker!" he grunted.

Agatha made a sound of protest and showed him the box, which he took reluctantly.

"Matches!" she said.

The word was unfamiliar, but the box was not. It had black stripes on the sides and a picture of a man's face on top: a man's round face with a brisling moustache.

The face made him shiver but another image superimposed itself upon it: a little boy's fingers holding a box just like that, striking a match…His own fingers.

In the city, matches were unknown. Stoves and heating appliances turned on when used, flambeaus shed illumination when asked. The city provided.

He gave the box back to Agatha and stared into the darkness while she rebuilt the fire, roasted the lizard on a stick, and baked the tubers. She offered him his share, but he refused. She needed food more than him.

"What's its name?" Kora asked Fiona. They were back on the train and the khrut-fowl was perched on the window-ledge.

"It's a she," the khrut muttered.

"Ask her," Adam suggested.

Kora looked at the bird dubiously. The encounter with the

khrut-fowl colony had left her uneasy. The idea that she had the power to "unlock" something was deeply disturbing.

Had she come from beyond the Divide? And what did it even mean? What *was* the Divide? Old Van had talked about it, implying that there had been some confrontation with Grandfather's people as they had made their way to the city. Thinking about it, she remembered that Peter had used the word as well.

What if Adam was trying to use her to "unlock" the Divide for some nefarious purpose?

Thinking this made her ashamed of her disloyalty. Adam loved the city. Adam loved…her?

Could anybody love her? Did she deserve to be loved?

With an almost physical effort, Kora wrenched her thoughts away from the dangerous track they were taking. Recently, she had become quite adept at that. The more time she spent in the country, the thinner the veil that shrouded her past. And the less she wanted to see what lay beyond.

She turned her attention back to the khrut and the khrut-fowl. She could not trust them. Even though Adam professed total confidence in his Guards, he knew little about the inner politics of the khrut nation. A majority of birdmen lived in the countryside. She kept asking whether they had a ruler – a hetman, as in a village; a mayor; or any other kind of central authority. He said no: every khrut flight was a law unto itself. She found it hard to believe but she did not know any better.

What she did know was that khruts hated humans. Nobody had told her that; she just knew it. And so their bird-kin must hate humans too.

"What's your name?" she reluctantly addressed the bird who cocked its small head. Its eyes were the color of amber with large liquid pupils.

It trilled a sequence of several notes that passed through Kora's brain without leaving any perceptual trace.

"So?' she asked.

"That's her name," Fiona muttered and repeated the sequence. Or at least, this is what Kora presumed she had done. She could not tell whether the sound was the same or different.

She discovered a new fact about herself: she was tone-deaf.

"Doesn't she speak at all?" she asked irritably. "What use is she, then?"

Fiona rounded on her.

"What use are you?" she cried. "You are an intruder, a monster! You don't belong here!"

Kora saw red. She stepped forward, her nails digging into her palms. She did not know whether it was anger or hunger that moved her. She did not know the difference anymore.

Fiona stood her ground, her beak clacking defiantly, the wings spreading, brushing the sides of the car.

Kora's hands clamped upon the birdwoman's forearms – and dropped. She forced herself to back off. Fiona lunged at her but was intercepted by Adam. He pushed the khrut away and unleashed a sequence of trills, clacks, and croaks that no human throat would be able to produce.

Fiona folded her wings and knelt awkwardly.

"Forgive me, human mistress. I acknowledge my infraction. I resign as the nav of my flight. I declare my Guard contract to be voided by my behavior and forfeit all the back pay that is due to me."

"I…I accept your apology," Kora mumbled.

Fiona slunk out of the car. Adam turned to her. He had his new face on: a patrician face with a thin-lipped mouth. It was a forbidding face, but she liked it because it seemed to be the opposite of the rounded features of Grandfather.

"Are you all right?" he asked.

She shook her head, hating him for seeing her like this.

The khrut-bird who had kept out of the altercation rose into the air with a whirring of wings and dropped upon Kora's shoulder.

"You can call me Dividing-the-Divide," the bird whispered into her ear in a high feminine voice. "Also, Light-in-Darkness. Also, Early-or-Late. Also, Near-or-Far. Also, Speech-or-Silence. We'll need all my names at the Divide."

Chapter 6. The Toad

He found the spoor of his prey again.

When he opened his eyes, Agatha was looking at him. In the bright light, the enchantment of the dusk was gone. The gauntness of famine and the remnant of baby fat struggled in her unformed face. And still, he was embarrassed to have her stare at him. He leapt to his feet and bounded out, searching for a secluded place to empty his bladder. And as he was pissing against a boulder, he saw it.

Here the limestone wall of the gorge was split by a crevice created by a recent rockslide. Because it was so recent, the tangled shrubs that choked the rest of the gully had not yet taken hold and he could see some way onto the lowlands below. And he caught a wiggling movement as the tail-end of something that looked like a giant snake disappeared from view.

But it was no snake. The Hunter knew what it was.

He scrambled up the slope, peered through the crevice. And yes, indeed, here it was. Bisecting the featureless fields, the giant twin worms crawled forward, their slimy hides glistening. They stretched out, anchoring themselves in the dry soil. And from beyond, a dead orchard of a puffing shape emerged, skittering upon the tracks, its eyes opening wide as it greeted the sun with a roar.

The Hunter turned away, unsure why it felt so right to see the creature – and so wrong at the same time. When he looked back, the train had disappeared beyond the foothills.

But, it did not matter. Now he knew.

He rushed back to the camp, startling Agatha who was washing her shift in the shallow stream. She blushed and pressed the wet fabric to her meager breasts.

Words deserted him once again. He grunted impatiently,

picked her up, set her upon the saddle of his shoulders and started running.

"Adam," she asked, "have you ever been married?"

They lay entwined and she was in no hurry to move away.

"Married? Of course not!"

"Don't tenants marry?"

He shifted his arm, drew her closer. It was pleasant.

"Are you jealous?"

He had on his default face: the dawn visage she had first seen him with.

"No, I'm not."

He blinked the patrician face on. His body remained the same, smooth and supple. It never showed any obvious signs of age.

"Tenants do marry," he said after a pause. "They can even marry humans nowadays."

"It wasn't allowed before?"

"No. After the Incoming, when Grandfather was still alive…he was very strict about it. They say he punished even occasional liaisons by public whipping. But, the last Mayor before Volk pushed through the Equal Rights Marriage Act. There were just too many half-breeds."

The terms struck her disagreeably, but he used it as a matter of course.

"Are you one of them?" she asked.

"No."

"So, who were your parents?" she asked.

Another face: a young dawn.

"The Pith," he said after a longish pause. "I'm a toad."

"How…I mean…how are you… people like you… born? Are you small, like human babies, and then grow up?"

He shrugged.

"Different in each case. Many are found in alleyways,

especially close to the Market, where the Pith is very active. Except now…it's active everywhere. Anyway, some new toads are small and helpless. They're gathered in orphanages. There are several tenant charities that do it, some connected to Buddha temples."

"Is this where you grew up?"

"No. I was…different. Some of us are…born…fully grown. I was found at the Market, wandering there. Naked, no speech, no memory."

"Like me," she said, as the realization hit her with full force. "You were found like me."

He nodded.

"Yes," he said. "But you're no tenant. You're human."

"How do you know?!" She sat up in bed, kicking the blanket aside, startling the dozing ceiling flambeau into full brightness. "Maybe I'm like you! Maybe I'm a toad, too! Maybe somebody kidnapped me in the city and dumped me by the Divide!"

Adam Malech shook his head.

"No," he said. "I can tell. You are human."

Deflated, she lay back. The train stopped for a second, waiting, as the tracks crawled forward and then resumed their skitter.

"Can you talk to the Pith?" she asked.

"Talk? Not like I talk to you, no. Nobody can do it. Some Buddhas claim they know what the city wants, but they're just fleecing stupid worshippers. I could…feel. Sometimes. Not for a long time, though."

He pulled the blanket over them and blinked the older dawn face back on.

"The Pith is sick. Restless. It calves all the time. Strange toads and ducks. Rogues."

"Like the ones that attacked your bungalow?"

"Yes, just like those. The Pith is supposed to be mindless. But there is a mind behind all of this. Somebody is planning this. And

I'll find out who."

He was silent for a while and then started speaking once again, slowly, dreamily, as if oblivious of her presence.

"I was found by the Triads. They are human criminals, working with khruts. Smuggling in illegal immigrants from the villages: construction workers, whores. Most are dawns, so I speak like them. They liked what I could do with my face. They had never seen this before. No tenant is like me. They helped me, trained me. I was running an immigrant ring first. But it was boring. I knew I could do so much better. And I could pass. For a human. No tenant could do it. I can. So, I made myself human."

"Are there people who know you from that time?"

He blinked on a new face, his equivalent of a smile.

"Not anymore."

She supposed she should be frightened by this disclosure, but she was not.

"Khruts know," he resumed his dreamy monologue. "But khruts are faithful. When you buy them, you get what you pay for. I pay for silence."

"But why?" she asked. "What difference does it make? This Equal Rights…whatever. I thought tenants and humans were equal now."

Another blink.

"Tenants can be businessmen, scholars, militiamen. Tenants can marry humans. But a tenant cannot be Mayor. Only a human can. This was Grandfather's will."

"You want to be Mayor?"

"I *will be* Mayor."

He turned toward her, trying to smile in a human fashion and almost succeeding, keeping his face on:

"So, you see, I could not marry a wife. A human would snoop me out, a tenant would be a hindrance. Still, it's not a bad thing."

"No," she said, pulling him close, one hand tangled in his hair, the other sliding down his stomach, "it's not a bad thing at all."

They were woken up by Dividing-the-Divide.

Of all the khrut-fowl's names, this one seemed particularly ominous to Kora. She did not know why. Perhaps it was just because she felt uneasy in the creature's presence. The mere sight of her brought the embarrassing altercation with Fiona back to her. And then Kora was angry to discover the fact that she possessed no musical hearing whatsoever. She did not need another handicap. She had hoped to learn khrut language in order to understand what the creatures were plotting. Now, it seemed impossible.

As if sensing her aversion, the bird made herself inconspicuous: just a fluffy, feathery ball in the corner. Occasionally, she flew out for a time but always returned before dusk. To Kora's surprise, she avoided the khrut Guards who were now headed by a new nav, a gnarled older male named Franz.

She was half-asleep, swimming in a sea of vague images that she now came to believe were memories. But there was something profoundly troubling about these memories and, just before Dividing-the-Divide perched on her face to wake her up, Kora realized what it was.

They were insufficiently strange. If she had in fact come from beyond the Divide, shouldn't she be plagued by visions of a world unlike anything around her? Instead, the interminable journey through the devastated countryside was making her dreams converge upon the depressing reality. Sometimes, when walking into a deserted barn, she almost felt the weight of a hoe in her hand or looked around expecting to meet the wet eyes of an Aunt Harrow.

Dividing-the-Divide was telling her something. Kora sat up in bed, Adam asleep by her side, the milky whiteness of his face-membrane contracting and relaxing as he breathed. It was morning.

Franz the khrut nav walked in without knocking. Kora pulled up the blanket to cover herself, even though Adam had told her that khruts neither cared for nor understood human modesty: like their avian brethren, they had their genitalia on the inside of their bodies.

"The hatchery," Franz said. "It's here."

The village was not there.

There had been a village once upon a time: a clump of gnarly apple trees designated a former orchard and piles of splintered boards marked collapsed barns and sheds.

But there were no houses. If the other villages they had visited were deserted, this one seemed to have been obliterated.

The visibility was terrible. When they had disembarked from the train, the air was laden with mist. But as they walked toward the village, she and Adam and five khruts, the haze curdled and solidified into a smoky vapor that burned the back of her throat. It stank of country things: mulch, and rotten leaves, and animal muck. And fire, as if all the desiccated vegetation of this blasted region had been piled up in giant bonfires and set ablaze. They groped through the yellow twilight, their footsteps muted by the dusty ground.

Franz suddenly took flight. His tattered wings unfurling, he launched himself into the dim air. The other khruts smoothly moved into a defensive formation with Adam and Kora in the middle. A reedy wail pierced the billowing fog.

Kora tensed and hated herself for that. A familiar, detested void rose up from the pit of her stomach. She had been fasting since the day of the battle. They had encountered no new bands and she had told the Guards not to seek them out.

And now, she was desperately hungry.

Something flapped over their heads; a squeal sounded so close that she jumped. She squinted up, trying to figure out what was going on.

Suddenly, the yellow fog curtains drew apart. A ragged mass careened overhead, shedding feathers. Adam caught her arm, pulled her away, as Franz fell heavily out of the sky, his wings smoking and curling up. The stink of burnt feathers filled the air.

She was buffeted and almost thrown off her feet as the rest of the khruts rose up. Coughing and tearing up, she ran toward an indistinct clearing in the fog. Suddenly, a furious flapping dove at her face and Dividing-the-Divide screamed in her high-pitched human voice:

"Look out!"

Kora rocked on the balls of her feet as she realized that she had almost fallen into a shallow ditch. She backed away. The murk was filled with khruts' piercing bird-calls, the flapping of their wings, and a hissing sound she could not identify. And underlying the pandemonium was the familiar, hateful keening.

There was a sudden flare ahead of her. Then, another one. She looked around: she had lost Adam.

The fog lifted again.

The ditch in front of her was half-filled with burnt skeletons, remnants of leather-like skin still clinging to their black bones. Most skeletons were small: children.

Beyond the ditch stretched a flat paved space. In the middle of it was a large, irregular structure like several buildings knocked together.

She called for Adam but there was no response. There were no khruts around either. Even Dividing-the-Divide had disappeared. Tendrils of yellow fog writhed around her in the harsh air.

Kora jumped over the ditch. The child skeletons stared at her with their empty eyeholes.

There was another blinding flash and she was bathed in hot light. Something heavy sent her sprawling. But worse than the pain of the impact was a blast of fire that clawed at her face like a beast. She rolled over, covering her head with her arms, and smelled the charred stink of her own skin. She felt her eyeballs shrivel and her skin crack. The fire embraced her with a furious voracity. She realized that she had finally found something hungrier than herself.

She screamed again, batting at the flames. From an inaccessible chamber of her memory came an image of a blackened corpse, its arms held up in a futilely defensive gesture.

And then she realized what she had to do.

She relaxed, forcing her muscles to become rags, her bone kindling. She let herself be consumed, opened the emptiness inside to the raging appetite of the flame. And the flame was sucked in, dwindling into the abyss at the center of her being. She was not a predator anymore but a limp need that could not be satisfied, a passive void that could not be filled. She drank the energy of the firestalker as her hair was sizzling and her skin blackening. She drank the roaring heat. She drank her own pain.

And finally, the pain and the heat were gone.

She scrambled up. Through the blind spots that clustered in her eyes like flies, she could see a lacy silhouette limned in fire moving away from her. The pain returned, stealthy at first and then brutal like a splash of acid.

Kora waited for the magic of her regeneration to kick in. Her pain lessened but did not go away.

She lifted her hand, focused on the puffy red skin, the black scorch marks, waiting for them to be erased. They were not. The pain was still there, and the burns were weeping clear liquid. Half of her hair was burnt to stubble. Her skin felt ill-fitting and tight. Still, she was alive and moving. It could have been worse.

Kora hobbled toward the structure in the middle of the paved area. No matter how close she came, she could not make out what it was. Looking like something abandoned half-way through, it had the woebegone air of an unloved dog. There was a greenhouse with filthy, rainbow-splotched glass panels. A little way to the left was what looked like an unpainted barn with no windows and a warped door. There was an unfinished walkway from the greenhouse to the barn. And beyond these two stood a low gray building with a flat roof and a single window covered by an ugly, institutional blind.

Kora went to the greenhouse first. She rattled the handle fruitlessly until it occurred to her to push it up. The wire-mesh door swung open. She stepped in.

Not for the first time, she wished she could vomit.

It was indeed a greenhouse of sorts. It was very humid inside, the air sweaty with the stench of diarrhea. The floor was bare gray soil that looked exhausted by its crop.

The Hungry Ones had been buried up to their waists and their uncovered parts had become shapeless organic sacks, bloated with the sticky lymph that seeped through cracks in their teguments. Their heads had merged with the body, giving them a spiderish appearance. Rudimentary faces seemed painted on their chests, but their maws were real, filled with broken teeth. Their arms now grew from the rounded tops of their head-bodies.

Kora's entrance caused a frenzy of activity as limbs flailed and bony fingers reached for her. But the zombies were firmly rooted in the soil and could not move. They were straining and keening in dove-like voices.

The sight was both pitiful and grotesque. But...she was hungry.

She approached the nearest creature, touched its slick pate...and stumbled back, her chest heaving. A ghost of memory rose in her mind: cramming her mouth with rotten, maggot-infested meat...

This is how it felt. The creature's vitality was spoiled and curdled, roiling with sickness. It should have been dead. It was dead...and was not.

But even rotten food nourishes you when there is nothing better. Kora took a deep breath, ran her hand over her head, and felt the fuzz of new hair pushing out.

She stumbled into the yellow fog outside, its chemical reek burning her lungs, and listened for the whirr of khruts' wings. The countryside lay silent and boundless around her.

She went into the barn.

The door was not locked. Tainted light seeped in through the doorway and through cracks in the walls.

The barn was filled with crates of eggs.

She picked one up and weighed it in her hand. It was bigger than a chicken egg and seemingly made of murky glass.

She put it back into its crate and walked out.

Only the gray building was left. There was somebody inside. There was no sound, the stained blind had not moved but she felt watched. She looked back. No cavalry to come to her rescue. No Adam, no Dividing-the-Divide.

She pushed the door. It was locked.

There were footsteps inside, firm but unhurried footsteps that meant business. The lock clicked, and the door swung open.

The man motioned her in.

It was James Wingate.

Chapter 7. A Conversation with a Dead Man

A meeting with a dead man went awry because of office furniture.

Wingate had an office: a real bureaucratic stronghold with a big desk, filing cabinets, and even a dispirited houseplant. But he only had one chair. He offered it to Kora but then she would have to crane her head up to look at him leaning against the wall. Nor would he agree to sit while she stood. Eventually, they compromised: she perched on the edge of the desk while he sat down. The ridiculous social faux pas, on top of meeting a man she knew to have been killed, made her lose whatever was left of her composure.

She tried to convince herself that Wingate had only been wounded but she knew better. The image of a glass shard sticking out of his throat was too vivid to rationalize away.

And he had changed in creepy ways as if he had melted down and solidified into a parody of himself. His face looked narrow and squashed, the parrot-like nose jutting out like a hook. His neck had elongated into a stalk of tendons, on which his head bobbed like a tethered balloon. Even his arms seemed longer and thinner than before, hands sticking out of the frayed cuffs of his worn gray shirt.

His insincere, servile manner, however, remained the same.

"I'm glad you're doing well, Kora," he said.

"By 'doing well,' you mean I'm not dead?" She wanted to add "like you" but hesitated because somehow it seemed a gratuitously insulting thing to say.

"That too. It was not obvious that you would survive this far."

"Not obvious to who?"

He did not answer, staring at her with fish-like eyes. One was now noticeably smaller than the other.

"You know that your former employer is here?" she asked after a pause.

"You mean, Mr. Adam Malech? Mr. Adam Toad Malech?"

Suddenly, he tittered. It was a horrible sound.

"You worked for him. You knew who he is."

"I do now."

"Come on!" she cried, exasperated. "You didn't know he collected faces to put them on? He had a whole display in that pavilion where both of you lied to me!"

"I believed what I said at the time," the creature that used to be James Wingate said with an air of injured virtue. "But he did not. And he's still lying to you."

"Really? What about?"

"He tells you that the Hungry Ones are coming from beyond the Divide, right? That they are a sent by some mysterious enemy, bent on destroying the city? That great city that he loves so much? The great city that has sucked the country dry, destroyed its people, starved its children, emptied the villages?"

Kora looked away. Her experience of the countryside was too raw to argue with him.

"If the Hungry Ones do not come from beyond the Divide, where do they come from?" she asked after a pause.

"From here, Kora. From the country. They are the revenge of the despoiled land."

The Hunter had lost his way in the fog.

He was so humiliated by it that for a while he pretended to Agatha he knew exactly where they were going. But he did not. The acid veils that whipped around their faces as they blundered across the marshy terrain disabled his sense of smell. Eventually, he had to concede he had lost the spoor of the tracks. He set Agatha down and squatted in the dirt.

She was upbeat, though, undeterred by the fact that all they could see was the pale orb of the sun floating in the sulfurous clouds like a spoiled egg-yolk. She pointed to something looming in the haze like silhouettes painted on glass.

"It's the Divide," she whispered with a mixture of awe and avid curiosity. "I know where we are. They said the Divide came to the village after it was deserted. The cursed village. They said they had brought the Divide close. Look at that!"

The Hunter was unimpressed. It looked like another dead copse of scraggly trees killed by the drought or by the people who had torn off their bark and dug out their roots to boil into a soup of desperation.

And then he blinked, and his sense of proportion reasserted itself. If this was a copse, its trees must be as high as the highest skyscrapers in the city.

Or was it that they were too close?

"The cursed village," Agatha went on. "This is where it all started. The famine."

"What village?" the Hunter asked reluctantly because he knew the answer.

"Edenberry."

"You're dead," she said.

"I *was* dead," the thing that used to be James Wingate corrected her. "But he resurrected me."

"I don't believe in resurrection of the flesh," Kora said automatically and wondered what she meant. So did Wingate, apparently, as he frowned and shrugged, all of his gestures slightly askew, as if he was clumsily imitating being alive.

"It was the land that has resurrected me. The land and its heart and soul. The Nestling."

"What are you talking about?"

Wingate leaned into her, his intimacy as odious as the sweetish odor that emanated from him.

"This is how the khruts call him now, but he has another name too. No matter. He is what this land is all about. Meadows and brooks, trees and plants. Wetlands. Silence and quiet. The whirring of wings. Birds and birdmen. Living in harmony as nature has intended"

"Not much evidence of this now!"

"That boil you call the city!" the Wingate-thing snarled. "The cancer that is devouring the land! The hungry stomach that can never be filled! Grown by the abomination your precious Toad Malech worships! Grandfather!"

"I was told the city had been here before the humans came!" Kora said. She was convinced the Wingate-thing was lying to her, but she had no criteria to distinguish truth from deception.

"It was, but not as it is now. It was kept within bounds. And now it is eating the land alive."

"If the Hungry Ones are really coming from here, as you say," Kora interjected, "then it is the other way around."

"The Hungry Ones are the city's own doing. It is the way the land strikes back at its despoilers. And you, Kara, you should know it better than anybody else!"

The shabby office, the thing's distorted face, all swam in spots before Kora's eyes.

"What did you call me?" she whispered.

"It was the biggest village around, and the richest too, my mam said," Agatha prattled. "Their hetman had five kids by his first wife and then he dumped her and married another and had three more."

Emotions for which he had no names were swirling in the Hunter's head like a cloud of stinging flies.

"But he could afford it because they were so rich. Corn, wheat, milk cows, berries. They were famous for their blueberries and gooseberries. This is why they were called Edenberry."

The shadow of the giant thorn-forest had melted into the fog and now they seemed to be stranded on a tiny island among the billows of darkening vapors. The Hunter sniffed, and a familiar bitter sting brought more tears to his eyes. It was not the fog that darkened the sky. It was smoke.

The Hunter knew they were in deadly danger, but he was powerless to run. Like a child mesmerized by the horror of a dark tale heard a hundred times, he hunkered down, listening to Agatha.

"They had a couple of bad winters and then the city khruts came."

"The Guards," the Hunter said.

"Yes. They had to pay taxes, of course, all villages do. But these khruts demanded more than was fair. They brought khrut-fowls with them and they ate the harvest in the fields. Cows started dying too because of a disease that jumped from the fowls to the cattle, and then dairy-women caught it too. They fought the khruts, but the disease had infected their 'arms and they rotted and the bodies rotted with them. Mostly women and children were left, and they tried to hide the seed grain but the khruts took most of it away, and they ate the rest, and when the spring came, they had nothing to sow. Except their dead."

"The dead do not come back," the Hunter whispered.

"Here they do. Here, so close to the Divide. Where the land is alive, where it defends itself from whatever is on the other side."

"Grandfather's world is on the other side."

"So, they say. But nobody knows what really happened in Edenberry. I wasn't even born then. My…my mam told me. Our hetman and other men came here in the fall, after we harvested our own grain. But there was no one around. The village was deserted."

"Come with me, Kara," the Wingate-creature said. "This is your only chance. To expiate your sin, to atone for your crime.

This is where you belong. On the land you cursed."

She bit her lip, and felt blood trickle into her mouth, and tasted nothing. She squeezed her burnt hands together, but they were already covered by fresh new skin.

"You mean *in* the land," she said slowly. "Under the soil. In the grave."

"Wouldn't it be just?" the Wingate-thing asked. "And the seed grain does not remain in the soil, in the dark. It sprouts and blooms."

"Like the creatures you are growing in your zombie greenhouse? Like the hungry locusts you are unleashing upon the city?"

"What has the city got to do with you?" the Wingate-thing asked. "You belong here, Kara. Here, in the country."

Hearing him mispronouncing her name was like having a rusty blade scrape the surface of her brain. But paradoxically, the pain centered her.

"It's all a ruse," she said. "A trap, laid by you and whoever your new master is. Because you're just a servant, James Wingate, a wage slave, whether you're dead, or alive, or something in-between. Your damned zombies would have killed me long ago if they could. But they can't. I'm their predator. They are as afraid of me as a flock of starlings is of a hawk. You know I'll try to defend the city from the Hungry Ones! Who knows, I may even succeed. And what if I discover what has made me what I am and learn to make more predators like myself? All this claptrap about the despoliation of the land and the crimes of the city is simply to make me roll over and die!"

"You're good at survival, Kara," the Wingate-thing said acidly, "nobody gainsays that! But do you really think the city will welcome you? You're not a citizen and you'll never be. The lowliest toad is more than you! You're country born and bred. This is where you belong. What is the city to you?"

Kora closed her eyes and saw the glittering splendor of the

flambeaus on the slender towers in the dusk, felt the invigorating bustle of the Market, saw the inhuman face of Irene the knitter turned toward her…

And Adam, flesh of the city's flesh.

Daniel…

Don't think of Daniel!

She opened her eyes.

"No," she said. "There is nothing for me here. It is all gone, all dead. The city is alive."

"Not for long, Kara," the creature said. "And you're quite wrong. We are not afraid of you. The Nestling is not afraid. You eat Hungry Ones, true, because your hunger is greater than theirs. But can you eat *this*?"

The door of the office swung open.

They emerged out of the smoke, developing like an image on a waking flambeau: indistinct smudges first, flat silhouettes next, three-dimensional presences in a heartbeat. They encircled the Hunter and Agatha, silent, seemingly staring away from them because their eyes were set into the sides of their heads.

Agatha made a strangled little sound as the Hunter pressed his palm against her mouth. His paralysis was gone; he gaze flitting from one khrut to the next as he counted them in his head. He noted their identical dappled feathers.

Finally, one of them spoke, his guttural words interspersed with throaty clicks.

"This is a proscribed village. You leave."

Agatha squirmed, freed herself, and unleashed a stream of indignant exclamations wrapped around a request for the khruts to show their papers! Birdmen could not laugh but their clicking sounds came close as they responded to her bravado.

"We are City Guards!" one of them said.

The Hunter finally found the words he needed.

"You are not!" he said.

The khruts exchanged twitting sounds as he pointed at them.

"You the same," he pronounced, groping for a way to string the words together. "Guards different. You rogues!"

The khruts who lived in the city succumbed quickly to its metamorphic influence and grew diverse, some more humanoid, some bird-shaped. Even within the same flight the differences would be striking. The uniformity of these khruts' appearances indicated they were of the country.

Another wave of twittering and clucking swept over the khruts. The speaker addressed him directly:

"You from the city? A toad or a duck?"

"A man!" the Hunter cried indignantly. "I am a man!"

Agatha laughed at the khrut.

"You blind? Does he look like a duck to you, you dumb bird?"

She was a country girl, and a duck to her was a creature swimming in the pond; a toad – something hopping in the grass. He was a citizen, on the other hand, he knew what the khrut meant, and was outraged at the insult. Couldn't he see…?

And then the slabs of his shoulders sagged as he saw himself reflected in the birdman's eyes, the hulking, stooping mass of him.

"I am a man," he repeated, still defiant. "A citizen. Not a tenant."

The khruts were staring at him now, all of them, their beady eyes the color of sloes and raisins.

"Come with us," the speaker finally said. "We won't hurt you. It is a dead place, a bad place. You can't stay here."

"Should we go?" Agatha whispered.

"We need humans," the khrut said. "We feed you."

He did not understand this but it did not matter. His path was clear now.

He would have to come back here, to this graveyard of a village. This was his hunting ground. This is where he would find his prey.

But not now. The smell of burning was overpowering, the smoke as thick as twilight. Birdmen could fly over the fire, but they would be caught. And Agatha was with him. She came first.

"We go," he said.

The door flew off the hinges. The thing that was behind it stepped into the room.

It looked like a two-legged spider: a rounded leathery sack tottering on spindly limbs, the equally thin boneless arms attached to its top. Its sagging body was its face: the toothed maw opening where the genitals should have been, the blinking eyes set crookedly in place of the nipples.

It was one of the creatures from the greenhouse but grown perambulatory and agile. Its tentacle swiped at Kora and she felt the sting of broken flesh, skin parting with a drip of blood. Her energy flowed to the creature; nothing flowed back.

Kora caught the edge of a filing cabinet and shoved it toward the Hungry One. The cabinet fell over, the paperwork fluttering in the air like many-winged moths. It slowed the creature for a moment, while she turned to Wingate and clasped him in her arms as firmly as a lover.

He was almost dead. But not quite as dead as the creature that flailed among the spilled receipts and memos. Death in the country was as gradual and complicated as life. Death had many stages and many forms.

She gulped his vitality and choked on it because it was as rancid as spoiled milk. But, when hungry, one feeds on offal. Hunger has no pride.

Wingate clawed at her. She shoved him at the Hungry One and the two of them tangled on the floor. The horrible thing was that, except for the rustle of paper, the room was silent, the twice-dead Hungry One having apparently lost the constant keening of its partially alive brethren. And Wingate…perhaps he no longer knew that people cried out in distress.

Powered by the dregs of Wingate's rotten vitality, Kora jumped onto the window sill, shattered the casement, and leaped out. She was running the moment her feet barely touched the ground, through smoke and bitter fog, away from the compound where Wingate and his new employer were growing their experimental crop. She was bitten, scratched, and burned but her injuries were healing fast. The aftershock of pain lingered for a while and then faded. The ache in her mind remained.

Chapter 8. The Khrut Village

The Hunter was shocked at how brutish and uncivilized the khruts' colony was: a pitiful cross between a village and a nesting sight, combining the worst of both. He distrusted all birdmen, even though he was not sure why. Now, he felt justified in despising them.

The colony was in a small valley bordered on one side by a range of low hills overgrown with wild mustard and parasol-shaped white flowers. On the other side stretched marshlands, still wreathed with what appeared to be smoke, even though he saw no sign of a grass fire. There were no trees anywhere. Perhaps they had been cut down to build the shaggy platform on which the khruts had erected their dwellings. They were tiny windowless cabins and untidy lean-to's, squeezed together and on top of each other without rhyme or reason. The platform and its foundations were streaked with white guano. A sluggish creek wound through the plain, a cane-bristling ribbon of shallow water.

The khruts were few in number. The flight that had brought him and Agatha in seemed to comprise the majority of the adult population. Several chicks flapped and scrabbled around the platform, and he looked at them curiously: he had never seen an immature khrut. They could not fly yet and looked like wizened rickety infants, their arms curving into sickle-like shapes and fringed with feathers, their pale thick skin dotted with red pustules where the adult plumage was pushing out. Their faces were more human-like than those of the adults, the nose and mouth not yet fused into a beak.

Agatha gaped at the whole thing with undisguised curiosity and her youthful resilience perked him up. The pain of losing her was almost too much to bear; and yet he could not see any way around it.

The nav of the flight, who introduced himself with a borrowed human name Vassily, offered them some grain mush. This hospitality made the Hunter suspicious. Clearly, the birdmen wanted something from them. But what?

It became clearer when Vassily explained the colony's situation to them – or at least tried to. His speech was not exactly clear (*who am I to complain?* the Hunter thought with a rare flash of self-deprecating humor). Still, it was better than that of his fellows, some of whom seemed to be able to communicate in the birdmen's clacking language only.

Apparently, the perpetually squabbling country khruts were being mobilized into a ragged army by some self-appointed leader. The leader's name was delivered in a succession of clicks and trills but Vassily tried to explain its meaning by pointing to a tottering child. Chick? Nestling? Neither made much sense.

In any case, a khrut army was being raised to attack the city. The Hunter was shocked when he heard it and so was Agatha. She did not hold back.

"Treason!" she cried. "Grandfather will punish you!"

Vassily trilled a sharp response whose meaning required no translation. The birdmen had always been notoriously resistant to the cult of the legendary human leader.

But in the case of Vassily's small colony, they had no desire to join the khrut army either. He was evasive about the reasons, but the Hunter gathered that they had sent their finest young to serve as Guards in the city and that their scraggly settlement survived only thanks to the money and provisions that flowed back from their prosperous kin.

Vassily also wanted to know what the Hunter and Agatha were doing in the uncertain lands so close to the Divide. The Hunter was surprised to hear of the Divide having a precise location.

Not sure how to lie his way out of it (since the truth was

unthinkable to reveal), he let Agatha handle the situation, which she did with an aplomb that instantly increased his admiration for her. Not only did she make up stories on the spot, but she displayed a genuine flair for lying. She spun a fast tale of loss and reunion, in which the Hunter played the role of her fiancé who had been to the city and come back just in time to save his beloved from the attack of the Hungry Ones that killed everybody else in the village. This part, at least, was true; and there was enough grief in Agatha's voice to lend the aura of sincerity to the rest of her unlikely story. The Hunter was afraid that the birdman would question their obvious age disparity but perhaps khruts knew as little about human mating habits as humans did about theirs.

She even came up with a name for him. She had asked him several times before, but he had refused to answer. Now, she blithely christened him Reggie, which was as unsuitable a designation as anything he could imagine. That would be a name for a rich wastrel from…yes, from up-levels! He was proud that the address popped into his head. Agatha, meanwhile, continued her flowery recital that seemed borrowed from some cheap romance. Vassily listened attentively and did not appear to doubt her.

She said they were making their way to the village of Lotus Pond where she had a cousin but that they lost their way in the smoke.

"What is burning?" the Hunter butted in.

"Fields," Vassily replied. "Firestalkers. Setting fields on fire."

The Hunter was astonished. Firestalkers were rogue flambeaus but, like all flambeaus, they belonged in the city.

At some point, Vassily decided he could trust them. Rummaging under the filthy mats on the floor of his hut, he produced the things that had prompted him to share his meager food with the two humans. And seeing them, the Hunter felt a chill creep down between his hunched shoulder-blades.

Kora limped along the dusty path that wound between overgrown hedges. The tangle of wild raspberry and thorny dwarfish trees spilled into the track, almost blocking the way. The air was still suffused with smoke. The sky was white and lifeless: no khruts or birds, not even insects buzzing over her head. The countryside was exhausted like a woman drained by uncontrollable miscarriages.

She was ravenously hungry again. The healing power that had covered her burns with fresh pink skin and stopped the flow of blood from bites and scratches had also depleted her resources. Her body was screaming for sustenance, overpowering her mind like a mad horse shaking and dragging its rider. It occurred to her that every thinking being was chained to its own Hungry One.

A rustle in the hedge, a whisper of sound. She stopped. Something was scrabbling through the bushes. An animal?

She had never seen animals in the city. In the place where everything was alive and potentially sentient, the flesh destined to be eaten had to come from somewhere else. She had seen meat in the Market and assumed it came from the country. Now, she realized that, with the exception of some birds and lizards, the countryside seemed to be stripped of animal life as well.

She stopped, silent and alert, a poised predator.

The scrambling in the hedge grew louder. And then a flapping shape fell onto the path. It was a chicken-sized bird with drab brownish plumage and an awl-shaped beak. One of its wings hung out, clumsy and broken.

It could have been a wild bird. It could have been a khrut-fowl. Or anything in-between.

Kora grabbed the bird, felt the rapidly beating heart in its soft breast. Its round black eye met hers. And without giving it time to speak, if it could, Kora drunk it, brutally and unreservedly, not holding back until the black eye was dimmed by the glaze of death and the rapid pulse dwindled to nothing. And then she tossed the bundle of feathers aside and walked on.

"'Arms!" Agatha whispered, awed, staring at the pair of skin-colored gloves.

The Hunter nodded warily. They were newer and healthier than the old exhausted things he had seen in her village.

Vassily pushed them toward the two humans with the tip of his clawed finger. The Hunter picked one up. It was pink and moist, newly hatched. Had the colony's urban kin managed to smuggle them out for the protection of their rural relatives?

If they had, they were stupid. Khruts could not wear 'arms. Nobody but humans could.

Agatha's face lit up with excitement as she caressed the soft tegument. The 'arm stirred under her fingers.

The Hunter dropped his.

"You'll defend us," Vassily said. "When the army comes. We give you food."

The Hunter shrugged.

"Fine," he said.

The life in the colony was so finely poised on the edge of starvation as to be indistinguishable from a slow death. It surprised the Hunter who thought of the birdmen as raiders preying upon the human villagers. But, now, he realized that if the prey was starving, so did the predator. The city, with its explosive growth, had sucked the country dry.

There were some pitiful vegetable patches around the colony but khruts were not agriculturalists. In olden times, as Vassily put it, as if speaking of some unimaginably distant past, they had hunted together with their bird-kin. Or had they hunted their bird-kin? His language skills were so rudimentary as to make both interpretations equally likely.

But, as human villages spread around the countryside and covered it with fields and orchards, their hunting-ground dwindled. Many khruts migrated to the city where they became Guards. And then they would be sent back to the country to squeeze food requisitions from the villagers. They were also supposed to protect them from the depredations of their wild cousins but knowing the birdmen's clannishness, the Hunter had no doubt that it was more likely the Guards colluded with the country khruts to strip away whatever was left of the harvest. In fact, he knew it to be the case but preferred not to think about it. Being with the khruts disturbed him deeply in a way that he could not articulate to himself and did not want to. He would have left immediately were it not for Agatha.

He could not leave her alone with the birdmen. If they decided they had no use for her, they would toss her into the desolate marshlands where the Divide was supposed to be hiding in plain sight. Or worse: they were meat-eaters, after all.

Nor could he take her with him. He knew now where the spoor of his lost prey led. The horror of returning to that empty spot sowed by despair was only mitigated for him by the inevitability of doing so. But, he could not lead Agatha back to Edenberry.

He procrastinated, not knowing what to do. At least they were only marginally hungry: Vassily shared grain mush with them and even let them occupy his hut (he slept with the rest of the adults in a pile of feathered bodies; khruts had little use for privacy). In the hut, the Hunter found several shiny trinkets, including an old sliver of mirror. He stared at what he had become for a long time.

He did not quite remember his face, but he knew it had been handsome. Women had thrown themselves at him; men had wanted to be his friends.

Now, he was looking at beetling brow-ridges above eyes set so deep in dark-ringed sockets that their color was impossible to determine. The muddy irises bled into the red sclera. The mouth was a mere slash above the heavy asymmetrical jaw. The entire face looked like a crude effigy chipped out of granite, and the pebbly skin also resembled unpolished stonework, all strange protrusions and rough patches. And below the wattled neck...he did not even want to look.

He tried to remember how it happened, but all he could conjure up was a smudged image of pungent smoke, oily flesh, and pain. The pain was the only reality; everything else might have been a nightmare. And he no longer had the words to tell himself a coherent story of who he had been and what he had become, a story that would fix the slippery images into an orderly progression of events. He no longer even had his name, though he was aware that it lay somewhere close to the surface in his word-chest. But he did not want to rummage in it because it would only bring up more pain, more regrets, more memories of intolerable smells and sharp teeth biting into his deliquescing flesh. He had a moniker given to him by Agatha and he accepted it because it bore no resemblance to his real name.

Chapter 9. The New 'Arm

She realized she was walking in circles.

It was impossible. The land was as flat as a pancake. There were no mountains, hardly even a hill. The upswelling of rock known as the Peak from whose mighty shoulders the city fell like a mantle was hidden beyond the horizon. The dry fields, dotted with thorny bushes and an occasional dwarf tree, stretched as far as the eye could see. The unpaved road ran ruler-straight.

And yet Kora had passed the remnant of a collapsed fence. She knew it was the same fence because a face was scratched into a post, a face with dark holes for eyes and a toothless screaming mouth.

She stopped and looked up at the sun. The sky was still veiled with thin parchment-like clouds, but the sun showed as a bleached orb. She should be able to identify east and west.

Until she realized the sun had been stuck in the same place for longer than she cared to remember.

She sat by the fence and tried to think. The screaming face leered over her. She touched it. The face had been carved in the soft, rotting wood with some sharp instrument and the grooves filled with a dark substance. It had been done recently.

The countryside surrounded the city on all sides. To the north, it was cut and gouged by some cataclysm, broken by fissures filled with boiling water and ash. Nobody went there. But, in the other directions, the land was flat and fertile. One could walk as far as one wanted – or so it seemed, until one would find oneself at the starting point. Or perhaps not find oneself at all. People, both humans and tenants, disappeared the further one went from the city. The countryside, so vulnerable in its simplicity, was roamed by…something. A force? A place? A confusion? A guardian?

The Divide.

Grandfather and his people were supposed to have come from beyond it. And so was she, Kora, even though in letting her through, the Divide had erased all memories of its nature, even of its existence. This perhaps was not so surprising. As Adam had hinted, the Divide bent time as much as space. People in the city thought the Incoming was part of recent history. Some, like Old Van, even claimed to have been participants in it. But, villagers in the countryside believed it had taken place in some legendary past. As far as they were concerned, the city had always existed and they had always paid taxes to it.

It was impossible to find the Divide, Adam had said. It found you instead. And since it had singled Kora out as it had done to no other human since Grandfather, perhaps it would do so again. Then, they could find the portal through which the Hungry Ones were coming to attack the city – if indeed they were coming through the Divide, which Kora no longer believed. But she realized that Adam had risked abandoning his political machinations in the city to embark on this open-ended quest through the countryside with her because he counted on the pliancy of time. Likely no longer than a week or so had passed in the city since they had left, and the Mayoral election was still a year into the future.

But, whatever Adam's calculations had been, he was no longer with her. She was alone. And the Divide, invisible though it may be, was crouching somewhere close, breathing heavily like a beast about to pounce upon her. About to reveal what she wanted to stay hidden. About to make her remember.

Kora got up.

There was only so much you can run away from, she told herself. *At some point, the track circles back.*

She touched the carving again and stared at the residue on her fingertips. Somebody had bled to make this sign. Was it a warning?

No matter. She was afraid of no monsters. She was a predator, a zombie-eater. The only monsters that could tear her to pieces were in her own mind.

Kora stretched her muscles, feeling supple strength flow back into her body. And then she started walking again.

Agatha loved the 'arms Vassily had given them: two flesh-colored gloves, ridged and wrinkled, ready to mold themselves to any hand. To any human hand, to be precise.

'Arms were actually toads, or so it was said. But, they were as nearly mindless as to make it possible to treat them as mere objects. Properly fitted, they would draw sustenance from their wearer and provide weapons of both aggression and defense. Different kinds of 'arms worked differently: some could project electric discharge, strong enough to kill a being of average size; some – like the ones the hetman of Agatha's village had used – could elongate into claw-tipped tentacles and slashing appendages. The electric ones were rarer and more tightly regulated: officially, only City Corps could wear them, even though the Triads in the Market had stockpiles of illegal ones.

Vassily's 'arms were of a more common hand-combat variety. They had not been cared for properly – something that the Hunter set out immediately to rectify. 'Arms could be deadly, but they were also delicate. They had to be cleaned regularly with pure water and carefully dried. They also had to be worn often, even if not used. Well, to be fair, this particular requirement could not be satisfied in the khrut colony. Khruts could not wear 'arms. No tenant could. In the militia, this meant that only human recruits could hope to reach officer grades. The City Corps did not bother to recruit tenants at all.

The Hunter stroked the soft hide. His fingers remembered the feeling of the velvety padding closing gently over his hand, molding itself to its contours, becoming one with his own flesh…

Agatha was watching him, her baby face aglow with curiosity. He offered her one of the 'arms.

"Put it on!" he said.

"Me?"

"Why not?"

Women wore 'arms as readily as men. Traditionally, there were more women in City Corps than in the militia but, in both bodies, female recruits were routinely trained in the use of, and outfitted with, 'arms. As long as they were human, of course.

She touched the fleshy glove, her kittenish tongue licking her lips.

"Put it on!" the Hunter urged.

She did, pulling it up with a short, snappy gesture. The glove flapped for a second on her small hand and then contracted sharply, outlining every knuckle and crease, the line of separation on the wrist fading. Except for the slightly darker color, her right hand now looked the same as her left. Agatha drew in breath and slowly made a fist, opened it, made it again, enchanted by the double sensation the Hunter remembered well: his own sense of touch overlaid and enhanced by the sparkly prickling of the second skin.

The next step was harder. One had to learn to command the 'arm mentally while treating it as if it were a part of one's own body. Some never mastered this technique properly. The Hunter rummaged in his word-chest, trying to scrounge up enough language to explain this complicated concept to Agatha when something buzzed by his head. He ducked automatically and stared in wonder at the pink tentacle snapping back and forth from Agatha's palm like a frog's tongue. She giggled, playing with it like a child with a new toy.

"Watch out!" the Hunter growled, filled with new respect for his companion.

He showed her the simple techniques of shaping the projection, enhancing its desired qualities – rigidity, sharpness, or stickiness – and calming the 'arm into a quiescent state when not needed. She was a natural, grasping his explanations instantly, cutting through the clumsy web of words to the kernel of meaning. By the end of their short session, she was as good as any of his former mates.

He crumpled up the second 'arm and shoved it into his pocket. There was no need for him to try it on, he told himself. He knew how to use it.

The road ran straight through the insipid terrain of yellowish grass and spindly weeds. No harvest in the fields, no animals grazing in paddocks, no people working the land. The quality of light was changing, getting murkier, as if ink was slowly spreading in the stale air. A smudge of gloom was spreading toward the zenith from the horizon on all sides of her in shades of purple and grey like a bruise. A tide of darkness, a circle of twilight. With her in the center.

Kora thought something was wrong with her eyes. Then, she realized something was wrong with the world. The horizon was shrinking, coming closer to her. It was as if she was standing at the bottom of a giant cup and its sides were curving out and over her. The lowering sky above her head still dripped dim light but around her, a wall of dusk was growing, cutting off the normal perspective, imprisoning her in a hushed, small, impossible space.

The rising darkness was not uniform. To Kora's right, it was denser and complexly layered, crawling with branching and intertwined strands like seaweed in polluted water. She strained her eyes but could not make out anything definite. The circle of gray light above her head was inexorably shrinking. The road ahead was stippled with shadows.

Suddenly, there was a flapping of wings above her head, as shocking as a scream. She instinctively covered her head with her hands.

"I am here!" Dividing-the-Divide trilled sweetly.

Kora lowered her arms and stared at the khrut-fowl. She was not exactly happy to see her, but her unexpected appearance signified that Kora was not as cut off from her companions as she had thought. Was Adam close?

"Where is the train?" she asked.

"I lead," the khrut-fowl sang, setting Kora's teeth on edge. "I lead you through. Dividing-the-Divide. Sooner-or-Later. Near-or-Far!"

"Where is the bloody train?!" Kora yelled.

"We are near! The Divide is near! Look!"

And she looked.

It was not only the sky that was tenting like a sheet of paper. The entire landscape rippled and elongated as if seen through a distorting lens. The space curved around her until she stood in a tunnel with the walls made of the darkened fields and the ceiling made of the gloomy sky. Only the road under her feet was still flat. The air was losing its transparency, filling with a muddy and purplish suspension like a very fine particulate. And with it came a smell of stagnant water and rotting things.

Something teased her sight, hiding in plain view like writing in invisible ink. A darker stain on the diseased duskiness of the distorted sky.

And, finally, she saw it. A gargantuan thicket of thorns.

"Lead on!" she said.

The army came when they were asleep.

The Hunter emerged from his dreaming, instantly awake and alert. For a long and blessed time, he had been free of dreams, but they had recently started again. They were mostly incomprehensible: a montage of filmy insubstantial images, like this latest one, composed of thorns and spiky shadows, filthy water and long hairy roots swaying in its depth.

At first, he thought it had been khruts' mating outside. He

had seen them do it before, to his total disgust, out in the open like dumb beasts, in full view of khrut-chicks. It involved some ridiculous dancing ritual, the male handing the female a cup filled with Grandfather-knows-what…but he did not stay to watch. Blushing furiously, he grabbed Agatha and pulled her away despite her giggling protests. Behind their backs, there was energetic clacking and loud rustling of feathers.

It sounded like this now but amplified a thousand times, a long uninterrupted noise of swooshing air. Their high-perched hut creaked and swayed.

He sat up. Agatha slept beside him, her face smooth and baby-like in the bright moonlight. The noise outside picked up. For a confused moment, he thought he was back in the city, the night traffic streaming in and out of the Market…

Vassily burst through the door-curtain, his feathers bristling. He was so agitated he seemed to forget human speech, issuing a rapid burst of twittering instead. The Hunter pushed by him and clung to the flimsy doorframe, awed by the view outside.

The night was alive. The rosy harvest moon flooded the fields with handfuls of light and shadow. The shadows streamed past him like a river, all in one direction. As he looked up, he could see what cast them.

Flying low above the tiny village was flight after flight of khruts. As their sharply etched silhouettes passed by the screen of the moon, they displayed their multiform shapes, from the standard winged-man to the humped, twisted, spread-eagled bodies that seemed impossible to lift into the air. And yet they all flew with the military precision, each flight led by its nav. There were more of them than the Hunter had ever imagined flocking together. And there was no mystery as to what their goal was. The city could not be seen from where they were, but the Hunter knew its location as well as he knew the location of his own limbs.

More hysterical twittering and clacking from Vassily. The

Hunter swerved around and squeezed his hand around the birdman's beak, silencing him.

"Shut up!" he hissed. "Lay low and they won't land!"

"Reggie!" This came from inside the hut, Agatha calling him by his pretend name.

The flight that was passing above them broke formation, its members – smallish, fowl-like things – wheeling above their heads, dipping low. The Hunter hissed at her to be quiet, but it was too late. She blundered into the moonlight, her smock hitching up above her bare knees, her right hand clenched.

The flight of six landed on the platform that sagged dangerously under their combined weight. Each of the khruts was no bigger than a ten-year-old, their heads crested with a huge bony sail, their toothed beaks gaping, their meager bodies supported on surprisingly shapely human-like legs. The Hunter was sure he could cope with them. But the seemingly unending stream of the khrut army above showed no signs of abating and if other flights came down…

Vassily struggled in the Hunter's arms and he released him, hoping the village chieftain would be able to say something to make his kin go away. Instead, he let loose a fearful squawk and dived off the platform into the melee of shadows.

The Hunter opened his mouth and no words came out. He made a vague gesture that he hoped meant peace. The small khruts dipped their crests but did not attack. One of them tottered forward, his skinny wings unfolding. The Hunter raised his opened and empty hands toward him…and then something swooshed past him and hit the khrut in the face, a supple tentacle winding around his scrawny body, lifting him off the platform and tossing him down, his wings broken.

Agatha! Her face was scrunched up in childish concentration as her 'arm, elongated into a formidable claw-tipped weapon, snaked through the silvery air, slashing and flailing. The Hunter let loose a roar that startled her and made her curl up the 'arm but it was too late. The khruts attacked, making coughing-like noises. The commotion attracted the attention of the khruts above, and several flights broke formation and circled back toward the village, their members folding their wings and plummeting down like black fruit off a shaken tree.

The Hunter pushed Agatha back into the hut and planted himself at the entrance. When the first crested khrut tried to bite him, he easily wrung the creature's neck and tossed him off the platform. But, all the while, his brain was working feverishly on how to de-escalate the confrontation.

He slammed another khrut against the doorframe and ducked back into the hut. The flight was between them and the shaky ladder to the ground. But, there was another way down and if they could just slink away, disappear into the rushes along the creek, lie low until the army had passed…He gave no thought to the khruts of the village, but if he did, he would reckon they were safe from their kin who clearly had a grander target to attack. In that he would be wrong.

Growling an order at Agatha to stand watch at the door, which she obeyed instantly, he struck with his fist at the thin wattle-and-daub back wall of the hut. It shook but did not break. Agatha laid another attacker low with a precise swipe of her 'arm. He struck again and punched a ragged hole. Grasping Agatha's hand, he dove with her through the hole. A sharp toothed beak snapped at his ankle and took a bite. He remembered that he also had an 'arm but it was too late to put it on.

The back wall of the hut was flush with the edge of the platform. It was too high for flightless creatures to jump. But yesterday he had tied a rope to the edge, prompted by an uneasy intuition that having another way out might be a good idea. Holding Agatha in the crook of one arm, he slid down the rope, taking a layer of skin off his palm but barely noticing the pain. Another croak, and he was attacked by a swirling, pecking cloud of even smaller khrut-fowls. They hit the ground and Agatha instantly engaged her 'arm, using it like a whip to pick khrut-fowls out of the air.

"Your 'arm!" she shouted at him and he knew she was right. The commotion was attracting the attention of bigger birdmen flying above. He pulled the balled 'arm out of his pocket, shook it out and slipped it onto his bleeding right hand. It squeezed as tight as a vise. The flash of pain was almost unbearable, frighteningly new to his experience, but in a second, he felt the familiar bonding sensation as if a forgotten limb suddenly announced its presence. It took!

He made the 'arm grow into a spear-point and impaled a khrut-fowl, shook it off, impaled another. And, all the while, he had been slowly retreating toward the creek, pulling Agatha with him, seeking shadows, glancing fearfully at the seething sky.

Apparently, the navs of bigger flights decided that a clash in an insignificant village was not worth a delay. The river of wings was still streaming through the black sky toward the city, only occasionally breaking into back eddies. But, the crested khruts and a flock of khrut-fowls were on the ground already. He could smell their angry stink. Clumps of bodies rose and fell like smoke amidst the trembling platform-posts. He blinked, cursing his worsening eyesight, another human birthright that had been – *stolen?* – from him.

No one pursued them. He kept sidling toward the belt of wild raspberries along the banks of the creeks. There were no woods in this blighted land, but there was a tiny copse downstream and if they could just get there, hunker down, lie low…

Another khrut-fowl flew at them and he swatted it out of the air with his 'arm. A shock-wave of pain traveled up and lodged in his shoulder. He winced and let Agatha kill the next one. The girl was fighting cleanly and adroitly, her lips pursed as if she were puzzling over her homework.

A din of squawking, croaking, and almost-human screaming

rose up from the platform. A couple of crested khruts who were trotting toward them hesitated, looked back, and took to the air to join the melee. The Hunter seized the opportunity and dragged Agatha toward the thicket.

They huddled in the cage of thorny brambles for an eternity, listening to the splashing of the creek and the screams of the dying village. Agatha fell asleep. The Hunter blew off gnats and mosquitoes that landed on her exposed flesh. He spent the time trying to tug off his 'arm. It would not budge. The blood of the rope-burn melded it to his skin. His only consolation was that it apparently recognized him as human enough to bond. On the other hand, it would not obey his mental commands. Could 'arms go rogue? He had never heard of such a thing, but in the world where an army of rebellious khruts was on its way to attack the city, anything was possible.

Finally, the dawn broke. Agatha woke up and smiled at him. Her face was the colors of the new day: pink and white.

They scrambled out of the thicket and stood together, surveying what was left of the khrut villages. The bodies of Vassily and other adults were strewn among the listing platforms, pecked to death, their eyes gouged. The khrut-chicks were little more than bloody skeletons. There was no sign of the assailants except piles of guano.

Chapter 10. The Marshland

The perspective shifted again. The land rose up in a wave whose crest was the road she was trudging on, then fell on both sides in indistinct rippling slopes that disappeared into darkness. Kora felt as if she was walking on a narrow bridge over an abyss. Her fear of heights kicked in and she hunched over, moving in mincing little steps.

The presence of Dividing-the-Divide provided little support. Despite her name, the khrut-fowl refused to fly. She hunched on Kora's shoulder, her talons tangled in the fabric of her shirt.

And then the road petered out.

Kora stopped, the tide of darkness lapping at her scuffed boots. It did not look like water or soil anymore: just a viscous, vicious mass of murk. She looked back and saw the curving bubble of black air. She shook the khrut-fowl off her shoulder.

"What the fuck do I do now?" she yelled.

Dividing-the-Divide flapped into the air. She was instantly magnified by the distorted space into a giant shadow, filling the entire "tunnel" with her beating wings. But as she flew on, the road reappeared.

Kora stared down in wonder. The road unspooled from under her feet in the wake of the khrut-fowl's passage. And while the rest of the Divide remained a cauldron of gloom, the firm surface of the road was clearly visible, as if giving off illumination of its own.

She stepped onto the new road and followed the khrut-fowl. The space around her writhed and contorted, expanded and contracted, teased her with hints of whipping branches, scudding clouds, convulsing bodies. The purplish haze stung her eyes; her nose was assaulted by a rotten reek; a whisper of a thousand voices hovered on the edge of her hearing, promising to say words that would drive her mad. But she refused to look, refused to smell, refused to listen. She just trudged on.

It took forever. The sun was gone; her inner clock had stopped. And still she went on.

And then a pale light spilled onto the road. It was as dim as the twilight of a cloudy day but compared to the darkness before, it felt overwhelmingly bright. She blinked, looked around.

Spatial distortions were gone; the land again stretched on both sides of her in the same flat expanse as before. But, instead of dry fields, she was surrounded by a low-lying marsh with rank tangles of greenery soaking in puddles of inky water. The rotten smell remained, though toned down to the natural intensity of a swamp.

There was no sun, no moon or stars. The sky was of a uniform slate-gray as if very heavily overcast but she could discern no clouds. Wherever she was, there was no day or night here. Just this maddening twilight, the fifth time of day, the never-ending hour of despair.

Dividing-the-Divide was huddling a couple of steps ahead, as indifferent as a barn owl. But, as Kora walked on, she rose into the air again and made the road appear as she flew.

The land was becoming more and more soaked, dotted with pools of foul-smelling water interspersed with the dark green of sedges and marsh-grass. The road was cutting through a dank labyrinth of channels and puddles, clumps of giant cattails, and tangled mats of some bubble-leaved plant. But it remained as dry as a bone.

Kora stooped and felt the road. It had been beaten earth and occasional cobbled stretch, but now it was something else. The surface under her fingers reminded her of an insect carapace, hard and faintly ridged. It was slick as if she were walking on chitin.

At least there was something ahead that could pass for a destination. The thorny thicket reappeared – or maybe it was another one; it was impossible to make out any details in the terrible light. But, there was a swollen tangle of shadows ahead of her, looking like a cloud-bank pregnant with a storm, unmoving despite the gusty, chilly wind which made her shiver in her city clothes.

She was trying to remember whether she had ever walked the road before. But, her memory was still occluded. She wondered for how long.

But there was nothing to do except to go on, toward whatever unbearable revelation awaited her at the end of the road. It emerged from the marsh in the wake of the khrut-fowl's flight and submerged again after she passed, so she was actually walking on a sliding stretch of pavement no more than fifteen meters long. It reminded her of the trains' method of locomotion and she felt a pang when she thought about Adam. Was he concerned about her? Was he thinking of her at all?

But Adam seemed unimaginably distant. Time, as well as space, was a plaything of the Divide. She did not know how long she had been walking. All she knew is that she was walking into the past.

The landscape around her was subtly changing, becoming even more grotesque. It was still a marshland but every part of it was metamorphosing into a caricature of its natural counterpart. The canes and cattails were gaunt, skeletal things that swished and dipped, even though the wind had died down. The pools of coffee-colored water roiled and bubbled. And the ground cover was now composed of a single species: a succulent plant, so swollen with juice that it looked ready to burst, its hand-shaped leaves colored splotchy green and filthy red.

Despite all this diseased lushness, there was no sign of animal life: no gnats buzzed in the dirty air, no birds other than Dividing-the-Divide cleaved the somber sky, no frogs or fish splashed in the water. But the smell of decay intensified. And it was not just the rotting vegetation; there was an unmistakable sweetish tang to the smell that told of the presence of dead flesh.

Suddenly, she wished passionately to be back in the Market, holed up in Irene's shop, falling asleep under the knitted blankets, listening to the unending buzz of the city…Why had she tried to find out who she was? Why had she gone back to the chairman? She could have vanished into the Market like so many had done before, found a small niche in its complicated ecology, hidden her gift – or her curse…

And then she remembered her meeting with Daniel and knew that her past – whatever it was – would have caught up with her. Even repeating his name in her mind brought up such a complicated slew of emotions that she automatically increased her speed as if to run away from herself.

Until the tips of her boots slid into the mud and she realized that the emergence and submergence of the road had stopped. She was marooned on a sliver of firm land surrounded by mud and succulents. And her guide was nowhere to be seen.

Kora swore. The sound of her voice came back to her as an inhuman croak, even though there was nothing here that could cast back an echo. She clapped her hand to her mouth.

She should call to the khrut-fowl, but somehow, she knew it would be of no use unless she could sing the creature's true name – and she could not sing.

Gingerly, she stepped into the marsh and was instantly engulfed in the peaty water up to her thighs. Giving an involuntary yelp, she scrambled back to the remnant of the road, shaking like a wet dog.

She squinted into the leaden dusk of the Divide and could see nothing. The grungy sky above was as empty and pitiless as a coffin lid.

And then she saw a coruscating spark in a clump of canes. For a moment, she thought it was an optical illusion brought about by light-starvation. But then the spark returned and was joined by others, all of different colors: citron, rose, amethyst.

They winked into being, scattered all over the dour marshland like drowned constellations.

The light was joined by a sound: the flapping of wings.

Dividing-the-Divide was back. She landed on the marsh and dipped her head like a heron spearing a frog. She picked up a sparkling jewel in her beak. But she did not swallow. Instead, with a sharp flick of her head, she tossed it onto her back. The khrut-fowl repeated it several times until she was festooned with beads of multicolored radiance. The light they shed was strong enough to dapple the black surface of the mire with bright reflections.

She hopped toward Kora, her drab plumage studded with luminescent creatures the size of a coin that crawled through the ruffled feathers. It was both beautiful and grotesque, as if the khrut-bird was infested with giant rainbow-bright ticks.

These were not ticks, though, but miniature flambeaus. Kora stared, spellbound. In the city, she had never seen flambeaus that small!

Either because the flambeaus were heavier than they appeared or for some other reason, Dividing-the-Divide declined to live up to her name by flying. First, she scuttled ahead with a pigeon-like gait and then leaped into Kora's arms. This was not pleasant. Kora hated the touch of her feathers and at closer inspection, the tiny flambeaus, for all their gorgeous luminescence, looked distinctly tick-like.

A stench hit her, burning her sinuses. She coughed and covered her nose. The smell was suffocating, as if a whole cemetery was suddenly stripped of its protective layer of dirt.

A sluggish creek cut the marshland ahead and the road stopped at its bank. There was a whitish structure looming in the fog. It looked like a pile of driftwood.

The sodden soil squished under her feet as she went down to the creek. The stench intensified until it almost choked her. Standing before the structure, Kora thrust the khrut-fowl with its festooning flambeaus forward like a torch, rainbow lights glittering with ominous festivity.

The towering thing was a made object rather than a random pile of driftwood. A carefully arranged structure of interlocking parts – a cenotaph. Made of bones.

The bones were scrubbed clean, scrapes and cutting marks still visible. It was not natural decay that flensed off the flesh so thoroughly. The bodies had been butchered. There were no skulls – the makers of the cenotaph had taken them away – but Kora had no difficulty identifying the bones as human.

"Was there a battle here?" she asked of Dividing-the-Divide and got no answer.

Grandfather and his people must have come this way. But perhaps the Incoming was not as triumphant as everybody seemed to believe. Perhaps the land had not welcomed the intruders. Were they ambushed here? And what had really happened when they got to the city?

But the terrible smell was not coming from here: these bones were old. She spotted something else: a shapeless, decaying mass by a creek. Kora forced herself to come closer, gingerly stepping onto the meaty leaves of the bog-plant that burst with a wet sound. Dividing-the-Divide, with her cargo of crawling lights, stirred uneasily in her arms.

The mass, bloated and puffed-up by gases of decay, was half-submerged into the sluggish water of the creek that lapped against its bulk. It looked like something that had crawled here and died, alone and abandoned.

And then it stood up.

Chapter 11. Edenberry

There was no food left in the despoiled village. The Hunter found some clay bottles and filled them with water. He also found two pouched belts that the khruts had used instead of backpacks and took one, giving the second one to Agatha. She did not seem unduly affected by the slaughter, but he was surprised to see her pause over the corpse of Vassily and whisper something. He grunted questioningly when she hurried back to join him.

"Grandfather Prayer," she said, blushing.

When they put some distance between themselves and the village, he went hunting. His right hand with the 'arm stuck to the scabbing skin was pulsing in waves of pain interspersed with abominable itching. The 'arm seemed lethargic and hard to control. He did manage to use it to lasso a chipmunk and to snag up a fat grey lizard. Both were cooked on the tiny fire he and Agatha made in the shade of a dying ash tree that offered a scant protection against eyes from above.

He ate half of the lizard, wrapped the rest in leaves and shoved it into Agatha's belt-pouch. She watched him with big round eyes.

He licked his lips. The words were there; it was something else that stuck in his throat. He coughed to clear it, but the obstacle would not go away. It was a lizard bone. Or perhaps grief.

"Lotus Pond?" he asked.

Her eyes lit up.

"Yes!" she pointed south-west. "I know how to get there! My cousin Stanislaus, he'll take us in, I know he will! There are no khruts there at all, no zombies, and the harvests are always good! They have fish-ponds too! Oh Reggie, we can have smoked trout!

We can build our own house! They'll help us! They are good, my mam's people, kind, she always said, hard workers but kind, and merry too, not like my dad's family, always complaining, and…"

He lifted his hand – the left hand, so she would not see how swollen his right hand had become – to stop her.

"How far?"

"Not far, maybe a day and a half walking, maybe two, but if we walk at night, it'll be shorter, and there is a road…"

Indeed, there was – a dusty country road running into the haze on their left, rutted and empty. He wondered how long ago it had seen any traffic. Perhaps it would be safer to walk in the fields but what difference would it make? Khruts had their own air-routes that did not respect human demarcations, and Hungry Ones swarmed where they would.

"Your 'arm?" he asked.

She showed it to him, proud and happy, its velvety golden tan blending perfectly with her own skin. It practically glowed with health.

"Wash it, remember? And take it off to rest…"

"I know, I know! Oh Reggie, I feel so good now! Nobody will bother us…and Lotus Pond, they'll take us in …"

She threw her arms around him, her smell – like ripening grain, or fresh hay, or long summer evenings – enveloping him in a moment of the forgotten past suddenly returned to him in all its sweetness. He held her and then let her go and, with a gentle pat on the back, propelled her toward the road.

"You go!" he said. "Lotus Pond!"

Her face went pale and her mouth formed a perfect "O" of protest. He had no need of her words. Or of his own, for that matter; he hoped they would go away and stop bothering him once she was gone.

"Go!" he roared.

She quietly collected her scant possessions – the pouched belt with water and meat, the shoulder pack with the odds and ends she had scrounged from her lost home – and walked to the road. She stopped there, on the verge, her back to him.

"Go!"

She walked away and he stayed there, following her with his eyes until she rounded a bend and disappeared from view behind a scraggly hedge. Then he stomped upon the remnant of the fire and scattered the ashes.

His right hand throbbing to the tune of his footsteps, he cut through the yellow stubble of the field, slinking low, keeping the sun behind him, going east, to Edenberry.

The thing was shedding pieces of itself as it came for her.

Kora backed off, her boots slipping in the mud. She knew that to fall would be to die. The thing was uncannily fast despite the fact that it could not run. Its lower limbs were fused together and it slid forward on a trail of its own slime like a snail.

Dividing-the-Divide squirmed. Kora had forgotten that she was carrying the khrut-fowl. She unclenched her fingers and let the bird fall.

But she did not fall to the ground; instead she rose into the air, hovering between Kora and the advancing mass of rot. The miniature flambeaus she was carrying flared brightly and illuminated the wet surface of the thing seething with beetles and maggots. At its forefront, the insects shaped themselves into a cartoonish face with darting worms in place of eyes and larval teeth.

Kora reached the road. Her left foot lost its purchase on the slick surface and she fell, her teeth rattling. The rot creature darted at her, sending Dividing-the-Divide into a spin as the khrut-fowl fought to remain in the air. Her cargo of tiny flambeaus were shaken off, falling onto the road in a shower of lights. And as they hit the ground, they exploded.

Kora had never seen a transition from a flambeau into a firestalker. The creature that had waylaid her near Wingate's farm had already undergone the full metamorphosis. Now, she was witnessing what, under normal circumstances, would be a harbinger of deadly danger. It was her own chance of survival.

The small luminescent tenants expanded to twice their normal size, quickly transforming into dazzling globes of fire. These globes were not uniform but composed of convoluted petals of different brightness, complexly folded and intertwined. The flambeaus' spindly legs and flat heads were absorbed into their new shapes. The globes rose into the air, spinning and darting like a school of flaming fish. They conversed upon the rot creature and it caught fire.

Kora was thankful for the fact that it had no mouth and could not scream. But the dreadful crackling noise, the sizzle of the frying maggots, and the flailing, smoke-limned limbs were bad enough. The stench was worse. She doubled up, coughing, tearing her sealed throat, and for the first time since her awakening faintly tasting something – her own blood. Tears were running down her face and blinding her to the stumbling torch that still advanced toward her. But then it collapsed in the avalanche of melted and smoking filth.

She scooted away on her behind, smearing soot on her face as she tried to clear her eyes. For a moment, she was afraid she had gone blind. Then, she realized that the unpredictable spacetime of the Divide had shifted once again, and night had fallen: a strange night with no moon and no stars but with a sickly puce glow coloring half the sky.

Unsteadily, she climbed to her feet. Dividing-the-Divide hopped toward her. The khrut-fowl's plumage was ruffled but otherwise appeared unharmed. The tiny firestalkers were crawling through the marsh, making for the cenotaph, creeping up the stacked bones.

Kora looked toward the glow. It looked as if a luminescent cloud bank was resting on the unnaturally close horizon. Or rather, something like a billowing curtain made of layers of semi-translucent dark gauze, lit from inside by purple radiance with flickers of green. And there were giant gantries within its layers: a spiky scaffolding, branching like an enormous thorny tree and bearing strange fruit.

There was nothing else around. There was no life on the gluey dead marsh for her to hunt. There was no place to rest. Mats of swollen scarlet plants and black mud everywhere; the flat night sky; and up ahead – the Divide.

She looked at Dividing-the-Divide.

"Lead on," she said, and the bird obeyed.

The Hunter reached Edenberry by midday.

The smoke that had obscured the ruined village before was gone, and the site was revealed in all its desolation. Most of the houses were gutted skeletons or collapsed piles of rotting wood. On some plots, creepers and weeds had grown over whatever was left of the original dwelling, turning it into a frozen wave on the green tide of rank vegetation. An apple orchard had become a zoo of gnarled shapes bearing sour, wormy fruit. The Hunter paused there, stared at the unpruned trees for a long time, then picked up a shriveled apple, bit into its rotten core, and spat it out.

Down the same street, he came upon a still-standing barn, retaining traces of red paint. He pushed the splintered door. Inside was a wheelbarrow missing its wheels, a rusty spade, and a cow skeleton. There was also a constant, busy rustling that stopped when he walked in.

He looked up into the bright eyes of rats festooning the edge of the loft. The whole barn was alive with their scrambling. He carefully closed the door and kept on walking.

He was looking for a specific house and could not find it. Then, it occurred to him to loop back, which he did. But his memory – or instinct, he no longer distinguished between the two – was too unreliable to guide him. He ended up on the village green.

Once upon a time, it was a handsome open space in the shape of a triangle, graced with mature chestnut trees, a duck pond, and several benches. The apex of the triangle was the village hall.

The hall still stood – barely. The villagers had invested the gains of their prosperity into this building, endeavoring to make it as imposing as they could. Of course, it was a pitifully dead hut compared to the living giants of the city, but they had not known any better. They had had no stone since the nearest quarry was far away and happened to belong to a hostile village, but they had done all they could with ceramic tiles that were hung on pegs driven into the wooden façade. The tiles, colored various shades of red, had mostly fallen off, lying in piles of fragments around the hall like permanent autumn leaves, but a couple still flashed proudly from the dilapidated walls and the steep roof. The windows were all broken; the door was missing.

The Hunter walked into the hall, quietly, as if paying homage to the authority that had once inhabited this place. But the authority was gone, together with most of the furniture. There was, however, a big and ugly painting still hanging on the wall of the auditorium.

The Hunter stared at it for a long time. It depicted a group of people – all humans, dusks, dawns, and noons in about equal proportions – standing on a flat, featureless terrain and looking toward something on the left side of the picture. This "something" looked like a hump with a fire on top, but it was probably the result of the artist's lack of skill in trying to represent a far-away mountain. The same lack of skill had made him or her exaggerate the gauntness of the people's features until most of them looked like walking skeletons. Their clothes were torn and bedraggled; some were carrying babies or dragging old people on travois. Many also carried strange implements that looked like double sticks.

At the head of the group, showing the viewer his profile as he gestured energetically toward the mountain, was a rather short man wearing a simple khaki tunic and pants. He was not quite as underfed as the rest and his clothes were in better shape. The artist had clearly attempted to endow him with boundless energy and so he looked almost spastic. His aggressively thrust-out nose and domed forehead dominated the rest of the generic round face, accessorized by a thin moustache.

The Hunter stood in contemplation of this dubious work of art for much longer than it deserved. But he had another reason for being still. His right hand was throbbing mercilessly like an inflamed tooth and every movement brought another surge of pain.

He sensed rather than heard purposeful movement behind his back. A shadow fell on the floor. A voice said:

"Raise your hands and turn around slowly."

He did as he was told.

A man stood at the entrance to the auditorium flanked by two khrut Guards carrying maces and long whips. He was dressed in immaculately tailored clothes and his arrogant face with icy-blue eyes practically screamed "up-levels"!

A citizen here, in this forsaken deserted village! The Hunter exhaled and squared his shoulders, trying to stand with the self-assurance of a militiaman. His body cooperated only marginally.

"Who are you?" the man asked suspiciously. "A tenant? What are you doing here?"

The Hunter noted an oddity in his speech: the man looked like a dusk yet spoke with a sibilant dawn accent.

"I'm a human!" the Hunter bellowed indignantly. "A citizen!"

At least this was what he tried to say but his word-chest clamped shut once again and what came out was mostly an inarticulate roar. He clenched his right hand and the jot of pain made his head spin.

"I'm a citizen!" he repeated again, more clearly this time. One of the Guards clacked, which he knew indicated amusement. But the up-level man regarded him curiously.

"What's your name, then?" he asked.

"Reggie," the Hunter replied.

"Reggie what?"

The Hunter was silent.

"All right, lower your hands but back off to the wall."

The Hunter obeyed. If his 'arm were functional, he might consider fighting but it had become an implement of torture, clinging to him like a poisonous tick. And in truth, he was as curious about this citizen's errand in Edenberry as the citizen was about his.

His shoulder hit the painting and almost dislodged it from the wall. The man smiled thinly.

"You were admiring this painting. Do you know what it represents?"

"The Incoming," the Hunter grunted. "Grandfather."

"Are you a believer, then?"

"No!" The Hunter himself was surprised at the force with which it came out. "Are you?"

The man did not answer but kept studying him intently.

"You're neither a duck nor a toad," he said softly. "But you don't look human either. I have seen…people being reshaped, taken in by the Pith and spat out…changed. Is this what happened to you?"

The Hunter almost nodded but did not.

"I'll answer all your questions," he said, "if you tell me your name and what you're doing here. You're not a procurement officer or a surveyor. Are you City Corps?"

The man smiled again, the same smile as if his repertoire of facial expressions was rather limited.

"You ARE from the city," he said, "if you know this bureaucratic lingo. Very well, my name is Adam Malech. You may have heard of me."

"I have," the Hunter said contemptuously, "and I know you're not him! Adam Malech is a dawn!"

Something changed in the man's posture, as if some tension had gone out of him, but his face remained expressionless.

"Then we're even," he said, "because your name is not Reggie either. As for what I am doing here – I am looking for somebody. They were with me, but we were attacked, and they got lost."

"I'm looking for somebody too," the Hunter said. "A criminal."

"A criminal? Here, in the ruins? This village was abandoned years ago!"

"Fifteen years ago," the Hunter said. "Because of her. Because of what she had done. This is why I'm here. Criminals always come back to the scenes of their crimes."

The purple glow intensified until the night dissolved into a feverish twilight. The hedge of thorns curled high above Kora's head like an ocean wave frozen in the act of breaking, dripping globs of sickly luminescence.

The branching structures within the purple cloud sprouted convoluted limbs, spreading like rime patterns on the window glass. She remembered rime patterns now. Close to the Divide, winter came sharp and deadly, cold sneaking in from the other side. The other world. The Divide would let snow and sleet through. Only people were barred from crossing. And to enforce its decree, the Divide had found new guards.

The guards were looking down upon her, unaccountable rows of them impaled upon iron thorns, crucified upon black wood. She could see their bald skulls and sunken mouths, the yellow parchment skin on their wasted arms and skeletal legs. They were men, women, and children, but children, especially babies, predominated. They were long dead and yet they looked down upon her, their shriveled eyes glittering with vengeance, their perpetual grins turning into snarls of hate. Scores and scores of Hungry Ones nailed together into a border fence: guards and posts at once.

Kora clapped a hand to her mouth, stifling a cry that would be lost in the rising susurrus of voices anyway because her approach awakened the flesh-and-bone blocks of the fence, starved of their screams by long decades of loneliness. Many simply keened because they had never learned to speak but some articulated words and phrases:

"…mummy!"

"…took my grain, took my animals!"

"…you bastards!"

"…he promised!"

"…Dada!"

"…water in the jug!"

"…gold!"

"…better life!"

"…hungry…"

She searched the serried rows for familiar faces but they all looked the same: marasmus, the mask of hunger, with big staring eyes and sunken mouths, multiplied endlessly.

"Let me through!" she cried.

"…father died yesterday…"

"…milk…"

"…a chicken and two geese…"

"…my baby!"

"…in the cellar…"

"…buried my wife, buried my mother…"

The surf of horrors, meaningless and repetitive like the ocean.

She stepped closer to the fence on the legs that trembled and folded under her as if she were paralyzed. There were gaps in the ranks of the crucified zombies and she could catch glimpses of the other side. Distorted by the purple light, the landscape looked like an expanse of wavy dunes. But the dunes were made of steel.

The flapping of wings startled her, and she lost her balance and fell onto the hard road, bruising her shoulder. She felt weak, as if her life-force was being sucked back into this prickly hedge of misery.

Dividing-the-Divide perched upon the shoulder of one of the Hungry Ones and casually pecked at its eyes. The creature gave a long wail and then crumbled in upon itself, its parchment skin folding like an empty bag, its bones tumbling down. Its fall created a gap in the fence, and the entire wall of twitching bodies was pulled into a funnel shape as if the air on the other side was thinner, drawing the flesh and wood outward. The khrut-fowl turned to Kora. She did not need to speak – her message was clear – but she did, in a rising musical trill that overrode the symphony of pain.

"Go!"

On shaking legs, Kora walked to the Divide. She was so close that she could touch the wasting bodies, the loose skin, and the hunger-distorted faces. Caught here, on the border between two worlds, perpetually hungry, denied both the pleasure of life and the solace of death, playthings of forces they neither understood nor controlled…The Hungry Ones.

The other side beckoned. She squinted but could not understand what she was seeing. A field of iron? An expanse of frozen water? A strange new city – *another* city – shimmering in bright inorganic light?

Whatever it was, she could feel waves of energy coming from there, beating at the pitiful wall of starving bodies that were pressed into this last unending service to the land. Clean energy that promised deliverance from the humiliating hunger that consumed her as surely as it had consumed the villagers. Whatever dangers the other world held, she knew she could overcome them – because she already had. The steely landscape, incomprehensible in its strangeness, was nevertheless perfectly familiar. She had been there. She had trod on the glittering soil she could not name. She had walked among the pulsating spires she could not understand. She had been to Grandfather's realm – even though she remembered nothing of it.

"Go!"

She stepped forward and the flesh of the Divide billowed out in front of her, the impaled bodies sucked into its maw and spat out in pieces. At least she was giving them rest, she thought – until she saw the pieces crawling toward each other like blind worms, reconstituting into the screaming guardians. The land needed them still.

But the land did not need her. It was letting her go.

"Go!"

She stretched out her hand and felt the electric air of the other world sparkle upon her fingertips.

"Kara!"

It was not her name. But she looked up anyway.

A scarecrow figure nailed to a fork in the black gnarly growth of the Divide; a woman or what once was a woman, clothed in rotted rags, her long gray hair falling in untidy hunks across her skull face. Her torn lips moved as she tried to smile.

Kora backed off, her feet slipping from under her, the bruised sky and the flapping bird-wings falling upon her like an avalanche, but not enough to obscure the smile. And the arms reaching out for her. Reaching for a hug.

Kora closed her eyes and dove into the darkness in her mind. The darkness parted.

Chapter 12. Men and Monsters

The up-level citizen who called himself Adam Malech had a train. He also had a full flight of khrut Guards who hovered the background when he told the Hunter that he was coming with him. And though the Hunter fumed with indignation, he obeyed.

He would not be so meek if the circumstances been different. Or rather one specific circumstance. The one attached to his right arm that coruscated with pain, sending messages of misery through his suddenly ungovernable body.

The man was quite decent, all things considering. He politely ushered the Hunter onto his train and invited him to share his dinner, which consisted of the kind of dishes the Hunter had tasted only once, when he blew half of his monthly wages on a hot date (nothing much had come of it but the up-level restaurant had been worth it). The Hunter was also grateful that pseudo-Malech did not invite any of his Guards to share their meal. He did not need their beady eyes staring at him. It was embarrassing enough to try to use the implements with his left hand and to make sure his heavy jaws did not produce any revolting sounds while he chewed. He sweated it out, but he managed to conduct himself as befits a citizen. The excellent wine helped.

"So, Mr....Reggie," his host said, pouring him another glass, "you're a bounty hunter, yes? And who are you bounty-hunting for?"

"Justice," the Hunter replied promptly.

His host cocked his head but his expression hardly changed. The Hunter had noticed already that his face seemed strangely immobile as if he had undergone a surgery to disguise his age. This physical handicap, no matter how slight, made the Hunter feel more self-confident.

"Does justice pay your bills? That is, if you have any bills to pay?"

"Of course, I do!" the Hunter said indignantly. "Taxes alone are eating half of my salary…and the bloody rent! And if I want to buy a place, forget it! The prices are insane!"

"I see," said the false Malech thoughtfully. "So where do you live? Cat Street or whereabouts, I'd guess?"

The Hunter snorted. Cat Street nested against up-levels; he would have to be of a much higher pay-grade to afford even a closet there.

"I wish! No, my place is near Fool's Errand. You know where it is? About five blocks up from the Pit, around where Skybridge Five meets the mid-level escalator."

The false Malech beamed at him and the Hunter realized he was an idiot. Clearly, the man was checking his knowledge of the city's geography! Well, never mind, just saying those familiar names gave him a sweet feeling of nostalgia. Fool's Errand, indeed!

"Yes, life in the city is hard," his host said thoughtfully. "But it is no better in the country, is it? Starvation, abandoned villages, violence…Hardly what Grandfather envisioned."

The Hunter snorted again.

"An educated man like yourself!" he chided the up-level impostor. "And you believe in this fairy tale?"

"And you don't?"

"No."

"Then how did we, humans, come here?"

"How did khruts, or Buddhas, or trains? Or the Pith, for that matter? We have always lived here."

"The land does not think so," pseudo-Malech said.

"The land does not think."

"Maybe it did not. No more than the city did once. But now that the city has awakened… The tenants…They say Grandfather was horrified when it happened. That he hated the first tenants. Tried to kill them, tried to pacify the city, to control it, to make it stop…"

"But he did not."

"No, just the opposite. The Pith is calving faster and faster, but its new get is…strange. And now it has started to make people like you."

"I'm a citizen!" The Hunter roared. "A man!"

Pseudo-Malech lifted a conciliatory hand.

"I know. I did not mean to impugn your humanity. But something has been done to you; you cannot deny it."

The Hunter dropped his eyes, staring at the floor.

"It may console you, Mr. Reggie," the false Malech said, "to know that you are not the only one. I have heard of many such cases. I personally witnessed one. The man was swallowed by the Pith, chewed up and will one day be spit out as something else. Neither a human nor a proper tenant."

"What, then?"

"A monster. No, wait a second! Do you know the difference between a monster and a man? Whether a man is human or tenant, male or female, he is the master of his own mind. He lives and dies for himself. A monster is a creature bound; a soldier in a war it did not choose. Like the Hungry Ones."

"Zombies, deadheads, locusts, train-fodder," the Hunter muttered.

"Yes."

"Are you saying the Pith is making them?"

"No, not at all. Something else is making them and sending them to savage the city. Something that hates the city and wishes it gone. And the Pith, being the flesh of the city, has to defend itself, to create its own army. And so it does. Only it does not realize that the only force that can defeat an army of monsters is an army of free men."

"I'm free," the Hunter said defiantly.

"Really? You said you're hunting a criminal, right?"

"Yes."

"Do you know what crime she has committed?"

"I…" the Hunter started and suddenly a jolt of intolerable pain went through his entire body, convulsing him so much that his flailing arm swept the glasses and wine-bottle off the table. They landed on the floor with a crash, peppering him with slivers of glass but the Hunter did not even notice the damage. The lance of pain that stabbed through his brain swept away the cobwebs of forgetfulness.

He stared at the swollen wreck of his arm. He felt Malech's gaze and knew the man was observing him keenly.

No matter. He knew who he was, finally.

He looked back at his host.

"Yes," he said, "I know. I know exactly what she has done."

He slept without dreams on the silky custom-made bedclothes. When he woke up, the pain was back. His right hand felt as if it were trapped in a vise. This was no longer the dull ache that could have been ignored by the force of will but rather a physical anguish that drowned everything else.

He examined his hand. The 'arm that fitted over it had become puffed-up and glistened like jelly. Up to the shoulder, his own flesh was swollen and tender. But the most alarming thing was that the boundary between the two was no longer clear. The 'arm was dissolving into his body.

He suddenly realized that the train was moving. The rocking, sliding motion calmed down the pain somewhat. He put on some clean clothes from the closet which the train thoughtfully revealed by withdrawing a fold of derma from the inner wall of the compartment.

He stepped out from the compartment and found himself nose-to-nose with Malech who regarded him thoughtfully.

"You're looking much better than yesterday, Mr. Reggie," he said. "Are you feeling better?"

"I'm feeling like shit," the Hunter said. "And my name is not Reggie."

"So I gathered. Sorry you're not feeling well. But you seem to have amazing powers of recuperation. Am I right in believing you no longer want to go back to Edenberry?"

"You're right," the Hunter said. "I no longer wish to hunt down the…that woman. Whoever forced that task upon me must have been some sick fuck. Unfortunately, I do not remember who it was. Equally unfortunately, I remember everything else."

"I can help you find out who it was. Who tried to make you into a monster."

"Out of the goodness of your heart?"

"Out of self-interest. I want to hire you."

"To do what?"

"I have to go to the Divide. I need a bodyguard. And I can no longer trust the khruts. I think they are in cahoots with the thing that lives there."

"And do you trust me?"

"Yes. You are a citizen."

The Hunter smiled crookedly.

"I was an illegal immigrant. But you are right, my allegiance is to the city. This is the only thing left to me. I have sworn an oath and I'll uphold it. But why should I trust *you*? You call yourself Adam Malech but you are not!"

"I am," the man said. "I am Adam Malech and I can prove it to you. Whatever you think of my business practices, you know I have dedicated my life to the city. I'm not like the Mayor and the up-level crowd who only think of their fancy mansions and their fancy mistresses! I care for the city, and this means I care for everybody who lives in it, human and tenant alike!"

"Spare me your election speech!" the Hunter sneered. "But fine, I'll accept that you genuinely love the city if you explain to me why you are here, in the deep countryside, instead of organizing the city's defenses. Don't you know it is under attack?

Two days ago, I saw an army of wild khruts flying toward it! Will the hired Guards fight against their kin? And if they won't, who is left to defend the city? The militia and City Corps? They are stretched thin trying to repel the Hungry Ones!"

"Look out!" Malech said.

He did and saw that the featureless plain through which the train was speeding was swarming with Hungry Ones.

"Yes," Malech said, answering his unspoken question, "they're going to the city. The war has begun."

"The war," the Hunter repeated, stunned. "There has never been a war since Year Zero."

"It is always Year Zero," Malech replied. "But there had been history before he took it away from us."

"What do you mean?"

"I'll explain later. But I want to know whether you accept my job offer."

"Why not?" The Hunter said. "I have nothing better to do. But I am a man, not a monster. I am free to make my own decision and to pay for my own mistakes. You cannot buy my fidelity."

"I don't need to," Malech said dryly. "I only want to buy your fighting skills – and only for a time. Contractual law, you know. Grandfather taught the city well. But I need to know your proper name for the contract to be valid."

"Daniel Moylan," the Hunter said. "My name is Daniel Moylan."

Chapter 13. Aunt Harrow

Agatha was pissed.

This was her normal state of being. As long as she remembered herself, she had been intermittently peeved, angry, resentful, or recovering from a real or imaginary injury. A third child in a farming family of five kids, with the weak mother and the tyrannical father, she had learned all the shades of neglect before she learned her letters and numbers. And she also discovered how to make use of her resentment, garner it as a precious resource. Victimization was power.

This skill came her in good stead now. What sustained her as she marched through the fields filled with slithering shadows was anger.

She had it all figured out, only to have it come crashing down. And she still did not understand how it happened.

He had been her lifeline out of the morass of famine. He had been her ticket to the place of salvation. To the city.

She had wanted to be in the city as long as she remembered herself. When her mother forced her to wipe the bottoms of her puling younger siblings, she consoled herself with dreams of urban glamour. When her father ordered her to bring him yet another glass of gassy homebrew, she imagined herself in some up-level fancy restaurant. When she had to work more and eat less, she visualized the boundless bounty of the mythical Market. And then the Hunter showed up.

She did not know who or what he was. At the beginning, she had doubted he was human, though later she decided he was. But human or tenant, it did not matter. He was from the city.

She had thought she had him and this had blunted the pain of her family's loss. She had not loved them, but they had been her folks. She had belonged. But she still had the Hunter. She had belonged with him and it was enough.

And now she had nobody, and the unfairness of it was enough to fan the smoldering coals of her resentment into the bright flame of near-hatred. He had abandoned her, sent her off with a pat on the back! Who did he think he was?

The fact that he probably could not have answered this question did nothing to calm her down. But she did not want to calm down. Anger was all she had.

A rustle in the hedge made her stop and look around fearfully. The gusts of chilly wind tossed pale light into her face. The road was bordered by prickly bushes that dipped and danced.

Agatha made a fist and was comforted by the velvety smoothness that gently squeezed her muscles back. Before the famine, when her family had been marginally prosperous, they had two horses: a mare and a gelding. This was uncommon as horses were useless, a vanity showcase. The land was plowed by Aunt Harrows, the massive toads leased by the city. Cows gave meat and milk. But mares' milk was scant and their meat tough. Some people rode horses, but it was dangerous. Train-and-track symbionts hated horses and often killed them on the spot. But Agatha was fond of their sway-backed mare named Rosie and enjoyed currying her silky coat and feeling the smooth muscles roll under the skin. The gentle squeeze of the 'arm reminded her of Rosie and she clung to these memories as she stood exposed in the middle of the darkening road.

The rustle was not repeated and she chided herself for a fool. With the wind, and the skittering clouds, and the whipping tree branches, how could the land be still? But the other noises were still too fresh in her memory: the flapping of the birdmen's wings, the moaning cries of the flesh-eaters, and the screams of her dying family.

Agatha angrily smeared tears across her dusty cheeks. She had nobody to rely upon but herself – but had it ever been different? The cousin she had told Reggie about was a fantasy: as much a fantasy as Reggie himself, the romantic image she superimposed upon the Hunter to hide his ugliness. The village of Lotus Pond actually existed, but Agatha was pretty sure they would turn away a useless orphan. Hunger made people clear-headed.

She had been tracking Reggie for a while now. After he had sent her away, she had trudged unwillingly in the presumed direction of Lotus Pond for a couple of hours, afraid he would follow her to make sure she obeyed him. Only when she knew she was alone did she double back. But by then she got tired and had to stop. There was an empty barn by the roadside where she took a brief nap in a pile of straw.

Agatha knew where she needed to go. She had seen the expression on the Hunter's face when she told him the story of Edenberry. He had banished her so he could go back to the cursed village unimpeded. Whatever he hunted was there.

Was it a treasure? Despite her fondness for cheap romances, Agatha had a very realistic idea of how poor the countryside was. All the treasures were in the city.

No, whatever the Hunter was hunting for was either knowledge or a person. If knowledge, Agatha would be there to share the profit of it. If a person – well, it depended on who the person was. If it was a female, she could not be younger or more determined than Agatha herself. If a male, the Hunter would hopefully kill him before she arrived and be done with his task.

But when she had finally gotten to Edenberry last night, she was too afraid to enter the haunted place in the dark. She had camped out under a tree, emptying her water bottle and finishing off her bread and meat. It was sad to fall asleep alone, with no comforting masculine bulk by her side, but she was too tired to care. And in the morning, when the sunlight dispelled the Edenberry ghosts, she walked in bravely, only to find the village empty.

But then she found the unmistakable signs of a train passing: the slime-covered grass and a pile of manure. She had followed the indentations left by the tracks in the increasingly soggy ground for a while now, coming occasionally on some minor sign of devastation: a heap of cow bones, bark-stripped trees, dug-up fields where somebody hunted for roots, a shallow grave. Nothing out of the ordinary except a huge patch of wet ashes where some isolated farm might have stood. This explained the acrid smoke they had seen on their first visit to Edenberry. Reggie did not want to tell her what made him so jumpy then – as if she did not know that khruts would raid and burn homesteads whenever they could! How stupid he thought she was!

Trudging through the bog, she clung to her resentment to counter her increasing desperation. She could not die here alone! She could not die before reaching the city!

And then she saw the road.

Agatha stopped and stared. There were roads in the countryside but not many. Trains and tracks did not need them and neither did the khruts and khrut-fowls. People who walked to neighboring villages utilized the elaborate system of paths that wound through and around cultivated fields. Agatha knew, of course, that city streets were paved but she had never seen such a thing. And yet here it was.

The road was quite wide and unnaturally straight. It made Agatha dizzy to look at it. Nevertheless, she followed it with her gaze to the horizon that seemed suddenly to jump closer. She attributed it to the rising fog that crept along the low ground and sucked the brightness out of the anemic sun. The surface of the road was hard and glistening like a beetle wing. She touched it gingerly. It was warm.

She did not want to walk on it but there was no choice. The ground was too soggy to bear her weight; her shoes and pants were already soaked. And the train had undoubtedly passed here.

Tracks avoided marshes and lowlands whenever they could.

Caressing her 'arm to give herself courage, Agatha stepped onto the sleek pavement. Nothing happened and as she walked for a while, she was beginning to like it. It was definitely easier that slogging through the mud! Her strained calves unknotted and she found her stride, devouring distance with a precise clip. The longing to be in the city where every path would propel her forward like this became almost unendurable.

And then she stopped abruptly as if running into an invisible wall. Or maybe not so invisible.

The terrain around the road was a wasteland of mud, puddles, rushes and some strange fleshy plant hugging the ground. There were piles of vegetation scattered here and there as if somebody had cut it for animal fodder but left it rot.

But ahead of her the marshland dissolved in in a steely-gray sheen. She squinted into it and had to close her eyes because of a sudden onset of vertigo. There was nothing there…or maybe something…or perhaps something that looked like nothing. There was a rotten, dusky softness in the landscape that hurt her brain.

And the light was outrageous. Like any countrywoman, Agatha had a perfect time-sense. She knew it was supposed to be just short of midday. But the pale sun was in an afternoon position, ominously hovering above the gray emptiness.

When did it happen? She looked back. But the horizon was creeping closer there as well, imprisoning her in a shrinking world.

There was a rustling in a clump of thorny bushes, as loud as a scream in the unnatural stillness of the marsh. Her 'arm unfurled, without her conscious volition, ready to stab and pierce.

The bushes parted with a crack. An ungainly bulk crawled out, shedding twigs and leaves. The creature was thrice as massive as Agatha and if erect, would tower a good meter and a half above her head. Right now, though, it crouched on all fours, its giant head, crowned with a blunt crest, tucked into its broad chest, its eyes glinting through the matted lashes. A long purplish tongue emerged from its bearded muzzle when it opened its maw.

"Aunt Harrow!" Agatha cried joyously and rushed to hug the massive body, her 'arm retreating from its fighting position.

The creature made a soft sound and rubbed Agatha's shoulder with its thick fingers. Its forelimbs, much longer that its hind legs, bulged with muscles and ended in spade-shaped hands. When it stood up, they would dangle well below its back-jointed knees. Aunt Harrows were mostly used for plowing but they could – and often did – perform just about any heavy agricultural labor the village required. They were sentient creatures, though not particularly bright, and were treated with respect by farmers because the harvest depended on them. Unfortunately, they were neither free agents nor village property. They belonged to the city. And when a village could not pay its grain taxes, the city would send in khrut Guards and take Aunt Harrows away. This is what had happened to Agatha's village and to Edenberry before it. She still remembered vividly the wailing of her mother and sisters when the khruts had herded away the massive tenants who were almost as distressed at being torn away from their adoptive families as the families themselves. No explanations concerning the fact that the tax default was the result of the depredations of wild khruts – probably the kin of the Guards themselves – had been of any avail.

But what was this Aunt Harrow doing here? And where was the village it had come from? The nearest one was Edenberry and it had been abandoned for as long as Agatha had been alive.

"What's your name?" she asked, instinctively adopting the singsong tone she had used with Rosie the mare and other barn animals.

The Aunt made another sighing sound. Agatha did not really expect an answer. Most Aunts could talk a little, but they were shy and would only communicate with their masters.

But then the Aunt did something amazing. It brought its rump down and crouching in the road, it started making patterns in the mud with its long, clawed finger. Agatha's mouth fell open when she realized the creature was trying to write!

Writing? An Aunt Harrow? Agatha had known plenty of illiterate farmers but never heard of a literate farm toad.

And yet here it was. The writing was clumsy but the squiggles in the mud were clearly letters. They spelled "D-R-I-S".

"Dris?" Agatha said dubiously. The creature tried to add something but made a mess. It mewled.

"I know!" Agatha cried. "Doris! Your name is Doris!"

Aunt Harrow's enormous head, almost one third of its body could not execute a human-like nod, but it managed a credible approximation.

"Yes, Doris!" Agatha said happily. "It is a good name!"

Indeed it was. Despite being dubbed "Aunts", the giant tenants were sexless; but by common consent, they were given male or female names according to their temperament. "Doris" indicated a pliant and agreeable disposition.

"What are you doing here, Doris?"

The Aunt wrote again. In her case, unfortunately, practice did not make perfect: the new letters were even more crooked than the previous ones. But Agatha managed to make out "B-R-D-M".

"Birdmen!" she exclaimed. "Birdmen brought you here?"

One letter, "Y". Yes!

"Why?"

It made no sense. The khrut Guards who had come to confiscate Aunt Harrows for tax default were, of course, supposed to bring them back to the city where they belonged.

Doris wrote again, its blue-black hide wrinkling with the effort.

"F-D"

"Fd? Food?!!?"

Yes again.

Agatha's head swam. The idea was inconceivable. Who would eat tenants? In her famine-stricken village, families slaughtered chicken, geese, rabbits, horses, and eventually milk cows. But these were dumb animals. Tenants were people!

"Who?" she cried, clutching Doris's arm.

And then her question was answered, as a thin moan rose around them.

Aunt Harrow's muscles twitched under its thick hide as Hungry Ones poured forth from their hiding places. The piles of rushes and cattails that Agatha had taken for abandoned animal feed fell apart like hatching eggs and released the zombie larvae inside. A thin maggoty figure wriggled out from one of them, flattening itself against the ground, and then gathering itself into a low-slung canine shape. But it was no dog. The face thrusting toward Agatha had once been human, even though its eyes were now bleeding pits.

More and more Hungry Ones hatched out of the piles, and others were crawling out of the mud pits. Some of them flailed around, unable to find purchase on the soaked ground. But others stood on all fours or upright. Their empty faces with huge eye-holes and broken teeth in receded gums turned toward Agatha and Aunt Harrow.

Doris stood erect, her long arms tensing, the shovel-like hands swinging. Her bony crest flashed deep red. She growled again and the foremost Hungry One leaped at her.

The Aunt Harrow's arm rose and swept the creature off its feet. It hit the ground with a wet sound and Doris followed the attack by smacking it down like a fly. It burst, leaking black blood. But this seemed to galvanize the others and they loped forward like a wild-dog pack. Agatha released her 'arm.

Killing with the 'arm did not feel like killing at all. She had slaughtered chickens and geese and assisted in dressing the carcass of Rosie the mare when the feeding of the family became more important than sentiment. She had done it because it needed to be done but she did not relish the blood and the reek of the animals' entrails. Now, though, she could kill at a distance and it was as exhilarating as a ball game. The 'arm when fully extended reached over two meters and its tip was as sharp as the sharpest knife. It could stab, pierce and impale. Some sensation reached Agatha through her interface with the 'arm's rudimentary nervous system but it was too faint to be disturbing, though just right for guiding the attack. She laughed as yet another Hungry One was bodily lifted off the ground, shaken and dropped like a sack of grain.

And then she felt clammy fingers close over her throat.

She would scream but her windpipe was blocked. Struggling, she waved her 'arm in the air, aimlessly slapping the road. Black motes swam in her vision. She kicked back, aiming for her assailant's crotch, but the blow landed harmlessly. Hungry Ones did not bother with such niceties as gender.

Suddenly, the pressure slackened and withdrew. She whirled around and saw another leaking body at her feet, squashed by Doris's mighty blow. But now the Aunt Harrow was trying to shake off a bunch of snarling Hungry Ones that hang off her like grapes. Where did they come from? Agatha glanced down the road and felt another wave of faintness wash over her.

She could not see the road at all. It was swallowed up in a stream of starveling, slate-grey bodies. The Hungry Ones who had crawled out of the piles were like a drop of water against a creek in full flood.

In desperation, she turned to her companion and the Aunt Harrow responded with a look as faithful as it was dumb. Agatha realized that the tenant would readily die defending her. But that was all she could do.

Another Hungry One loped toward them, its fangs bared

by the chewed-up lips. Agatha's skin was unbroken so far; no zombie had managed to sink its teeth into her yet. But it was only a matter of time. And then…she better hope she would be dead before the poison completed its work.

She looked into the silver mist of the Divide, the shiny nothingness under the wrong sun.

"Run!" she cried and sprinted through the line of zombies, her 'arm whipping them out of the way.

She did not know whether the Aunt Harrow would follow. But her footsteps not only kept pace but easily overtook her; Doris's clawed feet nimbly dancing through the crash of Hungry Ones, her mighty arms sweeping them to the sides. Agatha even found a moment to be amazed at the Aunt Harrow's speed. Soon, Agatha herself was beginning to lag behind, a stitch in her side developing into a knifing pain. She doubled over, gasping. The Hunter had told her that an 'arm fed on the energy of its wearer; now she was feeling the truth of it.

Something swept her off her feet, sky and land wheeling around in fragments of noise and fear, and then she found herself clinging to the loose skin of Doris' shoulders, lifted above the melee. The Aunt Harrow kept on running – further toward the Divide.

Chapter 14. Payback

Daniel nodded off, lulled by the swaying of the train. Sleep did not ease the pain but moved it to the edges of his mind where it lurked like a predator.

When he woke up, only minutes later, or so it seemed, his host had left and the train was slowing down. The 'arm – or rather, the arm, his own now – throbbed like a rotten tooth but the sharp stabs of ache had abated. He could think.

He looked out the window and was astonished at the change in the landscape. They had been moving through the familiar exhausted plain, the soil dry and fallow, covered by a thin matting of weeds. Now, they were surrounded by lush meadows.

Then he saw glints of dark water threaded through the vegetation like silver embroidery and realized they were in the middle of an immense marshland. The juicy green and bloody scarlet were the colors of some bog-plant rather than of grass and flowers. There were no trees; the monotony was only broken by clumps of skeletal cattails and rushes.

There was no movement in the marsh until he caught a glimpse of something giant rearing up ahead of the train. It took him a moment to realize that these were the tracks crawling back like enormous caterpillars. The train stopped.

Daniel hopped out and winced when he smelled the sulfurous, rotten odor that came at him in waves even though the air was unnaturally still. He looked up and was shocked to see the sun spread along the horizon like a broken yolk. It had been late morning when he talked with Malech. He could not have possibly slept the whole day sitting up in the dining car, could he?

And where was Malech himself? The train seemed abandoned; no sign of his master or of the Guards.

Daniel remembered his host's strange reaction when he had heard his name. Malech's unnaturally impassive face did not actually change its bland expression but something passed swiftly over it, something like a palpable shadow.

Could he possibly know who Daniel was? It seemed incredible. A lowly militiaman, he had seldom had any dealings with up-levels and none whatsoever with Malech Industries or their owner.

The train exuded a ladder again and Malech stepped down, nodding curtly to Daniel. They stood side by side, looking into the sunset that seemed glued to the pale sky.

"Where are we?" Daniel asked.

Malech smirked or tried to.

"Don't you know? We are not far from Edenberry."

"There are no swamps near Edenberry," Daniel replied.

"None that you can see."

"What do you mean?"

"We are at the Divide. Have you ever been here?"

"No."

"And yet you are from Edenberry."

Daniel looked away.

"The Divide is not a place," Malech said. "It is a being. An entity. It sucks in time and space and chews them up. It is the boundary between our world and the world of Grandfather, but it is not bound by geography. It manifests itself where it wills. Or when it wills."

"When I was growing up," Daniel said, "people seldom talked about the Divide and then they never actually named it. When the men at the pub started wagging their tongues about the Incoming, the landlord knew it was time to close up. Country people are a superstitious lot."

"Farmers have no reason to have good memories of the Incoming," Malech said. "They are the descendants of those Grandfather left behind as he made his way to the city. A bribe."

"A bribe to who?"

"The Divide."

"Why would it want humans here? Does it have a mind that it would need slaves or workers?"

Malech shook his head.

"Not at the time of the Incoming, perhaps," he said, "but…"

Malech suddenly lurched forward, squinting into the bloody light that had not changed through their entire conversation. Daniel saw two dark dots, wheeling and dipping against the immovable sunset.

"The khruts," Malech said. "They found her."

"Your lost companion?"

"Yes."

"Will they bring her in?"

Malech shook his head.

"They had told me they would not go into the Divide," he said grimly. "When I charged them with insubordination, pointed to their contract, they said they would leave. Such a thing had never happened before. The only commodity that they have to sell to the city is their loyalty. If it's compromised, they'll have nothing to trade. They'll starve. And yet they don't care."

"They don't care because they have rebelled against the city," Daniel said. "I told you, I saw the flying army. You are better off letting your Guards go before they decide to terminate their contract by tearing out your throat."

Malech nodded.

"I know. I *am* letting them go. This recon is the last thing they're doing for me. After that, it is up to the two of us."

"I haven't signed a contract with you yet," Daniel said dryly.

Malech shrugged.

"A mere formality."

"You have a touching confidence in my honesty," Daniel remarked.

"One of us," said Malech, "has no choice."

When the khruts came back, they were ready to go. Malech had two rucksacks with water and trail food. Daniel's respect for his new boss went up a notch when he realized they were the same size. This was how Colonel Shrimp had assured his men's loyalty: by sharing their hardships. Daniel wondered, nostalgically, what had happened to him

"Shouldn't we wait for the morning?" Daniel asked and immediately realized how stupid the question was. The sun had not moved an inch from its sunset position since he woke up.

The khruts stood in a knot by the side of the train. Malech addressed one of them, a bird-shaped thing called Fiona.

"Your contract is void," he said. "Nobody in the city will hire you or your kin."

She did not reply but another, somewhat more human-looking khrut intervened:

"If the city has no use for us, we have no use for the city," he or she said. "We have a new master."

Malech looked as if he wanted to ask something but then he shrugged, hoisted up his rucksack and started walking. Daniel followed. His pain had not gone away but he was beginning to feel used to it. It was as if the pain was slowly fusing with his body, outlining each nerve and muscle with its own fiery tendrils, *becoming* his body.

He noticed that Malech was not wearing an 'arm and asked him about his lack of weaponry.

"I have you to protect me," the other man replied. Daniel shrugged and they walked on.

At first, they jumped from hillock to hillock as the ground was becoming more and more waterlogged, studded with invisible waterholes and treacherous patches of slime. Daniel was sure they were not going to get far that way. But then he suddenly saw a relatively dry path. Malech leaped on in and started forward, with Daniel following.

The path was narrow, sunk into the ground between the

banks of tangled briars and prickly wild raspberry. But it was well-beaten and surprisingly firm.

"Who made it?" Daniel asked after they had walked for a while in silence.

"Grandfather and his people, probably."

"What? Are you kidding? It's fresh, recently done!"

In response, Malech just nodded at the eternal sunset. Daniel felt a chill of fear pass between his shoulder blades.

The immobile sun was not the only unnatural thing about the marsh. Silence was another one. Now that he had allowed himself to remember his country childhood, he knew that such absolute stillness had nothing to do with the peace and quiet of an evening in the fields filled with rustling of tress, buzz of mosquitoes, birdsong, snatches of people's talk and laughter carried by the breeze…But here the air was as still and close as if they were locked inside a cell.

He bent and touched the path, looking for signs of recent passage of feet, and saw that the trampled soil was thinning out, showing patches of something hard. It was as if there was a pavement buried under the earthen path and it was now emerging.

Pavement? Here? He suddenly realized he had never seen a pavement until he came to the city. And this material was nothing like the gray asphalt exuded by the Pith or the occasional flagstone used in smaller alleys or in the courtyards of the rich. In the bloody light, it gleamed with an unpleasant organic sleekness like a beetle wing.

Malech did not stop and Daniel hurried to catch up with him. But the other man suddenly started talking.

"When the humans came," Malech said, "they put their stamp on the city. Toads and ducks are what the Pith imagines men are: warped reflections of humanity in the mirror of its unconscious dreams. "

"What about trains, and Buddhas, and khruts?"

"Trains used to be giant worm-and-tick symbionts, scavenging the countryside. You would not be able to ride inside one of them except as food in its stomach. They were remade by the human desire to have reliable transportation. Buddhas were plant-like sponges sucking nutrients from the ground, just as flambeaus were luminescent crawlers, attracting flying creatures by their light displays. Khruts, though…khruts are different."

"Why?"

"They are intelligent in themselves, not just by borrowing from humanity. They resent humans because we have taken their world from them. "

"And yet they serve humans by hiring out as Guards."

"They did," Malech said.

The familiar vegetation by the sides of the path was flattening out and disappearing. No more raspberries and blackberries, nettles and briars. Instead, the marshland was becoming dominated by a single species: a succulent plant the color of jade and blood. Daniel had never seen anything like it.

"Khruts are perpetually squabbling among themselves," Daniel said. "I can't believe they would unite in attacking the city, no matter how much they hate humans."

"Not by themselves, no. Somebody must have united them."

"Who?"

"That's the question, isn't it?"

The covering of soil was gone; their boots rang faintly on the pavement. The path widened into something resembling a road. But Daniel could not see anything the road could possible lead to. It ran straight into the perpetual sunset and was swallowed up in its inflamed glare. The entire landscape felt small, as if the horizon was much closer than it should be.

"When the humans came," Malech spoke again, "the city was not alone in our world. It had an adversary – as mindlessly powerful as itself. The city was remade by the humans. But now it is remaking them back."

"What do you mean?"

"Think what happened to you. The Pith absorbing humans, spitting them back as monsters. Easy to control."

"Nobody is controlling me," Daniel said.

Something was happening; Daniel could feel it in the air that suddenly felt bristly. The marshland lay all around them, watching them with a million invisible eyes.

"The city subdued the countryside," Malech said, "because it was guided by the human mind. The mind is the most powerful thing in the universe. But not just mind. Desire. Appetite. Hunger."

"And now the countryside is striking back?" Daniel asked, skeptical and yet impressed more than he wanted to admit.

"Yes," Malech said. "The country has discovered a hunger of its own."

Ahead of them, the marshland roiled.

Chapter 15. The Disgruntled Employee

It looked as if a wave was gathering under the surface of the bog, a long rise, wrinkling the quilt of reds and greens. Perhaps it *was* a wave… but then Daniel realized that the rise crossed water and land alike. He did not feel in danger because there was no noise. When he had witnessed the hatching of the giant rogue in the city, the rumble, screech, and pounding of the Pith and the smash of dead stone and metal had compounded his fear. But this smooth puckering of the terrain looked odd rather than threatening.

Suddenly, the wrinkling stopped. On their right side, they now faced a long berm the height of a man that prevented them from seeing the rest of the marsh. And at the same time, the immobile sun that had been glued to the firmament for so long that Daniel started regarding it as a fixture jerked down and slid beyond the horizon with an indecent speed. They were now engulfed in a sickly twilight, emanating not from the darkening and empty sky but from the bog itself. The water in scattered pools shone with a rotten greenish glow while the succulent plant gave off a flickering copper luminescence.

Two giant pale spiders jumped onto the berm, paused there. Spiders? No, hands. Somebody on the other side was pulling themselves up like a child scaling a fence. A face swam into view.

It was a human face, though not an attractive one, with a parrot-like nose and weak chin. The man swung his legs over the top and sat astride the berm regarding the two of them with an imbecile smirk.

Malech gave a short gasp – more like a click, actually – and stepped to the verge.

"Wingate?" he said incredulously.

Daniel glanced at him and gasped too. The man standing beside him was his companion – same clothes, same body – and yet he was not. The face turned up to the stranger on the berm was not the same one he had looked on just a couple of minutes ago. Under the shock of black hair, a dawn's narrow eyes regarded the newcomer suspiciously and an unfamiliar broad mouth thinned in surprise. And yet, even though it was a stranger's face, he recognized it.

It was Adam Malech's face he had seen in pictures and broadcasts.

Daniel was still trying to digest this revelation when the person on the berm spoke and brought up a surge of adrenaline through his veins. Never had he heard a voice so grating. The screech of a nail on glass was music compared to it.

"You shouldn't be here, Mr. Malech. This is not a place for frogs."

Frogs?

"Is it a place for zombies only?" Malech lashed back.

The stranger tittered, which was an even less pleasant sound than his speech.

"You should go back to the city, Mr. Malech." He said. "To the city where you belong."

"And where do you belong, Wingate?" Malech asked.

"My name is not Wingate anymore. I have been remade. And renamed."

"So I see," Malech responded. "I thought you were dead. I even paid a fair compensation to your family. But you *were* dead, weren't you? I didn't realize zombies had names. What is yours now?"

The stranger's face twitched.

"This has nothing to do with you, frog!" he hissed. "Or with your companion, the traitor!"

"Traitor!" Daniel yelled in indignation. "I've been faithful to my oath!"

The misshapen face turned to him and Daniel realized that there was no human mind behind it. But there was something else that filled him with nausea. It was as if the rottenness of the marshland suddenly bloomed into self-awareness.

"Your oath? And what about your family, your friends, your village, your land? What about…?"

"Shut up!" Daniel screamed because he knew what the creature was going to say and he could not bear hearing it.

The creature smirked and waved its hands. Hungry Ones poured from beyond the earthen barrier.

There were relatively few of them. But even a couple of Hungry Ones would be an overwhelming force against two men who had nowhere to run and nothing to defend themselves with. Abandoned by his Guards, Malech had only his own physical strength that was no match for the famine-driven desperation of Hungry Ones. And he had no 'arm; now Daniel understood why. But Daniel was 'armed. And even though his 'arm, now fused with his body, was nothing but a white-hot concentration of pain, he stepped forward, instinctively falling into the fighting stance he had been trained to take. If he was not a militiaman, he was less than nothing.

Malech came to stand shoulder-to-shoulder with Daniel. His face had changed again – it had become a moist expanse of nothing. It was not pleasant to look at but Daniel had no time for such niceties. The nearest zombie was so close that Daniel could see the yellow rheum clogging its fishy eyes and the dry bumps on its hide. At least, he thought, the zombie poison was no longer capable of affecting him. He would just be torn to pieces, together with his toad companion.

The Hungry One made a mewling sound. Daniel lunged at it with his useless 'arm. And suddenly, with a wrenching jolt of pain that almost brought him down, it obeyed his mental instructing, lengthening and reshaping itself into a hard, pointed attachment, ready to pierce and stab. The pain did not go away: if anything, it had intensified to the point when he could barely bear it. But strangely, it made his 'arm more effective.

The Hungry One fell but another took its place. By his side, Malech dispatched another creature with a *Wushu* move the Triads often used. The creature rolled off the road and was torn to pieces by its brethren. But there were more coming.

And then something large plowed through the berm where the Wingate-thing was perched, flattening it into the black mud. Malech pivoted toward the creature that flailed like an overturned beetle and stomped on it. It broke apart.

Daniel, meanwhile, gaped at the sudden appearance of the galloping tenant. Its familiarity took his breath away. He felt broken fangs graze his shoulder but was too astonished to react swiftly, brought to a standstill by the miracle of the appearance in this nightmare of an Aunt Harrow, a faithful, forgotten helper of his childhood. The Hungry One fastened upon him like a rabid dog and another one butted his open flank when an 'arm whizzed by him and tossed the creatures aside. He was astonished that his 'arm had reacted without his conscious volition but then realized it was not his.

A small figure slipped off the Aunt Harrow's massive shoulder. Agatha smiled at him and dispatched another Hungry One with an easy flick of her 'arm, just as he had taught her. Malech changed his face in astonishment.

More Hungry Ones were pouring from the haze. Billows of yellow fog, shot through with lurid purple like frozen lightning, writhed above their heads. The pieces of Wingate-thing, trampled into the slime, stirred and started coming together: hands to legs, head to stomach.

Daniel pushed Agatha behind him. Malech, standing shoulder to shoulder with him, clicked on a new face.

They were surrounded by a circle of slavering grey bodies.

And then, through a chink in the barrier of Hungry Ones,

Daniel saw somebody walking down the road. A woman in black. Walking slowly, unhurriedly, her head bowed, her arms cradled as if she were carrying something. But no, they were empty.

PART 3. KARA

Chapter 1. Edenberry. Another Year Zero.

It was a slow accumulation of random disasters – not one decisive blow but small, insignificant strikes, each single one leaving almost no trace but falling upon the already tender flesh until it bled. First, a bad harvest. Then, an unaccountably larger than usual grain-tax requisition from the city. Then, the epidemic, killing a few, weakening many. Then, the animals dying. Then, the attacks by birdmen. Then, a cold fall and colder winter. And then, and then, and then...

Kara stood in the yard, furiously hitting her exposed arm with a switch, observing the rainbow colors of instantly blooming bruises. She stopped when the skin broke and a couple of drops of blood reluctantly crawled down to her wrist. Loss of blood had always made her faint and now it meant she could actually pass out. And she did not want to; not until she was sure the house across the road would remain locked down, the windows shuttered, the door latched.

Chances were it would. Very few people were out and about, especially not now, in the thin, papery-blue twilight punctuated by icy drizzle. The unfamiliar cold drove most families to huddle under their cotton quilts in front of the braziers that used to be adequate but now only mocked the survivors with their feeble warmth. Even ordinary winter would have been a challenge for their shivering bodies; this unseasonal freeze was busy finishing what the loss of the harvest had started.

Kara did not mind the cold. She had ceased feeling it a couple of weeks ago, at the same time her menses had dried out. All the other sensations had also dimmed: she had lost her night vision and her sense of smell dwindled so much that she almost set herself on fire when her braid fell onto live coals and started smoking, diffusing a pungent odor. She only jerked awake when sparks landed on her bare knees. She hacked off the singed hair with little regret: it had become so dull and brittle that she hid it under a scarf when loitering in the yard and hoping to be seen. The only things that she still felt keenly and therefore longed for were self-inflicted pain – and *him*.

The night was falling quickly; quicker than it had ever done before, or so it seemed. A faint movement above her head, a shadow on the iron-frozen bare ground…She looked up, her stringy muscles reluctantly tensing, preparing to dash inside. Even the hope of seeing *him* was no match for the fear of birdmen.

But there was only a heavier cloud drifting across the flat background of the overcast sky. The last birdman had been seen around the village more than three weeks ago and none appeared since. There was no more blood to be squeezed from that particular stone.

"Kara!" the voice from the kitchen window tore at her nerves. Her hearing, though good enough for the ordinary business of living, was blunt. She could not carry a tune, and used to smolder with jealousy at the other girls her age who compensated with sweet singing for their meager bodies and small minds. Many of them were dead now and those who were still alive could no longer sing. But for her, the one sense that remained unaffected by starvation was precisely the one she cared for least. Her hearing only served to alert her to the deathly pall of silence outside, and to the screechy voice inside, the house. She did not know what was worse.

"Kara!"

With a last look at the shuttered house across the street, she shuffled back. Opening the kitchen door let out the dregs of warmth that had accumulated inside from the body heat of the inhabitants as there had been no cooking done there for longer than she wanted to remember. Her mother clicked her tongue reproachfully at her. The baby in her arms woke and started wailing.

"Shut it up, will you!"

Her mother did not answer, just bent over the feebly moving bundle and kissed a tiny shriveled hand. Kara turned away, her hatred as physical as the greedy void in her stomach.

"Did you see anybody?" her mother asked after a long pause.

"This is why you called me in?" Kara's voice rose gradually, weak at first but ending in an undignified shriek that made her cough. Her mother sighed.

"The birdmen may come back," she offered meekly. "I did not want you to be exposed."

"Why would they be back?" Kara sniffled. "They have taken everything."

"…Well…" her mother did not finish but Kara knew what she meant. There had been persistent rumors of wild khruts actually preying upon people, seizing a tardy child here, a lonely shepherd there, carrying them away to their eerie which they supposedly shared with talking khrut-fowls, and there tearing them apart for a wild feast. Kara had listened avidly to such tales but recently they began to sicken her. Now that her best – and only – friend Masha had been dragged to the burial ground by her tottering uncle, she had nobody to share horror with.

"We could have been out of here," she said bitterly. "We could have boarded that train, been in the city by now. They say you can eat like Grandfather just by picking up what people leave on their plates."

"Trains…" her mother said. "How can you trust them?"

Kara shrugged. She knew, and her mother knew that she knew, that the fact that they were still here, in the dying village, had nothing to do with the distaste the country people had for the giant train-and-tracks symbionts. All such niceties had been erased by the famine long ago. No, the reason was right here, starting again its unendurable wail. The smuggler who came to the village after the first wave of the disease and offered passage to the city – for a price, of course – was perfectly willing to take two healthy women. But a newborn figured not at all in his calculations.

Kara plunked herself on the rug by the cold fireplace, staring fixedly at the thickening darkness outside. The temporary exhilaration brought about by self-punishment ebbed away. She dully remembered the time after the three-square meals a day had dwindled to one when she had felt euphoric. The school teacher – also dead now – had told her it was an effect of starvation when the body was beginning to feed upon its own tissues. Apparently now this self-cannibalism had come to an end. She had nothing to offer even to herself.

"There is some green soup in the stove," her mother said, lowering her voice as if afraid somebody would overhear, even though, except for the family across the road, their nearest neighbors were all dead.

Kara shot to her feet and then sat back with a groan. "Green soup" was an infusion made of stale hay from their empty chicken coop. The coop had already been cleaned out so thoroughly that its earthen floor shone like parquet. The hay offered no more nourishment than the bark they had stripped from the saplings in the yard – less, in fact, because the couple of times Kara had forced herself to drink the disgusting liquid she could not keep it down.

And yet it was tempting. She knew she would eventually gulp it eagerly, its stink burning her sinuses, cradling the warm crock in her shaking hands. She would do it. And then she would rush to the toilet, barely hitting the seat before it all went through her. She knew it and yet she also knew she would do it, no matter what. Hunger was a beast that could not to be reasoned with.

The baby stopped its reedy wail. Her mother got up with a groan, tottering on her grotesquely swollen legs. Many of the survivors were afflicted with edema that made parts of their bodies look unnaturally plump, fueling the suspicions of their fellow villagers that they had a secret stash. Old Mrs. Rogofff…but Kara did not want to think about her. She herself did not swell up. Her skin was dry and corrugated as if she was driven rapidly through the stages of aging by the whip of hunger. Her flesh clung to her bones like a worn dress. But she had good bones and, in the dusk, she still looked beautiful. Or so she told herself.

Her mother put the baby down, very carefully, so as not to wake him. She shuffled to the larder and, with a fearful glance over her shoulder at the curtained window, opened it. Kara watched her with dull surprise. She knew that the larder was empty.

With a painful intake of breath, her mother lifted something from the lowest shelf and gave it to Kara. She stared at it uncomprehendingly. It looked like a glutinous grey cake wrapped up in leaves.

"Eat!" her mother said.

"What…what is it?"

"I found some blackberry leaves behind the barn. Fresh, the plant was not dry at all. And I mixed them with mercy soil."

Mercy soil was a soft clay-like substance that lay in open pits around the village. In time gone by, school-kids ate it because they could and pregnant women because of their cravings. Now, people ate it because they had nothing else. In some places, the pits were excavated down to the rock and the rock scraped off.

Kara's mouth flooded with saliva. She snatched the cake and bit into its powdery substance. Her mother was watching her anxiously.

"Careful," she said. "It'll block you if eat too much."

It was true, but Kara felt another wave of irritation roll over her. Was her mother trying to tell her not to eat so she could have more for herself? And where was the second half of the cake?

"I ate it," her mother said apologetically. "My milk is drying up. The baby needs whatever I can give."

Irritation was supplanted by a burst of pure hatred. Kara felt like tossing the soil-cake onto the floor and grinding it with her foot in front of her mother.

But, of course, she did not do it. She ate her share of the cake and licked her fingers.

She finally fell asleep, but her dreams were of metal and brightness, strange lights glittering on vast expanses of what looked like a forest of sharp thorns. She woke up and her dry mouth was flooded with the taste of a wound. She shuffled to the kitchen and drank some water to wash it out. Her cracked lips dribbled blood.

When the famine was still new, Kara's dreams had been of sumptuous meals. Now her sleeping mind had given up all hope to ever be sated again. Instead, her nights were filled with lightning flashes of strangeness. She could have attributed them to the effects of starvation on the brain. But instead she had become convinced they were messages, coming from outside of herself. The problem was, she had no energy left to decipher them.

Still, it was tempting. There was something out there, and it was neither the unattainable city nor the dying countryside. Something was calling to her with images of flashing lights and flowing metal, something promising a deliverance from the stinking, hopeless trap her village had become. Edenberry was on the route Grandfather and his retinue of refugees had taken as his indomitable will drove them toward the city. In fact, the story was that Kara's village had been founded by the stragglers who could not follow the Incoming, too feeble or too craven to trust their leader. And now history had come full circle. She could not belatedly follow in Grandfather's footsteps: the city was guarded by armed militiamen and predatory Guards, too fat and smug to share their bounty with the desperate descendants of those left behind. But the Divide was there, she knew it; even though nobody could locate "there" on the crude maps of their neighborhood. She could cross back. Whatever it was that Grandfather and his people had been fleeing, it could not be worse than starvation.

And yet, she could not go. What kept her chained to the dull routine of suffering was a compulsion she could not break. Her mother thought it was family loyalty. Her presumption filled Kara with loathing, but she had no energy to waste in recriminations. She needed the last of her strength to keep herself beautiful.

She lifted the dingy curtain and peered outside. It was early morning, dawn breaking as grey and dispirited as everything else in her life – except for the one bright thing. It was the thought of *him* that made her pump more water, wash her face, peel off the sweat-soaked smock she had been sleeping in and put on fresh leggings and shirt. Luckily, the screamer – she refused to think of him as the baby, let alone her brother – was quiet, sleeping in his cot by her mother who stretched out on the platform under a pile of rags, her face as gaunt as the face of a corpse. But she was alive: Kara could hear her raspy breathing. She could not hear the creature, though; and not for the first time, the half-fearful, half-exultant thought that one morning he simply would not wake up crossed her mind. But then he gave a slight whimper, her mother stirred, and Kara quickly exited the back door into the garden.

The dank air made her shiver. The naked trees were garlanded with loops of unmoving fog. She reluctantly steered herself toward the outhouse. She fiercely resented the indignities of the famine: the blocked bowels, the stomach cramps, the bloating, and the pain. She would rather not eat than pay this price; but fasting turned her body into a wild beast that demanded feeding, no matter the cost.

"Kara!"

The familiar voice pierced her with an almost physical pang. She turned around quickly, blood rushing to her face. She was simultaneously mortified and pleased: blushing would disguise the sallowness of her skin.

He was leaning against the fence, his arm resting on the gatepost. His face was the only real thing in the world of fog and specters. And even when the pale light disclosed how haggard this face had become, the flush of desire that radiated outwards from her loins was as strong as ever. For a moment, everything else was forgotten. Even the hunger.

She walked unsteadily toward him, hoping he would attribute her awkwardness to the physical deprivation they shared rather than to shyness. She did not want him to pity her. She knew he despised weakness in girls; this is why he had dropped that crybaby Marie (*she is dead; but so what? No more than she deserved, bitch!*). He needed to see her as strong and competent. She was grateful that her long sleeves covered the self-inflicted bruises on her arms.

"How are you?" he asked.

She shrugged, tongue-tied.

"You know…"

He nodded and they stood in silence.

She was furious with herself. In their encounters, it was always like this: her fumbling for words, his effortless control of the situation. Afterwards, she would obsessively go over every word, ever gesture, reimagining the encounter with herself in the star role, finding a sparkling, witty reply to his every remark, wowing him with her nonchalant brilliance. She would wait impatiently for the next meeting, sure that it would go just as she wanted…and then the cycle would repeat again.

The silence went on for so long she was afraid he would just walk away but he did not. Instead he spoke again:

"My mam…she is not well. How is yours?"

"She is quite all right," Kara replied venomously.

He lowered his head, a shock of black hair falling across his forehead. Kara longed to touch it but did not dare.

"See," he said slowly and leaned closer to her, his proximity setting her heart a-flutter, "I was thinking…Edenberry cannot survive the winter. We will all die here."

Kara nodded. She often thought the same, but the despair of such thoughts was now drowned in the happiness of *him* confiding in her, seeking her support.

"I know," she said. "We need to leave."

He jerked upright.

"You thought about it too?" he breathed.

"Of course."

"So…if I…I mean…"

"I'll go with you," she said. And here it was, plain and simple, her victory. Nothing could stand in her way: neither the birdmen nor her mother. Not even the invincible famine itself. She would go with *him*. And they would live happily ever after.

There was something in his eyes that did not belong in that sublime moment, but she refused to consider it. Everything would go right from now on.

"How would we do it?" he asked dubiously. "Trains are gone. Even if we find a smuggler, we have nothing to pay him."

"We'll walk," she said.

"To the city?"

It gave her a pause. All the while she had been unconsciously considering their escape route to lie in the opposite direction to the distant city. The direction of the Divide. But now she quickly realized that raising this possibility would destroy that infinitely precious thing that was being created between the two of them. *He* was a practical, down-to-earth (*stodgy?*) sort. Along with the majority of the villagers, he probably did not even believe in the Divide. She had found out through the bitter experience of mockery and teasing that her vivid imagination only served to set her apart. *He* did not need a dreamer but an accomplice. And she had to be what *he* needed.

"We can do it!" she said, sounding more confident than she felt.

"But we don't have food or warm clothes," he said despondently. She suddenly realized – and it was an unwelcome realization – that he was trying to find excuses for not going. After suggesting this bold plan, he was now looking for a way out. But, at the same time, he knew this was the right – the only – thing to do in order to survive. When he confided in her, she thought he was seeking a follower. Perhaps he was seeking a leader. Very well, then, she would lead.

"We have…something," she lied, lowering her voice unconsciously as people always did nowadays when talking about food. "You must too."

"Something," he agreed reluctantly. "But I can't take it. This is for my mam."

"Then we'll use mine," she said with such an absolute faith that she believed it herself. "Until we can find something else. Other villages cannot be so bad."

"It was a bad year."

"But the birdmen…"

He lifted his hand, silencing her, casting a fearful glance toward the overcast sky. She shrugged. She did not know why the birdmen had singled out Edenberry for their depredations nor why the city militiamen had not come to the rescue as they had done in the past. Still, she refused to succumb to the superstitious panic sweeping the survivors. The birdmen were flesh-and-blood, just like people. Not demons.

"I'll find food," she said, putting all her passion into this simple statement. "I'll find food and then we'll leave. We'll go to the city. The city will provide."

He smiled, the first genuine smile from the beginning of the meeting, and for a moment, she was as happy as she had ever been in her life. Everything else melted into the blue of his eyes. Even the hunger.

"Tonight?" he whispered.

"Tonight."

"But your folks…" he started, and it was as if she were abruptly brought back to shivering cold and empty stomach of the present.

"They'll be OK," she said and meant it. She would make sure they would never come between them again.

He did not kiss her when they parted; just touched her cheek. But it was enough.

Kara knew they had no more food. The pit her mother had laboriously dug under the sleeping platform to hide the remnants of the un-confiscated grain was empty. They were heading into winter with nothing but a couple of pounds of mercy soil and some tree bark, grass and leaves. They were going to die. When she allowed herself to think about it, she knew her mother and herself were doomed.

And so was the baby – not that she ever thought of him as such. He was the parasite who had torn her mother apart on that horrible night she had been forced to help her deliver because the village midwife was too sick to come. She had cleaned up her mother's blood but refused to touch the squalling bundle that had come out of her worn body. She had held her mother's hand during the labor but stormed out of the house when she saw the blissful smile on her face and her arms gently cradling the red-faced intruder. Until then, such a smile had been for Kara alone.

And finally she was about to leave it all behind, to cut the sickening knot of love and hate that tied the three of them together. She was going to the city with Daniel. Nothing else mattered. Nothing else could be allowed to matter. And since she had promised him to bring food, food she would bring.

Lost in thought, Kara walked into the house and only then

did she register the strange silence in it. Her hearing always informed her where her mother was in their home that had shrunk to the empty kitchen and the sleeping/living room since they could not afford to heat Kara's bedroom anymore. If nothing else, the creature's feeble bawling would indicate where the two of them were.

But now the house felt empty. She stood in the chill, colorless light that seeped into the hallway, unwilling to cross the short distance that would bring her into its stilled heart.

Finally, she forced herself to walk in. The platform was neatly made up with rag rugs, and the wicker cot – the same cot that Kara had slept in a child – stood by the cold hearth. On the table was a piece of paper.

She had to fight the compulsion to turn around and run away, into the lilac twilight brooding over the empty despoiled land. Her head was suddenly painfully clear, her entire body shivering with little sharp bursts of energy. It was as if the early stage of hunger – the intoxication of ketosis in which the body is drunk on its own self-ingestion – had come back.

Still keeping an eye on the cot, she sidled to the table and picked up the note. In her mother's angular handwriting it said:

"Going to look for turnips in the Old Man's field. Give him water if he wakes up."

There were no turnips in the Old Man's field. Kara knew it because she had been there twice. The rotting turnip leaves that she had dug out of the frozen slush had been eaten a couple of days ago.

She let the note drop and stood still for a while. Then, reluctantly, she walked to the cot and looked inside.

The small face was as blank and sketchy as a newt's; the muddy eyes covered by translucent lids. Its toothless mouth sunk deep into the skull. Its little claws rested on the washed-out blanket, the skin and the fabric the same pinkish grey.

She held her hand above its face, then slowly it settled on, as light as the fall of snow, and quickly withdrew. Not a scintilla of warmth traveled through her shivering body; nor did the faintest whisper of expelled air tickled her fingers.

She brought a hand mirror from her bedroom and held it above the body far longer than it was necessary to make sure that its surface remained pristine.

She sat in the cold and dark room, keeping vigil as the anemic dusk curdled into the moonless night. There were no lights in the village because the lamp oil had been drunk and the candles gnawed away.

And then she lifted the body from the cot, carefully wrapped it up in the blanket, and walked across the road toward the house where Daniel was waiting for her.

Chapter 2. Survivors

Adam Malech was frying eggs.

The train's plushy warmth and softly rocking motion had put him to sleep but he woke up after a short nap with an unmistakable sensation of emptiness in his stomach. He was about to call Fiona when he remembered that she was not here. None of his Guards were. They had abandoned him.

He lay in the dark, alone. Kora – or Kara, as she now called herself – was not there either.

He stretched his hand and caressed the velvety upholstery of the sleeping car that gently rubbed itself against his fingertips. At least his train was still loyal.

He felt his eyes tearing up. Crying was a human skill he had learnt late in life and was proud of.

The train powered up the internal lighting and the inset strips in the ceiling shed a wan illumination onto his bed. Adam sat up and realized the train was slowing down until it finally stopped. He rushed to the window and saw the dull night and the gibbous moon swimming among clouds. They were out of the Divide.

He tapped on the wall and felt a series of contractions in response. Trains did not actually talk; they left complex communication to their tracks who could interface with the Pith and with other tracks. But they were capable of understanding simple commands delivered in a touch code and responded if they wanted to. Now, the train was telling him that his tracks needed rest after what had transpired. They were injured and torn and wanted time to heal. This place was safe.

Adam tapped a reassurance and consent. He got up, threw on some clothes, and went to the kitchen car.

In the kitchen, he made an omelet. He had briefly served as a short-order cook in his early days in the Market – before he had contacted the Triads and become the most accomplished spy and occasional assassin in low-levels.

Adam was about to sit down to his late-night meal when the car door whooshed open and the girl walked in.

He looked at her curiously. He had not had the time to assess her in the melee of their unlikely rescue. He had filed away the important facts: she was human; she was young; and she used an 'arm with astonishing skill. She was still wearing her 'arm, he saw, and filed away this fact too.

Apart from the 'arm, she was nothing much: scrawny but pretty in a rather ordinary way, with an unformed face, blond hair, and blue eyes. He was shocked, though, to realize that she was even younger than he had thought, almost a child. Adam was uncomfortable around children. He had never been a child himself and had none of his own. Many toads and ducks could reproduce sexually but he was not sure whether he was one of them. None of his girlfriends had ever gotten pregnant.

He put a plate with eggs and toast in front of her. She ate like a starveling. But surprisingly, she tried to keep her table manners, even though she did not know how.

"What's your name?" he asked after she had polished off most of the food.

"Agatha Rudenko."

"And your folks?"

"Dead," she said calmly.

"I'm Adam Malech," he said watching for a reaction and seeing none. She clearly had never heard of Malech Industries.

"Have you ever been to the city?" he asked, just to make sure.

"No. Are we going there?"

There was such an eagerness in her face that he felt immediately reassured. All relationships were relationships of power or exchange. He had learnt this lesson early and well. Each of them now had something the other wanted. She wanted to go to the city. He wanted her skill with an 'arm.

"Why do you want to go to the city?" he asked.

"The city provides."

Yes, it did. Adam felt a sudden pang of having been away from the city for so long. The Pith was the closest he had for a parent and even though he found the human sentimentality about family relationship ridiculous and off-putting, he also longed for the sense of warm communion he had occasionally experienced when touching the naked flesh of the city.

Not for a long time, though. There was a cancer growing in his mother's body.

"There is a war in the city," he said. "Are you willing to fight?"

She stroked her 'arm. This was a sufficient response.

Adam had gone into the countryside to find a weapon against the Hungry Ones. He lingered there because…well, because Kora. But he had realized already that his plan would not work. He had to fall back upon more conventional means of warfare.

And here was one.

Daniel was dead.

He realized in some corner of his pain-ravaged brain that this was a paradox. If he could think that he was dead, he must be alive. Dead men can't think. Some Buddhas taught that souls of the departed were absorbed into the celestial city, an eternal counterpart of the earthly city, but Daniel had no patience for this nonsense. Dead was dead. Just like his parents and his sisters. Just like…

Like the boy.

Carrion, inert and disposable flesh. Meat.

So how could he know he was dead, trapped in the disintegrating carcass? Struggling to get out of the trap and yet being aware that it was impossible because the trap was himself?

He reached deep within himself, trying to find something to cling to. And he found it. Pain.

It defined his muscles and joints, flowed through every bone, brought back his body inch by sore inch. The dull ache, interspersed with flashes of acid burning, varied by stabs of bright anguish, offset by a rhythmic throbbing…

And still he clung to it because it kept at bay the memories that circled him like a swarm of hornets. The pain could not erase them but it blunted them enough so he could reach out and examine each poisonous image one by one. His sudden arrival in the city as an illegal immigrant; his fortuitous enrolling in the militia that was short of recruits; the profound gratitude he felt to the city, the barracks, the service itself; the zombie bite; the deal with Madam Wren; his enforced metamorphosis into a creature of the hunt that scoured the countryside in search of the prey he had been sicced upon like a dog…And finding her. Finding Kara. And realizing that the criminal he had been searching for was himself.

She had done it for him. He had known her infatuation with him and had taken advantage of it. Not in the usual way – even though before the famine she had been the belle of the village. But the same boys who swapped stories, real and imaginary, of getting into the panties of every other girl would fall silent when Kara's name was mentioned. She was too much of everything – too smart, too handsome, too strong. Too strange. There was something about her that set her apart: a kind of smoldering intensity. He had been torn between attraction and revulsion when he learned just how much in love with him she was, the very strength of her feelings so spookily excessive that it dampened even his adolescent horniness. He had slept with a couple of other girls. He had never touched Kara.

And yet, that fateful evening when he sat in the lilac twilight of the winter day, hearing his mother's raspy breathing from the bedroom and knowing this was the end, he thought of her. She was his last hope. Escaping the famine was the only way but it was too late for him. He should have done it earlier but had not had the determination or the ruthlessness to leave his family. And now his father and his sisters were dead, and his mother was gasping her last, burning in the slow fires of one of the fevers that followed in the footsteps of the famine. He would bury her, but he no longer had the energy to undertake a perilous journey to the city. He would starve in the empty house, passively sinking into death through the layers of apathy and despair.

But not Kara. She had told him they would go to the city together and he clung to her promise with the tenacity he would despise if he could. Counting on a girl to save him? What kind of a wimp was he?

But he had looked into her emerald eyes that afternoon and saw determination, as hard as a gemstone. She would come. And she would make him leave. And she would lead him to the city. He was weak enough, desperate enough to admit to himself that this was what he counted on.

And so when he heard knocking on the door, he rushed there, almost tripping over the hearth-rug. His vision swam with the fireworks of hunger.

She stood there, pale and erect. In her arms was a swaddled bundle.

"What is it?" he asked.

"Food," she said.

And then…

She had done it for him and he had thrown her out, yelled at her, branded her with the most horrible of names. The name that was his own. Because as he looked at her, proud and erect, walking away from his doorstep, carrying the bundle, he opened his mouth to call her back. Because nothing was worse than hunger. This was the lesson of the famine he could not unlearn. Not the physical pain that had colonized his body, not the jabs of unwanted memories, not the remorse, the self-contempt, the pangs of regret…Nothing was worse than hunger. The Hungry Ones were merely an embodiment of this knowledge.

He would have called her back. But then the obscenely beautiful twilight lit up with a crimson glow and the earth buckled like a horseback.

Now having come close to the Divide, he could make better sense of the end of Edenberry. Then, he had understood nothing. He thought death had arrived as the earth moved like the living being that it was, and the flaming blanket of the sky fell upon him. The last thing he saw was a figure of Kara, black against the swollen sky, facing away from him…And then time and space folded and sucked him through a tunnel of nothingness. He came to, lying on the warm pavement and in front of him was the most wonderful thing he had ever seen in his entire life. Even now, as he was settling the final accounts with himself, the memory of that thing brought a spark of pleasure.

A trash can.

He crawled to it, and rummaged through its contents, and filled his mouth with a medley of things he could not name and did not care to because they all had one wonderful name. Food. He threw up most of it but enough remained to let him stand up and gaze in awestruck wonder at the towers of light that leaned over the crooked alleyways of low-levels. And there he was, in the city.

He had forbidden himself to think of her, had expunged her name from his memories, and had buried her, and the famine, and the dead body of the baby so deep that he had dared to hope they would never come back. But the Buddhas taught that the dead would rise one day. And this was the day for him.

Something touched his hand, eliciting a jab of pain that made him open his eyes. Light streamed in, together with the unwelcome realization that the darkness was inside, rather than outside, of himself. If he was dead, his body did not know it yet.

He was lying in a berth inside a rocking train. A woman was bending over him.

"Agatha?" he whispered hopefully. But even though the name

was back, scurrying in his mind like a spider, he still could not bring himself to say it out loud.

Kara.

She hated the woman immediately.

When Doris the Harrow carried her into the quicksilver of the Divide, Agatha thought she was about to die. She thought it but did not believe it. Death was not for her. Even as her family was being slaughtered by Hungry Ones, she had known she would survive. And this knowledge was still strong inside her as the world twitched and folded like a bad dream.

The ground under the Aunt Harrow's splayed feet was a latticework of stagnant pools, algae-choked streamlets, and bog plants. But the pools wrinkled with no wind, the streamlets burbled with human voices, and the plant observed her with malicious eyes.

The sky flamed with the colors of sunset even though the sun stood at zenith. And Agatha felt hot and cold waves pass through her body, clashing and pooling as if days and nights, months and years worried at her flesh like slavering dogs. She clung to the Aunt Harrow and survived.

The Harrow bowled into an earthen wall that gave under her massive body. Then Agatha saw two men standing in the middle of the road, fighting back-to-back. The sight of one of them made her heart flutter. The clothes he was wearing were as intimately known to Agatha as her own worn breeches and homespun tunic. She had washed them more than once.

The two men were surrounded by deadheads but Agatha was not afraid. The sweet sense of power filled her to the brim as she unwound her 'arm and felled one of them with a single flick. And then another. Reggie stepped between her and the next assailant. She appreciated the gesture; it gave her an additional sense of power. She also noticed that he looked more human now, the rough planes of his face smoothed over.

The other man was handsome and dressed in a kind of clothes Agatha had only imagined before. He looked like Petrus, the hero of her favorite flambeau romance. She wanted to impress him, and so she fought with renewed energy, but it would have gone badly for them had not the woman appeared out of nowhere. She was old, at least thirty. And she was both beautiful and ugly, in the way wicked women in romances always were. Her torn clothes clung to her curves but her green eyes were flat and opaque.

More Hungry Ones showed up then. One of them looked like a leathery sack with boneless tentacle arms attached to the top of its shapeless body. The body was the face, with blinking eyes where nipples should have been, wet pulsating nostrils in the place of the navel, and a giant toothy maw at the crotch. And this creature went straight at Agatha. She flicked her 'arm but it slid off the creature's tough hide.

The woman caught the deadhead in a disgustingly close embrace, almost nestling against its stinking leathery hide. Her arms went around it. The tentacled Hungry One shivered and seemed to collapse in upon itself like a pricked balloon. Its limbs went flaccid and the woman freed herself and stood up. And then the quality of light changed abruptly, the sun jerking across the sky and splitting into three discs the color of a bleeding wound.

"Run!" the woman shouted and looking back, Agatha saw a black line advancing across the marsh.

The Aunt Harrow snatched up both Agatha and the other woman in her powerful arms and sprinted forward, keeping ahead of the zombie army. The men kept up for a while, running low to the sleek surface of the road (the other man was faster than Reggie, Agatha noticed). But they would have probably run out of steam and been torn to pieces by the Hungry Ones anyway, had it not been for the tracks. Agatha used to be repulsed by the verminous, mile-long creatures who crawled through the fields where they pleased, destroying crops. But now she was overjoyed to see the dark lines undulating against the soiled scarlet of the sky, rearing up like caterpillars the size of mountains.

The other man called out to them in the voice of an owner like a farmer whistling to his favorite dog. Agatha realized then the extent of his power, for the man who could command such giants was clearly of the city – and could he, perhaps, command the city itself? But there was no time for such conjectures because the tracks whisked them up into the air, out of the way of the advancing horde, and delivered them safely to the waiting train. Agatha had never been inside a train and would normally be reluctant to enter its stomach of which such horrid tales were told, but everything had changed in those hours – if they were hours – at the Divide. And now she was safely inside the train, clean and warm and fed, and she never wanted to be anywhere else.

The other man – now she knew his name, Adam Malech, and it was just such a name as she would dream up herself for her favorite romance hero – was about to tell her more about the city when the door of the car sighed open and the other woman entered, followed by Reggie. Agatha felt a pinprick of jealousy seeing them together and chided herself for a fool. She should have gone to Reggie first! But then she would have missed the intimate meal with Adam. No, on the second thought, she had done the right thing.

The woman held her head up as rigidly as if it were stuck on a spike. She was dressed in black, her hair scraped off her face and tied back. She looked like one of the fabled demons that harassed Grandfather and his band of followers of the way to the city. Reggie slouched behind her, looking even sicker than before, his arm – or was it his 'arm? – swollen and puffed up. Agatha unconsciously stroked her own perfectly smooth one.

"Kora!" Adam went to her, making Agatha wish the tentacled

zombie had been stronger.

"Kara," she corrected.

"You'll always be Kora to me."

She shook her head wearily but Agatha, not to be outdone, rushed to Reggie and hugged him. He hugged her back, fiercely, and instantly calmed down her apprehensions. She dismissed a brief jolt of pain that went through her as a belated response of her battered body. And if Adam was made just a little bit jealous – well, nothing's wrong with that!

"Now that the reunion is over, can we please sit down and talk?" Adam said in his masterful voice. "Mr. Moylan, would you like something to eat?"

Who was Mr. Moylan? The answer was provided immediately with Reggie's reluctant nod. Adam gave him a plate with bread and meat and poured some golden liquid into tall glasses for both of them. He was about to pour a third glass but hesitated, glancing at Agatha.

"Farm children are given harvest wine before they're weaned," Reggie interjected. "She is not too young."

"I'm not a child!" Agatha cried indignantly but was mollified when she sipped the wine and felt the fiery sweetness diffuse through her entire body.

Throughout this interaction the woman, Kora – or Kara, sat immobile, staring into distance. She was not offered any food or drink.

She was the first to speak, though.

"He let us go," she said. "He could have killed us, but he let us go."

"He?" Adam asked.

"The Divide."

"The Divide is not a 'he'. It's unconscious, dreaming its soil and water dreams."

"It's conscious now," she said. "It is inhabited by the Nestling."

Adam nodded, as if it explained something.

"So this is why the war started," he said. "It has acquired sentience. But how?"

"What does it mean?" Agatha interjected.

The woman turned her dead eyes on her, but it was Adam who explained.

"When Grandfather came," he said, "the world belonged to two giants: the Pith and the Divide. The Pith sprawled on the mountainous slopes of the Peak and was a colony – like an anthill. The Divide grew like a blanket over the swamps on the boundary between our world and the world of Grandfather. The Pith had the power to shape living flesh. The Divide had the power to shape time and space. But both were animal-dumb, using their powers unconsciously, just to survive."

"They were better off that way," the woman muttered.

Adam shrugged and went on: "When Grandfather came, the city was born. Tenants split off the Pith, became intelligent and self-aware, joined with humans in building civilization."

"Don't tenants hate humans?" Agatha asked because this was what most farmers believed. Tenants were commonly blamed for the famine.

"No!" Adam exclaimed, sounding shocked. She nodded obediently and sipped more wine.

"But now the Divide has awakened, as you say," Adam said to Kora. "So, it's breeding its own army, the Hungry Ones. They are the dying whose agony has been stretched indefinitely by its manipulation of time. It has conscripted the khruts – I still don't know how, what bribe they have been offered…And it has sent its army to march upon the city. To win the battle that has been going on forever, beginning at Year Zero every year."

"I know why it woke up," the woman said. "It has a mind now. Stolen from the child who was left in the marsh."

"The child?" Adam asked.

"My brother."

Chapter 3. The Decision

Adam Malech did not like human beings.

As passionate as he was about the idea of humanity, he found that individual humans inevitably fell short of it. He would give anything to be one of them, to acquire, finally, that precious and elusive quality that set them apart from the tenants. And yet, as he struggled to puzzle out his human subordinates, rivals, partners, lovers and rare friends, he felt frustrated and disappointed like a child who pulls apart his favorite toy to find only cheap stuffing inside.

Take the three people who shared the dining car with him. The girl – Agatha? – was alright. She was so unsubtle in her attempted seduction of him that he felt a sort of adult tenderness, like watching a toddler take her first steps. He felt no attraction to her whatsoever: she was too young and too callow. But he could eventually mold her into something useful.

He was not sure about the man, Daniel Moylan. He had already been reshaped by the diseased intelligence inside the Pith and whoever collaborated with it. Adam had been shocked when Daniel had told him about the woman he called Madam Wren. He remembered Marika Fu, known as Madam Wren to her clients, from his days in the Market. A small-time people smuggler, a part-owner of a bordello, she was one of the innumerable petty criminals whose illegal activities smoothed the flow of the legitimate trade in the city. She had briefly taken him under her wing in the first days after his spawning, but he had had his eye on higher things even then and had quickly left her behind. And now she seemed to be at the center of a mysterious network that tried to do…what?

To get rid of Kora. Whatever else they had been dabbling in, this one thing was clear. They had remade Daniel and sent him out to find and kill Kora. It meant that they knew something about her. Something more, perhaps, than he knew himself? How was it possible?

Their plan had backfired, but he was determined to root out the conspiracy when he was back in the city. There were so many things waiting for him in the city, the election for Mayor being only one of them. He cursed his impulsivity in taking Kora to the country; even with the time dilation, the lost days were more than he could afford. Still…he did not regret it.

Kora…Or Kara as she insisted on being called now. Whatever history lay between her and Daniel – and by now he had a pretty shrewd guess what it was – had no relevance to the present. To him.

He had been in love with human women several times in the past, but he told himself this was different. How different, he preferred not to speculate. And anyway, she was not human anymore, not completely. Neither human nor tenant.

Was she a monster, then?

No. He would cling to his belief that she could choose. And to his hope that she would choose him.

He had read the official reports that finally reached the Mayor's office after the first starvation winter. An aid convoy had been sent to Edenberry and other afflicted villages. All the villages were found deserted. There were butchered bodies and raided graves. The official line had been that the wild khruts were responsible.

She sat at the table, her sleek black hair veiling her face like a folded wing. She was beautiful. This was the first thing he had seen when they had met in the pavilion. The reports from his Guards had never said that. He was prepared to meet a useful freak or a dangerous tool: not a woman as changeable as water. No matter how much he liked human women, there was always the lurking disappointment of their *sameness*. Kora was never quite herself.

"We are going back to the city," he said.

"I'm coming with you!" Agatha said promptly.

Daniel just nodded. He was hunched over like a man in constant pain who finds an awkward position that seems to ease it for a while. His face that had lost some of its cragginess, reverting to a more human-like outline, was beaded with sweat.

Kora said nothing.

He turned to her. She had said very little since they found her in the protean landscape of the Divide. He was concerned about her but not enough to repress his curiosity.

"Did you see what is on the other side?" he asked.

Kora finally lifted her head and looked at him. Her emerald eyes were ablaze above her hollow cheeks. Adam suddenly remembered how, after the first time they were together, he had experimented in private, trying to create a masculine version of her face. All his faces were based on actual models: dead men who would not miss their visage (some of them he had killed himself) or male fashion icons, too generically handsome to be bothered by a double. In his youth, he would scout the sex-trade quarter near the Market – called the Meat Market – staring at johns and rent-boys until he got tired of being propositioned. It had never occurred to him to try on a woman's face because it would be useless to him: his body was male and he could not change it. But he had tried it with Kora. The result still haunted his nightmares: the death-mask of a corpse.

"A field of steel," she said tonelessly. "A forest of blades."

Adam felt a shiver of excitement down his spine and Daniel stirred up from his slouch. Steel was produced in the city to supplement the Pith but it was never more than an afterthought for big construction projects. Dead materials were intrinsically inferior to living tissue.

"Is there anybody there who there can help us?"

She shook her head but did not elucidate whether it meant there was nobody or she did not know the answer. He waited for a moment and shrugged.

"Very well. We have to do it ourselves."

"Win the war?" Daniel said dubiously.

"We can do it!" Agatha exclaimed, and he smiled at her as one would at a precocious child.

"We have more resources than you realize, Mr. Moylan," Adam said. "Don't forget, you are still in my employ."

"You'll have to pay for my sick leave," Daniel muttered but Adam knew he had him.

He turned to Kora again who sat ramrod-straight with an absent expression on her face.

"Will you help us?" he asked bluntly.

"We had this conversation before," she answered in the same flat voice. "I'll do what I can. But I am only a single woman. And you cannot make more like me. Nobody can. Not in this world."

"Is that what you learned on the other side?" Adam asked.

She shook her head.

"I did not cross. Not this time. There is…a fence."

"A fence?" Adam leaned toward her. "Made of what?"

Her composure shattered, and she turned away from him.

"People," she whispered. "Hungry Ones. Dying but not dead."

"So it learned too!" Adam exclaimed. "The Divide learned the same lesson as the Pith! Stones are hard, steel is strong, but the hardest, strongest thing of all is flesh because it struggles to survive against all odds!"

Tears were now flowing down her cheeks.

"They want to die!" she whispered. "My mother wants to die!"

"Your mother is there!" Daniel exclaimed.

She nodded without looking at him.

"But you said…your brother…"

"My brother was…is…five months old."

Daniel hid his face in his hands and even Agatha looked faintly disturbed. Adam decided that enough was enough.

"We are going to the city," he said.

Chapter 4. The Flying Man

They had pecked him to death, tore out his eyes, and left the plucked carcass by the side of the embankment where trains ran no more. Peter tried to drag the body away into the bushes but his nav hissed at him and he desisted. What was the point, after all? Bodies were shit.

Except in the city bodies were disposed of with a Buddha ceremony. Many humans actually buried them.

His nav scoured his chest with her long claws – she was one of those True Wings, close enough to what humans called khrut-fowls to pass for one except for her larger size. He would challenge her, but he knew he had no chance. Not just because she had just come from the country, fed on stolen grain, fat and quick. The real reason was that he did not want to fight. And even if he did, he only knew how to fight a human way, with sticks and batons, the way Guards were taught. If he tried a Fighting Dance, puffing out his meager chest, striding in front of her with a flap of his small wings, he knew he would break hundreds of unspoken taboos. He would be mocked and pelted with excrement. He would be laughed at. And he had had enough of this.

He had volunteered for a recon. Actually, since his flight had gone back to the old way of having no chain of command, he did not need to report to his nav at all. He just rose into the air and flew toward the fire on the horizon. As he climbed up, the air felt thin and insubstantial, hardly able to keep him up. He felt a moment of blind panic when he realized he was actually afraid of *falling*. This was inconceivable: K'tua never fell! He repeated it to himself as he finally gained altitude and stabilized his lurching progress by beating his wings so rapidly, his muscles threatened to tear. Except Peter caught himself using the name "khrut"; the very name that the campaign against the city was supposed to expunge, together with the city itself!

He saw many signs of devastation below: charred ruins, fields of burnt stubble, and orchards of tree skeletons. Corpses littered the embankment like so many discarded food containers. From above, he could not tell human bodies from Hungry Ones, and was grateful for that. They were supposed to be allies, a gift of the Nestling, but Peter shuddered with disgust when he encountered them. He was disturbed, though, to see K'tua – khrut – bodies. Some were impaled on rough wooden spears or hacked by axes. Some – many – were clearly killed by other khruts.

The wall of flame where the city should have been was licking the foothills of the Peak and crawling upslope, toward up-levels. Peter wanted to come closer but was too tired. He realized that unless he turned back, he would have to alight and walk. His wings were not strong enough! He remembered the woman who he had failed to smuggle out of the city, the woman named Koraa. She had wondered as to how such small wings could carry both of them and suggested that the city helped, the Pith changing physical laws in its vicinity the same way the Divide changed time. He had been deeply offended by this suggestion. Now, it occurred to him that she had been right.

He still did not know why Koraa was so important. The order to take her away from his employer's compound and hide her in the Market had come to him via a chain of broken whispers from the True Wings in the countryside where the rebellion against the city was brewing. He caught himself using the human term "order". There were no orders in new flights, just as there were no inferiors of superiors, no discipline and no discrimination.

But without discipline, how could you ensure efficiency? And was not the disdain of the flock for him a form of discrimination?

Shaking his head, Peter forced his screaming chest muscles to contract. He was losing altitude. He realized he would have to go down and rest, perhaps hunt for a rat or a mouse. He hated the taste of bleeding rodents but there was nothing else to eat in the denuded countryside. He nostalgically remembered the bounty of the Fish Alley in the Market and his favorite sushi stall.

And that was when he saw the train.

Peter banked, helped by a lucky updraft. It was strange seeing a live train; MTT had been shut down after the major attack began. What was even stranger was that this train was busy scurrying toward the city rather than away from it. The train was short, only two cars, but it seemed young and healthy, and its tracks pulsed with vigor. Peter tried not to come too close. A track could lash out and bring him down.

He followed the train for a while, not knowing why. Shouldn't he just go back to his nav and report on what he had seen? But then he remembered that she did not care for his report. That was his Guard training speaking, the shameful remnant of his servitude.

But being a Guard had been a job. It had been an identity. And now, what was he? The weakest chick in the nest, the one to be pecked to death by its siblings or pushed out by its parents…

In the city, infanticide was a crime.

The train slowed down and stopped. From his vantage point, Peter could see a group of Hungry Ones on the other side of a copse that hid them from the train passengers. He could hear their soft cooing. But human hearing was not that acute. He landed behind a ruined outbuilding, peering cautiously at the train.

The train exuded a ladder and two humans stepped outside. Peter only just managed to cut short his trill of surprise when he saw that both were familiar.

The male was his former employer Adam Malech. And the female was Koraa.

Actually, he was not sure about Malech. His clothes and

figure looked familiar, but the face seemed different. Like all khruts, Peter had a perfect recall of human and tenant faces but he had only seen Malech once from a distance, as he had been hired by his assistant, an unpleasant creature called Wingate. But Koraa was unmistakable.

The two stood by the ladder, arguing. Peter crept closer.

"You must eat, Kora!" the man insisted.

"No!"

"What good would it do to starve yourself?"

She turned away, but he could still make out her almost inaudible answer:

"I should have done it before…"

The man clutched her shoulder and forced her to face him.

"Beating yourself up? All right, so you killed your baby brother…"

"I did not kill him!"

"Whatever. It does not matter. Not anymore. Only two things matter: the city and the country. The lives that will be lost, are being lost, while you are wallowing in self-pity!"

"I'm not…"

"Yes, you are! I am disappointed in you, Kora. You only think about yourself. Just as you did in Edenberry!"

"This was cruel, Adam!"

"Fine. I'm fine with being cruel. I'm not human, Kora. I'm not equal to you. I'm just a poor reflection, a second-hand imitation, a fake! But without me, the city will burn to the ground and the country will be eaten up by a living bog with the brain of an idiot!"

"Aren't you exaggerating your own importance, Adam?"

"No. I know what I am. I know what you are."

"A monster. A disobedient daughter, a treacherous sister. I broke the taboo that should never be broken."

"You'd be surprised how many have broken it. Hunger has the way…Anyway, so you are a cannibal…"

The woman gasped and Peter, in his hiding, gasped with her. Wild K'tua occasionally ate their own, but humans?

"I see you still don't like to say it," the man went on inexorably. "It doesn't bother me. We do what we do to survive. Nature doesn't care. Only people do. We have to rebel against nature if we are to survive as people. And that means doing hard things. Like eating when you want to starve. Like fighting when you want to make peace. And like hunting because others depend on what you kill. Look," he gestured toward the dozing train. "He is hungry. He needs to eat. He has carried us for miles and miles. And there are no Guards anymore to bring him food. You have to do it!"

The woman stood vibrating like a taut string for a couple of heartbeats, and then she turned around and sprinted toward the grove where a handful of Hungry Ones were hiding. The man looked at her retreating back. Something changed in his face, something that made Peter blink his nictitating membranes in astonishment, but then the man was on his way back to the train.

Cautiously, Peter flexed his wings. They were still sore, but the rest had done him good. He beat the smoky air as he flew toward the city.

Chapter 5. Soldier of Pain

Daniel had become a connoisseur of pain.

Pain came in many different varieties and each had its color, its taste, and its music. The stabbing through his knotted muscles was peppery-red, humming with the upbeat melody of a militia marching song. The dull ache spreading from his stomach to his heavy feet was the color of curdled oatmeal and sounded like the mournful dirge of a Buddha abandoned in its temple. The throbbing in his head was of a pretty rosy tint and buzzed like a hive of angry bees.

He thought of killing himself but could not muster the energy. He was a follower, not a leader. It had become clear to him during this interminable week as the train rolled back to the city and he lay in his berth, staring at the hanging folds of derma and exploring the landscape of pain that his body had become. There was no shame in it: no general could wage a war without soldiers. The problem for Daniel was that all his generals had abandoned him: Kora, Colonel Rosen, Madam Wren…They had all gone away, finding him unworthy of their service.

Adam Malech was the last one. He disliked the man – the toad – immensely. But there was this one last chance to give some meaning to his misspent life: to serve somebody.

So, when Agatha knocked on the door of his compartment, he got up willingly. He had not seen her in a while. Too sick to eat, he did not join them at dinners and she did not drop by. He accepted this. Having tried to take care of her, he screwed up. Again.

But he felt as a stab in his gut as she walked in. She looked wonderful: her body filled out in all the right places, her blond hair shiny.

"Adam is waiting," she said shyly.

Adam was in the dining car, his back to them, staring into the muddy darkness outside. Daniel did not realize it was night: he kept his own shutters lowered.

"Firestalkers," Adam said, turning to them, and Daniel's mouth fell open in surprise.

Adam's face was more familiar to him than his own – even his own as it used to be. Before he had become a Hunter, before the zombie scratch, he used to glance at this face every day as he showed up for duty at the base. It had stared blankly from the official portrait that had hung above Rosen's desk.

Agatha did not bat an eye – so she knew what Adam was! But Kara who walked in at that very moment, dressed all in black like a widow, stopped short.

"A new face for a new campaign?" she asked.

"A very old face," Adam replied.

"Mayor Volk!" Daniel exclaimed.

Kara exhaled slowly.

"I thought it looked familiar!" she said. "But why, Adam? Will the Mayor appreciate the masquerade?"

"The Mayor is dead," Adam replied.

"How do you know?"

Adam stroked the wall of the car that rippled under his fingers like the hide of a cat.

"He told me," he said. "Tracks communicate with each other within a certain distance. City tracks told ours and they told the train."

"How did he die?"

Adam shrugged.

"I don't know. The city is in chaos. The khruts are attacking daily, the Hungry Ones are already in mid-levels, and now there are firestalkers."

"And all this in a week?" Kara asked, incredulous. "You told me that time acceleration in the country will ensure we are back before anything significant happens."

Adam shook his head.

"That's what I thought. But time has shifted again. Either the Divide has slowed it down or the Pith has ramped it up. I hope not the second because if the Pith – or whoever is controlling it now – can play with time like a knitter with her thread, we are in a world of trouble."

"You can say it again!" this from Kara.

"Who is fighting back?" Daniel asked.

"Your militia buddies. Apparently putting up a good fight!"

Daniel grinned and even though this small effort sent a jolt of pain from his face down into his gut, it was worth it.

"Some City Corps," Adam continued. "There seems to be an issue about the chain of command, but several units are organizing guerilla raids. No Guards, of course; they have all deserted."

Daniel felt vindicated but this momentary pleasure was swallowed up in dismay. Without Guards' proficiency with dead weapons, would the militiamen's and City Corps' 'arms be sufficient? He knew the answer and it was "no".

"And the city, of course," Adam continued. "The city is fighting."

Daniel did not know whether it was a metaphorical flourish or something more substantial but Kara intervened, asking precisely the question that Daniel was afraid to ask.

"Will their 'arms be enough?"

Adam shook his head.

"Both humans and tenants have always been borrowed protection from the birdmen. And now they have come to collect their dues."

"Grandfather would not have left his people unprotected!" Agatha objected piously.

"He didn't mean to. Look!"

He got up and drew something out of a compartment under the table. The object was a piece of dead metal, shiny and curved, precision-tooled. It looked vaguely familiar and Daniel suddenly remembered why. Grandfather's people were carrying similar objects in the picture of the Incoming that hang in the Edenberry village hall.

Kara leaned forward with a catch in her breath.

"What is this?" Agatha asked.

"One of the very few such things left after the Incoming. Mr. Moylan, you're a militiaman. Can you tell me what it is?"

Daniel examined the object, his pain-swollen fingers sliding off the oily metal. Nevertheless, it fit snugly into his palm.

"It's almost like an 'arm,'" he said in awe, "but it is not to be worn but just…just clutched somehow. And it is dead!"

"It is a projectile launcher," Adam said, "meant to eject metallic ball with such force that they would pierce flesh and stone alike."

"But then it would…it would kill zombies and khruts!' Agatha whispered.

"It would kill anybody," Adam said. "And it is not human-specific, tenants could use it as well. If it worked, which it does not."

"Engineers…" Daniel started.

"I have the best engineers in the city in my employ," Adam interrupted. "They took this thing apart. There isn't much to it; they were able to build an exact copy very quickly. They were able to analyze and reconstruct the material that was to ignite and propel the ball out. They did everything right. And it did not work."

"Why?" Agatha asked eagerly.

"I don't know," Adam said. "Nobody does. It is part of the mystery of our world of which we know so little. We are made in the image of humans, reflections of them in the soft mirror of the Pith – and now of the Divide too who is manufacturing its own soldiers to battle its old enemy. But the humans had been traumatized by their passage, impacted so deeply that their memories were almost erased. And we are flawed copies of flawed originals."

"*You* are," Kara said, without lifting her head.

Adam shrugged.

"I'm only a toad among you, true humans. Does it make any difference now?"

Kara did not answer and Daniel looked away. How human was she anymore? And what about himself? Agatha, with her childish face, her innocence, was the only pure one.

"So where does this leave us?" Kara asked.

Adam turned to her.

"Back to you, Kora. If there is anything you know about what lies beyond the Divide, now it's the time to speak out. We are in desperate straits. If there is any way to call for help from Grandfather's world…"

"I know nothing," Kara said in a dead voice. "I told you, I did not cross the Divide this time. And yes, I remember now who I was in Edenberry, but this was not such a great mystery anyway. Daniel remembered it all along. Didn't you?"

Daniel turned away, staring at the inflamed sky outside.

"Sort of," he said.

"But I have no idea what lies beyond the Divide. If, as you say, I spent years in Grandfather's world, I have no recollection of it. If they sent me back as a living weapon to fight Hungry Ones, I don't know how they did it or why."

Adam looked at her for a moment longer. A new face slipped out – the impenetrable face of Adam Malech the businessman.

"Very well," he said. "So, we are on our own. With Volk dead, the election would have to be postponed, but it's moot anyway. I can just walk into the City Hall – provided it still stands – as Volk and assume power. The City Corps who are still loyal will be reassured by the familiar face."

"What are you going to do?" Kara asked.

He looked at her with his opaque eyes.

"Defend the city, of course." He said. "Now, the question is whether you are coming with me."

"I gave my word," Daniel said.

Agatha said simultaneously: "I want to come to the city!"

Kara was silent.

"Kora?" Adam asked.

"I will come," she said, and that was all.

He stared at her a moment longer and turned away.

"Very well," he said. "But it's going to be dangerous. I told the train to drop us at low-levels. We'll have to walk up."

"When?" Daniel asked.

"In two hours. I suggest you all take a nap or at least rest. We need our strength."

"But it's going to be dark! If the fighting is as bad as you say, no sane flambeau will be out!"

"We don't need flambeaus. Firestalkers are out in force. Look!"

The train lifted its shutters and they saw the red sky peppered with a scatter of fire-bursts and draped with drifting garlands of smoke.

The city was burning.

Chapter 6. Memories of Steel

Kara did not want to sleep.

She knew she had to. For all that her companions regarded her as some sort of a demon endowed with an almost supernatural power, the transformation inflicted by the Marching Blades upon her was not as radical as they believed. Apart from her hunger, she had the same needs as anybody else: sleep, rest, shelter. And love.

Unfortunately, the transformation precluded her receiving – or deserving – the latter. And since return from the Divide, she had been plagued by nightmares so vivid that even her waking hours, filled with fruitless rounds of self-recrimination, anger and regret, were preferable to the horrors crowding her sleep.

The worst part of it was that she was not entirely sure what the horrors were. She had not lied to Adam when she had said that she did not remember the steel-world or the reason why she had been changed into a zombie-eater. At worst, she just shaded the truth a little. She had her guess about the latter and would be willing to bet on it, but with the information she had already provided, Adam could have guessed the same. She was not sure whether he had but she trusted his intelligence.

The thing was, everything else remained as obscure as her childhood in Edenberry had been until she had looked into her mother's tortured eyes – and remembered. Now, she wished passionately for these memories to be excised again. But she could not do it. There was no mental knife that she could take to her brain to cut out the cancer of guilt and the shame. The cancer had been dormant for a while after the operation in the steel world, but now it was growing again. Whoever had performed that surgery on her had not done a very good job. Now, the unwanted memories returned to tear at her like a pack of hungry rats, while the useful information that could have perhaps helped Adam to defend the city was lost.

Or maybe they had done an excellent job. Maybe they had achieved exactly what they wanted to achieve.

They had remade her into a living weapon. If Adam was right, those dead 'arms – those *guns* – could not work in their world. Yes, guns. She realized suddenly that she knew what they were called, even though she did not know how she knew. She had heard the word "gun" in the Market where it was used as a mild expletive. Nobody had any idea what it meant. Except for her.

So, let's say it meant a mechanical 'arm. Grandfather and his people carried them across the Divide, only to find out they were useless. So, they learned to manufacture living 'arms that could bond with their wearer's flesh. Not as strong as real "guns", if Adam was to be believed, but strong enough.

But what if those who had been watching Grandfather from across the Divide wanted to punish the city he had remade in his image? If all they had was mechanical "guns", they would not do much good in this world. But what if a woman from Grandfather's world fell into their hands; a woman hungry enough to be shaped into a voracious predator, a living weapon that could not be stopped because her appetite was her power?

But they miscalculated. Because they had forged their weapon with a fatal flaw. A weakness that could derail their plans. A production defect.

Consciousness.

She remembered what Adam had once told her:

"Some say consciousness is a disease. The city was infected."

"Is that what you think?"

"No. I think it was a gift."

She was a conscious being. A person. She could choose.

A conscious monster.

No, monsters had no choice. She had. Just as she had had in Edenberry. The choice she had made had been horrifyingly wrong, but it had been hers.

And now here she was, at another fork in the road, another decision moment.

She could go back to the Divide and try to cross it back into the steel world where she could confront her makers and demand accountability. Or she could end the misery of the crucified Hungry Ones…but she knew she could not. She could not kill her mother, even though it was what her mother wanted.

Or she could follow Adam on his quest to save the city.

Kara did not really believe he could succeed, armed as he was only with the Mayor's fake face. But on the other hand…

Adam was incredibly resourceful, incredibly resilient. In their weeks together, her attitude to him had imperceptibly shifted from resentment to grudging respect to…love? No, she instantly recoiled from the word that rose into her mind unbidden. Love was not for her. She had loved Daniel, loved him enough to do…what she had done. And now she could barely look at his deformed face, torn between pity and revulsion. No, if she were to do it, to join the quest, she would not do it for Adam.

Who for, then?

She realized there was nobody in her life she could do anything for. She had betrayed everybody; destroyed every human connection she had had. Her brother…but she shrunk away from considering what he had become, his infant mind dissolved in the goo of the Divide…No, her brother was dead. Her mother, Daniel, Adam…she could not – or would not – do anything for them.

What remained?

Her mind was as blank as a field of ashes until something flickered there. An image. A memory.

The image of the city she had seen from her hotel window on the morning of her awakening.

It was beautiful. It was sublime. It was alive.

Kara's face was wet with tears. Wasn't it pathetic to come to the juncture when you discovered that the only thing that mattered in your life was an abstraction, a collective noun, an agglomeration of houses, people and signs?

But it was better than nothing.

Wearied by these endless ruminations, she realized she was drifting into sleep and let herself go, gratefully, hoping to get off the treadmill of thinking for a little while, to be ensconced in the black velvet of forgetfulness…

A rusted blade.

A thin sliver of cleared metal.

A drop of blood.

Cutting myself in the fleshy pad between the thumb and the palm where the scar won't be too noticeable. There is nothing to be ashamed of; that the woman's arms are a mesh of thin white lines and the man near her cradles his left arm like a swaddled baby with dark stains on the untidy bandages…Everyone does it. The only shame would be to have a scar on your wrist. This would indicate that you have tried to commit an unforgivable sin of theft. Stealing from the community. Stealing yourself.

I cringe when the edge slices into my skin, parting it with an almost audible smack. There is no pain, just a flash of heat. Pain will come later.

A round tray as shiny as the moon: the authoritative shine of naked metal. My blood drips, reluctantly, onto this pristine surface as if unwilling to pollute it. But when it is required, it is no pollution.

The dark crimson stain spreads for a moment, obscuring the silvery surface. But only for a moment. It disappears, absorbed into the metal, and it is pure and dazzling once again. More pure than before. More dazzling.

Kara woke up, her heartbeat thundering through her shaking

body. She sat up in her bunk, taking deep breaths, trying to calm down.

What the hell was that? A memory? A nightmare?

That was no Edenberry, for sure.

So much metal in her dream that her eyes still ached from its harsh brilliance. She looked around at the soothing organic curves of the train interior. You would never see so much exposed metal in the city, if at all.

And what with the blood? In her days of starvation, she would occasionally hit herself to restore her dulled sensations, but she had never cut herself. She was nauseated by the sight of blood. Indeed it was only recently that she had realized she did not bleed like other women and experienced nothing but relief. Her obscure makers got this right. Her refashioned body took energy in and gave nothing out.

Kara examined her palms and wrists and saw no scars. Of course. Just a nightmare.

But then again, her body healed so quickly and faded away all marks of injury.

She was still pondering her dream when she realized that the train was slowing down.

Chapter 7. The City Burning

The train crept closely to the boundary of the city through a field of ashes. Actually, the city had no defined boundary: it petered out in a wilderness of budding houses and aimless roads. By convention, the limit of the city was marked by the last span of Skybridge. But now most of the young construction had been burned to cinders, and Skybridge poked into the inflamed sky with its broken pylons.

Adam clang to the side of the train who had exuded a sturdy support for him to lean on. He peered into the smoke, nervously flicking Volk's face on and off.

The silence and the emptiness were getting to him. He had been ready to find himself in the thick of a battle, but now, it seemed the battle had been won – or lost. Apart from a troop of Hungry Ones that had been handily dispatched by Kara and fed to the train, they had seen little sign of combatants of any kind.

Had the City Hall been taken? Was he too late?

Adam refused to contemplate this possibility. Once you admitted defeat, you were as good as dead. The city gave no quarters.

But he was also realistic enough to see that his chances of victory were minuscule. Without his Guards, having failed to secure the secret of producing more zombie-eaters, out of the loop of the latest events…What did he have?

Well, he had Kara. Even this was doubtful. Nobody controlled Kara, maybe not even herself. Except, perhaps, those faceless entities on the other side of the Divide. A field of steel blades…He shivered in the dry heat. As eager as he had been to crack the secret of ancient 'arms, the idea of so much dead metal gave him the creeps. No, let them stay where they were.

Except they were already involved, were they not? Adam

thought he had a pretty good idea why they had remade Kara. And this idea was as horrifying as the butchered, bleeding houses the train wove his way through.

Somebody lumbered onto the step next to him. Doris the Harrow! Adam had all but forgotten about the clumsy tenant but now he looked at her with curiosity. The creature did not speak and though Agatha had told him Doris could write, he had dismissed it as the girl's flight of fancy. She was prone to self-aggrandizing fantasies – a useful ability if one was ruthless enough in their pursuit, a crippling defect if one was not. Adam suspected Agatha belonged to the second category but was not sure. There was something about the country teenager that gave him a pause.

"How are you?" he asked awkwardly. The creature just stared at him, its shovel-shaped head nodding stupidly. Adam felt a flash of irritation. This dumb creature – *thing* – was the same as himself! A tenant! No, surely not! He was a man, the owner of a company, future Mayor! This…it was hardly sentient!

"Go away!" he yelled, and the thing lumbered back into the train.

The train was slowing down, the tracks crawling back. Adam squinted into the murk and saw that their way was blocked by a barricade of house corpses interlaced with bodies of humans and tenants. The dawn was breaking, pale light reluctantly dribbling through the curls of smoke. He could see that the barricade extended across the flat stretch of what used to be the new development of Golden Fields, until it ran into a reservoir on one side. On the other side, the smoldering ruins bracketed his field of vision, but he remembered his city topography well enough to recognize the jagged remnant of a new MTT elevated line.

He gestured for the train to stop and went back inside. Agatha was already up, waiting for him. They were soon joined by Daniel and Kara.

"We will have to walk from here," Adam said. Kara said nothing; Daniel, his face beaded with sweat, nodded. Adam, who knew how to appreciate fidelity, smiled inwardly. The man was his now. Whether he would be of much use was a different matter but in his current predicament, even a broken follower was better than none.

"Why?" Agatha asked.

"Trains don't move on streets. Skybridge is splintered here, and it'd be suicide to go into tunnels."

Daniel shivered and even Kara's stony face showed a flicker of disquiet.

"I'm not afraid," Agatha insisted. "The city is ours; it cannot hurt us. Grandfather built it for humans!"

Kara snorted.

"He did not build it," she said contemptuously. "He took it over and made a mess out of it!"

"How dare you!" Agatha flared. "You blaspheme against Grandfather!"

Kara opened her mouth, closed it, and turned away. Adam decided that enough was enough. He could not quite fathom the hostility between these two – was it jealousy over Daniel or himself, or something more subtle? But the last thing he needed was a cat-fight.

"We walk," he declared.

It was only when they were out of the train whom Adam had ordered to go to sleep under the protection of the tracks, while waiting for them to come back, that Kara asked the question he had expected from the beginning.

"Where are we going?" she asked.

"The City Hall."

Adam, Kara, Daniel, Agatha, and Doris the Harrow scurried through the ruins on Virgin's Veil Avenue. Daniel felt dizzy as the devastation of the street he used to walk up every day *en route* to his base brought home just how bad the situation had become. Could it really have been only a week as Malech claimed? Or had the time in the city caught up with the time in the country?

There was hardly a single building left whole. So close to up-level, most structures were not tall, five or six stories at most, but they were all reduced to piles of dead brick and stone surrounding the ragged remnants of the Pith. Adam had repeatedly tried to contact his people in the city through the Pith but the communication system that the city depended on for its daily functioning had broken down. The first time Adam had touched the exposed flesh of the city he snatched his hand away as if burned. The Pith bled where his palm had laid. The second time was even worse: an exposed cable snapped at him, almost taking off the top of his head. Daniel, who had never been particularly good at touch-communication, did not even try. He had enough trouble keeping himself from howling as his pain intensified, building up to a point where he felt like curling up right in the middle of the street and letting one of the rampaging firestalkers burn him to cinders.

"Where is everybody?" Kara asked.

Malech shook his head, frowning.

"Some must have escaped into the countryside," he said. "Many are dead. But there should be street fights, more barricades. I expected better from the militia."

"I'm sure we put up a good fight!" Daniel flared up. "Better than the snooty City Corps! I bet they ran away when the first khruts showed up!"

"Your former colleagues are good fighters," Malech responded smoothly with a slight emphasis on "former". "But it's hard to fight flying attackers when you are on the ground. This is why the Guards' treachery is such a blow. If khruts were united – which they could never be, until now – the city would not stand a chance."

"Unless citizens had guns," Kara said. "They could pick out

khruts one by one."

"Guns?"

"The metal 'arm you showed us," Kara said. "It's called a gun."

Adam and Daniel spoke at once.

"Do you know how to make it work?"

"There is a saying 'dead as a gun' in the city!"

"I don't know how to make it work," Kara said to Adam. "And don't ask me how I know what it's called. I don't remember."

Malech's face flickered on and off and returned to what he had had on for the last couple of hours: Mayor Volk's. At first, it had irritated Daniel, but now it seemed almost reassuring: the face of authority.

They trudged on as Daniel pondered Kara's words. Did he believe her? He decided he did not. She spooked him, just as she had done all those years ago.

The sidewalk was littered with rubbish. Daniel stumbled over something soft which he thought was a garbage collector. He looked down. A little girl, her face crushed into crimson pulp under her braided hair.

Adam and the rest waited patiently while he retched into the gutter. They appeared unaffected. Agatha stared with open-mouth curiosity at the forest of slender towers slowly becoming visible as the sun climbed over the horizon.

There were other bodies scattered here and there but not many. Some of them were burned. Daniel looked around for a raging fire but none was to be seen, though a dense cloud of smoke hugged low-levels, obscuring Skybridge where it rose from the Three Pearls reservoir to join the Golden Flower precinct. But, other than the creep of the smoke and the monotonous flapping of a demented shop awning, there was no movement or sound.

"I wonder where all the khruts are," Adam muttered.

"You relied on your Guards too much," Kara said suddenly.

"They were faithful. It's the Divide acquiring sentience that made them change sides."

"When Wingate talked about the Nestling…" Kara said. "I thought he was just raving."

"What was your brother's name?" Adam asked. Kara turned away.

"He had no name," she said. "In our village a name was given at the age of one year. Until then, it was just 'baby.'"

"That's not right!" Agatha butted in suddenly. "Grandfather would not approve!"

Daniel opened his mouth to defend the customs of Edenberry but then something whizzed past his face and he ducked instinctively, the pain flaring up in a red-hot blaze. When it cleared, he saw a solitary Hungry One laid low by a swipe of Agatha's 'arm. Another one peeked from a narrow alley and Doris – Daniel had almost forgotten about the large mute tenant – slapped it down like a fly. Daniel tensed, preparing to repel another attack, but none was forthcoming. They exchanged puzzled glances – Hungry Ones seldom roamed alone.

Virgin's Veil Avenue at this point narrowed down and descended below a massive overpass. The black throat of the pedestrian tunnel gaped threateningly and Daniel paused, reluctant to go in. He had walked through the tunnel hundreds of times in his previous life but now it looked like a hungry mouth. He had never seen it dark before. Flambeaus would be there on duty day and night, but now, not a single one was around. In fact, he realized he had not seen any flambeaus at all: all their perch pylons were deserted.

Adam stopped too and was looking up into the pale morning sky. Daniel had a strong feeling that they were being watched.

"We need to reconnoiter," Adam said. "We are crawling down here like insects, not knowing what we are going to blunder into."

"Too bad you can't ask your khruts to fly up and tell us," Kara said sarcastically.

"No. But we can go up ourselves."

He pointed to the tower rising above the overpass. Daniel was so used to it that it did not occur to him that Honeywell Golden Emporium was one of the tallest structures in mid-levels, sixty stories high. From the top, the entire city – with the exception of the summit of the Peak and the City Hall compound – would be visible.

The tower glinted pink and bronze in the rising sun. Its outer cladding was dead ceramic tiles covering the tender flesh of the Pith. Its innumerable sleepy windows were shaded by lowered derma lids. Daniel scanned it for signs of rogues but could see nothing untoward.

"Let's go, please!" Agatha was almost jumping with eagerness. The poor girl had never been inside a proper city tower! Daniel smiled, and touched her shoulder, and felt an almost imperceptible flinch.

Oh well, so be it! But was Adam as set in his new role of her protector as Agatha seemed to think? Daniel had caught him glancing at Kara more than once. As for Kara, she was as much an enigma to Daniel now as she had been as the girl next door.

She spoke.

"Let's go!" she said and started toward the Emporium, the rest following. As with most city towers, the entrance was not on the street level but a story above it, reached from a pedestrian walkway that debouched from the same overpass they had been eyeing earlier. They climbed a flight of stairs attached to the side of the overpass and were confronted with a mazelike knot of shining posts, striped awnings and narrow catwalks.

Even Adam, the ultimate city dweller, hesitated. There used to be signs showing where each walkway led but they had been removed. Daniel found this almost more unsettling than bodies in the streets. Another thing that got to him was the profound silence. Even though the sun cleared the low-levels roofs and the city should be humming with the shuffling of crowds going to work, shrill cries of food peddlers, and the rumble of trains, it was as quiet as the countryside. The unnaturalness of this sent shivers down his spine.

Adam eventually chose one of the walkways. It crossed another one at a right angle. As he walked past the intersection, a post lashed at him, winding itself around his upper body like a snake. Adam cried out in shock, swept off his feet. The post whipped over the side of the catwalk above a sheer drop of more than twenty meters down to the pavement. Its coils relaxed and Adam would have plummeted down had he not managed to clutch the suddenly flexible tube that swung him like a pendulum in the air. But his hands could not find purchase on the slick surface and he was slipping down.

It all happened so quickly that Daniel, made sluggish by his unrelenting pain, failed to react in time. But Kara did. She ran to the base of the post and was about to grab it when she hesitated. Instead, she bent over the parapet, trying to reach Adam and failing. The post was too long.

Agatha was instantly by her side, uncoiling her 'arm.

"Don't!" Kara cried. "You'll kill the thing and it'll drop him!"

But Agatha did not try to lash at the post. Instead, she lengthened her 'arm into a thin tentacle and hung over the parapet, trying to reach Adam. She overbalanced dangerously but now Daniel shed his paralysis and rushed to help the women. Together, he and Kara held Agatha's feet as she flipped over the parapet and swung upside down. Her 'arm reached Adam just as the post shook him loose. For a moment, the two of them swayed in the air like circus performers until Kara and Daniel reeled them in.

Adam collapsed on the walkway; Agatha was petting her 'arm; while Kara turned back to the tube which now straightened up, snapped into place, and became another upright post, indistinguishable from the forest of them that supported the derma roofs of this aerial maze. She lay her open palm upon its silvery surface.

Daniel knew what she was doing but it was the first time he saw Kara feed. Torn between fascination and revulsion, he watched her – and was surprised when nothing in particular happened. Her face went blank for a moment and then she dropped her hand and turned to Adam who had meanwhile scrambled to his feet and was readjusting his face, which in the moment of mortal danger had reverted to the moist featureless mask of his default state.

"It's not an individual rogue," she said tonelessly. "I could sense…enormity. It's like the entire city is beyond it."

Adam, his Volk face back in place, nodded gravely.

"I know. I felt it too."

They commenced walking once again in the direction chosen by Adam. Honeywell Golden Emporium loomed tantalizingly close, but Daniel knew from experience that distances in the city meant little if you did not know the right route. He followed Adam closely, determined to do better for his employer next time, and overheard him asking Kara:

"Did you…?"

She snorted.

"It's like trying to drink the ocean," she said.

Daniel had no idea what it meant.

Chapter 8. The Firestalker

Adam was badly shaken.

Not by the fact that he had almost died – his belief in his own invulnerability was not so easily dislodged. He knew that tenants died, just like humans; but he did not feel his mortality in his guts as humans seemed to do. The city was immortal. And he was the city's son.

But now the city had turned against him.

He had been attacked by rogues before: witness the fiasco with the flying roofs that temporarily deprived him of Kora, turned his secretary into a bloody zombie, and made him rely too much on shifty birdmen whose betrayal still rankled. But the roofs were rogues: a cancer in the city's body. He would like to believe that the post was just another manifestation of the malady that he had sworn to cure but he could not lie to himself. One did not survive in the Market by pandering to one's illusions.

The post was not a rogue. The entire city was.

He could not understand how it was possible. The Pith was not self-aware, though its split-offs were. For as long as Adam had been himself, the Pith had been a well of inchoate warmth in the background of his existence. He knew that humans dreamed in pictures and sounds; he dreamed of rosy repose. And now the closest thing he had to a mother tried to kill him!

Honeywell loomed above him, so close he could almost touch its gleaming pink and bronze tiles. But the walkway suddenly dead-ended in a flight of stairs leading back down to the street level. Adam cursed in the dawn tongue.

Kora stopped.

"What's that?"

Adam cocked his head and heard it too: a silky, whispering

sound, quite unlike the regular city noises. At the same time, he smelled bitterness in a gust of wind.

Agatha, who was facing away from them, gasped and pointed at something behind their backs. Even before he turned, Adam saw the rippling light on the walkway.

Rising from behind the overpass like a tardy sun in the sunless sky was a sputtering, sparkling blossom of flame, composed of overlapping petals of bright orange, sunset crimson, and blood red. Its wheels-within-wheels revolved around their glowing center with a hypnotic grace, as the thing unfolded into a deadly rose, growing impossibly huge.

"Run!"

The bitter smoke lacerated their lungs as they stumbled back through the labyrinth of walkways. The heat of the creature wafted over them like the breath of a furnace. Adam snapped on one of his dawn faces whose epicanthus-shielded eyes allowed him to squint through the smoke. Kara stumbled and waved her hands to clear the air. The rest were invisible in the thick fumes.

The catwalk tilted dangerously and then buckled, throwing them off their feet and scattering them like pins. Its foundation wreathed in dark billows, Honeywell serenely floated above their heads. Kara rolled but managed to grab an inert post before the catwalk could shake her off. She propelled herself toward Adam and caught him in her arms. For a second, they clang together and then fell apart. Agatha was clinging to another post, using her 'arm as a guy-line. Of Daniel, there was no sign.

The firestalker loomed above them, its heat beating down. The core of the creature flared up. Blinking through the blue spots in his eyes, Adam saw the ceramic cladding of Honeywell shine like a pillar of pink fire. The glow limned a walkway to the right, leading away from the building, but then dipping down and connecting to a service ladder. The ladder led to a higher level where a wide straight path cut through the cat's cradle of walkways. He pointed to it and they ran.

Sparks from the firestalker rained down on them. Agatha screamed when her shirt caught fire. Kara tore the flaming cloth off the girl and sent it sailing over the side of the walkway.

But now they were on the upper level and suddenly the welcoming darkness of the entrance was within reach. Adam pushed the women toward it. And then he turned back and slid down the ladder into the dense swirl of smoke.

The firestalker was stretching its glowing arms across the sky, blooming into a fiery orchid the size of the world. Adam fleetingly wondered whether there was any mind left inside the creature.

The smoke hit him like a fist. He snapped on the toughest face he possessed, that of an old Triad smuggler who had been his first kill, and plunged into the acrid cloud.

He literally stumbled across Daniel and they both fell in a tangle of limbs. Adam was on his feet quickly, dragging the other man by the collar of his shirt. His hand slipped and touched Daniel's exposed neck. He felt a brief sting of the other's pain.

Daniel rallied up and together they scrambled up the ladder. A tentacle of fire swished above their heads, raining sparks. But then the gaping entrance sucked them into the dark cool of the tower's interior.

Kara and Agatha waited just inside the partially opened doors. There was an expression on Kara's face Adam did not know how to read as her eyes, green even in the meager light, darted between him and Daniel. But she said nothing, just took out her handkerchief and wiped soot and ashes off his face. She did not touch Daniel who slumped on the floor.

Agatha stood apart, arms crossed, her small breasts bound by a strip of cloth that country women used instead of the frilly undergarments of the city. But she was the first to speak.

"Where is Doris?" she asked.

Chapter 9. The Importance of Literacy

Irene Nitka crawled through the debris of her yarn shop.

The arcade where the shop was located had collapsed, showering her place in the hail of dead matter. The upper catwalk sagged through the hole in the ceiling. Fortunately, Irene could stretch the fibers of her body, flattening herself into an almost ribbon-like shape, so she wriggled under the sharp edge of the iron railing and peered through the broken door.

One glance confirmed that going into the Market now would be suicide. The place was in shambles. The crowds of angry humans that had rampaged through the duck- and toad-owned shops had left, carrying away as much booty as they could. But there were still stragglers, drunk on pilfered liquor, going after every tenant they could find. The toads who had enough resemblance to humans to try to pass, did so. Irene, whose body practically screamed to the world her descent from her own yarn merchandise, had no chance of blending in.

And in truth she did not want to. She was proud of her identity – a true daughter of the city, not like humans, the ungrateful foster children, tearing at the kindly flesh of their adoptive parent. She had been indifferent to humans before, but she hated them now.

Her first inkling of the troubles had been the arrival of that woman whom her khrut friend asked to take in. The khrut who went by the human name of Peter, even though his own trilling, whistling name was so much more attractive, was deeply enmeshed in some complicated intrigue. Birdmen were notorious for schemes that often came to nothing. Irene had never asked what it was. She just wasn't interested. But she liked

Peter, who played canasta with her, and she agreed to take the woman in. She came to regret her decision almost immediately. There was something off-putting about the woman; something not right. She was not a tenant but she was not quite human either. And then there was that strange altercation in the Incoming Sun café, in which four khruts and a harmless old man were killed. She could never get the details of that event straight: Alexandra, the human waitress who had witnessed it, claimed the woman killed all of them but that, of course, was impossible. Even if she had been wearing an 'arm (of which Irene had seen no sign), 'arms of such deadly capacity simply did not exist.

In any case, the woman had never come back and Irene did not miss her. But she did miss Peter, recalling with a twinge of sorrow their friendship – or what she thought was their friendship. Now, the birdmen had been revealed as the traitors the older tenants had always claimed they were. An army of khruts followed the invasion of Hungry Ones, laying siege to the city. The deadheads had been stopped by the City Corps and the militia (Irene had to acknowledge that humans fought well), but flights of birdmen and their disgusting fowl-cousins patrolled the skies, randomly descending to kill and plunder. And so, with the enemies at the gate and human looters rampaging in the Market; with flambeaus on strike because their hatcheries had been invaded, their eggs smashed, and many street hatchers killed; with Mayor Volk in hiding, the current Year Zero looked like it would be the wedge to stop the wheel of time from turning.

Irene peeked out again. The lane was deserted now, the sky inflamed, bleeding reddish-tinged light. She considered venturing into the greengrocers' lane to scavenge some food when she heard footsteps.

Somebody blundered into the alley, a silhouette too heavy and round-shouldered to belong to a human. A tenant but not of any variety Irene knew. She peered cautiously at it.

The tenant, whoever it was, was not a Market native. It seemed to be lost, its low-slung head swiveling around. It wore no clothes, so Irene was reasonably sure it did not merit a gendered pronoun. If truth be told, neither did she but she had adopted a feminine name and apparel as a business decision

The tenant was so clumsy it almost stepped on Irene who reared up indignantly. She had set free most of her semi-animate stock, but some yarn-balls still rolled around and she did not want her babies trampled by the newcomer's heavy feet.

The tenant started violently. It was so big it could smash Irene with one swipe of its heavy arm. But it made no aggressive move, just stared stupidly with its small, heavy-lidded eyes.

The stalemate continued for some moments. Not for the first time, Irene regretted her inability to communicate by voice as did most tenants and humans. But it was Grandfather's will.

The big tenant did not make any sound either. Suddenly, it bent down and with one large clawed finger scrabbled in the dust that liberally covered the shop-floor.

It was writing!

Irene's delight made her forget all caution. All humans and tenants were schooled but she had never met another being who communicated exclusively by writing!

"Lost," it wrote. "Mayor?"

Irene snatched one of her baby yarn-balls which she used to communicate. This one was not as nimble as her favorite green one, which lost its life in the pogrom, but it would do.

"Why do you need Mayor?"

"Lost," the creature wrote again.

Mayor Volk, elected due to extensive graft and voter intimidation by his Guards, had never been a favorite of the recently enfranchised tenant population who voted in low numbers and distrusted the human-run establishment. Now Volk's craven inability to stomp out the Market riots made him not just detested but universally despised.

"Where are you from?" Irene wrote.

"Country," the tenant wrote.

Irene's mandibles clacked in astonishment. She had never met anybody from the country!

"Who are you?"

"Aunt Harrow," the creature wrote and added: "Doris."

A lady, then, just like Irene herself. She remembered with a pang her best friend Lola, killed when a crowd of humans swept into the Market, trampling the barrier of courageous traffic cones who tried to stop them. The big tenant bore no physical resemblance to Lola but there was something in her demeanor that reminded Irene of her lost companion.

"My friends," Doris wrote. "Looking for Mayor. Lost."

Irene made a decision. It was madness to remain here, in the ruins of her old life, waiting for the human bands to come back and kill every tenant they could find. And come back they would, squabbling for food in the ruins of the Market like a pack of crows. Irene had no means of defending herself. Doris, on the other hand, seemed husky enough to stomp on a whole bunch of human killers. If, for whatever reason, she wanted a guide to the City Hall, Irene could oblige!

And she just did not want to be alone. This was a fearful time. For the first time since her birth from the warm matrix of the Pith, Irene felt lost and disconnected. The Pith itself seemed remote and diseased, peculiar vibrations emanating from its unquiet flesh.

"I'll take you to Mayor," she wrote and grasping the big tenant's mighty arm, led her through the wreck of the Market toward the looming Peak.

Doris was lost. They tried to call her name, peering through the tide of smoke, but it was useless. Venturing back onto the walkways was out of the question. Even standing by the door was too much as heat poured into the building from the inferno outside.

"We have to go," Adam said. He was prepared to deal with Agatha's resistance – after all, Doris belonged to her – but she said nothing as followed him into the dim interior.

Honeywell, like most towers in the city, was multi-use. The Golden Emporium itself occupied the middle floors. Other shops and eateries clustered in the lower level malls, while the upper floors were divided into layers of offices and apartments. The five uppermost floors were the viewing deck and restaurant, and this was where Adam planned to go to reconnoiter. But he quickly realized it was easier said than done.

When they turned away from the blazing entrance, they found themselves in a long, shadowy corridor lined with identical doors. It looked like a service floor. The corridor plunged into darkness ahead. Adam tried several doors, but they were locked.

They walked between two rows of featureless doors and stopped as the light from the entrance petered out. No flambeaus were at their appointed stations along the corridor.

"I think…" Adam said and choked on his words as all along the corridors the doors opened in perfect unison. Opened and then shut with an explosive crack that reverberated through the building. And then again and again, as if a giant was greeting them with a mocking round of applause.

"We must go back!" Kara said but then another wave of heat rolled down the corridor as the firestalker edged closer to the building. They rushed toward the indistinctly looming bank of elevators. The doors continued to bang, opening up a crack and then slumming shut. When it happened next time, Adam grabbed a handle and tried to keep the door open. It tore from his hand, but he glimpsed an empty office on the other side.

The elevators sat in a large landing decorated with paper flowers and a small Buddha in a niche. The doors of the shafts were closed but the call buttons glowed green: a welcome spot of light in the gloom of the building. Adam touched the button and snatched back his hand. A strange rumble rolled down the shaft from the upper floors.

He addressed the Buddha.

"Brother," he asked, "what happened here?"

The Buddha was silent. Adam bent over the golden, fat-bellied tenant. It lunged forward, dragging its root behind, and bit deeply into Adam's forearm. Blood spurted. Adam smashed the creature into the wall again and again until it let go and slid down in a heap of red jelly.

Agatha mouthed Grandfather Prayer, but the rest stood still in shock. Buddhas were the most peaceful of the city tenants. Kara broke the silence.

"The elevator is here," she said.

Indeed it was. The doors of the shaft slid apart with a soft hiss, inviting them into the dark plushy interior. A subtle rotten smell wafted out.

Daniel took a step and then paused.

"Something wrong," he said.

Adam lifted the smashed body of the Buddha and hurled it into the elevator cabin. The vertical lips of the doors smacked together and the entire structure convulsed, gulping it down.

Adam backed off.

"Stairs!" he yelled. "Dead, can't go rogue!"

The stairs were behind the elevators. The narrow stairwell had no windows, but some light seeped from far above. They were winded after the first ten floors but continued to climb, clinging to the reassuring inertness of concrete steps and aluminum rails. Adam called a halt when they reached a landing where shiny letters on the wall spelled "Golden Emporium" in all the languages of the city.

"There may be people in the mall," he said.

He cautiously pushed the heavy door but it opened with no fuss. They found themselves in a giant open space filled with displays, counters and groups of dummies. The place was bathed in a dim scarlet light that made heaps of clothing into piles of stirring shadows and painted with ruddiness the dummies' featureless faces. The windows were covered by derma but the inferno outside was so raging that its incandescence seeped through the building's blood-flushed lids.

Adam strode in and the rest followed. The emporium was eerily silent except for a stealthy cracking noise as if somebody was folding and unfolding sheets of packaging paper. Agatha lingered by a dress section, fingering lacy garments swaying on long rails.

Adam found a snack station hiding in the shadows of a kitchen-appliances display. Breaking the glass, he pulled out a handful of buns and candy and offered them to his companions. Daniel muttered thanks but winced when he bit into a donut. Agatha, who had meanwhile put on a sparkly blouse, daintily picked up a coconut roll. Kara, of course, did not even look their way. She glided closer to the shuttered window, trying to peer outside.

"Watch out!" Adam said between bites. "It may blink if you come too close. We are safe here, inside."

And then the tower shook.

Chapter 10. Honeywell Golden Emporium

Irene and Doris crept through the devastated streets. The pavement was littered with trampled scavengers, chunks of stone and concrete, and rotting hunks of dead Pith. And towering into the burning sky, dwarfing even the Jade Chopsticks, were walking maelstroms of fire, slowly rotating wheels-within-wheels of exploding stars.

The mid-level escalator sagged into the middle of the street, two of its lanes tied into soggy lymph-dripping knots. Fortunately, there were stone-carved dead stairs leading up to mid-levels. They started climbing.

They reached the top of the Cat Street Hill where the fallen canopy lay in pleats like a giant skirt. The City Hall loomed beyond a row of shuttered stalls, all hundred stories of it. Its bright colors shone through the smoky murk. The elaborate trusses exposed on the blocky façade, the giant pipes winding around its exoskeleton, and the toothy crown on top dominated the view.

Doris made an inarticulate sound, and Irene patted her hand. The Hall was impressive even to the city-born; how much more so to a country bumpkin? She had been subliminally afraid all this time to encounter a rotting corpse – the death of the Hall would have truly meant the death of the city. She was relieved to see that the building still breathed, lived, and fought.

The City Hall was the largest Pith-grown structure in the city. Other buildings, such as the slender towers of mid-level, the spacious villas of up-levels, or the hovels of low-levels, were the product of collaboration between human designs and the life-force of the Pith, channeled and shaped by city architects and engineers. Even Skybridge, though spontaneously grown to link different city areas, contained dead sections of metal, wood, and stone. The City Hall, though, was pure Pith. Its eye-popping cladding in washes of yellow, orange, and red was composed of thickened derma. Its dramatically exposed ribs were actual ribs. Its thick external pipes were its viscera, carrying water and nourishment throughout its mighty body. It had no head, but it had a crown, twenty meters high and composed of overlapping, flexible chitin plates.

The City Hall was reputed to precede the Incoming, but nobody knew for sure. In Year Zero, the past was a matter of idle gossip and indifferent conjecture.

They crept close to the Hall and peered from behind a stall. In front of the Hall was a large square with a statue of Grandfather, used for civic celebrations in ordinary times. But the crowd that filled it now was not in a celebratory mood.

The shockwave that passed through the Emporium was strong enough to dislodge goods and crack display cases. Something fell with a bang. The dummies swayed.

Adam was thrown off his feet but fortunately fell into a pile of clothing. Righting himself, he listened for a tell-tale rumble. Earthquakes were rare but not unknown in the city. Instead, however, he heard a thrum of many feet on the stairs, the sound coming from below. Then a piercing, rusty screech – and then a wave of moaning and cooing.

"Hungry Ones!" Agatha cried.

Load bangs came from below. Adam blinked his youngest face on and off in distress. He had forgotten that most towers had underground entrances connected to the web of MTT tunnels that run underneath the city. Somebody had just opened the underground gate to Honeywell.

"We must go up!" he yelled.

Daniel stumbled and went down. Adam thought that the

other man had somehow tangled with a dummy. But then he realized the dummy had its arm around Daniel's neck in a chokehold.

Throughout the Emporium the dummies were twisting and stretching like a band of suddenly waking gymnasts. The dim space was filled with creeping movement.

Kara hit on the glass wall and the lid-shutters lifted, flooding the Emporium with fiery light. It revealed that what they had taken for dummies were nothing of the kind. The figures that stumbled toward them were faceless indeed; their bald heads carrying smooth ovals on their fronts. Their long hands thrust from their ill-fitting suits and dresses. But the heads oozed blood, as if their previously human features had been scraped away. The hands were raw claws. They came in all shapes and sizes: men, women, children; old and young; fat and thin. They had no eyes, but they homed in on Adam and his companions.

He moved to help Daniel, only to see the former militiaman shake off his attacker who curled up on the floor like a tortured animal. Daniel whirled around and felled another pseudo-dummy. Adam could see that he did not actually fight them. It was enough for his swollen fingers to brush a creature for it to convulse as if struck by an electric discharge. The current of pain flowed away from Daniel into whoever he touched – or whoever touched him. Adam's bet on his new bodyguard paid off.

As the pseudo-dummies realized what was happening and started to edge away from Daniel, they run into Kara who pulled them into an obscenely close embrace. The two of them did not exchange a single word or glance yet they fought with an uncanny coordination that reminded Adam of a pack of feral dogs.

Agatha, open-mouthed in surprise – or was it disgust? – was uncoiling her 'arm. Adam shook his head at her.

"Let them!" he said and pulled her toward the door to the staircase. For a moment, he was tempted to leave these two –

the predator and the soldier of pain – behind. His lover, his bodyguard – they felt more alien to him than the Hungry Ones.

But rationality won. He needed them, now more than ever.

"Run!" he yelled. "Zombies are coming! They opened the tunnel gate!"

Kara leaped over an overturned counter and joined him and Agatha. Her movements were a little sluggish. Adam had already realized that her power was quite limited in certain ways. She could not simply kill – she had to feed. And while hunger was irresistible, it was also self-consuming. You could only stuff yourself with so much.

But Daniel kept lunging at the dummies, mowing them down like bowling pins. He practically glowed. Gone was the sickly pallor, the fragility – he was draining away the pain that had been gnawing at him since the moment his ill-fitting 'arm blended with his body.

"Come on!" Adam yelled. The melee outside had reached the landing.

Daniel grazed a child dummy – but then another one attacked him from behind with a curtain rod picked from a display. The feeble blow only glanced off Daniel's shoulder but he doubled up in anguish. For a moment, his scream drowned the moaning outside.

So, this was the limit of *his* power, Adam realized. He had no resistance to injury. He could inflict pain, but he could not withstand it.

Kara grabbed him and hauled him to his feet, flinching and gasping as she did. But Daniel revived somewhat and followed Adam and Agatha as they ran to the door to the stairs.

The door flew off its hinges as the slate-grey flood of Hungry Ones poured into the Emporium.

The four of them were caught between the pseudo-dummies and the zombies. It dawned upon Adam that he could actually die here.

Kara stepped forth toward the Hungry Ones, and Daniel whirled around to face the dummies, holding Adam and Agatha between them. Adam picked up the curtain rod; Agatha readied her 'arm.

But instead of attacking them, the pseudo-dummies skirted their small group and fell upon the Hungry Ones, swiping at the zombies by their half-made claws, trying to trip them, or battering them with random objects.

The fight was pitifully uneven as Hungry Ones bit into the others' rubbery flesh, worried at them, and tore away chunks of bleeding meat. But there were a lot of pseudo-dummies and they fell in the zombies' path, delaying them. Adam motioned to the others to follow as he led them to the back of the Emporium.

He hoped there would be stairs there as well but there were none. Instead, the gaping lips of the cargo elevator parted as they approached. The cabin was empty and as opposed to its passenger sibling appeared to be properly dormant. There were no dripping secretions on the floor and its light strip was glowing evenly.

Adam risked a glance behind and saw that the Hungry Ones had smashed the dummies' defenses and were advancing through the shop floor. Being country creatures, however, they did not know how to navigate the landscape of city luxuries and were floundering through carpet rolls and tangling in clothes racks. This won them some precious seconds but not enough to seek another exit.

Adam stepped into the cargo elevator and the rest followed. Kara paled visibly as she felt the floor yield softly under her feet.

The cabin did not try to eat them but neither did it close its door. Adam looked around desperately for a bank of buttons but saw none. Apparently, it was one of the more advanced devices that were operated by voice commands. There were more and more of those in the city as the Pith doled out awareness with increasing generosity. It was supposed to make life easier for citizens and tenants, but it now occurred to Adam that perhaps there was a darker design at work.

"Up!" he yelled. The cabin quivered but remained stationary, the door gaping open.

"Up!"

The first Hungry One reached the threshold and was felled by Agatha's 'arm. More crowded behind it.

"Up!"

The elevator stirred and smacked its lips closed, spitting out a small Hungry One that had pushed half of its spindly body inside. Groaning and trembling, the cabin rose through the shaft.

Chapter 11. The City Hall

Irene had seen Hungry Ones before but never in such numbers. The square in front of the Hall was crawling with low-slung, emaciated bodies; the air was thick with their stench. Some of them had even climbed the Grandfather monument that was tilting dangerously under their weight.

She crouched behind the row of shuttered stalls and made Doris do the same. But while the stalls may have concealed them from the zombies, there was another danger aloft – literally so. The darting, sweeping shadows on the littered ground were cast by khruts who wheeled above their heads, cawing and screaming.

Fortunately, both khruts and zombies were too occupied by trying to get into the City Hall to pay attention to the two tenants. The scene before them was so strange that Irene forgot her fear in a rush of astonishment and pride.

The Hall had no defenders – no militiamen or City Corps were lined up to repel the attacks. But the building itself was fighting back – and winning.

As the ladies watched, the toothed top snapped at the wheeling khrut-fowls, snatching two of them out of the air and crushing them into bloody rags. Opening and closing with a supple grace of an anemone, the toothed crown strained toward its aerial enemies who retreated further up, their hoarse noise deafening as they voiced their frustration in a mixture of words and squawks.

The grand entrance to the Hall was blocked with a sturdy gate that Hungry Ones attacked with their usual mindless ferocity. At one point, they seemed to lift it a little off the ground but then its horny edge smashed down with enormous force upon the grey bodies that tried to worm their way underneath it.

The black-bleeding pieces were spat out and landed in a crowd of their fellows who fell upon them.

Doris made a sound of distress and Irene – a vegetarian – turned away in disgust. But inside she bubbled with ferocious happiness. She had been afraid to confront the rotting corpse of the Hall. But seeing it active revived her civic pride. She was flesh of the flesh of the city and she would not let human interlopers, zombie invaders, or treacherous birdmen rob her of her patrimony. She would fight! She had mistrusted Mayor Volk and planned to vote for his challenger Adam Malech, but right now, she did not care who was inside the Hall. The Hall itself, the heart of the city, was all that mattered.

One of the pipes that wound around the Hall's exposed ribs tore itself from its matrix and reared up. A mouth opened at its blunt end and spat a steaming jet upon the intruders who retreated pell-mell.

Irene saw her chance. As the Hungry Ones ran away from the scalding water, and the khruts milled impotently high above, afraid to be caught in the building's jaws, she made her move. She scuttled toward the Hall, wading through the puddles of black zombie ichor and boiling water. Doris picked her up and carried her like a baby.

The bloated worm of the pipe swayed above them. Irene lifted her no-face, hoping that the city would recognize its own. The pipe let them through.

There was still the question of getting inside. The gate had snapped back down. But Irene who had been to the Hall before knew there was a side entrance. They skirted the Hall's ribbed façade – and almost ran into two Hungry Ones in the side alley, one of them seemingly headless but with two wriggling tentacles on top of its trunk.

Irene was defenseless. Not for the first time, she cursed Grandfather's decree that prevented tenants from wearing 'arms. She backed off. But her companion did not. Doris lifted her massive forearms and brought them down upon the headless creature. Its companion snapped at her and managed to take a bite out of Doris' thigh before it, too, was smashed.

But more zombies were appearing at the bottom of the alley. Irene looked around for the entryway and saw a partially lifted bone grill masked by the hanging folds of derma. The grill was beginning to descend but Irene flattened herself on the ground and squeezed her fibrous body through the gap. Afraid that Doris would be left behind, she tried to send a wordless plea to the Pith but felt it rebound like a ball thrown back off the wall. But there was no need. Doris' country-fed muscles stood her in good stead as she shoved the grill up and lumbered through the opening. The gate fell down with a bang as more Hungry Ones arrived outside, attracted by their fellows' sweet smell of death.

They were inside the Hall. And it looked nothing like Irene's memory of it.

Chapter 12. On Being Stuck

The elevator puffed asthmatically as it dragged itself and its cargo of four upward, and she felt dizzy. Kara thought that soon enough bad memories would bar her from being anywhere at all: caves and tunnels crawling with the black images of the reeking train; the ground treacherous with the living marsh; the air…But she did not know what trauma had made her flinch away from the sunlit emptiness as she stood on Skybridge. Was it part of the missing fifteen years? Should she be grateful for her remaining amnesia? Recovering her identity had brought her nothing but grief.

She stole a glance at Daniel who had slumped against the wall, the animation of the fight fading away, the clenched tension seen on faces of the chronically ill reasserting themselves. He had cut away the right sleeve of his shirt and his puffed-up arm dangled off his body like an alien appendage, which it was. King of Pain and Queen of Hunger, two country kids unwittingly crowned as royalty of death by a faceless and anonymous parliament. She felt a stirring of pity toward him, though she had none left for herself. The love she had had for him was a dead husk like the mummified insects one finds in a dusty attic. But the bond remained. There were just the two of them left: the surviving children of Edenberry.

The elevator shuddered and came to a stop. Adam, who had been listening intently to its wheezing ascent, swore. He wore the likeness of Mayor Volk and despite everything she knew about him, Kara still found it hard to separate the man and the face. Volk's face was cowardly and grasping; she would feel better with Adam wearing the likeness of a young patrician or an avuncular Asian businessman.

"We are stuck between the floors," he said. His voice, his

accent, never changed and Kara wondered how he had planned to pull it off if he had to impersonate the Mayor. On the other hand, maybe seeing the familiar face of power would be enough to rally up the city's defenders.

"Can we climb up?" Agatha asked. The girl was compulsively stroking her 'arm but other than that, she seemed composed. Kara did not like her but regretted that the feeling was mutual. She would like to acquire a friend. But Agatha plainly regarded her as a rival, though Kara was not sure whether in relation to Adam or to Daniel. Or perhaps to both.

"We can try," Adam said dubiously. He pressed his palms on both sides of the elevator's vertical slit of the door, his lips moving. The door remained shut.

There was another surge of running footsteps outside. Now, Kara realized what was strange about them: it sounded as if all the runners were barefoot. Adam dropped his hands.

"Perhaps we better wait it out," he said.

"The Hungry Ones can climb the stairs too," Daniel remarked, sitting upright and squaring his shoulders. Agatha's eyes lingered on him, and Kara felt a ghost of jealousy stir into existence and quickly fade away.

"They can. But if we reach the roof first, there is a skywalk. It leads to Skybridge."

Daniel nodded.

"True. I remember I went shopping here once and then walked all the way to Golden Flower. There was that famous café down under the overpass…"

"Grandfather's Rabbit," Adam said and flashed on a young man's face in lieu of a smile. Daniel smiled back, the two urbanites united by the common knowledge that excluded the women. Kara felt the ghost of jealousy stir once again. They were of the city; Agatha – of the country. She belonged nowhere.

The elevator dropped down.

Somebody screamed – Kara hoped it was Agatha and not

herself. The elevator stabilized after a long, stomach-churning lurch. The noise from outside rose like a tsunami.

"We must get out now!" Adam roughly pulled at the elevator's tight lips and managed to part them enough to insert his knee in the opening. Kara joined him and together they made the slit wide enough to get through. The dead metallic struts of the shaft were on the other side.

"Go!" Adam commanded Agatha, the smallest of them, and she pushed through and started climbing the cage.

Daniel was next. And then Adam and Kara were alone in the cabin, both straining the keep the elevator's vertical mouth open.

"Go!" he yelled at her. She shook her head. It was clear that whoever was the last one would be trapped in the cabin.

"You go! You're the Mayor now!"

Muttering incomprehensible dawn curses, Adam wedged himself sideways in the opening. He flashed the blue-eyed face at Kara.

"Come on!"

She jammed herself in, side by side with him, feeling the elevator's horny lips cut into her flesh. Dimly, she sensed an enormity of life-force raging around her like a turbulent ocean. And then the lips closed, squeezing both of them out like watermelon seeds.

The landing seen through the struts was empty. Noises were coming from below, moaning and wet slaps. They started climbing up, following the lead of Agatha who had already reached the landing above. She peered outside and waved frantically at them. This floor, apparently, was not deserted.

The atrium, when Irene had last been there in order to renew her business license, had been thronging with people: humans and tenants both. There had been a huge desk manned by two unfriendly Guards, and a giant flambeau scrolling the names of applicants and numbers of offices. There had been two running elevators, a whistling fountain that sung a tune while blowing a jet into the air, and flesh flowers growing out of the brightly colored derma walls.

Now the fountain was dry, its plump lips shriveled. The derma hung in tatters. The elevator shafts gaped open with no cabins in view, and the desk was overturned and splattered with dry blood. At least the flambeau was still there and doing its duty by lighting the windowless atrium, but instead of legible messages, its flat body intermittently flashed gibberish and obscene pictures.

Doris tried to write with her finger on the floor, but the self-cleaning surface showed no trace. Irene took out her yarn and wrote: "If Mayor is here, he is in the Chamber. Up we go!"

But how? The butchered body of an elevator cabin hung on the cables inside the shaft. Irene did not remember where the stairs were. She tried to signal to the flambeau, but it was lost in its own world.

Then she saw a lacy staircase spiraling up the far wall. Screwing up her courage, she led Doris to it.

They were halfway up the five-story-high atrium when the flambeau leered at them with a giant picture of an erect penis and then blinked out. They found themselves in total darkness, clinging to the fragile railing.

Adam peered through the struts and recoiled.

The landing was packed with a jam of figures. They were emerging from the swinging doors and streaming down the stairs to the floors below. The stairs were too narrow to drain the crowd which should have reacted with curses and complaints. But it was eerily quiet.

Adam was born in the city, *of* the city, but he had never seen anything like the creatures on the landing.

They were not humans but neither were they tenants. All tenants, no matter how bizarre – from the human point of view

– their shapes were, shared a certain quality of being themselves, being comfortable in their skin, whether this skin was glassy or pebbled, velvety or rough. Even the rogues – the wild, unregulated spawn of the Pith – were instantly recognizable as the entities or objects they were meant to be.

The creatures that pushed against each other in total silence were all the same – and all twisted.

They looked like peeled two-legged carrots, their inflamed skin oozing blood, their faces almost gone but for a faint sketch of obliterated features. Their stick-like arms flopped tonelessly by their sides, but Adam noted that they had a glossy sheen that sharply differentiated them from the rest of the sketchy bodies.

The things were wearing 'arms!

Agatha, who clung to the cage by his side, looked at him questioningly but he was more concerned with Kara below him. She was pressed into the grillwork, her face obscured by her hair, her fingers white as they dug desperately into the metal. He knew she was afraid of heights.

The stream of the creatures was unending, but they showed no interest in the non-functioning elevator. Instead, they seemed hell-bent on reaching the lower floors on foot. The moaning and cooing of Hungry Ones was overlaid with the noises of a scuffle.

Adam pressed his finger to his lips indicating that they should wait it out. And they would have had it not been for Kara. He saw her bloodless fingers uncurl and with a muffled scream she slipped down. He lurched down to help her, but she found another grip and hung on.

For a moment, he hoped the creatures had not heard the commotion. But they had.

The stream of them flowing downstairs slowed down and stopped. They turned their no-faces toward the elevator cage, all together in a weird unison.

And now Adam suddenly realized what they reminded him of – the half-girl in the Colonel's house, semi-absorbed by the

Pith.

They rattled the elevator cage, reaching over each other's shoulders with their uncoiling 'arms. Yes, indeed, these were functioning 'arms! Adam did not want to think about the implications of this.

He gestured for his companions to crawl down the cage but immediately realized it was useless. The noise of fighting intensified as the commotion rolled up.

Kara slapped at the 'arms reaching through the grid-work but she could not sap the vitality of their wearers, insulated from her by their symbionts. Agatha's 'arm swished through the air but tens of 'arms rose to lash back. The elevator cage rattled alarmingly and then another sound came from down below, filling Adam with horror – a wizened, puffing ascent as the elevator cabin they had left was now rising through the shaft. It could squash them like flies against the unyielding roof.

He pushed open the cage door and leaped into the landing, clutching the pathetic mechanical weapon he was ashamed to wield – a knife. The rest followed and were instantly engulfed by the melee of raw-meat bodies, slick with blood. Adam felt the sting of innumerable 'arms winding around him, biting into his unprotected flesh…and then they fell away.

It was Daniel. The militiaman used his diseased limb like a club, lifting it awkwardly and bringing it down with force onto the attackers. Adam blinked a young face on in shock as he saw Daniel's skin crack, and blood and pus ooze out. But if the militiaman was in pain, his attackers received the pain tenfold. They fell away from him, curling up on the ground, being trampled by their fellows who pressed forward, only to be hurled back by another blast of anguish emanating from the man.

He cleared the path for the rest of them toward the door and they followed. Adam cut off one creature's 'arm and felt a wave of savage pleasure mixed with bitterness. How inefficient mechanical toys were compared to the power of the flesh that was, infuriatingly, denied to him, a true son of the city!

Another creature careened into him and sunk its needle-like teeth into his shoulder. Adam yelped, flashing on the rough-and-ready face of a Triad enforcer he had worn in his youth in the Market, and with an upward swipe plunged his knife into the creature's belly, gutting it. It would not have worked with most rogues who had their digestive apparatus distributed in random parts of their bodies, but it worked here. The creature made a mewling sound and collapsed, its guts unspooling out of it, splattering Adam with its human-looking blood – more human-looking than the blackberry-colored ichor that flowed through his own veins.

He hurried after the rest toward the heavy swinging fire door. They pushed through and found themselves in a long dim corridor. Adam expected to see many more of the creatures coming toward them – they had been emerging from here, after all – but all was quiet.

Daniel collapsed on the floor, while Agatha and Kara tried to latch the door against the horde pressing from the outside. Adam added his efforts to theirs and together they pushed the heavy lock-bar into place. The door vibrated under the onslaught but held – it was a heavy, inert thing made of dead steel. And then suddenly the creatures on the other side stopped hammering at it, silenced by the familiar moaning. The Hungry Ones had reached the landing! Adam never thought he would be happy to hear them, but he was. Let your enemies devour each other, as they said in the Market.

He looked around at the neat taupe walls and the doors accessorized with name-plaques, Grandfather's portraits, or good-luck charms. They were on a residential floor of the Honeywell Tower. But where were the residents?

Chapter 13. Office Furniture

In total darkness, Irene and Doris clung to the wispy stairs suspended above the floor of the atrium four stories below. Doris shifted her heavy bulk and the stairs creaked alarmingly.

Irene steadied her with a pat on the arm but she herself was trembling. The blackout was so absolute that even her compound eyes were useless. She was afraid to move, because every time they did, the stairs lurched.

And then she had an idea. She got out her yarn-ball and tied one end to her wrist. The yarn's dim consciousness flowed into hers and she gave it a wordless command. The yarn was not truly sentient, but it understood pleasure and pain. And it loved her. Nosing in the dark, finding its way by the texture of the surface, the yarn crawled forward. After what seemed like an eternity she felt a tug on her wrist. Tugging back, she discovered the yarn had tied itself to something solid on the other end and was now taut. Holding Doris' paw, she advanced cautiously on the juddering structure.

And then the light blazed back, so bright that Irene almost lost her balance. Fortunately, Doris' bulk steadied her. She focused her compound eyes, trying to make sense of the overlapping fragments of vision.

Finally, the dance of multiple images coalesced into a single picture and she discovered they had reached the top landing of the stairs. But the light was not coming from the deranged flambeau who had collapsed into a heap on the floor below. Instead, the door on the landing had opened and the light was streaming from it, pure white unlike the colored radiance of most flambeaus.

Irene tried to remember the layout of the Hall but could not. Was the Mayor's Chamber on this floor? The Chamber was the hub of the Hall and, some said, the hub of the city. This was where Grandfather had sat in his day, issuing the decrees that had transformed the wilderness of flesh into a living body politic. This was where his corpse had lain in state before being interred in a secret location as he had ordered it to be in order to avoid his tomb becoming a site of pilgrimage. And this was where the current Mayor Volk showed up to accept petitions and argue with council members on those rare occasions when he deigned to show up at all. Irene could not wait for him to be replaced with Adam Malech who, if the rumor-mills of the Market were to be believed, had *really* close connections with tenants. But, right now, she did not care who was in the Chamber as long as there was *somebody*. The empty but alive and active Hall started creeping her out. She was beginning to realize how the first human settlers must have felt when they ventured into the expanse of the Pith. And to her mortification, she realized that she, a tenant but yet a self-aware individual, had more in common with those humans than she had with the Pith itself.

Holding on to Doris as much for her own reassurance as to calm down the country bumpkin who shied away from everything she saw, Irene walked through the door – and found herself in the familiar antechamber. This was where her business license had been renewed by a surly human clerk. At the back were the huge double doors leading to the Chamber itself, but they had been firmly closed at the time. Now, they gaped open. But she could not see inside the Chamber because of the impossibly bright flambeau standing at the entrance. Apart from it, the antechamber was empty but tidy, with desks, chairs, filing cabinets and everything else in their proper places. The derma shutters on the windows were lowered and shuddered from time to time as they repulsed the khruts beating against the building like moths against a lamp.

Irene waved at the flambeau. It did not reply, standing there as stiff as a pole. She advanced cautiously – and discovered it *was* a pole. And pinned to it with giant metallic screws was the corpse of a firestalker, consuming itself as it poured forth a flood of harsh radiance.

Irene recoiled in shock. With everything else going on in the city, it was this desecration that dealt the final blow to her hopes of things returning to normal. Firestalkers were dangerous criminals, hunted down and arrested or killed by the militia and City Corps. And this was how it should be. But they were still tenants! Using their bodies as if they were dead wood or metal was beyond callous. And doing it here, at the heart of the city, the place that symbolized civic order! This was unbearable.

Shock turned into anger, and she marched into the Chamber. But suddenly something coiled round her ankle and sent her sprawling on the floor. And, at the same time, she heard Doris' heavy body crash into an obstacle that should not have been there.

Adam cautiously advanced along the corridor and pushed one door. It opened. Beyond was one of the standard mid-level apartments where the bulk of the city's human population lived: two or three cramped rooms with a bathroom and a kitchen. The human elites, of course, could afford mansions on up-levels similar to his own, while the poor, the illegal immigrants, and most tenants were crammed into the chaotic mazes of low-levels or the teeming alleys of the Market. Judging by the prominently displayed Grandfather icons and expensive furniture, the owner of this apartment fancied himself to be on his way up. But now he was nowhere to be seen.

Or was he? Adam ventured inside and had to fight back the milky, featureless caul that always snapped on in moments of stress. He could not show any more weakness in front of his three humans! But what he saw was almost too shocking to believe.

Hanging from the back wall like a rotten fruit on a vine was the upper body of a flayed bleeding creature. As it sensed their approach, it lifted its blind, unformed head and feebly snapped with its toothy mouth.

Adam turned away and met Kara's eyes.

"Colonel Rosen's daughter," she said.

"Yes. She must have been one of the first."

"What does it mean?" Daniel demanded, his voice hoarse as if he had been biting back a scream for a long time.

"It means that this has been a long time in preparation," Adam said gloomily. "It means that the things below are former humans who have been digested and spat out to fight the Hungry Ones, also former humans. It means that the Pith itself has gone rogue."

Agatha gasped and Adam wondered how much she actually understood about what was going on the city.

"How do we get out of here?" Kara asked and Adam was glad to hear that her voice was rational and calm.

"Skybridge. There is an air exit on this floor – I saw a sign. We must hurry. I don't know how long the ex-citizens and ex-farmers below will be busy with each other, but whoever gets the upper hand will be after us."

Kara nodded and they followed Adam as he strode out of the apartment, eager to be out of the stink of hot blood and vomit. But, over his shoulder, he saw Daniel turn back to the human fruit on the wall and put his swollen hand, gently, onto its raw pate. The creature shuddered and gave a mewling cry – almost, not quite, a woman's name. And then it drooped lifelessly, its skinless fingers brushing the floor.

As they hurried down the corridor, Daniel stopped by, and pushed, every door. Some were locked but most gave. In every apartment, its former owners hung on the wall, sometimes singly, sometimes in family clusters. The worst was the cluster of a mother with two toddlers who gnashed their toothless gums like gutted fish. Daniel laid his hands upon the things, oblivious of their scratches and bites. His pain pouring into them overloaded their already strained nerves and burnt them out in a final burst of anguish.

Adam knew they could not afford to tarry but said nothing.

Finally, they were at the swinging door with a symbol for air painted on its white surface. Adam pushed it and they found themselves high above the city.

A flimsy ladder led down to Skybridge that flowed below them like a steely river, its surface dancing with reflected flames as the city burned. Smoke was so thick it veiled the sun, but enough light was provided by the madly rotating wheels of fire that prowled the streets below. Many towers had collapsed in huge piles of steel and bone, blocking the alleys and trapping people who tried to scramble over them, only to be picked out by khruts, flocking and cawing like hungry gulls. From where they stood, it was not clear whether these were humans or tenants. Adam doubted it mattered.

He stepped onto the surface of Skybridge. It was as slick as ice and had no guardrails. Adam winced. *When I'm Mayor, I'll fix this*, he thought. And then he realized he *was* Mayor.

Agatha followed with surprising nonchalance, even though she had probably never been higher above the ground that the top of a tree. Again, Adam was surprised at the little country girl's unexpected resources of strength. Daniel followed. He looked so exhausted that Adam doubted he cared much whether he tumbled down or not.

It left Kara. She stood still at the juncture between Skybridge and the tower, her hair covering her face as she turned away from the void.

"Go!" she said, her voice hoarse. "I'll cover you. I'll delay them…"

"Coward!" Adam said.

Her head snapped up, her green eyes blazing.

"Don't pretend to be a heroine! You're afraid of heights, that's all!"

"But if they follow us…" Agatha said timidly. He ignored her.

"Don't play games with me, Kara! Dizzy? Too bad. You have to see it through. You owe it."

"Owe it? To who? You?"

"Your family."

"I betrayed my family!"

"And now it's your chance to make it right."

She stood still for a heartbeat and then stepped onto Skybridge. She advanced with mincing steps, hunched over, her eyes glued to the bridge, not looking right or left where smoke-streaked emptiness yawned. But she did advance. Adam would have offered her a hand, but the bridge was only wide enough for a single file. He led the way.

The swirling dark cloudlet seemed just another one of the puffs of smoke and pollution that streaked the air until it fell apart, resolving itself into a multitude of khrut-fowls. Rain of guano dropped around them. Adam covered his head and trudged on. But then he was assaulted by a confusion of flapping wings, cackling, and insults. He waved at them in annoyance, tottered and almost slipped off the bridge. He managed to steady himself, arms windmilling, but then he heard a scream and, looking back, saw Kara obscured by an angry flock. She swayed and went over the edge.

He tried to go back but the fowls formed a jabbing barrier between them. Pulling out his knife, he slashed at them and saw a pair of white-knuckled hands clinging to Skybridge and sharp beaks pecking at them. He saw Daniel reaching out to her and then hesitating and pulling back as he realized that touching her would give her a jolt of pain. He saw Agatha unleashing her 'arm and trying to…it almost looked as if she were trying to push Kara off but surely she was just failing to loop her 'arm properly around her wrists in order to pull her up.

Adam struggled through the curtain of birds when a larger body fell from the sky, scattering the khrut-fowls. It dived under Skybridge and then rose up again, Kara clinging to it as tightly as a lover. The creature's plucked-chicken wings beat furiously but it had no apparent difficulty in keeping the two of them aloft.

It – he – landed and deposited Kara on Skybridge. She turned to her savior.

"Thank you, Peter," she said.

It was the office chair.

It tried to stomp on her with its wheeled legs. It reared and buckled, lunging at Irene. Fortunately, while very strong, it was not agile. She kicked it in the seat and overturned it. It lay on its back, its legs twitching. Doris was pounding a file cabinet that snapped at her with its drawers.

She rushed to help Doris, but the bulky tenant had already subdued her adversary. Irene looked in disgust at the oozing ichor and raw flesh emerging from beneath the veneer of pseudo-steel. It was unseemly for objects created by the Pith to flaunt their origin so blatantly!

But then again, nothing was seemly anymore.

They moved into the Chamber but suddenly the dead firestalker pinned to the post dimmed its radiance. Its festooned front flattened out and letters ran on its sallow surface.

If Irene could, she would cry out in horror. Corpses should not talk! Dead was dead; or had been until now.

The letters spelled a phrase, but Irene had to read it twice because it made no sense:

"Has the quota been met?"

Quota? What quota? Irene's faceted eyes dimmed in despair. The city, *her* city, had turned into a nightmare of unreason!

She sensed a ponderous movement by her side and then Doris stepped forward. The big tenant leaned forward and wrote with her finger on the firestalker's skin:

"Yes."

Irene made to stop her – this was not the way; one communicated with flambeaus by voice; they did not allow themselves to be touched...but the dead thing accepted being written upon. It dimmed again and new letters formed:

"Is the harvest as plentiful as promised?"

Again, Doris wrote:

"Yes."

"Are the saboteurs defeated?"

What saboteurs? What insanity was that? But Doris, the country innocent, seemed in her element now. Without hesitation, she wrote again, in a firm cursive:

"They have all been eliminated. There is so much food that cakes are animal feed and wine is used for bathing."

The dead firestalker flickered as if making a decision. Its blackened edges shed a light rain of rotting skin.

The words were traced in an unfamiliar angular font, but the meaning was clear.

"You may enter."

And they did.

Chapter 14. Old Friends

"Peter!" Adam slipped on his business face, seething with anger. The khrut with his ridiculous plucked wings was smaller than himself but he stood his ground, glaring at his former employer.

Peter had disappeared after the roofs' attack and Adam assumed that he had absconded – an event that had been unthinkable even a short time ago but was becoming more common, a forerunner of the Guards' massive betrayal. When Kara told him she had been saved by Peter and brought to the Market, he filed this fact away together with the rest of inexplicable occurrences plaguing the city. She was evasive about where she had stayed in his aerie, and he did not want to pressure her. Now, he regretted his soft-heartedness.

It was Peter who spoke first.

"You won't get to the City Hall this way, Malech."

"Really? And I should take your word for it because you have reneged on your contract?"

"A contract signed with a double-faced toad is invalid."

"Double-faced! You dare speak about betrayal? You, a khrut! Look at what you are doing to the city! Grandfather should have exterminated all of you as he wanted to do!"

Peter's wings twitched nervously.

"It wasn't for want of trying!" he replied sarcastically. "Had he not lost his mechanical 'arms, we wouldn't be talking now! But no matter, this is ancient history. This is Year Zero, a new beginning. I want to help you!"

"Why?" This was Kara, surprisingly recovered from her near-fall. "You worked for the Divide, didn't you?"

Khrut faces were as expressionless as birds' but somehow Peter's stance managed to convey unease.

"Yes," he said. "When I took you away, I had orders from my

nav to bring you to the country. But I didn't. I knew something was going on. Something bad. You accuse me of disloyalty, toad, but loyalty is our greatest virtue. We cleave to our families and our flights. Even when our bird-cousins had dealings with the things beyond the Divide, we stuck with them. We knew these things were dangerous. But I thought: it cannot hurt. Grandfather and his people came from there, how bad can it be? I know now. It is very bad. And …I have to go against my flight because my nav has been seduced by the dead thing inside the Divide and is leading us to destroy the city. And I don't want the city destroyed."

"Why not?" Adam asked.

Peter's beak clacked as if he were searching for human words. But then his golden eyes dilated as he saw something behind Adam's back.

"Never mind," he said. "It is too late. They are here."

The Chamber was as impressive as Irene remembered: a sweeping, circular space topped by a transparent dome. In ordinary times, the petals of thick derma that formed the toothed crown of the building would fold back and let the light of the day flood the Chamber. But now they were firmly closed around the dome and the illumination was harsh and glaring, coming from the firestalkers crucified on tall metallic posts ringing the room. It was bright enough, however, to see that the pictures of former Mayors that used to be displayed on the walls had been removed. So had been the Year Clock – a brightly colored dial that displayed hour, day, and month and that had been ceremonially reset to zero every Incoming anniversary. The only familiar object was a giant painting depicting Grandfather entering the city that pullulated at his feet as a reddish mass of inchoate meat. But in addition to this official work of art that had been an object of derision to even the most law-abiding citizens, the Chamber was cluttered with other paintings and posters, haphazardly propped against the walls or pinned to the podium. They all depicted Grandfather. Some looked familiar and Irene blinked in surprise when she realized these were the posters from the Incoming Sun café in the Market.

The podium was empty but below it was an ordinary office desk and seated at it, engrossed in some files, was an ordinary-looking human male. He lifted his head and glanced incuriously at the two tenants. He was a dawn in his late fifties, with a balding head, round face, and a small priggish mouth under a scrawny moustache. A severe pair of glasses was perched at the end of his nose. His face scrunched in distaste when he swept his eyes over Irene but lit up when he regarded Doris.

"A country worker, I see!" he enthused in a somewhat squeaky voice. "Big and strong, huh? The slackers won't have any more excuses when we send them such labor force!"

Irene clacked her jaws in distress. Who was this person? She was a well-informed tenant, determined not to waste her recently-won vote, and she followed all political debates. Not only did he bear no resemblance to Mayor Volk, but she was certain his face had never appeared on any flambeau cast.

"How is the harvest?" the man chattered on. "Exceeds all expectations, I believe? Oops! You can't answer, of course!"

Of course? Irene's muteness was rare; most tenants, toads and ducks alike, could speak from the moment they were born, even if they came into the world as small babies. Irene had been spawned full-grown and self-aware but unable to speak – the disability she had always borne stoically. Until running into Doris, she had never encountered another mute tenant.

Doris lumbered toward the desk, picked a pen and a blank sheet of paper, and started writing. The man's face underwent a rather unpleasant metamorphosis, his mild features sharpening and setting into a ferret-like mask.

"You can write? Who taught you?"

Doris continued to scribble busily. And then she held up the sheet of paper. Written on it in her firm hand were the words:

"Are you Grandfather?"

The man nodded:

"I am."

Chapter 15. The Dangers of Peasant Revolts

Three figures emerged from the coiling vapors and smoke that masked the end of this section of Skybridge. Two of them were familiar dummies – raw, bleeding human carrots with featureless faces, gaping maws, and sparkling-new 'arms. And slightly ahead of them, busily toddling on short legs, was a small woman in a brightly colored padded pantsuit.

Or rather, so she appeared. When she came closer, Kara gasped. The garish jacket was, in fact, a part of her hide, blending with the wrinkled skin of the neck and face. The face itself was impossibly aged, folded and creased in parchment yellow. Her eyes were two slanting strokes of black ink; her mouth – a lidless gash; her hair – a solid helmet perched on top of the bald skull. And yet she was instantly recognizable in this cruel caricature of herself.

"Marika!" Kara cried.

"So we meet on Skybridge again," the woman said. "And to think how much trouble I could have saved had I pushed you off, then. But my good heart was my undoing! I helped you – and see how you repaid me. But all for the best. Grandfather is wise. Here we are, all together, no matter how you all ran away like mice. A traitor birdman, a bad Hunter, a hungry demon woman. And you, Adam Malech, a Market toad who wanted to be Mayor. Grandfather has brought you all where you need to be."

"Grandfather is dead, you stupid bitch!" Adam yelled. "What are you doing? Look at yourself: a rogue! Surrounded by human rogues! Look at these things! They will chomp you up, together with your rotten dinner, Madam-Stinking-Wren!"

She shook her head smugly, invulnerable to his insults in her new shape.

"I'm saving the city," she said in an oily sanctimonious tone. "After your precious Guards sold you out and ran to the corpse in the dirt; after you, and toads like you, contaminated the city with your lawless pollution; after you enlisted a cannibal to your service…Grandfather came to us, the last humans. He called upon us. We serve him now like our honorable ancestors did."

"Grandfather came to you? You've had too much rice wine to drink! Grandfather is dead!"

"No."

"Well, if he is alive, where is he in the city?"

"He *is* the city," Marika said.

"You see," the man who called himself Grandfather chatted animatedly, pacing back and forth in front of his literally mute audience, "people need to eat. There wasn't enough food. We needed more food, so everybody can be happy and healthy!"

Irene felt her compound eyes glaze over. So, this was the reward of her epic journey through the besieged city! She had battled khruts, zombies, darkness, deranged furniture – only to have to sit through the most boring lecture of her lifetime. The fact that the lecturer was undoubtedly delusional did not make it any more exciting. He had to be seriously unhinged to call himself Grandfather when he was nothing but some small-time bureaucrat left behind in the bowels of the Hall when the Mayor and his retinue had run away! And all he could do was spout a stream of platitudes. Surely, the real Grandfather who had crossed the Divide and brought humans to the city had been more inspiring than this mousy pen-pusher!

She could not interrupt him, but she would have gotten up and left long time ago had it not been for Doris. The big tenant sat on her haunches, leaning forward, apparently hanging on to every cliché that fell from the man's lips, and scribbling notes on a piece of paper. Irene clacked her mandibles. She had grown fond of her companion but now she realized Doris really *was* a country bumpkin.

Suddenly, Doris raised her paw like a pupil ready with an answer. Irene who had had to suffer through the six years of basic education mandated for all tenants, swatted her on the backside but the man beamed and pointed at her as if they were in a crowded classroom. Doris lifted the page she had been writing upon. In large letters, it said:

"How many died?"

The man frowned and Irene revised her opinion somewhat: he was mad, true, but not harmless mad.

"It is better that some die, so others can eat and live!" he barked.

Doris nodded, and scribbled quickly, and lifted the page again:

"So you could eat the dead."

Irene would have gasped if she could at the change that came over the man. She was used to the plasticity of the flesh in the city and would not be surprised to see his features flow and reshape themselves. But it did not happen. His was the same face but so swollen and darkened with rage that she had to look away.

"Lies!" he barked. Doris kept on writing.

"The Divide let you through because it did not recognize you as people. Only animals eat the flesh of their own."

"Lies!!!" the man bellowed.

"You left people behind as hostages to the Divide. And it learned to prey on them. It learned from you."

The man exploded.

He rushed around the Chamber, picking up pictures and posters, pointing at the heroic figures of Grandfather leading the Incoming, leading his ragged band of followers into the city. He yelled incoherent snippets of sentences, disjointed words like "salvation" and "promise" and "refuge". His face swelled with dark blood. Spittle flew from his mouth.

Irene trembled. She could stand up to zombies and birdmen but human madness frightened her. She saw again the faces of the drunken human mobs that chased tenants through the Market. She shook Doris' arm, trying to drag her to the exit. But the big tenant would not bulge. She straightened her ungainly body and faced the man steadily. And then she picked up one of the black-and-red posters that used to hang in the Incoming Sun café and, with a bold stroke, crossed out the image of Grandfather.

The man stopped his rushing around and stared at her. The rage had drained away and something else had taken its place, an expression that Irene had never seen and that terrified her more than a murderous anger.

But Doris was not done yet. She also crossed out the stylized wavy lines that represented the countryside. And then she painstakingly drew a couple of figures that, Irene thought, must be her idea of a human being and a Harrow like herself. They stood together in the middle of a blank expanse, neither city nor country, facing away from Grandfather's beckoning arm.

The man who called himself Grandfather shook his fist and Irene almost laughed at the impotence of his gesture, as he strutted in front of the hulking tenant, twice as large as himself. But the laughter died in her throat as the Chamber quivered.

It was not the occasional tremble as the Hall swatted at the khruts and zombies outside. Nor was it the bump of an attack on the impregnable building they had sensed before and learned to ignore. No, the entire Hall shook in perfect unison with the man's raised fist, as if he were the conductor of an architectural symphony. He stomped his puny foot and the giant structure groaned. He crossed his arms and, with an alarming creak and rumble, the exposed ribs of the building bent inwards, penetrating the spaces inside and piercing the body of the Hall. Irene ducked as the bony spears crossed above her head, clashing and ringing, loud enough to deafen but not enough to disguise the shriek of mindless pain as the Pith obediently mutilated itself.

She rolled away from Doris who stood her ground steadily. One of the dead firestalkers on the pole tottered and crashed into the files-laden desk. The corpse burst into flames and the paper caught fire. The man who called himself Grandfather jumped away from the whoosh of the sudden conflagration. He was not fast enough: his eyebrows got singed. But he still managed to raise his hand and point at Doris. The flaming desk lunged itself at the tenant, enveloping her in a shroud of fire.

Her entire life Irene had tried to be as pliant and adaptable as her yarns. But now the fibers of her body were unraveling in anger. The man who chuckled as Doris burned melded in her mind with the human marauders who had trashed her shop and killed her friends.

She tottered to her feet and sent her last ball of yarn spinning toward the man who called himself Grandfather. It caught him squarely in the forehead, and he flicked off the soft globe contemptuously. But it hung on, quickly unweaving into a mesh of loose threads that engulfed his head and grew in a fringe of tangled tendrils toward his feet. He roared in anger and swiped at the cat's cradle of yarn that spun around him like a loose cocoon. But he could no more get rid of it than a fish ensnared by a net. He tore at the threads and they parted and then grew together again. He lurched toward Irene, a windmilling, bellowing mass of loose yarn, and she stepped back and willed her threads to squeeze tighter and tighter.

But he was strong, tearing at the filaments, tossing them aside in handfuls. Irene felt their pain in the very fibers of her being. They were her children, and their deaths reverberated through her in jolts of anguish. But it was the fight for the city itself. She did not know how she knew it, but this was so. Her own life no longer mattered.

The man savagely tore away the remaining threads that

curled at his feet like a handful of dying snakes. He stepped toward Irene, his teeth bared. And she let go of herself.

The life force that kept her woven body together leached away, and she felt herself unraveling, falling apart into bundles of tough filaments, ropes of living tissue. Her consciousness flickered and went out but with the last effort she sent the yarns that had been herself strike at the man like a nest of hissing snakes. Rearing and weaving, they fell upon him, binding his hands and feet, tripping him and sending him sprawling onto the floor where the smoking bulk of Doris the Harrow still flailed mutely.

The big tenant's hide was charred and blistered, her eyes gone, her mouth gaping in a rictus of silent pain. Flames enveloped her like a cloak.

But she sensed the man's struggle. Rolling over, she grasped the fringes of his web in her flaming paw. The threads that had been Irene caught fire and burned with a smoky, fatty abandon.

The man screamed. And the city screamed with him.

It explained so much.

The frenzy of the Pith. The proliferation of rogues. The roofs' attack.

If the Divide could channel the pain of the dying, why should not the Pith channel the madness of the dead? If the Divide could absorb the mind of an infant, why should not the Pith absorb the mind of an old man? If the countryside now seethed with the rage of the victims of the famine, why should not the city heave with the ambition of its perpetrator?

Adam cursed himself for his blindness. But it hardly mattered now. As they said in the Market, it is foolish to hit a dog with a meat-bun. The past devoured the present if you let it.

He looked at what used to be Marika:

"Let us pass," he said. "We are going to the Hall and you cannot stop us. The city is ours. Grandfather is just another

Hungry One, feeding off our flesh. We are done with him."

"No!" Agatha cried in protest, but Adam had eyes for Kara only. She stepped forth, oblivious of the slick surface underfoot, her face drained of color as she grasped his hands.

"This is why…" she whispered, her voice rising until she was almost screaming. "This is why…"

"What?"

"They sent me. Remade me. The Marching Blades. This is what I am for. Not to kill Hungry Ones. They are not important."

"So why?" Adam asked but he already knew the answer.

"I was sent here to kill Grandfather."

A whip whizzed by them, striking Adam on the shoulder and almost dragging him off Skybridge. He balanced back but the 'arm was not meant for him. It wound itself around Kara who swayed and threw herself down flat, clinging to the edge with her fingertips.

"Blasphemer!" Agatha screamed.

Kara tried to pull off the living weapon, but Agatha made a slight gesture and the tentacle closed upon her upper body, cutting through clothes and skin. Adam yanked at it, but it was as hard as steel.

A dark shape careened into Agatha. Holding her in a bear hug, Daniel squeezed her 'armed hand, wrenching it away from Kara. For a moment, the two of them were poised delicately on the edge of Skybridge like a pair of dancers and then their combined weight toppled them over and they plummeted down, disappearing into the billows of ash. Kara cried out. Adam peered down into the smoke-veiled street but could see nothing. Peter, who had been hovering nearby during the entire altercation, dove into the murk and emerged back quickly.

"Gone!" he said.

Kara sobbed but Adam, disengaging himself from her, faced Marika again.

"Let us go," he said. "Whatever lies beyond the Divide – you are no match for it. If the world Grandfather came from has passed a judgment on him, why should we stand opposed?"

Marika made an awkward gesture and the two 'armed dummies stepped forward, unleashing their serpent-tongue weapons.

And the city screamed.

Chapter 16. The New Mayor

Skybridge shook and convulsed. A slow noise rose in pitch from a whimper, to a low growling, to a shriek so full of chaos that Adam, who had fallen to his knees, clapped his hands to his ears. His collection of faces flickered randomly over his features, no longer under his control, and he felt his own personality dissolving in a welter of borrowed identities. And all the while the shriek went on, unendurably long, impossible to issue from any pair of lungs, and yet undeniably human.

Skybridge trembling, he felt rather than saw Peter beating his wings desperately, trying to stay aloft, but listing and plummeting like a wounded bat, as if some support had been removed from his body. He felt the Pith disintegrating under his fingers…

And then a hand closed over his wrist and hauled him upward.

Kara stood on the palsied surface of Skybridge, her black hair whipping in the cold wind that had no place in the balmy air of the city. Something passed from him to her, but he did not know if it was his life force or an emotion for which he had no name.

"You're the Mayor," she said. "You have to stop this."

He looked around. The sky was darkening quickly but unevenly, as if a cloud of ink was dissolving in the air. And then he saw something so strange that his brain refused to process it. The tower which anchored Skybridge on the other end was bending and whipping like a stalk of wheat, even though the wind had died down.

The mechanical sounds of pulverized stone and stressed metal blended with the unending shriek into a jarring cacophony. Something whooshed below, in the airy gulf they were perched upon. The rotating wheels of fire that patrolled the streets bloomed into uncontrolled conflagrations. Clouds of khruts and khrut-fowls rose, flapping and squawking, into the sky layered with darkness.

A mighty screeching came from the Honeywell tower. He turned back to look at it – and froze.

Shedding its bright cladding, the multistory building slumped lopsidedly like an underdone pudding. Its windows popped. The web of walkways that anchored it to the streets cracked and collapsed. The entire tower was losing its definition, subsiding into an enormous pile of undifferentiated goo.

And then, just as quickly, it reshaped itself. Rearing on a snake-like neck as tall as a skyscraper, a giant screaming face rose into the black sky. A human face, with small bulging eyes and a torn mouth. It screamed its rage, buffeting the insignificant creatures clinging to the vibrating bridge. And when it seemed that the scream could no longer go on, it was echoed and multiplied.

Blinded and battered, Adam squinted into the smoke and saw versions of the same face all around him, all screaming the same defiance. Each tower was reshaping itself into a simulacrum of Grandfather. Some had completed the metamorphosis and were twitching and flailing on their long necks, like human snakes, reducing their subsidiary structures to rubble. Some were just hatching.

The metamorphosis was not limited to the big towers. Every building he could see, from the stand-alone shops and stalls to villas and hospitals, was undergoing the same process. The city was becoming a nightmare jungle of endlessly replicating face, multiplied thousands of times, its rage feeding upon itself, its scream looping around itself in a feedback loop.

Something twitched under Adam's hand. He looked down and saw that the sleek surface of Skybridge was bubbling and roiling. Miniature versions of the face popped from the bubbles until the entire walkway was paved with its scream.

"No!" Marika fell to her knees, scratching and clawing at the faces that kept rising up like soap suds in a tub. "This is not what you promised! You promised purity, making humans like our honorable ancestors, getting rid of toads…"

One of the struts supporting Skybridge from below snapped free and rose up, the screaming face at its end tearing the black hole of its mouth until it was big enough to swallow the woman whole. And it did.

Skybridge dipped sickeningly, sending Adam and Kara on a vertiginous skid. He grabbed her, held her tight. Her arms went around him and they clung together, all questions answered in that one moment of pure flight, as they were blown in the smoky wind, as weightless and powerful as birds.

The surface of Skybridge rose toward them and they landed with a jolt, separated, rolled aside. Adam clutched at the viciously snapping miniature faces that still grew under his palms. But their bubbling seemed to be losing momentum, their teeth only grazing his skin. He raised himself to his knees.

Kara was kneeling, her palms flat to the surface of Skybridge, her face scrunched up in concentration. The bridge shook in palsy and the nature of the shriek changed. What had been a bellow of rage and defiance was now a pure howl of pain, as instinctive and uncontrollable as the cry of a woman in childbirth. Adam's flesh was traversed by lightning strikes of agony and momentarily he felt sympathy for the vast creature bound to the torture rack of its own devising.

The scream of the city rose up to such a pitch that khrut-fowls and khruts rained from the sky, knocked out by the sound. Adam clapped his hands to his ears, regretting that he had no deaf faces in his repertoire. He could no longer endure it – and yet he was enduring it because there was no choice.

And then it stopped.

The city lay around them in mountains of rubble, rivers of fuel and blood, broken beams of bone. But it lay quiescent. The last vestiges of the screaming face dissolved on the slumping towers.

Skybridge plunged down when its supports came loose and now hang perilously close to the river of wreckage that used to be the street. A fat Buddha wriggled out from under a fallen awning and waddled past them, staring fixedly ahead with his round-shaped eyes. Otherwise, there was deadly silence, shocking after the scream. Adam thought he might have gone deaf but then he heard a scrabbling and turned around, helping Kara to her feet.

"Grandfather is dead," Adam said. "You killed him."

Kara shook her head.

"No. Not me. It was too much…I couldn't have…They miscalculated."

"But he is dead." Adam said flatly.

"Yes. He is dead. What will happen to the city now?"

"I don't know. We have to go to the City Hall."

"You are the Mayor," Kara said.

"I'm the Mayor."

Chapter 17. The Opposite of Hunger

They scurried through the ruins like vermin in a dead body. Adam was afraid to touch the exposed Pith and to sense the slow pulse of rot. But when he did brush against it, he sensed instead a life energy: erratic, unfocused, but still there. It gave him hope which the sight of bleeding stumps of towers, sidewalks cracked like old skin, and rogue bodies littering the ground seemed intent on denying.

They saw no humans or tenants. They heard screams in the distance and a couple of times smelled the charred stink of burning flesh. Apparently, some firestalkers were still around.

As they came close to the mid-level escalator, a lonely figure emerged from behind a pile of derma. It was a khrut, and Adam tensed, drawing out his knife. He still held it on ready when he recognized Peter.

The khrut's wings looked singed and crooked, the down on his body had fallen out in patches. But he was alive, waving his hands when he spotted the two of them.

"The thing inside the city is dead," he said.

"I know," Adam said. "Kara killed it."

Kara started to protest but he squeezed her hand, forcing her into silence. The fear of a weapon was as good as the weapon itself.

"The city killed many K'tua but many more remain," Peter said. "They will pick over the corpse."

"Can you convince your kin to withdraw?"

"No. The khrut-fowls won't let them. They speak to the thing in the marsh."

"Yes, the Nestling…What does it want?"

"What does a wronged child want? The world to cry as he has."

Kara bit her lips.

"Never mind," Adam said. "Maybe we can talk to him."

Even as he said it, he knew it was impossible. Talk to the mind of a five-month-old? But he had to have hope in order to give it to others.

"We are going to the City Hall," he said. "Come with us."

Peter nodded and followed, his singed wings fluttering in the sooty air, as they started the climb to Cat Market Street.

Kara felt bloated. The life energy she had consumed in the fights in Honeywell sloshed in her veins like undigested, sour milk. She knew she would be useless if they ran into another contingent of enemies, whether Hungry Ones or dummies.

But she did not care. The leaden depression that had hovered over her since she had woken up at the Divide with her memory restored finally settled on her, smothering her mind under its grey-washed cloud. She saw herself as she really was. A monster. And a failed one at that.

She had failed at everything she had set her mind to accomplish. She had wanted to win Daniel's love – and now he was dead, and she could not even mourn him. She had wanted to escape to the city – and here she was, and the city was an alien graveyard. She had wanted to find out who she was – and now she knew and wished she had not.

So why was she still stumbling through the ruins, following the chairman? He had become the chairman again instead of Adam, the man she had thought could love her. But he was not a man; and she was not worthy of love.

She started lagging behind them, inconspicuously at first, just a couple of steps that grew into a real distance. Bone-tired as they were, stumbling through the ruins, they did not notice.

Adam finally stopped at the crest of the rise where Cat Market Street's stairway joined the flat expanse of mid-levels. Above him, the Peak rose up into the darkening sky, blending into the undifferentiated mass of angles and shadows, and Kara suddenly realized that the sun was setting, and apart from the sporadically flaring firestalkers, there would be no illumination. Flambeaus were dead or in hiding. The country night was coming to the city.

A bony hand clutched her from behind.

Kara pivoted, pushing away the emaciated body pawing at her. A familiar reflex rose up and subsided, filling her with a roiling nausea.

She could not eat.

The Hungry One pushed its broken-toothed maw at her and she could smell its cloacal stench. It was the odor of famine. It was familiar. It was what she had been running from her entire adult life. The running had brought her to places she did not remember, delivered her into the hands of unseen powers, made her into the monster she was.

Not anymore.

"Take me!" she said to the creature.

It stared at her with its rheumy eyes. Its black swollen tongue darted out, touched her cheek clammily.

She waited.

And felt the hateful bloat of the life-force she had ingested drain out of her as gently as breast-milk, drain into the hungry emptiness of the creature, filling its void. As the violence of the transformation brought her to her knees, she felt a jolt of vitality from the splintered sidewalk go through her body.

The city was alive!

Adam's arms closed around her and raised her up. She looked down, at the dead man.

There was still a hint of the Hungry One's starveling mask in his features, but it was a human face: a stolid, patient, deeply furrowed face of a countryman, a farmer. He was naked, his ribs standing out against his leathery flesh. Adam took off his jacket and covered the body.

They resumed walking.

Chapter 18. Agatha

She had been badly winded by the fall and splattered by the blood of Daniel's exploded body that had hit the pavement with full force. It had cushioned her as had perhaps been his intent when he had twisted before the impact, raising her above him. She lay on his corpse, playing dead when the runty khrut fluttered above, looking for her. When he had gone away, she rolled off the body and raised herself laboriously to her knees. Every muscle ached but there were no broken bones.

She looked with dry eyes at the Hunter's smashed features and spat on him. When push came to shove, he had chosen the demon woman before her.

Agatha hobbled away into the shelter of a semi-intact kiosk where she found a bottle of water and a packet of sweet cakes. She ate slowly, caressing her 'arm from time to time, feeling the pleasurable shiver of power travel through her aching muscles.

She was alone. But she had always been alone. She had been looking for protectors her entire life but they had all betrayed her. Her parents, the Hunter, the frog who called himself Adam Malech. They had abandoned her. The only one left, now and forever, was Grandfather.

They said he was dead. Fools! As if Grandfather could ever die! He had made this world, her world, and he could no more die than the air she breathed.

She nodded off but woke up alert in the predawn hush. Some creature scrambled through the litter; she felled it with a single swipe of her 'arm. Fine drizzle hung in the air.

The city spread before her, dark and majestic, lit with flashes of guttering flame, sloping away in fields of spires and forests of towers. It smelled of rain and blood.

She stood, contemplating the living landscape in repose,

feeling rather than hearing its deep regular breathing and the throb of its mighty heart. Much of the urban body was torn and wounded but as the sky lightened, she could see sidewalks knitting together, towers righting themselves, cleaners venturing out to unclog street arteries. Life was all around her: not the feeble life of the country where her parents had scrabbled at the unforgiving soil but the abundant vitality of urban power.

Agatha padded up the street, deftly avoiding the stirring debris and the chattering scavengers. Her country-adapted eyes made it easy for her to navigate in the thin darkness.

She was neither awed nor afraid. They had thought her a country bumpkin, a village idiot who would be overwhelmed by the city and agree to do anything just to earn their protection! Well, they did not know her! And they did not know the country, for all that the demon woman claimed to be from there!

Agatha's village had been battered by the random fluctuation of time coming from the Divide, but it was fortuitously positioned just at the right remove to keep its collective memory reasonably coherent; much more so than the luckless Edenberry. And as opposed to the city where all the records had been destroyed on Grandfather's order, in her village, some handwritten books survived. Agatha, the only reader in her family, had gone through them before her twelfth birthday. So, a lot of what Adam imagined was a revelation to her was, in fact, familiar. She knew that the city was alive. She knew that the Divide was alive as well, though the idea that it now had a mind of its own – and that of a puling babe! – struck her as disagreeable. And she knew what Grandfather and his people had done, how they struggled through the morass, leaving some of their people behind as ransom. Those left behind were, in fact, the lucky ones because many of those who straggled after Grandfather but had no strength on the march were eventually eaten.

Agatha knew all of this, but it only increased her admiration for the leader who had prevailed so spectacularly, becoming the god of both the city and the country. Grandfather dead? Never!

The street was leading up, steeply, and Agatha, still winded by her fall, was getting out of breath. She sat on the pavement, leaning against the standing wall of a partially collapsed building, and unfolded her packet of cakes. The sweet dough melted in her mouth. Eating like this her entire life! Never going hungry! Just thinking about this made her head swim. This is what Grandfather had given to those who followed him. And what had he gotten in return? Disobedience and ingratitude; lawless spawning of ugly toads; and the demon woman assassin, sent by his faceless enemies! Agatha bit into the last cake angrily and winced: her cracked tooth responded with a jolt of pain.

The surface she was leaning upon was warmer than the drizzly air and pleasantly soft, cradling her bruised back. She touched it, curious. It was pinkish-orange and slick. The cladding of the demolished building had fallen off, exposing the living tissue underneath. Agatha stroked it and it gave under her fingers. Indeed, it yielded almost purposefully, cupping her fingers in a little hollow. Agatha smiled. It felt as good as having the mighty bulk of the Aunt Harrow obey her wordless orders. She remembered Doris but quickly dismissed the memory: the tenant was probably dead, and there was no use moping after her.

The living wall reshaped itself into a convex structure that softly drew Agatha inside until she was reclining on her back. It tilted, taking the pressure off her aching spine. She was held in a gentle embrace of warm tissue that brought back inchoate half-memories of being an infant in her mother's arms – before those arms withdrew, sapped by hunger and toil.

The tissue was getting softer, drops of opaque liquid running down and gathering at the bottom of the convex. Agatha sniffed it, dipped her fingers in the liquid, and brought it to her lips. It tasted salty and sweet.

She was lying on her back now, looking into the sky. A ragged silhouette crossed her field of vision: a low-flying birdman. Agatha tensed, trying to release her 'arm – and could not. Her right hand was encased in the tissue that had crept up her wrist. Panic and indignation welled up in her as she struggled against the squishy bonds.

The tissue shuddered and the top of the wall exuded a thick tentacle that swished in the air, bringing the khrut down with a single swipe. The body of the birdman flopped on the pavement, squashed into a mess of blood and bones. In her cradle, Agatha drew in a sharp breath as the power coursed through her veins: the power in comparison with which her previous mastery of her 'arm was like a drying creek in comparison to a river in flood.

The tissue had crept up to her waist. The pain that had throbbed in her from the moment of the fall was gone, and so was the hunger, only barely dulled by the cakes. For the first time in her life, Agatha was neither cold nor tired, or achy, or hungry. She was complete.

The sky lightened to milky-grey and suddenly something shifted in Agatha's brain and she saw the city as no human had ever seen it before: the pit of low-levels and the heights of the Peak; the web of tunnels and the skein of roads; the soaring arches of Skybridge and the crawling web of train-tracks…All of it together, all simultaneously, filtered through the blinking headlights of a train and the luminous eye-spots of a flambeau; captured by the exposed Pith of a budding tower and a scavenger creeping through garbage; pouring into the reviving body of the Market as its innumerable derma-lids lifted at dawn…The body of the city, still alive, still healing…And blindly groping for a guiding intelligence, now that the mind that had animated it for so long was dead.

The shock of being in the city, being the city, wiped out the vestiges of the girl named Agatha Rudenko who had once cooked gruel for her family and gone hungry so her siblings could eat. But the resentment remained. And as the Pith drew her body into itself, the self-awareness that used to be a country girl went out with a last image: the city growing, spreading over the barren fields and mean villages. Eating them up.

Chapter 19. Unanimous Vote

They slept in a gutted grocery shop. After the dark, when Kara almost fell into an open sewer hole, Adam called a halt. Peter still could not fly; and they were worn out by the day that seemed to go on forever.

The morning air smelled like smoke dissolved in water. The rain had put out the remaining firestalkers. The city was still empty, but signs of life were beginning to appear in the streets as humans and tenants, emboldened by the spreading calm, started crawling out of their hidey-holes. Surprisingly, the sky remained empty. Adam asked Peter why the khruts had retreated but he did not know. His hunch was that the death of Grandfather had shifted something in the web of power between the city and the country and the birdmen, already riven by rivalries and erratically guided by the mind of an infant, simply did not know what to do.

They resumed walking toward the City Hall. Adam ahead, Kara lagging behind, mechanically putting one foot in front of the other. After what had transpired yesterday, Adam was worried about her. But while exhausted and gaunt-faced, she seemed to exude renewed determination

After a couple of minutes of walking, Peter suddenly flapped his chicken wings and rose into the air. He listed alarmingly at the beginning but then righted himself and flew above and somewhat ahead of them. Adam flicked his dawn face on and off – his equivalent of a smile. The Pith was healing. He brought back his Volk face and kept it on.

The streets were no longer empty. The pavement crawled with scavengers stuffing themselves on corpses and litter. Some of the towers that had dissolved into piles of jelly under the onslaught of Grandfather's agony were beginning to right

434

themselves, growing new backbones of beams and struts, opening up their multiple eye-windows and blinking at the sunlight. And humans were to be seen, singly or in family groups, groping through the chaos, as shocked as their ancestors had been during the Incoming.

Finally, they came to the City Hall that loomed before them, dazzlingly bright despite the lowering sky. Kara slowed down, craning her head to take it in, and Adam remembered that she had never been here before. But his heart was beating so fast he had trouble keeping his face on. Here it was: his destination. His legacy. The seat of his future power. The heart of the city.

The plaza before the Hall was thronged with humans and tenants who swarmed around the toppled statue of Grandfather in the center, trying to right it up. Adam pushed through the crowd, leaped onto the pedestal.

"No!" he yelled.

The crowd fell silent.

"Mayor Volk?" somebody yelled, the question hanging in the air. Adam could almost see it: the name and title of the Mayor. All he needed to do was to stretch out his hand and grasp it…

He flicked on his Adam Malech face. The crowd gasped.

"I am Adam Malech," he said. "I am a businessman. I am a citizen. I am a tenant."

The crowd surged forward and he thought, *how stupid, to die here, after the Divide…* Kara's pale face swam in his sight. *What would happen to her if they attacked?*

But they did not attack. They milled around the pedestal, bewildered and unhappy, but the impulse of mob violence had dissipated.

"Where were you when we needed you?" a silvery-skinned toad yelled.

"I went to the countryside," Adam said. "To find out where the Hungry Ones were coming from. I wanted to be Mayor and I felt I had to do what a Mayor was supposed to do. To protect the city."

"Did you find out?" asked a human female holding a baby.

"Yes."

"Did you destroy the source?" a duck shaped like a road sign.

"The source of our troubles is dead. But it was not in the country. It was here, in the city. A dead man took possession of the Pith and reshaped it in the image of his own insatiable appetite. He destroyed the countryside and then started devouring his own children. We have been ruled by a Hungry One."

"Who?" a noon male.

Adam pointed to the prone statue of Grandfather whose blind eyes stared into the sky.

"Him!"

Another ripple of exclamations, cries, and whispers.

"Blasphemy!" yelled a short Buddha, hobbling on its tiny uprooted legs.

"Since when do we worship our Mayors?" Adam countered. "We all know who he was: a man. A man who led our ancestors across the Divide into a new world. But why did he do it? Do we know who he had been before he came here? The Divide wiped out memories. We have no history: only the cycle of Year Zero. He may have been a criminal, a fugitive, an outcast!"

The crowd seethed and Adam risked one glance into it, seeking out Kara. She was still there; but would she vouch for the truth of his words? He did not know; and he dismissed the question. It was between him and the city now. Before the Buddha could whip up more indignation from the believers in the crowd, he raised his voice.

"But it does not matter! We are here! We are free! Who cares about the past? The city is ours, to build a better future, humans and tenants together! But he would not let us. He would not let go of power. He became a cancer in the body of the city: an undead abomination feeding on our weaknesses, sowing discord, whipping up the hatred between the city and the country, all the better to control us. Would you be ruled by a corpse? Would you worship a zombie?"

There were feeble voices of protest, but Adam knew he had them. And then a gnarled old man – a tenant or a human, Adam could not tell – stepped forward.

"And what about the Hungry Ones?" he asked. "They are still ravaging the city. Will they go away?"

Adam hesitated, just for an infinitesimal moment, but he felt his control of the crowd slipping away. He pointed to Kara:

"She killed the undead creature. She can kill the rest of them!"

She did not stir. Suddenly and vividly, he remembered a game of Liar's Dice he had played in the Market in the first year of his life: bone-colored cubes suspended in the air, falling down to reveal whether his bluff would pay off or he would be stripped and thrown out into the gutter…

Kara stepped forward.

"The Hungry Ones will go away," she said. "I can make them go away. Now that Grandfather is dead, they don't need to be here."

"Who are you?" the silvery tenant asked.

"I am a countrywoman," Kara said. "The city starved my village and killed my family. But it was not the citizens' fault. You were ruled by a cannibal and you did not know that. Now that he is gone, we can have peace at last."

He had called "two fives" and the dice had rolled to reveal six on one, four on the other.

Adam spoke again.

"I am a tenant. I am flesh of the city's flesh. You all know me: I trade with you, feed you, fight for you. The rules established by the cannibal are dead and gone. I want to be your Mayor. I ask for your vote!"

The moment of silence went on and on. And then a hand rose up. The woman holding a baby.

"My great-grandmother told stories of the Incoming," she said. "Stories you never read in schoolbooks. You have my vote!"

Another hand. A wide-shouldered man in filthy overalls.

"I work in the Market. We throw away food every day and the Guards bring more and more. And then children slip in from the countryside and they're so thin you can count their ribs. You have my vote!"

Another hand. The duck whose body was shaped like a road sign.

"We were never allowed to vote before. Now we can. You have my vote!"

More and more hands rose up. The gnarled man hesitated, looked around, and then slowly raised his as well. The crowd cheered. The Buddha's round eyes rotated in disgust, but it did not interfere.

Adam smiled, feeling the tight muscles of his face loosen up a little as he forced himself to accept it as his own, a permanent one, forever and ever. The face of the Mayor.

"The city belongs to you," he said. "I am your Mayor. I am your servant, not your master."

And jumping off the pedestal, he strode to the gate of the City Hall. The crowd parted before him and surged forward, and he felt himself borne on the wave of their love. For the first time in his life, this love was not for his money, or one of his assumed personae, or the strength of his Guards. It was for him, Adam Malech.

He paused before the gate whose faux-bronze surface was embossed with images of the Incoming. But the moment his fingers touched it, the images wavered, flattened and disappeared, absorbed into the Pith. The gate shuddered and then started, slowly, to rise.

But as Adam, followed by his voters and Kara, walked into the devastated interior of the Hall, a blurry image emerged for a moment on the gate, pulsed for a second and smoothed out. The gate was shiny and blank once again.

The image was of a human figure standing in the iconic Grandfather posture on the threshold of the city with its back to the viewer. But the raised hand was elongated into a sharp-tipped tentacle.

Chapter 20. Family Reunion

"Stay with me," Adam said.

They were sitting in his old pavilion on top of the Thousand-Buddhas stair. The pavilion had been repaired after the roofs' attack, the walls plastered anew, and the splintered furniture removed. There were painted cityscapes where the chairman's collection of faces used to hang. The Mayor needed only one face – his own.

"No," Kara said.

He sighed.

"I have to pay my debts."

"Look at yourself!" he yelled. "You are starving! Feeding Hungry Ones – and for what? They are dead already; they just don't know it!"

Kara shook her head. She was huddling under a heavy shawl. Being constantly cold was one of the symptoms of starvation but it still surprised her that it did not matter whether the air outside was sharp with winter frost or balmy with the city's perpetual summer. Hunger was its own season.

Adam shrugged and turned away, motioning to the house's flambeau to dim its light. Kara was grateful; she did not want him to see her lifeless skin sagging over sharp cheekbones. Vanity was the last thing to go.

In the days while Adam was busy settling into his new role, she had been wandering the city, seeking out the few remaining Hungry Ones. The rest had melted back into the countryside, drawn back to the Divide, she imagined. When she found a solitary one, she would grasp it in her arms, pouring life-force into the empty husk of its being. The scarecrow creature would fill out, its beaky mask smoothing back into a human face. Most of them died on the spot; but some remained alive. They were disoriented, not remembering where they were from or what they were doing in the city. Kara just left them where they were. The city, with so many killed in the fighting, was hungry for immigrants.

There were a couple of untouched dishes on the table: Adam's dinner. He had been staring at her hopefully when she came in, as if she could be tempted by roast chicken into changing who she was. When she shook her head, he pushed the dishes aside. Kara appreciated the gesture but wished he would eat. It did not matter to her. Her own stomach had been locked for so long that food had lost its ability to entice her.

"How is it going?" she tried to change the subject by pointing to the Mayor's official regalia – the embroidered cloak of office and the ceremonial wand – lying on the sofa. The official inauguration was two days off and Adam had already appointed a new personal assistant to take care of the preparations: a duck named Bryn, shaped like a road sign, who had been one of the first ones to vote in the impromptu elections on the City Hall square. Kara liked him much better than James Wingate despite the tinny voice issuing from a round orifice in the middle of his square body.

"It's going well. We'll have a great parade. But..." he hesitated.

"But what?"

"There were some...rumors. And more than rumors. Disappearances. Weird pictures on public buildings. Some of my Buddhas are gone and nobody knows where."

"Do you think...?" she asked. Adam did not answer but they both knew.

They had retrieved Daniel's broken body before the city scavengers got to it. He was given a private burial outside the city in a small farmland cemetery where the dead remained dead. But they had not found Agatha.

"She is just a country girl," Adam said. "What can she do?"

Kara could not help herself. She laughed – and Adam,

realizing what he had said, laughed with her.

Something shifted between them; a barrier melted away.

"Please don't go," he said.

"I have to. You know I do. And what can I do in the city? Hungry Ones are not a danger anymore."

"What difference does it make?"

"You are the Mayor. You have to defend the city. Isn't it why you don't want me to go?"

"I don't want you to go," Adam said, "because if you do, I'll never see you again."

The glitter of the city night outside spangled Kara's face with stardust. When he took her in his arms, he saw that some of the stars were tears.

The train took her as far as Lotus Pond. She had slept for most of the journey. Her energy was running so low that she was afraid there was not enough left for what she had to do. But she had to try.

When the train stopped and blinked opened the door, Kara came out and stroked its down-covered face. She was still not at ease with trains and could never be. But it occurred to her that it was the last time she was seeing one. Its powerful vitality throbbed under its derma and she was tempted: just a single sip, it would not even notice, what difference did it make…But she abstained. The time for self-justifications was over.

Peter was waiting for her at the outskirts of the village, his winged silhouette stark against the sunset. She paused, a ghost of memory slipping, elusive, through her mind: spread-eagled giants, the blaze of furnaces…It teased her and was gone.

They embraced silently and he lifted her in his arms. She was surprised how easily he took off. The renewed vitality of the city had flown through him, expanding his chest muscles, beefing up his wings.

They flew over the flat fields and Kara forced herself to open her eyes, to look for one last time as the emptiness of her birthplace. But it was veiled with shadows as the night descended, and the moon lingered on the horizon.

"Here," she told Peter.

"Further?" he asked in his abrupt way.

"No, here is good."

He set her down among the mosaic of the marsh. The moon had finally climbed higher and, in its silvery light, the red-and-green patches of the bog plant that housed her brother's mind looked like a game board.

"Thank you," she said to Peter.

"Can I..?" he asked.

"No. Go back to the city."

She wanted to add a message for Adam but realized she had already said everything that needed to be said.

The khrut nodded and took off, disappearing in the clouds. Kara trudged on. The track was littered with dry leaves and smudged with muddy footprints.

The purple glow was strong now, crisscrossed with the black scratches of the living fence. And here it was. She stood looking up into the yellow skulls of their faces. She was too late. They were all dead.

She sunk to the ground. And then a faint voice called her name:

"Kara…"

She lifted her head and one of the skeletons was reaching down toward her with its twig-like arms. She reached up and embraced her mother's corpse.

And felt the remnant of her life-force pour out in an uncontrollable flood. She was glad that it was leaving, purging her of her guilt, her rage, her hunger. It was going, going, gone.

And as she sunk into darkness, she heard a baby's wail.

When she came to, her head was cradled in strong, warm

arms. She wondered, confusedly, whether it was Adam or Daniel. And then she opened her eyes and saw a woman's face bending over her.

"Mama!" she whispered.

Her mother put a small piece of bread into her mouth, and Kara wanted to spit it out. But one did not spit out Mother's food. And so she chewed obediently, expecting her body to rebel and eject it any moment. But the chewed-up piece slid smoothly down her gullet, into the mysterious warm interior where life fed on life. It was the most delicious taste she had ever known.

"More!" she cried like a baby.

Her mother shook her head.

"Enough for now. You'll be sick if you have more."

Kara sat up and looked around. They sat on the verge of the road. The fence had fallen and lay askew the muddy tangle of the bog-plant. The moon shone wetly in the sky. Her mother stroked her hair.

There was a bundle wrapped up in her mother's torn shawl lying beside her. The bundle squirmed. Her mother lifted it to her breast. Kara reached out, pulled away the shawl and looked into the baby's red face.

"What's his name going to be?" she asked.

"Felix," her mother said. "It means lucky."

"In what language, Mama?"

"In the language of the Steel World. The world we left behind when Grandfather led us out of the massacre of the Marching Blades. The world we escaped from because it could not feed us anymore."

"And now we are here…"

"Yes," her mother said, "but not for long."

"What do you mean?"

"Look," her mother said, and pointed to what lay beyond the fallen fence.

Kara looked at for a long time, squeezing her eyes against the glare, feeling the unaccustomed heaviness in her stomach grow even heavier.

"Are they coming in?" she whispered.

Her mother shook her head.

"I don't know, daughter. When I was one of the guardians, we did not know much. Only that we should let through those from our side who have the password, whether they be humans or birdmen. And that we should never, ever let anybody from the other side. Except for one. I let you through when you came to the fence, crying in despair."

"Why?" Kara cried and her mother only shrugged, as if it was a stupid question, which of course it was. The baby at her breast squirmed. Kara felt the old anger returning.

"He put you there!" she cried. Her mother shrugged placidly.

"He is only a baby," she said, patting his head. "He'll learn!"

Kara smiled and realized that she would never be free of jealousy and that it was just fine. She gently touched her brother's smooth cheek. And looked again at the cruel landscape of the other side.

"What is the password?" she asked, getting to her feet.

"Hunger," her mother said.

Kara nodded. Of course. She walked to the Divide which was now a real divide, as clear and obvious as if it were drawn with a ruler. The heat from the other side scorched her face. She looked back at her family.

"What will you do?" she asked.

"Survive," her mother said.

"Talk to birdmen. They are no longer enemies of all humans. They'll have learned their lesson. Tell them to take you to the city's Mayor. His name is Adam Malech. He'll take care of you."

Her mother nodded and got up, cradling the baby in her arms.

"Be careful, Kara," she said.

They embraced briefly and she turned toward the scorching

brightness that was now pulsing with waves of heat and noise, rolling closer to the line where the fence used to stand. Her mother's voice stopped her.

"Remember, Kara," she said. "Whoever crosses the Divide, forgets. Even khrut-fowls and birdmen come back with their memories almost wiped out. But they are stupid and persistent; and they hear a call from the Steel World that they cannot resist. But you, you have to remember."

"Remember what, Mama?"

"Remember who you are."

Chapter 21. The Empty Hotel

She woke up hungry.

An anonymous hotel room lay still and bright around her, the chandelier with its metal refractors blazing, even though a harsh light from the outside seeped through the drawn curtains. She got up and went to the window.

END

Kara's story will continue in
THE MARCHING BLADES.

About the Author

ELANA GOMEL has taught and researched English literature at Tel-Aviv University, Princeton, Stanford, Venice International University and the University of Hong Kong where she spent a memorable year. Since then, she has visited Hong Kong, mainland China, Japan, Thailand and Cambodia many times, both as an academic and as a traveler, immersing herself in these countries' cultures, histories and present-day struggles. *The Hungry Ones* reflects her fascination with Asian cityscapes and dreamscapes.

She is the author of four academic books, including *Bloodscripts: Writing the Violent Subject* (2003), *Postmodern Science Fiction and Temporal Imagination* (2010), and *Alien Encounters, and the Ethics of Posthumanism: Beyond the Golden Rule* London (2014). In 2009 she published *The Pilgrim Soul: Being Russian in Israel*, which is one of the first comprehensive treatments of the subject.

She is the author of more than 40 fantasy, horror and science fiction stories, that appeared in *New Horizons, The Fantasist, Timeless Tales, The Singularity, New Realms, Alien Dimensions*, and many other magazines; and in several anthologies, including *People of the Book, Ink Stains, Zion's Fiction*, and *Apex Book of World Science Fiction*. Her story "In the Moment" won second place in the 2009 Short Story Competition of the British Fantasy Society. Her fantasy novel *A Tale of Three Cities* was published in 2013, and her standalone novella "Dreaming the Dark" came out in 2017.